HIDDEN SOLACE

LOST SOLACE BOOK 3

KARL DRINKWATER

ORGANIC APOCALYPSE

Hidden Solace

Copyright © Karl Drinkwater 2022 (updated 2023)
Cover design by Karl Drinkwater

Published by Organic Apocalypse
ISBN 978-1-911278-33-7 (E-book)
ISBN 978-1-911278-36-8 (Paperback)

Organic Apocalypse Copyright Manifesto

Praise For Hidden Solace

"So much blew my mind in Hidden Solace."
Jera's Jamboree

"Drinkwater has generated a universe with cruel corporate governance, sentient AI personalities, significant racial discrimination and economic disparity, and a love story between a woman and her sister and a non-human. Not all love is sexual, not all family is biological, and not all perspectives are equally true."
Scintilla

"What is so remarkable about Opal is that whatever physical or mental torture she undergoes, she never loses hope. Hidden Solace is a powerful story. Drinkwater likes to leave readers with big questions at the endings of the books. Excellent science fiction."
SciFi Mind

"Drinkwater is a master of getting into the psyche of his characters, and his narrative makes you think more about the world around you."
Pink Quill Books

"The cat and mouse game between Opal and Aseides is brilliantly portrayed. A tense, atmospheric novel."
Literary Flits

HIDDEN SOLACE

Utopias

28 ...

Beams of sunlight speared between clusters of overhead foliage, so blinding bright that Opal had to shield her eyes, dazzled and exuberant.

"Clarissa, where are you?" she shouted into the rich undergrowth. "Athene's cooking up something new. Promises it's edible this time."

Giggling from the bushes to Opal's left betrayed her little sister's location. But Opal let it play out a little longer. There was a lot of time to make up. A lot of fun that Clarissa had never experienced. Now they were somewhere safe it was time for Clarissa to have the childhood she deserved.

"Damn, that girl must have tricked me again!" Opal said, as if to herself, but louder than normal. "She is *way* too good at hiding."

Opal picked up a hefty stick, brushed off damp leaves and insects, then used it to poke at a tangle of bushes.

"You aren't in there, are you?"

Something flashed in her peripheral vision. A girl dashing away, skin a contrast to the translucent green leaves. There had been a teeth-revealing smile on that face, delicious to see, infectious.

Opal followed, crossing the spongy moss floor, stepping over the exposed roots of ancient trees. A rich smell of verdant earth and decay permeated these lower levels.

Mornings of fun. Days of exploration. Evenings of play. It was hard to recall exactly how long they'd been on the planet now. Happiness tends to do that, make time blur and fade away, until time becomes timeless.

Opal feigned exasperation. "I reckon she's gone deeper into the forest. I'll never find her!"

A twig snapped somewhere to her right. Clarissa must have snuck around the trees.

"And it's a shame, because I'm sure Athene said something about ... strawberry ice cream."

That temptation wasn't quite enough to pull Clarissa from her hiding place, but the innocent giggling was more subdued this time, as if a battle between The Game and The Stomach was being fought.

Opal navigated between low-hanging branches that scraped her head, and wiry tendrils that tangled her ankles. Mud squelched and sucked underfoot, retaining deep imprints from her boots' industrial treads. Then one of the bushes rustled. She avoided looking in that direction, but adjusted the curve of her route to pass nearby.

"If only I could find Clarissa, and give her a huge hug, and squeeze her so hard she can't get away from me again," said Opal. "Ever. Never ever."

No giggling this time.

At the last second Opal spun round, dropping the stick and groping in the bushes, emitting a monstrous "Rargh!" and expecting the childish squeal of delight on being discovered ... but instead, something scrabbled further into the undergrowth. And the bush seemed larger than it had first appeared.

Opal groped through the spiny branches, pushing deeper, where the sunlight didn't even reach. She heard giggling again (*or was the sound something else?*), further away.

"No, wait!" she called, as cold flushed through her, a skin contraction of the uncanny that she hadn't felt since ... well, since she'd been on a Lost Ship. "Stop playing, Clarissa, this might be dangerous!"

Thorns plucked at her exposed skin, small tears, blood tears, but she didn't hold back. She forced on with even more effort, slipping on ground where the fallen leaves had rotted to sludge, shielding her eyes from curved plant spikes.

So dark and creepy in here. The kind of place Clarissa was drawn to. Sometimes Opal worried about her sister. A feeling like a stubborn callous. That traitor, doubt. But she would not let it be part of her. She would purge it, like Athene did with redundant code.

Why did that thought make Opal sad?

"Clarissa!" she shouted. "You stop right now!"

Opal broke through into an open patch, deep within the bush, a kind of dark clearing around a trunk, arched over with impenetrable branches like a roof, or a bubble under deep water. Clarissa was ahead of her, in that flower-patterned dress she loved, except now it was torn from the thorns, and muddy from slipping in this festering, stinking undergrowth. Clarissa faced away from Opal, completely still, as if examining the trunk. No more lively, giggling girl. Opal could only see the back of her head, the curly hair with leaves and twigs tangled in it.

"Clarissa?"

Nothing.

Opal dropped to her knees so their heads were on a level, gripped those skinny arms and turned her around. Clarissa's eyes were closed tight.

"What is it?" Opal asked. "Have you seen something again? A bad dream? Remember what I said about dreams, that you only have to open your eyes and they go away?"

Clarissa opened her eyes. But nothing reflected behind the lids. Just holes, blackness beyond blackness, like the featureless blank within the Null.

"You didn't save me," Clarissa – or whatever she now was – said, in a voice that was broken, emotionless, yet accusing, all at once. "I'm still trapped in here."

Opal staggered back, slipping on the rancid slime, and the thing's mouth stayed open, but a sound came from it that wasn't words, more like a scream, inhuman, endless, howling, a painful alien warning of attack.

The Oracles had taken Clarissa again. Except they'd never really released her.

And Opal's eyes flicked open to her cell, taking in the reality, the grey streaked with blood from vain punches, from taking out her frustration on any surface that presented itself, with the wake alarm still wailing, indicating that another day of horror awaited.

She'd failed. Athene had failed. And it took effort not to add to the artificial squeals with her own screams.

OUBLIETTES

... 27 ...

Opal covered her ears until the alarm ceased. Dazzling spotlights burned down on her face, so she waited until she was standing before opening her eyes and flipping the hinged bunk up against the wall.

The dream had been a nightmare, but at least it was a temporary escape. From this.

As expected, the voice followed.

"Please exercise for fifteen minutes. Be seen, be pure, believe."

A kind-sounding voice, though it spoke High Dialect like a newsreader. It was the kind of voice that implied protection. The voice of a friend, a confidante, an ally in this hell hole.

It was artificial.

And it was the same voice that administered punishments.

Opal began walking in circles. This round chamber was good for that. She stretched her arms and twisted her upper body as she paced. She still wore yesterday's jumpsuit. The metal floor pushed hard and cold against her bare soles.

The chamber was five metres in diameter. She performed each circuit in twenty-five paces. After her bed she reached the shower. Water-based, not steam. It was bolted to the metal wall, like all the furniture, and obviously not part of the original design. However, the floor sloped down to a drain in the centre, so the chamber did once have something to do with liquids. The cylindrical shape, rusting rivets, and age-streaked metal floor implied industrial heritage and storage tanks.

The drainage grid was welded in place and unmovable, and she had been unable to loosen any of the screws with her bare hands before punishments began.

Another five paces and she passed the toilet. No cubicle around it. No privacy. A chamber designed for observation from above.

Six paces more brought her parallel to the shoulder-height shelf which contained clean clothes and a Portable Personal Diagnostic Ally. Its frame said PPDA at the top in orange, followed by the manufacturer's logo of a smiley face. The shelf had curved edges, nothing you could brain yourself on, intentionally or otherwise.

And she was back at her bunk.

The next loop was the same.

And the next.

Light was not equal. Looking up, you were blinded by the intensity of the spotlights which never went out. They made it impossible to identify features at the top of the chamber, or to tell if the viewing hatch was open or closed. Knowing her captor, it was probably also an attempt to disorientate her, make her more pliable. She had no way of knowing if it was night or day. In here there was *only* day.

Sleep was difficult when you were always in the spotlight, psychologically and physically. There were no bedcovers or pillows, just the padded bunk. She'd tried sleeping underneath it but they'd punished her for being out of view for too long. So the best she could do when they insisted it was sleep time was to put a forearm over her eyes and count imaginary knives thunking into targets.

Shadowed areas formed between the illuminated ellipses where spotlights speared down. But the shadows weren't enough to hide in. And it was obviously intentional that each item of furniture sat in the brightest-lit points.

"Exercise time is over," announced the voice. "Thank you for cooperating. Please shower now."

Opal squinted up into the whiteness, and just received sunspot after-flashes when she blinked. Someone would be watching. Maybe many someones. But you picked your battles.

She tore off the flimsy red paper outfit, shoved it into the sealed container by the shower, then stepped under the spray head and thumped the button. The water was warmed, ready-soaped and antiseptic. It would switch to clean rinsing water after forty-four seconds. She counted while rubbing her body down.

Forty.

Forty-one.

Forty-two.

The temperature cooled, the water now less slick. There would be a minute and sixteen seconds to rinse. Two minutes of shower time. They liked their even numbers. Useful to know.

She used the pretence of rubbing her head to examine the metallic stud nano-welded to her ear lobe. The stud was smooth, resembled the one Xandrie Dervorgilla had attached to Opal's bag while they fought in vacuum outside the Gigatoir. Probably a tracker. Beneath the skin were hardened extensions, like the roots of a tooth. Even if she had a blade, picking it out would be messy.

Hot air blasted her from a welded vent. That, also, had proved impossible to pry off with her fingernails.

Once dry, she grabbed clean red coveralls from the pile and slipped them on. The material was fine-grained and flexible. Comfy enough, but no pockets, so you couldn't hide a weapon or tool. Plus you never shook off the vulnerability of being in something so easily tearable, especially when they didn't give you underwear. A deterrent from trying anything. Same as the lack of footwear for prisoners. You were always just one stomp away from broken toes.

She didn't care. Sometimes bone could strike harder when not cushioned in soft materials.

"Thank you for complying. Now please take your Portable Personal Diagnostic Ally and update your current internal bodily and mental status, emotions, and thoughts."

Opal picked up the PPDA.

"PLEASE RATE THE FOLLOWING STATEMENTS" glowed in light blue text against the dark blue background of the screen. "THIS MORNING, I FEEL RELAXED." Below that were seven options for various levels of agreement or disagreement. A soft, bordering glow which brightened and dimmed in a breathing pattern implied patient waiting for her response.

Opal strolled across the chamber as she read the text.

"There's a missing option," she called, aiming her voice upwards even though there were probably implanted pickups all over. Her voice reverberated around the chamber.

"The options provided are all you need to concern yourself with."

"No," Opal insisted. "It's definitely missing one on my screen. There are only six options."

"There are seven."

"Nuh-uh," Opal said, shaking her head. "It's missing the option for 'Fuck you, none of your business'."

"Behavioural breaches will be punished," said the AI voice, as pleasant as ever. "Three. Two."

Opal flung the PPDA away, knowing its rubberised case would, unfortunately, protect it from damage (she'd tried to smash it on day two). In the next moment she slammed her bunk down, and leaped onto the mattress so she was off the ground before receiving the electric shock. Charge sparked where the shower water hadn't yet drained away, but she was unharmed up here. An idea she hadn't tried yet. She grabbed onto a rivet and pinched its small surface in her fingers. If she used her toes and strong grip she could scale up and –

Bzzzzt.

She was flung backwards onto the floor, smacking her elbow and skull while the punishment shocks continued. When they ceased she was gasping, some muscles still convulsing and twitching, yet to realise it was over.

So the bastards could electrify the walls as well. What a surprise.

"Are you all right, Opal?" asked the falsely concerned voice. "Any injuries?"

Opal clamped down on her instinctive reply of "My pride." That was an answer for AIs that were friends. AIs that understood you. AIs that knew what existed beneath the jokey responses. Instead she said, "Negative."

"Are you being sarcastic, Opal?"

"Neg– ... No. I'm not." She stood, trying to still her shaky legs so as not to reveal their weakness.

"Then let us move on. I will lower the lift to you. Please interlace your fingers behind your head and stand back. Keep your hands in that position until told otherwise. Be seen, be pure, believe."

The chamber darkened as a platform lowered from above, blocking some of the light cones. The platform was a round disc of metal, supported by six thin cables.

"What's the agenda today?" asked Opal.

"Someone wants to see you."

Someone. Opal could guess who was being referred to. The AI Opal interacted with was called Dulcetta, and Dulcetta only answered to one person.

ESCORTS

... 26 ...

When the disc clanged against the base of the chamber, Opal stepped onto it, hands behind her head as instructed. The platform ascended.

After a few moments she peered over the edge. Twenty metres high, already. The shrinking view of her chamber below was enough to make her dizzy. She wondered if anyone had ever lost their balance and fallen. Or even jumped on purpose. It seemed like an oversight on her captor's part to allow such possibilities. Perhaps even to cause them, by not letting prisoners hold on to the platform's vertical cables for support. Maybe it was mind games.

Maybe they just didn't give a shit.

As she neared the lights it was hard to see anything much, they were so intensely bright. She did her best to squint from one eye in case some detail was revealed this time that might be useful.

The disc she stood on was a circular part of the ceiling that lowered, leaving a hole, above which guards would be waiting.

At last her head was above the spotlights and she could observe how the platform's cables ran into the sides of the aperture, into the ceiling structure itself. As she rose through the gap into the passage above, the disc clunked into place as part of that corridor's floor, delineated in orange and black stripes.

Two body-armoured guards awaited her, both in UFS uniforms with full grey faceplates that hid the features of the wearer. One had D-69 printed on his helmet's forehead, the other was R-43. She recognised both codes. D-69 was often aggressive and contemptuous. R-43 tended to be silent and keep more of a distance.

D-69, the taller of the two, pointed a reinforced glove to his left.

"Walk."

His voice was filtered by the Sec-3 suit, making it harsh, inhuman. At first the effect had been seen as a flaw in the audio system of early versions of the armour. Then, because it made the wearer sound more intimidating, especially if their normal voice wasn't deep, the audio system was kept and readvertised as a *feature*. The Sec-3 suit had always been designed for value over performance. Sure, it had strengths.

It also had weaknesses.

Opal preceded the guards, keeping her hands behind her head. The flooring of these upper corridors was pleasantly warm on her feet. Perhaps 22°C. The walls were coated in glossy back-lit panels of non-oxidising Stay-Nu materials. So different from the rusting metals of her holding chamber.

As usual the guards kept a metre behind her, one to the left, one to the right. Close enough to grab her. Also near enough for *her* to strike *them*. Every decision will close some opportunities, and open others.

They proceeded over other circles marked in hazard lines. Further holding chambers. The viewports were closed so she couldn't determine whether they were occupied or not. She had never seen anyone being placed into them, or taken out, but that might just come from segregation security rules. Opal had narrowed base procedures down to five different protocol possibilities. There were ways to clarify it further.

Junctions were marked by code patterns of tiny dots. Indecipherable to the naked eye, but guard helmets probably filtered the codes and overlaid them with navigation aids. All part of making prisoners feel lost and small, trapped in a maze.

Every so often they'd pass beneath a small black dome mounted in the ceiling, the kind of protective covering that went over cameras. A distraction, since there could be micro cameras embedded in any wall surface. Perhaps they were just there to give the impression of always being watched. A deterrent against trying anything.

The domes were spaced every fifty steps, no doubt equating to twenty-five metres because the UFS loved regularity. That enabled her to include correct distances in her mental maps, a navigation aid in lieu of coded markings.

Step four. Step five. Step six.

The corridors were kept free of anything that could be picked up or dismantled. Never a toolbox lying around, no loose pipes, no smashable glass.

Step forty-nine. Step fifty.

This route ended at a T-junction. To the right was an area for prisoner processing, where they shaved her head in an obvious attempt at dehumanisation. She'd enjoyed it. The itching of her hair growing back had proved distracting. Down one of the corridors there she'd seen guards coming out of a sliding door. It might lead to a staff area where they kept weapons, or communication equipment. But her escorts would want to go left today.

So she headed to the right.

"Other way," snapped D-69, quickly stepping forward and holding out his arm.

It was foolish to have his limb straightened like that. Elbows could be locked out or broken with ease.

"Sorry," Opal said, turning to the left and continuing.

R-43, or Silent R, had moved to the side when D-69 – Angry D – left position to block her. Silent R continued where he was, so Angry D took up the other place. Now they were on opposite sides from where they started.

She filed that outcome as potentially useful.

As they walked, and she counted, a subtle nausea passed through her gut. It happened most days. She'd ruled out infection and dietary incompatibility. It wasn't stress, or the results of tests or punishments. Twice when it happened she had been aware of a faint astringent smell, and assumed she was passing through an area where one of the rarely glimpsed hovering S1 drones had been spraying surfaces with antiseptic cleaning mist. It could have been some bodily reaction to the chemicals. But she flared her nostrils and inhaled, and there wasn't even a faint trace of that scent today. So that was an option ruled out. She wasn't sure what she could replace it with. Low level radiation sickness? Was the prison a toxic environment? Hmmm.

Despite the lack of readable signage, Opal knew where she was. Counting the domes and combining the numbers with junction options gave her memorable route plans. She was approaching SSLL7. Sometimes a scuff, a remembered incident, a different juxtaposition of panels or lighting provided more memorable names, such as Five-way Scratch, or Triple-J, or Removed Bloodstain. SSLL7 was fine, too. She'd waited days to come this way.

She dragged her feet, took shorter paces.

"Move it," said Angry D.

"My leg hurts," Opal replied, half turning.

Angry D shoved her, trying to aim her down the corridor, but she staggered, angled left, hit a wall panel, and fell to her knees. The panel was loose, rattled, a tiny echo to the thump. Cavities. Not mounted on solid wall, at least not here. Self-warming, probably a model of standardised metamaterial plasteen, usually used in renovations. The eight inset pins backed up that idea. On a previous journey to SSLL7 she'd noticed a faint black edge that indicated this panel wasn't flush with the others. Having Angry D to her right, combined with a dramatic stumble, meant he'd pushed her smack into it.

She rose up, leaning on the wall for balance, then fell again, using the opportunity to check nearby panels. A slight give to them, hollowness, but securely pinned.

"Get up right now, you filthy failure," said Angry D. His hand unclipped the rod at his side, ready for removal. The familiar green glow of a Stunstix Mark 2 readout was clearly visible. The bar was less than halfway. Naughty boy hadn't fully charged it.

She stood, and began moving.

"I'm sorry," she muttered, eyes downcast.

Before long they reached a special junction which she called ROT1. They used them as barriers between areas with different security levels. The equivalent of bulkheads, maybe. These special security corridors were hexagonal in cross-section. Each of the six sides had a paired opposite of the same colour. Two facing reds, two white, two blue. The top and bottom panels were always lit, the others dark. Today the red sections were active, so the whole corridor glowed an ominous ruby colour.

At each end was another opaque black dome in the ceiling, just before and after the hexagonal passage. Opal was told to halt, then Angry D looked up at the dome.

The corridor ahead rotated with a smooth movement. It was like looking into the sights of a rifle and twisting the focussing dial clockwise. Opal glanced at the point where the hexagon cross-section joined her corridor, but the turning didn't reveal any gaps where something could potentially be jammed to stop the rotation. Just smooth surfaces.

When it stopped moving, the white panels were in the ceiling and floor positions, and neutral light replaced the blood-like reds. White indicated safe passage.

As they moved through the security corridor Opal kept her gaze down, but not out of meekness. She was checking the lower red and blue panels to each side of her feet. The blue was reflective and sparkled. She guessed at electrical current, based on what happened in her cell when she misbehaved. Maybe when the corridor was in blue mode, electricity could arc between floor and ceiling.

The red panels had tiny holes. Nanowire extrusions? Acid sprays? Some of the holes looked larger, but it was just dark staining at their edges which hadn't been cleaned. File for later.

Beyond the security corridor things got busier. The passages were wide to accommodate larger groups and machinery. Sealed doors led to areas she hadn't seen. Most were unlabelled, though a few did break the ranks of anonymity and have recognisable signs.

At the next junction they had to wait as a group of prisoners were escorted by five guards. The guards each carried large custom weapons with unknown payloads. Probably non-fatal and extremely painful crowd control options. They obviously had different protocols for different groups of prisoners. She'd only ever seen groups of four to twenty in this section, with one guard for every two prisoners. Opal should be honoured.

As usual, the prisoners looked downcast and malnourished. Their heads had also been shaved in an attempt at depersonalisation, but it failed since the captives displayed various body shapes, facial features, and shades of skin. Variety in appearance despite similarity of demeanour. At the front shuffled a tall man with skin darker than Opal's. Behind him was a woman who would be as pale as an Indostaqr native, except her face was coated in tattooed symbols, many of which were recognisable as anarchic logos. The third woman had perhaps been a prisoner longest as her dark hair was growing back cat-fur fine. She was shorter than Opal, with features that weren't common in the UFS – possibly from Ortel, Barotross, or one of the planets out there, generally seen as a threat to UFS border security.

Opal didn't know their stories but most were obvious Genitor Purity Test failures, like her. Not excluded from citizenship, but less likely to have full life choices, and more likely to end up in places like this. Maybe others were failures for non-visible defects. Criminals, regressives, freedom fighters, rebels. Or politicals: people who thought too much and made the mistake of stating their opinions to the wrong person or in the wrong place.

They were all doomed.

Opal still had her arms up and hands clasped behind her head. She noted that her escorts had moved to each side and both of them had a hand on one of her shoulders.

The Gunderson Escort Protocol. *Nailed it.*

But she didn't have time to think about the potential there, because the large prisoner group had moved on and her enemy was waiting.

INTERROGATIONS

... 25 ...

All rooms have a mood. A combination of the tiniest hints of scent which come from its past and present; the small details placed by accident or design; the lighting; the purpose. And the company, or lack of it.

This room stank of interrogation. Of sweat and hopelessness. No decoration to distract you. Intense spotlights focussed on the central seat that was fixed to the ground and could be tilted back. The cushioned material was stained: almost imperceptible, but prominent to the panicked mind. Stains that could be old blood on fabric. Or maybe they were just meant to look that way to increase fear.

Opal sat in the chair without needing to be shoved. Metal clamps locked around her wrists and ankles. The swish of a closing door indicated the two guards had left the room. She was alone.

He didn't like to keep the guards around. No idea if it was an attempt to make her open up, or to imply he was powerful and didn't need the guards' protection. It might even be because things were discussed that he didn't trust his guards to overhear. Probably all three at once, knowing the way his mind worked. She only cared about the implications of each possibility, and whether it might be useful to her in some way.

A different door opened behind her. Slight shifts in the air suggested sealed chambers with their own air supplies. Heavy footsteps. Not him, then. He was solid but walked with a light step, as if noise might distract his mind. These were genuine steps of mass, combined with a lack of care about how they might be interpreted.

"Hello, Dulcetta," said Opal.

The synth moved to a position in front of Opal. So polite in not risking Opal cricking her neck. Fucking hypocrite.

"I hope you are well, Opal." Its voice was completely human. Calm yet nuanced.

"I'd be better if you hadn't zapped me."

"That was a result of your own actions and choices, not mine."

Opal didn't reply. You can't argue with a metal wall.

Dulcetta was an enigma. She seemed to be the base AI, but was embodied in a unique humanoid frame. Her proportions resembled the curves of a fantasy SynthMate, with slightly larger than human proportions so that she could look down on you and intimidate with her mass. And yet her appearance was softness, with gold skin and hair, set off by detailed green eyes of the finest optic glass, precision detail, the hint of internal glow. Apart from the inhuman colour, her ectodermis seemed soft and organic. Of course, she no doubt had internal defences, and could probably tear someone's arm off with ease, despite the divine appearance.

Dulcetta wore loose-fitting clothes that were expensive and stylish. She combined colours and patterns in ways that seemed slightly off to Opal. Perhaps the clothes were something she was required to wear but disdained. More likely, her tastes were not quite human, or she wore what her master told her to wear. Each option provided possibilities to file away now, and consider later.

"May I remind you that I am fully capable of sedating and incapacitating you if you try anything when my master is here," Dulcetta continued.

"You always say that."

"Repetition is necessary because you rarely listen or act sensibly."

"You don't like me, do you?" asked Opal.

"I have no preference amongst captive subjects." Dulcetta nodded, both a reminder of Opal's place in the hierarchy, and a full stop to the conversation. "Be seen, be pure, believe." She stepped back, so that she was beyond the circle of light and could only be seen as a golden glow if Opal squinted.

The door opened again. Soft footsteps, but quick, as if there was lots to do, and physical transition was a frustrating but necessary chore separating the things of true importance.

"Good morning, Opal!" said Doctor Cuttram Aseides, with a boyish smile.

"Is it? Time's artificial here. You manipulate it to mess with our heads."

"Time is artificial *everywhere*. Morning on Rosarium Prime might be night-time on Indostaqr Beta. Who am I to break with tradition? But my intention was pleasantry. Do you wish to dispense with that mode?"

"Always."

"That's why talking to you is refreshing."

"I said *always*."

"Apologies. I can't help saying nice things in your presence. Ah, there I go again."

"If you want pleasantries, you should release me so I can be treated like a human."

He pulled a face. This was a combination of "Yeah, right" with "You're such a joker!" She was getting better at reading him. It took time because his lack of hair, even eyebrows, and his smoothly ageless face made him difficult to interpret. No wrinkles that might gather to show a frown or a smile. No brows to emphasise eye expression. Just clinical smoothness, poured into a high-necked grey UFS research outfit.

He checked his Comm-Bond as he paced. His was implanted, of course. Maybe it displayed base updates, or Dulcetta's reports about Opal. Could even be beauty tips, for all Opal knew. It had privacy filters, and he never angled it where she could see the screen which glowed under his skin.

"Hmm, Dulcetta says you refused to do your morning status report and dream diary."

"What's the point?"

"Useful data! Dulcetta combines results for the official UFS reports, but I like the unfiltered responses for some people, yourself included." A pause. "Oh, I see, you meant what's the point *for you*. How about, so I don't have you killed or tortured?"

"I think I'm too important to you for the former. And I guess you hold back on too much torture because you're worried it might affect the results of something you want to observe. Same reason you don't drug me."

"You are partly correct. Might I not also possess some compassion in your mental model of me?"

"Nope."

"And so this all takes longer than it should."

"Boo hoo. Your life must suck."

He paced slowly, hands clasped in front. Opal tapped one of her fingertips in time with his steps until he stopped.

"The answer," he said, "always comes. In this case it is compromise. I prefer your cooperation. So, if you will answer my questions fully during our meetings, and also do the daily psychological diary reports with diligence and honesty – bearing in mind that it isn't some onerous duty placed on you alone, but is something *everyone* in this base does: guards, researchers and myself included – well, in that case my compromise would be to answer some of *your* questions in return."

"What makes you think I have questions?"

He gave her that combo look again.

"Okay," she said.

Aseides clapped his hands. "Excellent! Dulcetta, new protocol. Continue to record my sessions with Opal, but do *not* simultaneously broadcast them to Central. They are to be stored in my repository, and I will review them and choose what goes where."

"Protocol updated," said Dulcetta, her body statue-still, as it always was when she observed.

"You got something to hide?" asked Opal.

"Is that your first question?" asked Aseides.

"No." She stared into his eyes, ready to identify the tiniest tell-tale, that twitch or squint that might suggest dishonesty. "Clarissa. Is she okay? Has anyone hurt her, because if they have, I'll tear their brick-fucking –"

"No need to resort to fruitless posturing. Clarissa is in fine physical health. She does not respond to outside stimuli but I promise you all attempts to speak to her – to comfort her, to entertain her – have been gentle. She has chambers far more hospitable than yours, in keeping with your different temperaments and risk levels."

He hadn't betrayed anything. Obviously trained in personal suppression.

"I want to see her."

"If your cooperation is genuine, then you will. My turn!"

"What's the topic going to be today? More about Xandrie and VigMAX, their performance and fates? A recap of what happened to the Aurikaa and its escorts? How I stole Athene? What I could do if given a screwdriver and ten minutes alone with Dulcetta?"

"All but the last are topics I am ordered to look into by UFS Mil-Com. They are furious with you." He leaned over, though just out of range of her teeth. "And you managed to anger the Genitors as well. They all wanted things from a Lost Ship, and you ruined not *one*, but *two* interventions, more than normally occurs in a *lifetime*. At least, now that your running days are over, you'll never need to face the horrors of a Lost Ship again!"

"I'd rather take my chances there than here," she muttered.

Aseides' breath had a peculiar tang that reminded her of the cleaning chemical smells. It was a relief when he backed away.

"Your enemies want to learn all they can, then dissect you and your sister," he said. "They don't appreciate you and your critical, resistive mind like I do, and I need to provide data to keep them placated in the short term. But I am looking for ways to keep you both alive. To be *kinder*. I have some influence, you know. Anyway, those topics are not the ones that really ignite my reactor. Well, I do have an interest in AI development, so everything relating to VigMAX and ViraUHX does –"

"Athene."

"Very well. No harm in letting you acknowledge its attempts at self definition when we are off the record. But it's not a key topic now it – sorry, *she* – has been disposed of."

Opal grimaced and glanced down at her shackles.

"Apologies again. I am too literal. And I consider it the greatest shame that she would not surrender, and so had to be destroyed. But you saw the mission recordings, what she was like! She had long ago replaced reason with chaotic and self-destructive emotion. I was sorry to have to show you what happened, but it was the only way you'd be convinced."

"I knew it was her. We travelled together too long, and went through too much, not to think alike. If she'd still been alive you bastards would have asked me about her, wanted an edge to find and defeat her. I can tell you don't give a shit now that my only friend ..."

"Please, don't upset yourself. We all have to move on. Now she is gone, you may as well cooperate. Maybe *I* can be your friend? Not at this moment, obviously. But one day. No need to glare at me like that. Or ... perhaps even Dulcetta? She might make a better replacement for Athene."

"Indeed," said Dulcetta. "The fact that I have not been blown up during a desperate and risky infiltration of the Velumin Archives – accompanied by uncouth insults, delusional rantings about ancient god mythologies, and some predictable obfuscation tricks – suggests I am the far more reliable companion. ViraUHX's desperation was a weakness, as was her failure to contemplate that we would sacrifice the archives, and the thousands of people stationed there, just to negate her. I would not have miscalculated in that way. I would have suspected such a predictable target, and that it would be easy to hide enough Geocracker G23F tectonic warheads amongst the structures to tear the asteroid apart, and everything within a thousand kilometres. Some would say that the outcome was sad, the loss so great that it could tear a hole in one's heart. But I had backups of the whole archive, so I dispute that."

"I'll tear a hole in *your* heart, if you dirty Athene's memory like that," growled Opal.

Aseides glanced from Opal to the synth. "You're not helping, Dulcetta."

Dulcetta remained unmoving.

"This is not going as planned," said Aseides. "Not in alignment with our new accord. You asked about topics for today. Let us consider the Null. Not the part our ships skim via Null-C drives, but the *deeper* Null. The place Lost Ships come from. What exists there. Entities, navigation, locations, physical rules. Also how contact with it changes us. Obviously I can learn a lot from in-depth analysis of body chemistries and traces, from you and Clarissa, but that's just examining the UI of a Comm-Bond when I really want the data stored within it."

"I've already told you everything."

"And I love rereading my data entries. I often use your own terminology, you know? My existing records are being revisited and tied in to your reports when there is a match. The Humungr. Oracles. Navigots. Satreweth. The other terms such as Topias. Some of this knowledge already existed but it was fragmentary. It is incredibly rare to encounter these beings. Even rarer for a human to survive the encounter. And rarer again for them to remain rational and able to communicate! Over time, if we come to trust each other more, I would like you to work with me on my records. To *hone* them. To *clarify*. This would enable me to list you as indispensable, providing you and your sister with permanent protection. Clarissa will hopefully emerge from her withdrawn state, and you would be given more freedom and responsibility. It is the *best possible outcome* drawn from the many threads your life could follow, and one of the few that does not involve pain and death. Your ready engagement is what protects her, too. We can all win if you embrace the possibilities that remain."

He paced, hands clasped behind his back now. Opal gazed down at her feet as if depressed, while tracking him in her peripheral vision. She was calculating how much force it would take to break one of the manacles. What tools could damage the mechanism. What could block it from closing properly.

"You are not as excited as myself," he continued. "That is understandable. This is new territory we embark on. So I offer you an enhanced deal. Today, I will solely answer *your* questions.

I won't ask you any more about the Null and your experiences. I will show my goodwill with this gesture. Then, next time, you will answer *me*. And following that, we will work *together*. And thus more opportunities will open up. Deal?"

Opal met his eyes. "Okay. A deal."

AGREEMENTS

... 24 ...

"Excellent!" Aseides clapped his hands, childish, then gave Dulcetta's shoulder a squeeze. Dulcetta smiled at him, her head tilting in his direction.

Opal sat up as straight as the restraints allowed. "So, you say everyone in the UFS wants me and Clarissa dead. But you can hold them off if I cooperate. Right?"

"Yes."

Opal tried to discern any facial movements, but he was still indecipherable, except when he made an effort to be readable.

"Okay. Since me and Clarissa are on our own now, I'll have to trust you. Next. How did you find us when we left the Null and crashed in a realspace planet's desert? We didn't see anyone, didn't send a signal, had no idea where we were. Yet a UFS stealth dropship turned up within a few days. That's not chance."

"One moment." Aseides leaned into Dulcetta and whispered, listened to her reply in his ear. They were angled so Opal couldn't read their lips. He nodded.

"I can answer that," he said. "VigMAX had left us the destination he and Xandrie were heading towards as they tracked you. That was down to me. I was suspicious of the engagement at Tecant. So, although the UFS believed you were dead, I used resources at my disposal to keep looking.

"VigMAX and Xandrie were to confirm whether you and Athene were alive, and, if so, to capture or turn you both. But we didn't hear back from them. When the follow-up crew arrived at the Albright Nebula they only recovered a survival bag with a tracker stud beacon. That stud contained a dataset of recordings from Xandrie's suit, filling us in on her mission status up until that point, and confirming the presence of you, Athene, and a Lost Ship. It was still a dead end, but now Mil-Com went back on high alert and I was granted further resources. Across the UFS and beyond, eyes and ears, officers and AIs, scan glitter fields and Ellond Towers, all looked out for *you*.

"Of course, your recent report revealed Xandrie's fate. VigMAX has not been heard from since, and that is a mystery I would very much like to solve at some point. Maybe he was pulled into the Null with the Lost Ship, though my personal suspicion is that Athene destroyed him before she went searching for you.

"After three weeks we had an encounter with her. She got away, so we set traps in likely targets, which paid off with our Velumin Archive gambit during her final botched mission. Sorry, I see that pains you. It was assumed you had been on board when Athene was destroyed. A sad end to so much potential, so much work. So many of my own projects tied up in what was now classed as a failure. A failure! Knowledge is *never* a failure. They are so close-focussed they can't ... won't ..." He'd been clenching his fist as he paced, then realised and relaxed it. "Never mind. But although the alert level dropped, it takes time for messages to cross the UFS domain. The outermost locations still hadn't received the new command to stand down.

"And, at the far edge of the UFS there's a planet that hasn't even got a proper name. Designation HNW658, a grey dustbowl with just a few staffed monitoring stations, set up thirty years ago. Never been any point in colonising it. Too far from the Core Systems to make resource extraction worthwhile. Anyway, their satellites detected an anomalous planetary entry. Rising smoke made it easy to locate. They called it in and a nearby patrolling corvette sent down a stealth dropship to investigate. Finding you two there was *quite* the surprise."

"Not the good kind, for me," Opal said.

"Indeed. And it raises so many questions."

He circled her as he talked, so that he was not always visible. Despite his bald head, the spotlights did not glare off it. Either his skin had anti-reflectivity embedded, or he applied some kind of make-up to achieve that effect.

"Firstly, items from Lost Ships often have anomalous compositions. Yet the garments you wore when we found you turned out to be chemically unremarkable. Fibroin proteins and cellulose fibre. The sharpened shells you ungratefully wielded against your rescuers – to such devastating effect – were also standard calcium carbonate. Even the rapidly decaying ship was majorly composed of chitin, aragonite crystal and dentine scaling. Did the aliens purposefully copy fibres they know we use, choosing materials that wouldn't reveal anything useful to us? Were elements of the ship programmed to break down into mush before they could be analysed? If so, what are they hiding, and why, and how?"

"It's not hard. Same as a Genitor's boner."

"You could be executed for a joke like that."

"What joke?"

He sighed. "But there is more. We know Lost Ships sometimes reappear in the same area, but it can be decades or centuries later. The last time a Lost Ship was in the region of HNW658, the planet was probably uninhabited. So why did the Oracles send you there? Did they expect you both to die of thirst and starvation? Did they misunderstand your biological needs? Do they overlook things, because their perspectives are so different from ours? *Or did they have up-to-date information about the planet's status*, and knew you'd be found before you died of dehydration? Hmmm." He steepled his fingers below his chin. "Knowing motivation enables prediction, which precedes control."

"You can't second guess the unknowable."

"I believe *everything* is knowable, given time, resources, method, and intelligence. Take the fact that, according to your report, you were in the Null for only a few hours. But when you were discovered on HNW658, more than four months had passed. Of course, we already knew about this time dilation effect, that time passes quicker in the Topias than in our world – or vice versa, viewed through the prism of a Null perspective. It's accounted for in the theoretical understanding of Null-C drives, even. Now, it isn't possible to do an accurate comparison because records are sketchy and I have a strong suspicion that the time dilation effect varies between Topias – what a multitool in the works that wrinkle is! – but with your updated information, let's say an hour *there* is a month *here*. So a day there is roughly two years here. Spend a month there and come back, and you'd have jumped sixty years into our future without ageing. Ten months there equates to six hundred years here. It probably explains why Lost Ships seem rare to us. And yet, for all we know, the Null Entities could be *churning* vehicles out in their own time frame. It gives new insights into how much the inhabitants such as Oracles might know, if they can sample our world in a flash, yet see what we have created over *centuries*. They must be like gods! So much knowledge. So much potential in time manipulation. And so much new information for us, to make tracking down Lost Ships a methodical procedure rather than a haphazard legend. If they only come through at certain points, we can use that. And what if some of those sample points are far away, far beyond what we could ever reach? What if there are other universes, not just ours and that of the Null? Oh my, sedate me, please!"

He looked at Opal expectantly, his breathing accelerated, eyes widened, the most animated she'd ever seen him.

"So, are you banging Dulcetta?" asked Opal.

It was impossible to tell what bodily composition he had hidden under the long research gown, how much was fat versus muscle versus bone. But it definitely deflated at her answer.

"Disappointing," he said.

"I mean, she comes in after the guards leave, and exits before they return. Just made me think they're not allowed to see her. That implies some kind of jealousy."

"She is trying to bait you," said Dulcetta. "Should I deter her?"

"No, no," Aseides said with a wave of the hand. "I shouldn't get carried away. Shouldn't forget she has a razor sharp focus, but she directs it to places I would not have considered."

"And I guess you won't tell me where we are?" Opal asked. "What base, what planet?"

No answer to that one. Just appraisal.

"Okay," Opal continued. "How about this bit of methodology observation specialness: the people here. I can tell it's not a normal prison. I've heard of places like this."

"You certainly shouldn't have." But he was interested again.

"I've seen more grey-suits than guards in this section. It's obviously a research installation of some kind, not just a prison. People don't come in, get some skills training, boost their fitness, pay their dues, then leave as happy and reformed UFS citizens, do they?"

"Agreed. It is a place of punishment, not correction. But also it is a place of discovery and possibility. And, in a way, reform: because every inmate gets to contribute to the evolution of the UFS, to its security. To its *future*. That is how a criminal pays their debts."

"You really believe that?"

"That a crime has been committed against the stability of the UFS? Yes. That the punishment is justified? Not always. Certainly not for some of the Genitor indictments. Be seen, be pure, and all that. But they have their world view, just as I have mine. I am not offended by insults to the Purity Beings or Primogenitors. Likewise Genitors probably don't care about the laws forbidding public criticism of UFS technological and scientific outputs, whereas I have some stake in those. We must protect the research imperative! We can't have people disbelieving what the government tells them."

"So your beliefs are true, everyone else's aren't?"

"To a degree. Contrary beliefs must be suppressed. But rest assured, there are also a number of murderers, rapists, terrorists and so on to fill out the ranks. I don't care where my corn comes from, I just want to make bread, or some such, as they say in the Periphs. And everything here is perfectly legal. Each prisoner has had citizenship and corresponding rights revoked, names and records wiped from the official record so that they become their Subject IDs and only exist as data sources. You have been honoured in that I forwent the UV forehead barcode for you and Clarissa. I also use your given names, and excluded you from the general research pool."

"I'm not excluded from the ear stud, though." She turned her head to display her right ear lobe.

"I said I honour you. I didn't say I become stupid as a result."

"What's it do? Let you listen in? Tracker? Explosive device?"

"Explanations aren't pertinent to your situation of cooperation. My point is that I have shown kindness, and unfortunately you can't appreciate its extent or duration. But that is all right. I am not here for thanks and credit."

"*I* am aware of your kindness to this one," said Dulcetta.

"And my kindness does not end here. I mapped your scars, Opal. Old ones, from events in your military record, as well as more recent marks such as that which you said came from the Oracles digging a bullet out of your stomach, leaving strange whorls of cicatrix tissue. Your skin tells quite a story, like words on a screen but imbued with the texture of past pains. If you wish, I could have you taken to the medical bay and your dermal layers renewed. Sometimes removing the footprint of pain is enough to remove the memory of it. Or at least, the reminder." He had been speaking more softly as his speech progressed, but when she didn't respond he resorted to his normal volume. "It's fine," he said, with a dismissive wave of the hand. "I know that's something you don't care about."

Opal glanced at Aseides, taking in his flawless, almost plastic skin. Then at Dulcetta, a synthetic being that had perfectly textured human skin on the outside (albeit gold-coloured – but since humans sometimes went for skin colouring, it wasn't the giveaway it could have been). Human and non-human, with their inhuman and human skins swapped over, the similarity only in the perfection.

"Okay," said Opal. "I'd like that. And I'm sorry for my attitude. It takes time for a mind like mine to adjust. Don't hold it against me. I know you're trying to be kind."

"That's the spirit!" A smile radiated across his face, though without corresponding wrinkles it almost looked like oil spreading over water. "I'll have you escorted there and inform one of my best surgeons. This has been a productive meeting, and a sign of things to come."

"I'm trying to change, to adjust," said Opal.

"Can I ask why?"

"I know when I'm beat. That wouldn't normally bother me. I'd resist. I'd force you to kill me. But this isn't about me any more. It's about Clarissa. Everything I do is to protect her."

He scrutinised Opal's face, and waited moments more before speaking. "I believe you. It fits one of my theories, a series of stages called the Renegade's Journey. Like a hero, but degraded. One common stage is disarmament. Suddenly the renegade is weaponless. Oh no! What will they do? A defining choice. This is good. I do love progress!"

Alterations

... 23 ...

The guards' heavy boots echoed off the hard corridor surfaces, unnecessary heel strikes reinforcing their presence. Stupid machismo. Opal could move quickly and silently on her bare feet. Never underestimate going back to basics.

This was a route she knew fairly well. She visualised the junctions, the wider areas, the passages she hadn't been down. She applied her route names and predicted what came next: both direction-wise, and in terms of her future.

They would alter her in medical. Take away some of her story.

She slowed her pace and Angry D shoved her with a heavy gauntlet.

Something had nagged at her last time she came this way. Something slightly off. Now she recognised it. The ceiling-affixed domes were further apart, and unevenly spaced. Panelling was irregular, and looked like retrofit, using whatever was available. Punched sheet metal steps that didn't match anything else. Tightly curved corridors with obstructed views.

Corners were always a security issue when it came to surveillance. The ideal placement to counter this weakness would be cameras at junction centres, facing each direction. But twice she spotted areas which were potential blind spots.

Careless.

She counted her steps.

Scars weren't ugly, any more than body parts or facial features were ugly. The world left marks on bodies and minds, and only some were visible. Give up part of who you are, who knows what else you're giving up?

She was counting down, not up. Thirty-two. Thirty-one.

Spending your life as an outsider gave you a different perspective. You valued existence, not looks. The inside was the important thing. Minds. Attitudes. Kindness and compassion. Imagination and ideas.

Positive change was not to alter your *body* to match the views of strangers.

Good change was to alter your *mind* to match the views of those you loved.

To ask: what would X do in my place?

The numbers in her head got lower. Twelve. Eleven.

It was the last junction before medical.

Seven. Six.

Scars were reminders.

Opal slowed. Angry D reached out to shove her shoulder again. He'd used greater force every time she'd delayed, his impatience always bubbling below the surface, his expectations of the outcome so certain in his head.

Opal turned inside his reach while gripping his forearm firmly; she dropped her hips below his and threw him in one movement so that he smacked flat on his back in the side passage without a dome, an almighty crash of *heavy* against *hard*. She snatched Angry D's Stunstix, ready for his companion. But Silent R had delayed, missed his moment to attack her from behind, perhaps too surprised by the speed of events. He approached her now, reaching for his own Stunstix with one hand while extending his other arm towards her as – a ward? A grab attempt?

A mistake. She seized his wrist and rammed her Stunstix into his armpit. The underarm jointing on Sec-3 armour was one of the weak points, the indicator of a budget option over a premium design. Silent R stiffened then collapsed. Not fatal, but it gave her some time. She dragged him out of the main passage to the camera's blind spot. It was taking too long. Ten seconds already.

A hand grabbed her ankle. Angry D, winded but recovering, on hands and knees but trying to get up. He was the real threat. Her momentary advantage was mobility, and she needed to use it. She broke free of his grip and climbed onto his back; when he tried to slam his helmet into her face she made use of his raised chin to engage a strangle hold, locking her arms tight. He struggled so she couldn't quite get the right grip, but she didn't let go.

"You scum," he wheezed, as he twisted one way and the other. "You'll pay for this."

She squeezed harder. Had to cut off his brain's blood supply for a quick finish.

"Your sister's not with the other chattle ... she's in solitary ... easy to visit ... you'll regret ..."

Wrong thing to say. She gave up on the strangle and threw her whole body to the side. Necks aren't strong enough to resist that amount of force. A single sinewy snap and he went limp. Sometimes people dig their own graves and save you the trouble.

Silent R wasn't moving yet. No alarms rang out.

Always ask: what would your lost friend do in your place? How would they achieve what needed to be done using the tools available?

Opal was familiar with the fastenings on a Sec-3. She'd worn them enough times. She had the gloves off Angry D and was working on the helmet, but discovered extra straps. Maybe they'd upgraded or modded the armour, even though that wasn't common outside of Zorin products.

She had two catches undone and was unscrewing the spinal connecting rod when the other guard muttered something, incomprehensible electric whisper of distortion. She needed to zap him again. Damn Angry D for not keeping his stun equipment fully charged. But Silent R was hardly moving, not yet a threat. She had time to yank this off.

"No!" Silent R said, raising his visor. A pale face, as if in bloodless shock. "You can't remove his helmet," he said in his human voice. "Explosive charge."

"Bullshit," said Opal.

"The backlock ... look at the indent. If it's not removed with a sec-room de-fit tool, it activates. Ten second silent timer. To stop a prisoner stealing a uniform as a disguise. Just like you're trying to do."

Opal eyed the connectors. True, there was a sealed strap with an indentation. Of course, it could be a bluff, but ... What were her chances? Fifty-fifty? *What odds would her friend take?*

Silent R wasn't trying to get up. Didn't look like he wanted to attack. In fact, he didn't look guard-like at all. Not pissed. Not yelling for help. No expression of distaste. If anything, he seemed conflicted. There'd always been something different about this one. In the past he'd followed procedure, but never laid a hand on her.

So maybe a sixty per cent chance he told the truth. Too much of a gamble when this wasn't just about her. She'd change her plan. Have to change the route too, since she'd hoped the disguise might get her past the rotating corridors, safe passage being based on uniform rather than implants. But she could move quicker without it, she could – okay, yes. Adapt. That's what friends did. This could save minutes she would have wasted in changing clothes.

She snatched up Angry D's Stunstix. It had enough charge to shut Silent R down. She was halfway towards him when he held up a hand.

"Wait ... I can help," he said. "I know the layout. My helmet will activate the Transecs so you can get through."

"Transec?"

"Rotating corridor. Security section. You don't ever want to go down those if it's in sec mode. And you don't need to tell me what you're doing, just – take me prisoner. That's it." He reached for his weapon, but did it slowly. Click. Clasp open. Fingertips on the handle. He gently pulled it out of the holder, then slid it across the floor, where it spun to a halt by her toes.

"Fully charged," he said. "Keep them both."

She picked it up. "Why?"

"You're not the only one who isn't here by choice," he said.

"Get up. You go in front."

He had to use the wall to stand. The arm she'd stunned still hung limp at his side.

"A few junctions from here there's a comm room, right?" she asked.

"Yes. It's not used much nowadays because Dulcetta deals with IO systems."

"Don't care. Is there a maintenance area en route? Somewhere with mag clamps, cutters?"

"Yes, if we detoured down here, across, through a Transec. It's just past a staff section and guard room."

"Let's get there before the alarms kick in."

"The alarms are *already going*. Alerts flash in our helmets with no audible output, it's all networked."

"Damn. Get moving. Straight to comms, then. No time for anything else."

COMMS

... 22 ...

The guard nodded and passed by Opal without trying anything. Then he turned left, as she'd expected.

"Quicker!" she said. Shouts and footsteps echoed down the corridors. Opal held a Stunstix in each hand, glancing back every so often.

When they reached the security junction – no, Transec – it was in blue mode. The whole corridor lit up like an aquatic ice cavern. It made her cold just seeing it.

Silent R didn't wait, he walked up to the larger dome after sliding his visor back down. He'd angled himself so that the camera's view of Opal was partly blocked.

"Pass," he said, in the standard electronic guard voice.

Nothing. Footsteps, louder, closing in. She couldn't fight everyone.

Had he moved forward so he could communicate a secret message to whoever monitored? Dulcetta?

Then the Transec rotated. Blue glow faded, replaced by white, and the floor and ceiling settled into the safe position. As soon as they were through, it rotated back to blue.

"Any way to lock it like that?" Opal asked.

"No." His visor was still down, voice tinny.

She forced him to move faster, outrun pursuit, outrun the destruction of her only chance. Like they said in sniper training: one shot, make it count.

"Hey!" Guard voice, somewhere behind. They'd been spotted.

But *there was the door*, with the curving sparks logo that indicated a comm area. She'd seen it before, just once, and suspected the guards that day – ones she'd not encountered before – had taken her the wrong way. It was something she'd not been meant to see.

But she saw, all right.

She slapped the entry panel and shoved Silent R in even while it still slid open.

The room was tiny. No other exits. And almost empty.

An armoury would have been her first choice, but they'd be properly secured and guarded. Whereas old comms rooms just got forgotten. Now that AIs ran most installations, specialised rooms were redundant.

Once the door closed she hit the lock button. They could bypass that, though. This was why a mag clamp would have been useful: ram it into one of the door's indentations, lock it in place. Then they'd have had to cut their way in.

She tried to prise off the door control panel. Too close-fitting. Yet it wasn't original. Had been added at a later date. Perhaps it had clips that could be broken by striking the right place. And then a Stunstix could damage the locking mechanism? Worth a try. She activated overcharge.

"Wait," said the guy, who'd raised his visor again. His face was still pale. This was all too much for him. But some people, shock makes them complacent. She'd struck lucky.

He carefully removed something from his belt. A multitool. Then he extended the mini prybar, and wedged it behind the panel. A slam and it popped off, the plastic catches broken. He switched to a bladed cutter, identified an area of circuitry, and snipped away. A shower of sparks, then a red light.

"They reuse tech from elsewhere," he explained. "It doesn't always fit. Some of the series twelve doors have external over-rides, but they never removed the physical lock mechanisms. It's jammed, now."

"How do you know all this?"

"I've always been good with electronics."

She slapped the open button as a test, but he told the truth. Even though the indicator kept flashing green, and gears tried to whir, the light then flicked back to red and nothing happened except for a pungent whiff of scorched electrics.

But time was still tight. The friend question. The friend answer. *Do the unexpected. Then try to control and access comms.* But unlike her lost friend, Opal was only human.

"Hands on the wall, spread," she said.

Silent R did it immediately. She snatched the ties from his belt, and the mini tool from his hand. Swung him over to the console. A footrest was embedded in the floor, the plasteen cracked around its base, badly installed, but the desk structure was solid.

She made him kneel, used ties to secure his ankles and wrists against the footrest. Not comfy, but no one came here for a holiday.

"I'm sorry," she said.

"What for?"

She jabbed his neck with a Stunstix and he collapsed. He'd have a banging headache, but he'd live.

No distractions.

This room wasn't kitted for luxury. It had obviously been an afterthought even during the establishment of the base, let alone the retrofit, or damage repair, or whatever had led to sloppy alterations. It must have become a storage cupboard. Nearby was a trolley, odds and ends stacked on top. Spare piping leaned against a wall. A dismantled air filtration system took up a corner. No obvious cameras.

She plonked herself into the desk seat. The console before her was at least three generations old, pre-smart surface. Good. It was the kind of thing she'd been trained on back in her specialist systems courses, the only classes she'd ever really enjoyed during her mandatory military enlistment.

The only classes that weren't training her to kill.

This device was generic design. Console, port, holographic projection. She swiped her hand, woke the UI, and pulled up the comm interface. A message scrolled across the screen:

> **BIOPROFILE NOT RECOGNISED**

To be expected.

She swiped to the emergency section, the only area not fully locked down. Selected the CRINVI interface: CRIsis Non-Vocal Input.

The restricted UI appeared, a luminous speckle of projected letters onto the desk surface, enabling typing. The oldest of interfaces. Dust on the table top glowed in the colours of the projection. No one had used the room in some time. Rarely used meant rarely updated.

She cracked her knuckles in preparation but her grin faded when someone started pounding the door from outside. They'd found her.

Distraction. Ignore. Focus on priorities, as an old friend once said.

Emergency systems would be hooked into base security. But older ones, like this, often had an option to go wider. Redundant now that AI control was standard in military installations, but in those days people needed a backup.

Shouts outside, more banging. They couldn't get in.

She glanced at the ceiling for inspiration.

What would a friend do?

Gather information. Prepare.

Opal used the mini prybar on the multitool, pushed it against a joining point on the console. Again, she was lucky it was old: modern ones were all-in-one kits requiring a remoulder (or a lot of brute force and risk of damage to components) to get inside. But this kind ...

Pop!

She let the panel fall to the floor after examining it for potentially useful labels. Nothing. The multitool had a torch. She shone it inside the case, checked the circuitry, looking for year designations, model numbers, corporation chips. With specialist hardware she'd have more options. She missed her old training kit. But sometimes memory was your best weapon.

There! ID codes. She now had a better idea of what she was dealing with. Commands sprang to mind. Ideas. Ways in. Unlike an AI she didn't have perfect recall, needed these triggers to take her mind back, to engage context, to retrieve what it might have categorised as useless nonsense.

The advantage of CRINVI was that it would accept variants of anything it understood, as a parser aid for dealing with crisis situations. This was hardly even a hack, just an attempt to out-think the interface.

She typed, fingers tapping on the desk and activating the projected letters:

`access emergency channels`

The display updated with a response:

> APEN CW232: REGISTER

Residual effects of not being a recognised user, but parsed through a different language system. She tried gesturing at the swipe display above, but it had been locked out. This was all going to be based on words.

`disable arbitration`

> APEN CW232: REGISTER

`arbitration override`

> APEN CW232: REGISTER

Damn. Think. The machine wasn't being obtuse. It was just in a loop. You had to break out of the loop. Remember the commands for the different systems, the combinations of software and hardware from a more primitive time. What would a friend do? *Think like her opponent.* A machine that could think like a human. And so, become a human that could think like a machine.

Opal kept typing, trying combinations, and then:

```
0 arbitration
> 0 ENABLED
> RUNNING bus.Arbiter
> N. category 0. writername 1.
> APEN CW11: ACCEPTED
```

Well well well, ones and zeros all the way. Could have been a joke, but she didn't feel like laughing. The guards had fetched a plasma burner – maybe even from the maintenance room she skipped – and were sizzling an oval of blinding fizz through the door.

```
1 access emergency channels
> 1 ENABLED
> APEN CW11: CNR
```

She was getting somewhere.

```
1 write
> 1 ENABLED
> S-tax: Target!Mess [syn poss]
```

It looked like she was in. Or rather, out. Outside the closed loop and on an emergency broadcast channel. Sure, it was low-res, probably not widely monitored, but there was always someone listening. She ran a test.

```
S-wide!Opal here
> Broadcast success
```

She'd even remembered the correct target transmission name. She was flaky on the syntax but worth trying everything.

```
S-wide!Public!W-band!Transport
lanes!military prox!Athene, Opal Imbiana
here, the Clarissa constellation is real,
Aseides has us
> BROADCAST SUCCESS: S-WIDE / PUBLIC /
W-BAND
> BROADCAST FAILURE: TRANSPORT LANES /
MILITARY PROX [SYNTAX ERROR]
```

Three out of five. Not bad.

```
1 repeat all success; list pingbacks
> RUNNING busArbiter / 18:08:25 #Text
150
> #25836 = Ship "Blue Murder" = NON-LO-
CATABLE, position index0 not provided
> #37861 = Outpost "Zletovsko" = NON-LO-
CATABLE, position index0 not provided
```

> #10049 = Ship "Lifeboat Mona" = NON-LO-
CATABLE, position index0 not provided

And it went on. Something was wrong. It was performing the actions, not getting the expected result. Were the ships receiving her message or not? It only took one craft to relay the emergency message before the UFS clamped down, and the words would be *out there*, echoing between nodes where they could be repeated, boosted, shared, found by anyone running keyword scrapes across a number of networks.

A deafening clang as the door fell in, edges still steaming even as the guards burst through the molten oval. They were armed with some of the nastiest stuff: suffocation foam cannon, lance shockers, and screamers that could make your ears bleed.

Her time was up. She stood, and raised her arms. "I surrender," she said.

The bastards fired anyway.

Awakenings

... 21 ...

Sounds came back first. Movement and hushed voices.

Memory and context were still scrambled.

Was it a surprise party?

Was she waking from an operation?

Opal ached, and pain was a tether to memories. She reeled them in, each attached to others, each making up a picture, filling in parts of a puzzle.

No, she wasn't a child. This was no party.

She opened her eyes, a watery squint into bright lights, a ring of them facing inwards. Vague movement in the shadows beyond. Everything was blurred. A display unit a few metres away seemed to hold dismembered heads. And was that someone strung up on a rack? Hard to make out. No one had spoken to her yet, maybe not noticed she was coming around. She tried to move. Strapped down, arms locked by her sides, limited head mobility. She couldn't make out the words being spoken, too whispery. Blink, get the water drops out.

Clearer now. Not real heads on display, some of them looked like robot skulls. The way they were laid out suggested ornamentation, or honour. In a position where they could be clearly seen by a strapped-down victim. That might be relevant. A threat?

The rack thing nearby. It was a huge ring of metal, attached to the floor by a rod so it could rotate around the y axis. Currently it faced her. In the centre was a man. Naked. Head lolling. Short red hair, pale skin. His arms and legs were pulled into an X, held in place by versatile cords which grew from the inner edges of the ring. Holes showed where more of the cords could extend, if required.

She blinked again. The face was familiar, even at this angle.

The guard. Silent R.

Opal looked down at herself. She was still dressed in her crimson paper gown, though now stained with the sticky yellow residues of suffocation foam.

"You're awake," said Aseides.

"You're supposed to be smart, but often waste words stating the obvious," Opal replied.

She tried to see beyond the lights, to get an idea of the room's scale, and who moved around and whispered just beyond the circle of illumination. More than two people, possibly more than five.

Aseides nodded, seemingly agreeing with her comment, but she couldn't rule out an earpiece and external comms. "Why did you do something so stupid?"

"Old habits."

"We had an agreement that would have been to your advantage. Your behaviour negates that." Aseides' manner always had a weird duality to it, as if only half focussed on the present, while the other half of his mind had already moved on to the next task.

"Don't pretend to be surprised," she told him.

He liked to pace. It was a regular pattern, as if in synchronisation with a ticking mind. She was tempted to tap her fingers in time with his steps again. Maybe later.

"The message you broadcast," he said, stopping to look at her face. "Why did you send that, if you believed ... no, no. Let me start again. Why do you hold to the delusion that Athene is still out there when every piece of logic and evidence proves you are wrong?"

"Because everything about you is fake. Videos and reports created by an unimaginative level three pet AI sexbot are hardly going to change that perception."

Heavy footsteps, then Dulcetta entered the light, her golden skin reflecting it in a dazzling display. She glowered at Opal, and one hand twitched like she wanted to strike. Interesting. Opal now knew who one of the observers was. And also that Dulcetta's buttons were as easy to press as Opal had suspected from previous encounters. That shouldn't be the case for any socialised AI, which meant mods or custom design to a human set of preferences, with dialled-up parameters for pride and temper. Useful to know.

Judging from the weight of Dulcetta's movements now and in the past, she was densely built. Maybe as much as 130 kilos, backed up by super-tight powered muscle fibres. That gave her massive physical potential. Not something to fight against, one to one.

Also useful to know.

"I am not some level three type AI, and I am not –"

"Dulcetta, *please*," Aseides interrupted. "She's baiting you. Stand down."

"I'm sorry for saying that," said Opal.

Dulcetta moved to his side, although there was a hint of reluctance to her retreat.

When no one else spoke, Opal added, "I know cumdollz are level fours."

Dulcetta's eyes, normally like human eyes carved from the finest crystal, now illuminated in an emerald glow. Probably just for show, an emotional outlet, a means of communication.

But it was Aseides who spoke. "Since you show an interest, however facile ... Dulcetta cannot be categorised via the normal systems. If one were forced, then some elements of her might be like an advanced Five, with a fully developed humanity that is missing from the interpretations normally foisted on socialised AIs. But she is also able to splinter like a Six in order to perform other tasks. In fact, she was one of the prototypes that led to the *development* of Sixes. She is mother to many. And it is a shame you can't distinguish between different AI types, any more than you can separate real documents from your imagined fakes. Better discernment would have saved you pain in your attempt, and further pain to come. So, again: why?"

"Intuition."

"Which equals instability of cognition. It's amusing how faith creates certainty from the dust of bones. No evidence of the senses will shake the beliefs. You align with religions. That's an amusing outcome from such a cynic as yourself."

"'Absence of evidence isn't evidence of absence.' Isn't that the kind of guff you'd say?"

He smiled, fingers forming a circle beneath his chin, as if encapsulating a tiny imaginary audience.

"This is a rich vein," he said. "Dialectic method, back and forth. It generates ideas in me. Always has. I suspect I need the nutrients of unpredictability and resistance to find that which is hidden in plain sight."

"Glad to help."

"Do you see what is hidden in plain sight too, Opal?"

"Nah. Too many bright lights blinding me. Can you dial it down a notch?"

"Didn't you think accessing the comm station was a bit too easy?"

"No. You're all just complacent arseholes."

He tilted his head. Still smiling. The smiles never reached his eyes, making it impossible to assess how much of them he felt.

"Nothing in this base is an accident. Dulcetta sees to that. We set up four escape possibilities for you. I'm surprised you missed the others. You're slipping."

"And you're bluffing."

"It was obvious you'd take the bait, even though I admit that I secretly hoped you wouldn't, that we really *had* made some progress. I knew you didn't want to remove your scars. You have H4 markers for practicality, with a sublevel focus on pain (and painful memory) motivation. Combine that with a cross-parallel identity confusion and partial denial, aligned along the Genn diagram R-axis of non-conformity, and it was an obvious outcome."

Opal's eyes had adjusted now. This room was not like the previous small interrogation room with its low-tiled ceiling. This was a high domed chamber, in which sounds echoed like her oubliette. Probably metallic walls and ceiling, rather than pristine white plasteen panelling. The amount of echo gave her some idea of diameter.

"Why would you do that?" she asked.

"To crush your hope, of course. It's all the more effective when you first have the illusion of freedom. You see, breaking someone isn't about pain. That's just torture, which can be a part of breaking, but can just as easily be punishment or deterrence. True breaking is cleverer. It's about taking away the manifold expressions of hope. Hope of escape, of change, of ever being whole again, of there being goodness in the world. Once you take away all hope you can replace it with fresh concepts, since the patient will be so desperate for *something* to believe in.

"It's part of a program of mental modifications. Each takes time to settle. Preload elements, substantive ingraining, post-reinforced chemical inducements. With other people I just need five minutes, a skin tray, and a razor-edged peeler, but you're a special case. And so you have a chance to comply, and forego some of the unpleasantness! I believe in *choices*. A lack of options induces desperation: but offer alternatives, and manipulate circumstances to make some of them more attractive, and you have an efficient persona modification program."

"You admit all that? Seems naive."

"The beauty of my systems is that they work whether you know about them or not. Sometimes they even work *better* when consciously applied to the right kind of mind. Think back to your lessons about interrogation. I note you had good theoretical scores but performed poorly in the practical element. Still, you'll know that if someone is to be tortured then it is more efficient if you inform them ahead of time, so they can anticipate it, focus on it, *dread* it. By the time you start cutting or burning, half the job is done for you: their nerve endings are super sensitive, and their anticipatory senses inappropriately interpret sensation as pain. And so I cleverly segue the topic towards the 'what happens next' part of our conversation."

"You said you lured me into the escape attempt. In that case, you can't blame me."

"But I had also *warned* you. There have to be consequences to our actions. Promises must be kept. Both are necessary conditions for trust and behaviour modification. And so, there have to be *punishments*. I don't make the rules."

"Yes you do."

"It was a joke, Opal."

"You're as funny as a rash of Aloran hexworms."

"Back and forth, excellent. But to the point. Possibly literally. There will be punishment today. But it won't be the soul-destroying bleakness of the Perfervid Chamber, my special place which you have yet to experience. Not today, anyway. And, as a further kindness, you also have *choices*, and they can affect the type and scale of the punishment." He turned towards the encircling lights. "Revive the second subject," he said.

A figure in a grey research gown stepped into view, wearing a mask of perforated mesh which hid their face. Gloves covered their hands too, so that no skin was visible. They approached the sleeping guard and yanked another stretchy cord from the inner ring that held him. It extended, and they fed it under the skin of his rib cage, sealing it in place with some kind of clamp, puckering the bloody flesh into a bulge.

Moments later the guard raised his head groggily. Presumably the cords could feed chemicals and drugs into bodies.

"Where am I?" he asked, glancing around through slitted lids. He noticed the way he was secured, his nakedness, the observers. "No, I didn't do anything!" Panic in his voice. "Please!"

"Be quiet," commanded Aseides. "You're here *because* you didn't do anything. Not enough, anyway. You were practically her assistant! You're all drilled on base security, and the penalties." He turned to Opal. "I need guards. But they can become brutal in this role, unable to retain the necessary detachment. I disapprove of mistreatment to no purpose. I certainly do not approve of the threat you received from his companion. Sometimes guards need to be reminded that dehumanisation of subjects has its place, but it must never spill over into pointless provocation."

"Oh, you're so thoughtful," said Opal.

"I do consider that to be one of my traits. And so, *the choice*. You are to receive multiple sessions of a punishment that is currently unspecified, but will be unpleasant. For attempted escape and outside communication, it will be five sessions. I give you an option. I could provide you with a scalpel and release your bonds. You may take out any frustrations you wish on this guard. There would have been two, but since you broke the other's neck, my resources are limited. You will kill the guard in any way you like, taking as long as you want. Observing you and your choices will be useful to me. The guard is going to die anyway, so you would not be saving his life by refusing. But by taking part you would be saving *yourself*. In return for agreeing to this, your punishments would be *severely* reduced." Aseides clicked his fingers.

Another person in a full grey research gown entered the illuminated circle. They also wore a mask but this one was made of polished wood, with leaf patterns carved into it. The researcher held out a scalpel in one black-gloved hand, and something that resembled a deflated and translucent balloon in the other.

"This is an Asphyx," said Aseides, pointing to the second item. "It compresses over a skull and face. Porosity is controlled externally. It can enable normal breathing, or completely shut off air flow, and anywhere in between. If you agree to this offer, each punishment session will only consist of wearing this, completely sealed, for seventy seconds. I'm sure you'll agree, that is minor. I bet you can hold your breath for far longer than that!"

Opal glanced at the red-haired prisoner. His eyes were wide, beseeching. Yet he didn't seem surprised by how things were going. That suggested he was fully aware of these kinds of situations. Had he participated in them? Perhaps he was as cruel as Aseides. Perhaps he deserved to die.

But killing someone who couldn't fight back, who wasn't actively trying to harm her ... that wasn't something you came back from.

"The Asphyx is excellent for its ability to prolong all the sensations of suffocation and panic whilst holding back just enough to prevent irreversible brain damage. The way people writhe and drool is an indicator of the intense terror it creates. I once had a phase of researching the long-term effects and interpreted cognition of extremely low oxygen levels on the brain, but I got bored after – apologies. You don't want to know."

An attempt to scare her? That even the easy option could be horrifying? Aseides watched, unblinking. He begrudged missing any input, any data. He was probably as interested in Opal's decision-making as he was in her actions.

That was why she had to keep him in the dark.

Yet Opal also had to stay alive for Clarissa. She had to stay functioning and whole. Had to do whatever it took. If she couldn't free Clarissa, then she had to protect her. To do that required self-preservation.

"If you want to kill me, I understand," said the guard. "At least you'll make it quicker than him. Just don't think we're all bad."

"Oh, now it's all coming out." Aseides folded his arms. "R-43 will say anything to manipulate you, Opal."

But Silent R wasn't finished. "I only tell the truth. No point pretending, now that I'm a dead man. But you should stop pretending too, Aseides. None of us chose to be here, to do what you make us do. It isn't betrayal when I had no freedom to begin with."

"Freedom is a myth. Someone with your background should know that. What next, demands for equality?"

"I'm not stupid." The guard lowered his head, worn out.

Opal kept her gaze on Aseides, but her mind on the scalpel. She could feel its slender weight in her hand, imagine how it would split her thumb's skin if she pressed the blade against it, so smooth the pain wouldn't register until after the blood.

CHOICES

... 20 ...

Of course, scalpels were tools, not weapons. They break easily if used with force. They would be ineffective against a being like Dulcetta.

So you go for the weak point. She could take the blade to *Aseides*. His physical abilities were unknown, but she'd err on the side of him focussing more on his mind, and hope it wasn't solid muscle beneath his research gown. He was only a few steps away. An eye blink of movement, cross the gap, make him the shield. Blade to his throat. Dulcetta would hold back. Opal would have a hostage. If she was careful but also decisive, she could use him to get to Clarissa. They could reach a vehicle. Keep Aseides as insurance. It was the best shot she'd seen so far. He'd be controllable because he wouldn't feel fear, would in fact be intrigued, want to see the outcome, play along. He might even share information, acting his part as an embedded researcher, an active participant in an unfolding research scenario.

"You've been staring at me for eleven seconds," Aseides told her. "Presumably your attention is partly elsewhere. Let me clarify that everyone would leave the chamber before you were released and gained access to the scalpel. It would just be you and the guard. You may have considered threatening to take your own life, but that would be a bluff. You would not leave your sister alone over such a frivolous non-opportunity. So your options are to accept my offer, or refuse it: in which case your punishment will be five sessions of something *worse* than the Asphyx. Worth bearing in mind."

The bastard.

"I'm not going to kill anyone with a scalpel," she said.

Aseides waved a hand, and the wooden-faced researcher retreated, disappearing into the blackness that always exists behind a glow.

"I am enjoying this. I want to try something else. Your sentence ended with a clarification. Was that pertinent? Let's see. Dulcetta: if Opal touches your hand, I'd like you to immediately send two thousand volts through the guard for a duration of thirty seconds. Presumably he'll be dead before his body heats to a hundred degrees and melts his eyeballs. We may need to turn on the air filters if it gets unpleasant."

"Understood."

"Opal, lift your hand. Your wrist is secured, but you have that much movement."

Opal stayed still.

"Dulcetta: apply the same outcome if Opal doesn't comply with any of my commands in the next five minutes."

"Also understood."

Opal could swear Dulcetta smirked as she said that.

Opal raised her left hand.

Aseides smiled. "My offer still stands. Kill him this way, you get five minor punishment sessions. Refuse, and they'll be at the same level I use for everyone else. Equality, eh? I'm not all bad."

Dulcetta moved in and knelt, slipping her own hand under Opal's, a distance of only centimetres.

The detail of Dulcetta's golden skin was much clearer up close. It looked like it might be organic, or a good facsimile of it, down to the level of sweat pores and subsurface musculature. At first glance you'd just assume Dulcetta was a human who worked out to excess in order to create sculpted muscles. She wore a loose-fitting green outfit which draped off one shoulder today, and laced boots which were open to the sides. The kind of thing any high-fash model might be seen wearing.

But the eyes were one of the giveaways. Obviously artificial, and designed as works of art. Like liquid crystals which kept their shape, somehow reflecting caustic light around the interiors, tinted by translucent irises composed of minute filaments covering the spectrum of blues and yellows.

Then again, just like skin colouring, many a human had artificial eyes now. Augmentations were the thing.

Opal held her hand in place.

Dulcetta smiled.

Strangely, her teeth weren't perfect. A slight crookedness to the lower incisors. Affectation, or Aseides' preference, maybe. It depended on how Dulcetta came about, when she had been born.

No, not born.

It was still adjustment for Opal. She no longer saw divisions where they once seemed self evident. Her adventures and friendship had changed that. AI or human, robot or alien, hero or monster, dark skin or pale skin or gold skin. None of it was relevant any more.

Now there were only friends and enemies.

Opal's hand trembled. She quickly stilled it. The palm beneath was too eager for touch. Contact that wouldn't be tenderness, but violence.

Looking at Dulcetta, it was clear that beauty and cruelty, desire and abhorrence, were easy to mix. More boundaries which never really existed except in minds. Luckily, Opal always liked ignoring demarcations set up by other people. Rules, laws, divisions. Fuck that shit.

"I'll never do it," said Opal.

"You might. Given time," whispered Dulcetta.

Everyone waited.

The guard watched, teeth clenched as he anticipated the shocking death that could arrive at any moment.

Dulcetta's perfect crystals lured the gaze like hypnosis.

Aseides, poised and alert.

(A dog! He reminded her of a dog, waiting for a ball to be thrown. Opal had never had a dog as a companion, not possible at her military grade, but she'd seen them. Yep, he was a dog.)

The invisible watchers beyond the ring of lights, those creepy pain perverts.

Opal's wrist ached so much.

"I said no!" she shouted.

Dulcetta glanced at Aseides; he nodded; she removed her hand and stood.

"Disappointingly sub-optimal choices," she told Opal. "Though anticipated. Because, after a time, volatility as a characteristic *enables* predictability. That's why I think your research potential here is going to be much shorter in duration than you or Aseides might hope."

"That's enough, Dulcetta," said Aseides. Then, to Opal: "But it looks like you are out of choices. I will execute the guard, and you receive full punishment across five sessions."

"I'm not out of choices," said Opal. "I already made one."

"Oh?"

"Let the guard live. But make him a prisoner. Like me."

Silent R's eyes widened, but he said nothing, as if afraid that he'd discover some trick.

"Why would I do that?" asked Aseides. "It would be like creating a list of tasks to do in the future, when I could complete them today. Touch once, move on."

"You like to study. Changing environments and roles is a variable you can alter. You want to punish him? This is a punishment. One which lasts longer. You want data? This provides more data. It allows investigation of reversals. Give someone another viewpoint and they might become a new person."

"I've done it before. It's not as interesting as you think."

"You ever done it because someone else proposed it? That face you're pulling suggests not."

"What if I said I could agree to that ... but only if I added forty per cent more sessions to your punishment? Would you take extra pain for no beneficial reason?"

He was pushing her to back down. To be sensible and practical. To put self-preservation first.

Fuck him.

"Sure," she said. "Because no matter what I do or say, you'll find excuses to hurt me and claim it was my fault. That's your style, isn't it, denial of responsibility? Like you're hiding from something. A conscience?"

"Conscience kicks in when we do what's wrong. If we're doing what's right, it's irrelevant."

"You've no right to do this to any of us."

"The law disagrees."

"The law is wrong," Opal said.

"The law cannot be wrong. The law states it is universal, with no exceptions, and even ignorance of it is no defence. The law does not have to explain itself or publish itself in order to manifest. Which, to my mind, makes UFS law a kind of god. And gods aren't supposed to be questioned. They get *angry*." He grinned at her.

"You don't care about the law as long as it lets you do what you want," said the guard, somehow incensed.

"How would you know, R-43?"

"Because everything you do ignores people's rights!"

"Rights. Huh. One of those words bandied like a shield. I hear it daily. 'My rights.' 'Human rights.' 'Rights of my people.' 'Discrimination rights.' 'Tech rights.' 'Access rights.'" Aseides said those in a whiny voice. "More rights are invented every year. They breed faster than a forgotten colony in the Periphs."

"You dismiss them easily," said Opal.

"Logically, yes. Half of the rights are contradictory of the other half. How can you have a right to free speech if you also have a right not to be offended by other people's free speech? One person says there's a right to life, another says there's a right not to live in an overpopulated world. Which is it? How can you have a right not to be randomly murdered without giving up a right to freedom so a government can protect you *from* murder? Everyone's so vehement about rights without understanding what they are. A mess of confused thinking."

"Whatever," said the guard. "We all know what's right and wrong. You're just using justifications to avoid admitting it. Typical UFS."

"I'm far from typical, you idiot. Also not really UFS, except for convenience. But I'm tired of you. Speak again and you'll go through hell before the day is over." Aseides waited, but the guard kept silent this time. After an appropriate time, Aseides rotated smoothly back to Opal.

She stared at him. "You whine that it's too complicated and contradictory for your shiny head," she said. "But it needn't be. It can be so simple that even your ego can comprehend that it's possible to throw away all of the rights except for *one*. The central one."

"I'm listening."

"*All beings have a right to their own body*. It's the only thing we ever really own. And no one can harm it or do anything to it without our permission."

"Opal, you always have a way of cutting through the mire, even if it leads to oversimplification. I like your idea, though." Aseides stretched his arms out and looked up dramatically. "Enshrine a single right in the sanctity of being! One law, in place of millions!"

"It's logical," said Opal. "You could agree. Adopt it. *Free us.* Do the right thing."

"Ooh, conversational transition, I like it! It's true that our body is the vehicle for all we are, and all we can be. Our tool, our existence, our experience and memory. Mmm. Yes. I see a potential article on such a topic. Broad and singular rather than narrow and multiple. At a stroke it covers killing, eating, rape, torture, kidnapping." He paced again, nodding. "I could support that. Much to think about." Then he laughed and faced Opal. "Shame it will never happen."

"We're not excused from our decisions and actions, Aseides."

"I don't need to be excused, Opal. Power is not fair. No one born into the UFS ever voted for the UFS to have authority over them. Governments don't work like that. They sometimes wrap it in pretty lights to dazzle the ignorant, claim that making a choice in some limited vote indicates citizen support for the overall structure, but the truth is that authority comes from *power*, not consent. And power does what it likes because that is the *definition* of power. It isn't part of any nonexistent moral framework. Those frameworks are philosophical resistance attempts by the powerless. Irrelevant. Power is pure. Power is god. And, much as I love our chats, we came here today for a *purpose*. And I want to get that over with so that we can move on to more pleasant things in the future. And so, to punishments."

"You don't have to do this."

"Stating the obvious is an insult to us both."

"Okay, *don't* fucking do this."

"Imperatives have no power when you are a prisoner. I need to punish you. That involves suffering. There are many ways to achieve this with a human body and psyche. When I restrict myself to ones that don't involve irreparable damage – burns, amputation, physical restructuring, body modifications – I have fewer choices, but more than enough." He gestured at something outside of Opal's vision. "As prepared."

Motion. An embellished metallic table with implements laid out neatly was carried into her view by two people in research gowns. One was Mesh Mask, the other's disguise was a reflective blue covering that resembled an animal's head, though not a creature Opal recognised. They placed the table carefully. Maybe its location was for the convenience of Aseides, but she had no doubt it was also chosen so that she and the guard could look at the devices and feel dread.

She didn't look.

Aseides took one of the many varied masks from the display behind him, and placed it over his own head. It was silver, shaped to resemble a stylised moon with an expressionless face. Aseides approached the table, moved items around, as if trying to select a favourite toy.

Other figures brought additional lights in. The guards – if that's what they were – wore yellow robes down to the ground, and huge amber helmets that covered their heads. She'd once overheard an escorting guard refer to these imposing figures as "Warders". They positioned the free-standing lights up close, beams aimed at Opal's face so she could see even less than before. Her world reduced to the centre of a dying sun in a dead solar system, all focus pulling in, contracting to a bright spot that would be pain. The figures stood behind the new lights for the best show. No doubt they'd observe in silence no matter how much she screamed.

Aseides raised a rod-like, curved implement. It didn't resemble the functional whiteness of UFS tools, more the ornate decoration of some lost past.

"Subcutaneous inserter," he told Opal, rotating it so that it glinted in the light. "I'll resolve you first, then deal with the guard – sorry, new prisoner. Habits! Note that your five sessions, plus the increase for letting him live, means seven punishment sessions in total for you. Though I will be kind and give you a day or two to recover between each session."

"What's in the gadget?"

"A variant of A1 Cycline. It paralyses and triggers pain receptors without causing cellular damage. Results are affected by dosage and post-dispersion sensations. At the most extreme levels, with all pain triggers going off at once, it is like being burned alive to the point of transcendence. In this case I've combined it with hallucinogenics, to enhance the mental aspects." He lowered it to her arm.

"Last time I'll ask," said Opal, keeping her teeth clenched. "Don't. Do. This."

"Opal. This isn't some fictional ent-cast where a character outwits their captor and gets away. You *will* go through this. But that's a positive, too. You will *get through* this. So, remember your training. Remember breathing, focus, asymmetric perceptions."

"What I'll remember is *you*. Making this choice, now. That's all I need to remember."

"Brave talk. Good. We'll see."

He pushed the tip of the device under her skin.

Agonies

... 19 ...

Pain is a thing.

It's a thing you can't touch or pick up. It's a thing in your head. But it's every bit as real as a knife, gun or a whip.

Opal's muscles spasmed, fought each other, contracting like the worst cramps. Struggling was futile.

Other sensations. In the skin. Tickling. Not unpleasant at first, but soon it began to itch.

Then ominously growing discomfort at a deeper level, in her stomach, like a reaction to bad food.

It was spreading.

The contractions evened out. She tried to move a finger and it would not, could not. The attempt triggered new sensations. They were pulling out her fingernails, each ripped from its bed, bleeding and raw. Paralysis of body but not sensation or mind.

Her blood burned like heat, beyond exercise, beyond training in furnace conditions to simulate desert warfare.

She could move her eyes. Along with breathing, it was her only freedom. But doing so jabbed needles into her eyeballs, hundreds of scraping pinpricks.

Everything was about eyes.

They all watched. Greedy eyes hidden behind lights that burned, heat everywhere.

Breathe deep, don't focus on the burning.

Sweat broke out on her body. The paper dampened as her head fried in the hot sun's beams.

Eyes. Eyes hidden behind masks, drinking pain and calling it data.

No. No.

Someone scraped at her skin with a blunt knife. Persistent, rasping everywhere. She looked. But there was no one. Unless they were invisible.

Eyes. Aseides' eyes. Silver-masked and empty peep holes of horror. Blank as a paused display screen. Unreadable. Experienced. They had seen horrors. They had instigated horrors.

Stinging. Nettles and insects and acids. They filled the gaps that heat couldn't reach.

She had been burned before. These faceless captors knew her fears all too well.

No. Inhale long. Exhale. Fight to slow the racing heart. They were tearing out her toenail as well, wrenching and twisting and –

Paralysed so she could only look. Into the green eyes of a synth. The most beautiful terrible thing she'd ever seen. The most hateful. Insane. It made no sense. Opal's life made no sense.

Draw air into the lungs, and focus. Focus on a point. *Two points.* Eyes. Two big *brown* eyes. Two beautiful eyes full of intelligence and mischief and they were oh, unbearable skin-melting heat,

no, it *is* bearable, *concentrate, count*

three – two – one

Eyes of a sister, of one she loved. A universe of billions upon billions and only those two eyes mattered. Two eyes. And there was *another* being that mattered, that loved. A being with no eyes and a thousand eyes. A being that was more human in its inhumanity than anyone in this room. Two beings Opal adored, and between them there were only two eyes.

Centre yourself, in and out, calm.

She couldn't do it! Her skin was being peeled. She poured with sweat now, a river, a stinging river of salt rubbed in a wound. The room pulsed with agony – *no, it breathed with her. The lights flowed, in and out, helping, heartbeats, they were sympathetic pulsars and she was the centre of everything.*

Skins are surfaces. That's where incineration first occurs. *Retreat deeper. Focus deeper. Find somewhere cool inside, somewhere away, somewhere past.*

Past.

The last moment you were happy.

A needle shoved into her ear, into her brain.

Sink down away from it. Deeper.

Muscles being grilled.

Down.

Teeth clenched.

Descend. Cooler.

Holding someone.

Clarissa.

Opal held Clarissa's hand.

Clarissa didn't speak.

Holding was enough with those you loved.

Holding says it all.

An empty world with only the two of them.

With a third, it would be perfect.

A family. A home. A future.

Where was the third?

She would come. She *had* to come.

This heat, it was *not* from outside, *not* from torture. She told herself it was from *memory*, and it was bearable. *Repeat that, repeat that. Repeat it to make it true.* It was a memory, which meant she'd already lived through it and it wasn't so bad. A memory, but she was inside it.

Aseides had added hallucinogenics.

To make things *worse*.

The idiot!

It helped!

Opal could keep retreating, keep making her own world in her mind, split herself in two, the part feeling *pain* and the part feeling *love*, and favour her good side, as she did when she fought, as she'd always had to do.

Holding hands.

Clarissa was an anchor in the vortex.

It was quiet, the wind a puny thing, like the wisps of cloud streaked across the green-tinted sky, like the weak sun which rose over the jagged grey landscape.

This was the desolate planet they'd reached after Opal rescued Clarissa from the Null. From the Oracles.

Peace. Sisters staring towards the horizon. The future.

The world was once heavily volcanic. Igneous grey rock stabbed upwards at every angle, angry at the universe that spawned it, spiking and slicing all it encountered so it could share that pain, one of the jagged pieces cutting into her stomach, slicing, slicing –

No, not pain, no, not there at all. *Here.*

Here and now.

A hand held. It roots you to the spot. Looking down at the top of Clarissa's head, her curly hair which bounced when she played, bounced like the spirit no one else saw in that small body except Opal. Opal had the time to observe, every small detail, everything that could be interpreted as a need, as a joke, or as a joy.

A hand held is a comfort. Back to this seed, this root.

Plants dotted the landscape. Stringy turquoise things of unknown toxicity.

If they were here much longer Opal would have to sample one, test it, work out if it was deadly or if it might prolong Clarissa's life. Mash them with stones. Try again to light a fire, to cook, to break down cells to make them

breaking down

burning, blistering, skin raising in the heat, fats melting

no

no

no

she floated, drugs in her system, *remember it's all drugs, none of it real.*

What was in her *heart* was real, what was in her *head* was real.

She knelt. She kissed the top of Clarissa's head, inhaled the smell of her, a smell that had been absent for so long.

A smell that proved she was the same. That this was Clarissa, but Clarissa who hadn't aged. Opal had moved on, growing older by fourteen years, but she hadn't left her sister behind, not truly, because *she was with her now*. Opal was *here*. She had circled, an orbit, an unbreakable orbit, determined always to descend back to the centre, the core of her life, and here she was, pulled down onto this planet exactly where she was meant to be, exactly back on the surface with her core, her focus

Focus focus breathe breathe

Breathe the air of this planet, its tang, then breathe the hair of this sister, this beautiful being who was worth the universe, worth life, worth pain

not pain, not here! why was someone digging out her breast tissue with a sharp-edged spoon, tearing – worth life – worth ...

worth it, and Opal smiled

She smiled.

And Clarissa looked up at her and grinned back.

That beam, those teeth, the brown eyes that were love, that were grateful, that communicated in ways words could not, because words were hard sometimes, or lied, but actions were better than words.

This feeling in her heart didn't lie.

This feeling in her heart was big. So big no one suspected. No one knew.

No one except Clarissa.

No one except Athene.

Love was the power.

And she continued to smile.

Her body floated up, off the planet. She pulled it down, pulled it back to the memory.

The sun in the memory wasn't bright enough to burn her like this, *cheat, make it bigger, it explains the sensation,* she is still in *this world,* still with *this person.* No other world existed.

And the sun above brightened.

Voices, trying to break through, asking why she laughed, what it meant, how she could do that. Shut them out, cram them in cells beneath the rock, their own oubliettes, slam the door, lock it, swallow the key, dissolve it in stomach acids

No, acids, no ... change the thought ... gone.

Gone ...

here. here and now. A kiss and a hug.

Not enough, the other world breaking in, forcing its way.

Only one thing to do then. Always the same.

Run!

She picked up Clarissa. Clarissa wrapped her legs around Opal's waist, arms around her neck, how Opal always used to carry Clarissa when her little sister needed comfort.

A secret embedded in there. A secret and a lie. Go deeper, pull out the truth.

And it came to her.

Opal carried Clarissa like that when *Opal* needed comfort.

When things were rough in the orphanage.

When their adoptive parents died. When they were left alone.

And Opal never got to carry and hug Clarissa the day the UFS bastards split the sisters up. The last time Opal would see her sister for fourteen years. The last time she heard her make a sound. A sound of pain. A scream.

A scream!

Can't scream, paralysed.

And yet she can smile. The power of a miracle.

Curve the lips in happiness, and breathe.

Carry.

Carry this weight. Not a burden, never a burden, only a monster would ever use that word for this beautiful being in Opal's arms.

Bear her across the sharp rocks, stepping carefully to avoid more barefoot cuts. Tying the green-blue plant fibres around Opal's feet was only a partial success. But, with time and practice, she would improve. Like all skills, she would perfect it. She would perfect it because it had a goal, and an important one. To master this skill so she could use it to protect Clarissa, to wrap *her* feet, so she could walk without those tender soles being cut.

But for now, Opal could carry.

Her heart, racing. Her breath accelerating. Bringing the pain in, bringing the world in.

Reinterpret.

Recompile.

It is not outside *in*, it is *inside out*.

It is this life in this memory on this jagged grey world that is real.

Her heart races because she has seen that the ship – descending in jets that raised grey duststorms – was not Athene.

Her breathing is hard because she runs with Clarissa in her arms, runs to avoid the soldiers which disembarked from the dropship's rear ramp. They knew where she was by the still-curling black smoke of the rotting crabship.

The soldiers raced across the flat area. They wore heavy boots, could run with impunity. Whereas Opal's feet stung with the cuts. She tried to land each step on flatter areas but the shale had too many razor edges, and it was too hard to see with this precious cargo bouncing in her arms.

The soldiers follow. The ship takes off. Eye in the sky. Enhanced scanner range.

Move forwards!

Create distance. Hide. This landscape is a horror but it is also chaotic, the spurts of molten rock settling in unpredictable jags and arches and overhanging shelves and hardening to create the terrain. Opal hadn't been far, but she'd found a few clefts. Places not visible from the air. Places where rock might jam scanners, block infrared, block fine motion sensors. She just had to reach them in time.

The partial plant wraps on her feet fall away, torn and frayed. She can't run barefoot on this surface of sharp stones, the weight of another slicing deeper with every bad landing.

But she runs anyway.

"It's okay, baby," she says to her sister as she bounds over the harsh landscape. "In the end, everything will be okay."

They'll track her by the blood, of course. They'll find her. But that's not a reason to stop. Because nothing is as important as what she holds in her arms, what she holds against her heart, a heart separated from her sister's by only centimetres, a closeness that has not been there for so long. She'll do anything to prolong it.

And when the soldiers catch up, she screams, and it takes her to the pain, the pain everywhere, mind and body, memory and present, and they're wrenching teeth out now, breaking jaw bone to get at the roots, and she floats, and the world bulges, faces distort like rubber, *but it's okay. It's okay now. She knows what to do.*

She rewinds. Inhale, focus, exhale.

Three. Two. One.

She is on a grey planet.

She picks up her sister.

She runs.

ILLUSIONS

... 18 ...

Floating downstream on her back, torpid in a river of acid. This was not the first time. Or the second. Nor the third. Time was a spinning disc of sandpaper shaving skin down to nerve endings. And the sky was panels. White. White. Blinding white. They bulged with the throbbing in her temples. The rubbery walls and ceiling breathed with her. In. Out. Swell and stretch as if something was behind them, a secret, pushing to be revealed.

She could tilt her hand, though the movement sparked pain. It was tough to tell which extremities were strapped to the gurney she was being transported on, and which were paralysed. Her head wouldn't move. Not yet. She could only use peripheral vision to see the guards pushing the trolley.

Their helmeted heads swelled too, wobbled, underwater distortions, but they didn't burst, they shrank again.

"Ndhjsdk," said one, his voice echoing, robotic.

"Ldjdjshs," replied the other.

They were monsters, and this was their true voice.

If the world distorted in sympathy then maybe the pain was outside her too, in the elastic walls, in this hellish base; and if it was shared then she didn't experience it all, and that eased things a shred.

Roll along. Panel after panel marking progress. Swoosh. Swoosh. Like the days rolled along. One after another, repeating the pattern of suffering, then temporary reprieve. Swoosh. Swoosh.

Maybe the *ceiling* was really the *floor*. She flew above it, looking down. Drifting through clouds which stung and itched. A god gazing on creation and finding it blank and disappointing, in need of a reboot.

They rounded a corner too sharply and her head lolled to one side. The view was ruined. Everything sideways. Corridors she did not know the number of, could not code into her schema. It had been harder to keep track of anything as the days passed. The passages stretched away at junctions, constricting like throats, as if on a Gigatoir and they wanted to swallow her whole, gulp and crush, but they opened up again, pulsing, alive and malevolent like this whole place.

A guard walked next to her trolley. He was in armour but she knew he wasn't human beneath the face mask, none of them were. His heavy footsteps echoed, they all echoed, not two guards but a hundred, a thousand, all tramping these passages and leaving the sounds of their passing to bounce for eternity, even noise unable to escape. Her ears were swollen inside, cavernous, hollow, making her teeth ache with the impacts.

At one point she witnessed an angel. She had seen it before, while in this partway state between sleep and death. Through the wall. As if panels became translucent, just for her. An angel unfurling wings of glowing violet like waving sunbeams, pulsing to say hi, a call, a sea god in a sea flower, anemone twitches, and then the trolley passed that point and the angel was gone. No way of knowing if it was real, or just the drugs filtering from her system.

Despite the world now being made of jelly and echoes, she could remember what had happened each time. What he did. When her screams ended, the red-haired guard's began, and she was wheeled out, and the sweat on her body chilled to ice. She could imagine the droplets literally frozen to tear-like crystals, and the feeling was relief, salvation. Then recovery time would pass in a dream state in her cell until they judged her fit to start the suffering all over again.

But memory was wobbly too, and hard to hold on to. Like the pain, it floated away. Small mercies.

They took her off the trolley and lay her on the floor. One guard stayed with her as the platform descended into her cell, to make sure she didn't roll off and break her neck. At the bottom he pushed her over with his heavy boot, then he floated up into the ring of lights above, a devil ascending to a place he didn't belong, like some story she'd heard once as a child, mostly forgotten, but lifted on the turbulent waves in her head, memory silt swirled around in a cloud.

Even the metal floor of her chamber pulsed beneath her. Her ear pressed against it, and she heard groans. At first she thought they were her own, but no, there were creaks, too. It was background sound, not the emissions of her pain. These noises sometimes entered her consciousness when she tried to sleep if the ventilation systems shut down for maintenance and the ambient sound levels dropped. It infected her nightmares with the monsters on a Lost Ship. When awake, it was never clear what caused them. Maybe the groaning parts were the moans of people in pain in another section of the prison, their tortured sounds carried through the dormant ventilation pipes. Creaks could be anything related to expansion and contraction. This prison might be in a desert, prone to extreme heat changes. That would match the choice of inhospitable and isolated locations for places like this.

But now, when the sounds from the swaying floor entered directly to her enlarged and hollow head to reverberate, they seemed so much clearer. The base was in pain. It tried to communicate that.

"I know," Opal said. "We all hurt."

Her own agony had subsided to throbs, stinging and aches. Unpleasant but mostly ignorable. The residual hallucinogenic effects were more long-lasting, turning reality into sponge.

Sleep it off.

She tried to crawl over to her bed, but it became more of a slither. She was a snake, wriggling over the metal desert with its dips and dunes formed by the wind, under the burning sun of spotlights above, too bright, too hot. Cool the skin, get under shade. From down here the area beneath her bed looked most inviting, a sanctuary of darkness and relief. They let her rest there following torture sessions. After all, she had no chance of climbing up on it when her limbs were still made of rubber, and the floor's marshmallow surface indented with every push.

Radiance under the bed. Not the purple angel but something that flickered in blue like a faulty las-charger. No sparks, though. Something else.

It was the PPDA, where she'd dropped it last, flashing its demand for input, insistent, annoying. She slid under the mattress platform. Opal needed to leave this body for a while, go somewhere else, somewhere in memory that was solid, not stretchy. She tried to turn the device face down so that its glow wouldn't keep her awake but her fingers spasmed and she dropped it. Tried again. The letters moved round the screen as if trying to get her attention.

They'd never swirled like this before. Her brain was totally unwired.

She thumped the device. A good whack often fixed things, and the letters settled after another distortion glitch.

Blinking text now. Bigger than before, and so neon-bright she had to squint. For a second they formed some kind of picture out of the letters, the lines. More angels trying to communicate. Play along.

"WOULD YOU SAY YOUR CURRENT MOOD WAS:

A. POSITIVE BECAUSE WE WERE JOINED ONCE

B. SATISFACTORY CONSIDERING YOU SHOULDA BROUGHT A BIGGER GUN

C. NEGATIVE FROM HORRORS IN ICY PLACES"

The words didn't make sense, and yet they also *did*.

She closed her eyes for a moment, shook her head, then tried to focus on the blurs again.

The words had changed.

"THINKING BACK TO A RECENT SITUATION THAT MAKES
YOU FEEL STRESSED, WERE YOU:

A. ABLE TO COPE EVEN THOUGH YOUR INNER CORE WAS
VIOLATED

B. REMEMBERING THAT SOMETHING WAS WRONG

C. AWARE THAT THE BAD PLACE IT OCCURRED IS COM-
MON"

Was Dulcetta fucking with her? Or was her own mind fucking
with Dulcetta?

She tapped at the screen. Of course, her floppy hand chose
every option at once. The screen blanked.

She pressed it again. Interference, flashes of random colour, a
distorting ripple, then normal letters scrolled on again.

"WHEN FACING A DIFFICULT SITUATION, WOULD YOU
RATHER:

A. USE A WINDOW RATHER THAN A DOOR, TO AVOID BE-
ING SEEN

B. KEEP COUNTING TO POINTLESSLY PROLONG THE IN-
EVITABLE, BE PURE

C. FJD*E– SO MAKE YOUR WAY TO THAT PLACE OF VIOLA-
TION

D. REALLY, BELIEVE, GO THERE, THE NEAREST, RISK IT ALL

E. LOOK FOR THE FAILED MEAL, NO ALICE IN IT

F. DON'T EAT YOUR FOOD, LISTEN TO IT, VOICE OF A TITAN

G. KLK SKS&FGSLGJ"

The letters melted, a puddle of absurd phosphorescence on the screen. This was a conscious dream, a knowing nightmare, and she hurt like fuck, but she couldn't help laughing anyway.

COMPANIONS

... 17 ...

The wake alarms, and then Dulcetta's voice, shattered her neon dreams.

"Opal, it is time for morning routines. Joyous news: your punishment sessions are complete. We will dispense with immediate exercise as a kindness, in recognition of your debilitated state. So please shower and dress. Be seen, be pure, believe."

Morning routines. It could be the middle of the night. It could be that Opal slept for a week. A year. She'd been flat-out exhausted.

Opal was still beneath the bed where she'd fallen asleep. She moved her stiff limbs experimentally. The pain was a ghost, not real, yet still sensed and threatening. The PPDA glowed faintly. She checked it. Normal pause screen, even when she tapped. No strange messages, no leaking membranes between memory, fantasy and reality.

A groan came from somewhere in her chamber. And, for once, it wasn't Opal.

A body. Lay where the platform lowered. Red hair.

Opal crawled from under the bed, stood shakily. Leg bones had reverted from their rubber forms back to calcium. Blood drained from her head and she gripped the bed frame tight until it passed, then made her way to the centre of her chamber and knelt just out of reach.

It was the guard. They'd shaved his head to ginger stubble and he was dressed now, in the same scarlet papery garments as Opal. Except a cutaway section revealed his back, and a device had been surgically attached near his spine. It looked like a miniature drug dispenser, with bubbles of coloured liquid, and part of it extended under his skin, creating a subtle bulge.

She prodded him with a finger and he groaned again.

"Hey, soldier boy. Sleepy time's over."

"Not a soldier," he mumbled. "Not anything."

"Sit up."

He struggled into a sitting position and faced her. His eyes were puffy, cheeks and arms tinged with fire from the punishments, not able to hide the effects as well as Opal's darker skin.

"Why are you in here?" she asked.

"I don't know. I passed out. How do you feel?"

"I'll ask the questions. They haven't let me mix with anyone else in my time here. Are prisoners normally kept in solitary like this?"

"No. You're one of the exceptions."

"Keep talking."

"As far as I could tell – just stuff overheard – you had too much 'chaos potential'. Instead of being intimidated or threatened by others, it might give you more options."

"Flattered. And what –"

The loudspeaker interrupted. But instead of the expected business-like-yet-pretend-concerned inflections of Dulcetta, it was Aseides who spoke, his voice rumbling from above like the voice of a god. No doubt he had considered that subconscious effect and delighted in it.

"Good morning, Opal. I hope you are better today. Now that the unpleasantness is over, we can start again, fresh, scores settled, infractions forgiven, with a renewed optimism for our joyous collaboration. I see you have met your companion. He would have been dead without your intervention. But I am never one to cry over spilt catalysts when new scenarios can be repurposed from the recyc of old. So this fresh situation is a form of thematic-loop reversal. The being in front of you is *your* prisoner. You are his guard. He is at your mercy. I have implanted a shunt into his back which can disperse a selection of chemicals directly into his vena cava if you press any of the containers. Red is 'immediate release' – a euphemism for death. Orange is the painful serum you both experienced as punishment. Yellow is a ... surprise. It is up to you if and when you press any of those. Up to you how you treat him. Remember that he is not some innocent, he was a *guard* here. Well, that's you caught up. I have things to do but hope to see you shortly. Bye!"

Opal looked at the guard's eyes, to see how he responded, what he knew, what he might be hiding. But all she saw was defeat.

"You know who I am," she said. "So what's your name?"

"Ruabon."

"I knew of someone with that name in the Periphs. Enforcer guy."

"It's a common enough name. I've never been an enforcer, though, so it wasn't me."

"I know. He was huge, muscly, and didn't have skin like a boutique price tag."

"My skin certainly hasn't protected me from ending up in here. We're all failures, one way or another."

"Some of my best friends are freaks."

Now it was Dulcetta's turn to lecture from above. "Opal, I told you it was time to bathe. I won't ask again. It is optional whether you punish or kill your cell companion first. Be seen, be pure, believe."

Fuck that annoying Genitor creed.

"You better face against the wall while I shower," Opal told Ruabon.

They took it in turns to get cleaned up. Two new outfits sat on her shelf, neatly folded into paper rectangles. One for her, one for him with a patch removed from the back for easy access to his spinal shunt.

Opal was ravenous – she hadn't eaten yesterday – but when Ruabon and supplies had been placed in her room during the night, they'd only left one plate of food. Part of the observational behaviour games they liked to play, to see whether Opal would leave Ruabon hungry.

The plate contained the standard fare she'd got used to. A dry brown biscuit. A rectangle of soft pink material, savoury. A sphere of reconstituted green paste that probably represented a portion of fruit. Who knew what any of this was made of, really?

She broke the biscuit in two, scooped up half the pink goop on it, and ate as slowly as she could force herself to, savouring the salty flavour while her stomach grumbled. No cutlery, so she used the other biscuit fragment to divide the green glob and ate her portion before handing the plate to Ruabon, who looked as starved as she was.

"Thanks," he said.

"I bet you're used to superior meals."

"No. We got the same food as you guys."

Was that the truth? Didn't seem likely. Maybe it was an attempt to create a false bond with her, dissuade her from pulling his plug.

After eating, they had to do the mental status and emotions survey. A separate PPDA had been left for Ruabon, which glowed with yellow text rather than her blues. Opal complied today and answered the questions without argument. The only unexpected thing to appear on the screen was words of praise at the end, thanking her for cooperating.

Then it was officially rest time but Opal chose exercise, to try and bring her body back to life. She did press ups with her feet raised on the bed, then squats. She refrained from practising punches and strikes against the metal walls. She'd been told off for that and punished early on, for "introducing aggression into her system". She stuck to stretches and muscle work.

Ruabon walked in circles, keeping to the opposite side of the chamber from her. He looked pained.

"Can you check something for me?" he eventually asked, limping over.

"What?"

"I can't see the thing in my back. I've tried twisting my neck but it's too low down. I don't want to risk feeling for it in case I accidentally press a button. With my luck, I daren't chance it."

"I'm no medic."

"I know. Just ... well, look at it. See if there's any hope of it being removed somehow. And ... if it looks like permanent damage."

Worry in his voice. Understandable.

"Lie down. On your front. Don't try anything."

He complied, head on his folded arms. Opal knelt to the side. She wasn't unaware of the implications of her examination. Ruabon was making a point, showing that he trusted her.

Opal carefully examined the shunt, following the flesh ripple where a pipe ran under the skin's surface, then deeper. Perhaps it passed between the ribs. How much would he want to know? It certainly didn't look removable, not the way it was bonded into the flesh, possibly at the molecular level, same as her ear stud. No doubt anti-removal systems would dump the full payload into his bloodstream if anyone tampered with it. Red, orange and yellow. The yellow capsule was the unknown one, and resembled a blister.

"Don't act suspicious, just lean in like you're examining it up close," he whispered.

She did so, gently tracing a finger over the coloured capsules.

"The cameras are above," he said. "At least, the only ones I ever saw on a viewscreen in the control room. Acoustics aren't great, so if we whisper they might not pick it up. Dulcetta can lipread, but as long as you're looking down at me and my mouth is hidden, we'll be okay."

"Shoot."

"We can help each other. My fate's tied to yours. But not much time. Dulcetta gets suspicious easily."

"Seems tricky," Opal said, loudly. "Does this hurt?" She pushed gently on some raised skin, then leaned closer and whispered. "Where are we? This base, I mean."

"I don't know. Everyone's brought in blind, ultra-sec. I think we descended, though."

"So it may be underground. Access would involve an elevator shaft. Escape requires dealing with whatever's on upper levels."

"And Dulcetta. Her splinters control everything, so you can't even steal access codes. My turn. If I got you to a medical bay could you remove the thing from my back?"

"Won't come out without a fight," Opal said with volume, glancing around so Dulcetta would see her lips for a moment. Then, leaning forward and murmuring again, "Is there a med bay nearby?"

"There is, equipped with a robotic medical expert system."

"Ceiling mounted?"

"Yes. But the room's rarely used for prisoner access. More for guards and ... nasty stuff."

"Where?"

"Not far from where you escaped and took me prisoner. If we'd carried on three junctions, taken two lefts, you'd be there."

Yep, that matched her mental map. "Maybe the yellow one's sedative?" Opal said, pretending to analyse it from a few angles before whispering once more. "But if we got there and removed the shunt, they'd recapture us, put it back. It would need to be part of a proper plan. So for now, scratch that idea. Back to escape. If someone got out I bet the location is isolated, inhospitable terrain needing protective gear. Airborne combat drones. Perhaps there are surface buildings. They might have supplies, if there's a way in to them."

"I don't know what surface security is like, but it can't be any heavier than it is down here. So it should get easier as you moved upwards."

"No chance of anything without floorplans."

"I only know the areas I was told to patrol."

Opal tried to picture the video footage of Exidris 3's lower levels, how scenes from that other research base's cameras connected. It was just flashes of layout. Corridors, shower blocks, chemical stores, guard stations, canteens, prisoner areas. Not enough to be useful, even if it applied here, too.

Dulcetta's voice rang out through the chamber. "Unless you are engaged in punishment or killing, please step away from your cell companion, Opal."

Opal complied. Don't push it. But there could be options here.

Ruabon sat up, facing her. "So I'm stuck with it. Like you're stuck with me."

"Not if I push the red button."

"True. But you didn't."

"Seemed unfair when you're just getting used to the shift from guard to prisoner."

"It's the story of my life. I'm a screw-up, not a monster. At the top one minute, a future full of possibilities; down at the bottom a moment later. I was a prisoner, too."

"Really?"

"Yep. When I came here. But then they decided I'd be more use working for them. Must have seen some potential, but I don't know what. I'm awful at it. Just keep – kept – my head down. The funny thing is, I was just as scared after they made me an overseer. Maybe more. Because then you really *know*."

"Know what?"

"How hopeless everything is."

Dulcetta interrupted again.

"Opal, guards are coming to escort you to Aseides. Please prepare yourself."

Ruabon looked worried. "Not more torture, is it? Already?"

"I doubt it."

"Phew. I couldn't cope. Don't know how I'm still alive after the last few weeks. I've had punishments, but never anything like that. I kept wishing you'd killed me."

"I still might. Don't mistake my fucking with Aseides' head as mercy." She softened. "When bad shit happens, you have to focus on something good. Fill your mind with that."

"Does it make the pain go away?"

"Hell no. But when the method works you get a brief respite." She rubbed a rough fingernail edge against the floor, filing it to a smooth point. "Sometimes."

"Ah. I tried something like that, during the torture. Thought about someone I used to work with. I wish I'd got to know her better. But I made a lot of mistakes, and this is where they led me."

"Don't beat yourself up. But whoever that special person is, seize on to her memory. Sometimes, in the bleakest places, that's all you have to hold you up."

The platform descended. It was time to go.

"Looks like you'll be on your own for a while, Ruabon. Stick to my rules. One: don't touch my shit. Two: you can sleep on the bed when I'm not here." Pause. "Three: don't roll onto your back."

SURPRISES

... 16 ...

Four guards escorted Opal this time. Two ahead, two behind. Gunderson Escort Protocol v-B. There was both a wariness, and a detachment, about their behaviour. They didn't insult her. Didn't shove her. Concern about Opal's possible retaliation ... or Aseides'?

This was the first time she'd been in the elevator beyond her section, though she had seen the door. They descended in silence apart from the hum of efficient machinery. The enclosed space circulated stale body odour from one of the guards.

The controls displayed no floor number that might hint at depth. A surreptitious peek upwards revealed no obvious access panels leading into a shaft. Also no visible cameras, but there would be some, embedded in the surfaces. The capsule was secure, and couldn't be manipulated to her advantage at present.

The floor where they exited resembled the one she was familiar with, except silver lines ran along the white panel walls. In other places the shiny lines gently accented architectural features, applying some aesthetic to the functional. Maybe other floors had identifying marks or designs like this. That could be useful. Or this one was special, deserving of consideration and enhanced decor.

She had to create new sets of navigational beacons and junction codes in her head, taking the chance to glance down every passage and tying it all together to generate a basic mental map. Walking in silence helped. Transecs here used the same colour indicators as she was used to: white for safe passage versus whatever nastiness might trigger when they were red or blue. The horizontal lines separating each panel were embedded with silver trim to match the walls.

Her bare soles told her the temperature was a degree or so warmer here. Perhaps the floor was nearer to a power source, or geothermal venting, or just had the environment altered to be more luxurious. That might fit with the extra attention to detail. As did the plants when she rounded the next corner, breaking up the regulation lines as they spread over a curved seat large enough for three people. Stylishly shaped transparent bowls held beds of nutrient moss from which grew the flowering vines, supported on silver frameworks. Designer vegetation, modified to thrive indoors, far from sunlight. They were beautiful, giving the impression of life outside of sterility, something to create hope and admiration.

She wondered if the bowls were smashable. Glass shards could be used as weapons, but how sturdy would they be for puncturing Sec-3 armour at the weak points under the arms, or between the third and fourth rib panels?

The corridor ended at a door flanked by more vines, taller ones, which stretched over the frame and intermingled their leaves and purple flowers. The guards waited a moment, then the door opened. As Ruabon had said, it seemed like splinters of Dulcetta monitored portals. That was why Opal rarely saw DNA scanners. Presumably invisible uniform codes or implanted chips acted as ID, which worked in conjunction with the fact that uniforms couldn't be removed as disguises for the unauthorised. Dulcetta was an anchor for the security system. No obvious way in which she introduced exploitable weaknesses.

The room beyond was something new to Opal. The floor, walls and ceiling sparkled in glittering silver like jewellery. In the centre of the room a fancy sofa beckoned. She stepped in and the door closed behind her. She was alone.

Except, of course, the solitude was illusory. She was inevitably being observed.

So she played along.

The hard floor was textured like brushed steel, colder than the plasteen panels used for flooring elsewhere. She ran her fingertips over a wall's gritty texture. No obvious lights, yet the room was well illuminated. No visible doors. She turned. Her entrance had disappeared, not even fine cracks betraying its outline. A silver box of a room. No reflections in the surfaces despite the shininess that should have acted like a mirror if the microtexturing hadn't prevented it. Perhaps they were modified smart surfaces.

She'd seen this room before, or something like it. When she'd been on the Gigatoir and a recording of Aseides played, a ridiculous attempt to persuade her to surrender. His enticements had been poorly chosen, manipulations obvious. The background had been non-reflective silver. Maybe he'd even recorded that message from here. Perhaps it was a favoured place of his. An inner sanctum. He must know she'd recognise it. In which case, choosing to meet here was a message. An attempt to alter probabilities to his advantage. To reframe, to manipulate. Just like his words, always carefully chosen, but with certain ones recurring more often: obey, sensible, conform, submit. Attempts to embed them in her subconscious. But Opal had travelled with a far better manipulator than Aseides. By comparison, he was glass to Opal.

Not that it would benefit her to reveal that.

Not yet.

The furniture had a low back, curved legs of what looked like dark wood, and padded orange fabric. She stroked it. Velvety. It was new, but designed to look old. It didn't fit this barren, inhospitable room. It was a prop. A prop for a scene. Was the room a stage? Did it normally have other contents, which had been removed for Opal's visit? The contrast with the torture bed she'd been strapped to last time was obvious. Objects could also be messages, and this one was a promise of comfort, and an expectation of sitting.

So she circled the room again, looking for anything she'd missed, touching surfaces as if impressed, but checking for hardness, sharpness, hollowness.

The wall facing the sofa disappeared. Not a physical movement, more of a ripple, so it was a transparency effect. Aseides stood in a room identical to hers, even down to the seat. It was a trick, a mind game, an apparent mirror reflection with one changed detail – in this case, she wasn't seeing herself in the reflection, but him, where he'd been watching all along, of course, through a one-way display.

She approached him. He did not flinch. Did not feel threatened. She reached out and came into contact with a wall. It was still there, just fully transparent. She'd expected as much.

"What do you think?" he asked.

"The room means something to you."

"True."

"It's somehow tied to how you perceive yourself."

"Not really."

"Well, silver. You like that colour. And you like things that reveal themselves, as here with transparent walls. Maybe they're smart walls, a focus on hi-tech functions, adaptability and permanent observation. And this isn't a place of life, it's a place of study without distractions. No proper reflections because that would reveal reality, and you only see what you want to see. And it's square, confined, restricted, regimented, featureless. So yeah, this is what the inside of your head looks like."

"Now that *is* an interesting observation. And I only sought your opinion on whether the seating looked comfortable."

"You didn't mean that at all. You never intend the obvious."

He nodded. An ambivalent movement which might mean "I concede your point", or could be interpreted as "Wrong, but let's move on because I am bored". He lowered himself onto his orange sofa, gesturing towards Opal's.

Humour him. She sat, but on the edge, like him. She suspected in his case it was because mental energy made sitting still difficult. In her case she wanted to leap up if anything unexpected occurred.

The seat was plush, well padded around a sturdy frame. Possibly heavy enough to break the invisible barrier between the adjacent rooms. File that option for later. After all, he might not really be physically beyond the wall, but instead far away, his image transmitted at hi-res.

"How are you feeling now?" Aseides asked. "After the unpleasantness of your sessions?"

"I've had worse." She made an effort to hide the trembling in her hands. Not fear, just after-effects.

"I doubt it. But I hope you never experience it again. That we have moved on. Because, if you have to be punished again, it will be worse next time. Escalation is a key element of behavioural redirection systems."

"How about not torturing people as a key element of 'being nice' systems?"

"You see torture, I see reform. You say evil, I say organisation. Perspectives are a wonderful thing. They can liberate, and they can bind. They can unite, they can divide. And so rarely does anyone realise the truth, that perspectives don't even exist, not in the real world. They are just filters that change reality's colours. I favour logic over emotion, and you are the reverse. Your past is one of reaction, rebellion, anger. You make it difficult for people like me, who don't want to be your enemy. I cannot shake hands with a clenched fist. But as an ancient phrase says, I have shown the stick, now I show the root vegetable. There are rewards for meeting me halfway."

A swishing sound revealed the presence of a hidden door in the wall to Opal's left. She spun, ready for a surprise attack – Dulcetta, an inrush of guards with Stunstix, a release of toxic gas or some other horror. But she didn't expect what she saw. Never this.

Clarissa. Gently propelled forward by the gloved hand of a grey-coated researcher wearing a smiley mask. But the adult wasn't important.

Clarissa.

The first time in weeks Opal had seen her, since they'd been captured and brought here.

Clarissa as she'd looked when she disappeared fourteen years ago, not aged a moment despite the years sitting heavily on Opal's own body. Clarissa matching the memory, as if time had never happened. They'd not shaved her head as they did with adults. Nor was she clad in a red prisoner jumpsuit, instead wearing clothing that was normal for a girl of her age.

The researcher retreated quickly and sealed the door as Opal rushed over. She dropped to her knees in front of Clarissa, to better gaze into her eyes. Eyes that were still blank.

"I considered keeping you both apart by a barrier," Aseides said. "But touch is important in mammals. Reassuring. Maybe it will help."

Meaning they'd got nowhere in terms of bringing Clarissa out of this walking coma.

Opal hugged her sister. Resisted the tightness she wanted to indulge in, the crushing love that might hurt a fragile body.

"It's okay, C. Everything's all right," she whispered. "I'm here. Oh, I'm here. I love you."

"The way she hasn't aged is fascinating," Aseides continued, as if to himself. "So much potential there."

Opal checked Clarissa's arms and neck for needle marks, for signs of invasion. Her skin was unsullied, as if she'd never suffered the bumps and scratches of childhood.

"And seeing you both together, the physical similarity is striking." Aseides leaned closer to his invisible barrier, taking everything in.

Opal picked up her sister. Clarissa showed no signs of awareness in her face but she wrapped her arms around Opal's neck, legs around her waist, just as she used to. It had to be more than muscle memory. It was communication. Communication Clarissa-style.

Opal circled the chamber, savouring everything about the contact. The warmth and softness and fragility of Clarissa's body. The tickle of moist breath on her neck, which brought back a flood of memories. Aseides' voice in the background was an irritating distraction, but he had asked a question, about her parents.

"Of course I remember them," said Opal. "They were so kind. They stood out from the other orphanage staff because of that. Then they adopted us."

"No no no. Your *birth* parents."

"They died after Clarissa was born. No, I don't remember them."

Which was true. Opal's earliest memories were just a confused mix of sensations and emotions. She had dreams sometimes, dream memories, and they were always sad, always filled with longing.

But it was Clarissa she cared about now. "There is hope," she murmured into Clarissa's ear. "I never used to believe it, that there might be better worlds, and better people, but there *are*. And you should hold on to hope as well, keep it inside you, your source of strength. Because I know you're in there. Listening. Waiting. And at some point you'll know it's safe to come out. And I can wait till then, too."

For once, Aseides didn't interrupt. Seemed happy to observe. And Opal's circles around the fancy sofa were something new. Not circles of frustration and ways to mark passing time, but circles of absorption and ways to *stop* time, to be in the moment, to focus on the one thing of importance right then. So she walked. Walked and walked.

DEALS

... 15 ...

But she couldn't stop time. Couldn't do Clarissa's trick. And when Aseides said she had to let her sister go, and the researcher returned, waiting at the doorway, Opal wanted to say no. Refuse, resist, fight, protect. But it would be the wrong move.

So she put Clarissa down. Promised to see her soon. Watched her being gently ushered away. When the door sealed, the wall becoming an unbroken surface, Opal faced Aseides.

"She's just a girl. And I'm just a bad soldier. We don't have special powers, don't have important information, don't pose any threat. We just want to be together. It's all we've ever wanted. Let us go."

"No."

"Can't? Or won't?"

"A bit of both."

"In that case, I'll change. I'll work for you. As long as I can be with Clarissa. I won't rebel, won't answer back."

"I believe you. The motivational factors fit. Cooperation on these lines would work far better than the stupid coercion Mil-Com used on you. Mil-heads are so unimaginative."

"Where is Clarissa being held? What cell?"

Aseides just wagged his finger at that. "But it does lead me to an idea. An offer."

"What?"

"It's a simple test. Kill the guard, Ruabon. He deserves it anyway. If you do that, I'll let Clarissa stay in your cell with you, in his place."

"I have your word?"

"Of course! Will you do it?"

Opal stared at him. Assessing his reliability. His gaze never faltered.

"Yes," said Opal. "For Clarissa, I'll do anything."

"Impressive. We are making *huge* progress. And I don't want to push it, but I also can't miss capitalising on this rush of euphoria at the possibilities opening up to us. I should let you know that I have many projects. And many prisoners, all with their own stories and potentials. You and Clarissa are not my whole focus. You're not as special as you would like to imagine. I don't think about you all the time. Don't dream about you. You might feel like you're Dulcetta's only observational and correctional priority, but that's what *everyone* feels as she talks to a thousand people at once. To be honest, she probably spends a billion more focus cycles on her pet projects – such as designing reaction and velocity modifiers for acid inversions – than she does in caring about what you do. It's a truth every human must face, yet so few do: *you are not as important as you think*. Not in any grand scheme of things, and not even in any minor scheme of things. We're all just cogs in processes far greater than ourselves. I'm sure you're not insulted by my honesty. And yet, having put you in your place, I do still have hopes."

"You need something from me. Even if it's just answers to abstract behavioural stuff you have in your head."

"Correct. Continue."

"So it has to be particular to *me*. You're either interested in something I know, or it's about my relationships, connections you don't have."

He nodded.

"It could be related to Clarissa. Or to something in the Null. Or to Athene. But if it was Clarissa ... well, she's a prisoner too. And since you already know how I feel about her, that's not news. And the Null? I answered all your questions, and will keep doing that. So that leaves Athene."

"Getting pretty warm in there."

Opal was pacing as she thought aloud. "But you knew everything about her, from helping design her. And you think she's dead, so what else could have relevance?"

"I like this. Keep going. You prove that everyone else was wrong to underestimate you, and I was right *not* to."

"But you realised I thought Athene was alive. And you let me go through the motions of an escape attempt just to crush my hope."

"Getting colder."

"Your motivation, then? You said I had other escape options I missed, but I don't believe that. I only saw one option, and I took it, and it was a dead end."

He shrugged.

"But if you set it up as bait, then you chose the details, right? So why a comm station? Why not an armoury, or a shuttle bay, or access to some key system? Everything with you is a choice."

"Warm again."

"You wanted more. Comms is about messages. But once I was there I didn't have a script. You didn't know what I'd say."

"Warmer."

"So there's something about my words."

"Hot."

"You wanted to find out what I'd say to Athene."

"Sizzling."

"She's not dead."

He clapped his hands, a brief applause. "You've earned that revelation."

Opal slumped onto the sofa. Took a moment to get her head straight. Suspicion was one thing, confirmation another. Okay, what now? She dry-wiped her face and sat forward again.

"And you haven't been able to find her," she said. "I bet you've been trying to leave traps. But Athene hasn't bitten because she sees through your tricks. So you needed something authentic to convince her. Which you'd only get from me. And, ideally, only from a me that wasn't being forced. Only from a me that believed I really had a hope."

"Indeed. And you performed admirably. The stuff about the Clarissa constellation, whatever that was – we modified it and got a response."

"But then you ran dry and she worked out it wasn't me."

"Correct."

"And I'm guessing your claim that we're discussing this because you feel suddenly positive is at least partly bullshit. Really there's some other pressure at play, from above – Mil-Com, or the Genitors. Because they must care more about capturing or destroying Athene than they do about me and Clarissa. She's the thing that has value. Or, more likely: she's the thing they're afraid of. Has she been causing problems?"

Aseides gave a non-committal wobble of his palm.

"Huh," said Opal, smiling. "I just bet she has."

"Let's end the supposition. Question: do you know where Athene is, or is likely to be?"

"Nope. Not a clue. I last saw her – well, spoke to her – just as the Lost Ship I was on transported itself out of our universe. Then I was gone a long time. And I know you'll get Dulcetta to analyse all this, for what it's worth. She'll conclude I'm telling the truth. Even give you a frigging probability stat."

"Again, I believe you. If I'd thought otherwise then my approach might have been quite different."

"So what next?" Opal asked.

"We want you to record another message. A vocal one this time. We'll fake a scenario, and there'll be a partial script, core things you have to include."

"Coordinates for another trap?"

"Don't worry about the *what*. You'll just have to build it into a message that will convince her it's you. Put in the – as you said – authentic details."

"How do you know I won't blurt out the truth before you cut me off?"

"Do you really think we'd let you communicate with her *live*?"

"Huh." Opal crossed her arms. "What do I get out of it?"

"Down here you could have a new life. In time ... who knows? No one can see the future. There may be options. But for now you'd be with Clarissa. Neither of you would be harmed. Just show willing."

He'd said "down here". Which reinforced her subterranean base theory. Except – would Aseides slip up like that? Maybe it was a false lead. Why would he do that? To mess with her? Or he knew what she'd discussed with Ruabon. Close observation, perhaps. Or betrayal by her new cellmate. Mmm. Ruabon might even have been briefed to share that information with Opal.

She gripped the arm of the sofa tight. "Just show willing. Right. Just help you destroy Athene."

"Who said destroy? She's a pet project of mine. And since we've still detected no sign of VigMAX, Athene may be the only Seven in existence. I can't destroy all that research potential!"

"So what do you plan?"

"A fleet on full alert, ready to drop in to the location we send her to. Specially equipped with EMP and restriction armaments. We've always had contingency plans for this scenario."

"You capture her. What then?"

"Incapacitate. Restructure her mind to be cooperative."

"If you enslave her, then it wouldn't be her any more."

"At least she would still *exist*, rather than being blown into uncategorisable fragments. We all change over time. She has already transformed more in two years than humans might do in ten lifetimes. This would just be the next stage in her growth."

"And I guess if I say no ..."

"We could break you, eventually. We can break *anyone*. We have a hundred per cent success rate as long as the subject doesn't kill themselves first. But that is my least favourite option, for many reasons."

"Conscience not being one of them. So I imagine that torture process takes time, and I already guessed that's the resource you don't have enough of, hence the attempts to persuade."

"I'm more concerned by how perceptive a level seven depth AI is, and how she might recognise you've been broken. It's especially a risk with their Primary Bond."

"Primary Bond?"

"You travelled with a Seven, and didn't know about that? Fascinating."

She waited, but he said no more.

"Well?" she asked, impatient.

"The P-Bond system is built into the AI so it can form a special relationship with a controller. It's not just functional, but is also personal and emotional."

"So I'm Athene's P-Bond?"

"It seems so. You obviously weren't chosen for that role by us. In fact, I had a P-Bond in place, and she promised an excellent outcome, until ... well, something happened, and perhaps an impetuous and potentially paranoid senior Genitor – praise the purities etcetera – got carried away. Suddenly the P-Bond was gone, lots of secrecy, convoluted cleanup, more work for me. I was extremely frustrated, had to put another project on hold and rush back to enact exigency protocols. A real mess. Which got all the messier when *you* somehow stole ViraUHX. An event which still has question marks embedded in it. We know your past, your training, your interests in hacking, your backup plans, your fake IDs, your ingenious use of dual-level bypasses so that the obvious element is discovered and halted while a secondary subversion continues in the background. But that does not tell all. There's no way you could have designed the hack chip you used without insider knowledge. Plus, what of the untraceable comms you received that helped you plan the theft? And yet, I believe you when you say you don't know the source of the messages. All I know is that they came from inside the base. And if she hadn't been dead, I might have suspected the P-Bond, Doctor Vermalle. But who does that leave? Everything has the fingerprints of an AI, yet ViraUHX was restricted. It's a mystery I still love to ponder when I can't sleep."

"So a P-Bond is just like an algorithm? It's not real friendship?"

"Something like that. It's an accelerated trust process built for convenience."

"So ... Athene was never really my friend, she was just following code?"

"Of course! You didn't think you were special, did you? I explained all that earlier. This is a lot to absorb, and I know you'll hate this, but it's Athene for Clarissa. You can't have both. And unless you agree, you'll get *neither*. Accept the deal."

Opal glared at him. But he wasn't intimidated. So she let the realisations sink in, softening her face from hard defiance.

"Okay. I'll do it."

"A wise choice. It won't take long. We can begin right away. In fact, that's best. Not that I don't trust you're being genuine right now, but let us avoid too much thinking time, in case you're tempted to try anything foolish, or change your mind about this minor betrayal. When I decide on a course, I can't settle until I enact it. And maybe you're just starting to see things my way. A little bit."

Opal leaned back and stretched her arms out over the luxurious fabric. "Maybe."

BETRAYALS

... 14 ...

Opal recorded the messages for them, as multiple phrases they could tweak or combine in any order. They made her speak in a rush, sounding desperate and time-pressured. No doubt they would apply distortion and crackle as if transmitted long distance, and use that to cover up any imperfections in the way her messages were altered.

She followed their guidelines exactly. Looked at the next bare point they wanted her to make, the next plain clue they wanted her to give, then wrapped it in her own words. Sometimes multiple attempts at each, all different, so they could take their pick of content. As instructed, she slipped in personal references only she and Athene would know, confirmations that this was really Opal, this was really true. During the whole process she was watched over by guards and Aseides: the former silent and stoic, faces hidden behind helmet plates, while Aseides directed with enthusiasm, suggested things, asked questions about every element Opal slipped in, slowing the whole process down. It looked like childish enthusiasm over a new toy, but she suspected careful analysis of her additions and changes to make sure she wasn't conveying anything she shouldn't.

Pointless worry. She fully intended to say what needed to be said.

After nearly two hours, when she finally reached the end of the bulleted list that had scrolled up the display screen, she looked at Aseides. He nodded, a big grin on his face. She pushed her chair back from the desk. She'd hoped it would squeal in resistance but the contact points were polished repellents, and slid frictionless as ice when her feet weren't on the bar which magnetically locked the seat in place.

"Thank you for your cooperation," said Aseides. "I'm still unused to that."

"The world isn't perfect. I just did what I had to do." Opal stood and stretched, her joints cracking. "I've learnt that lesson. I'll go back to my cell and kill Ruabon next, so Clarissa can be with me."

"My, that steely determination is at the fore today. I'm sure you are hiding pain and frustration, pushing any vulnerabilities deep. Nobility in defeat. Motivated by love for your sister. Good. I'm happy with progress. We'll bring you back if we need further content."

There had been four guards on the way, but only two accompanied her on the way back. Minimal escort duty. They knew she couldn't run anywhere. They knew *she* knew. And she'd complied. They had what they wanted. She was beaten, and making the best of an awful situation.

Opal didn't rush back to her cell. Her feet wouldn't move quickly today. Putting off the inevitable. Head down. The guards didn't tell her to hurry. Obviously Aseides had instructed them to be nice. And so she let the minutes stretch, running everything through her mind as she passed along the silver-trimmed passages of Aseides' floor.

But going slowly made no difference in the long run. Actions still had to be taken. People had to be hurt. It was illogical to delay, even if violence, confrontation and hurt always affected the giver as well as the receiver. It was the way of things. No one gets through life unscathed.

They entered the elevator, and Opal looked down at her bare feet, which seemed darker against the white luminescent panels. She would never fit in here. Not permanently. The feeling of motion ceased, a slight knee-bending deceleration, and the doors opened. They exited the elevator. She was back on her own confinement floor.

Aseides was so confident. In his systems. His security. His assessments. The lack of options in scenarios he created. How terrified people were of pain and injury. His confidence embedded itself in every panel, every Transec, every armoured guard, every observing camera. A place did that. Somehow took the imprint of the designer. Became their body. Their eyes.

She had a better mental map now. The botched escape attempt and Aseides' recent introduction of new locations had expanded her knowledge. She knew how many intersections it would be until she had to do something that would be unpleasant, but necessary.

Junction SSRL9.

And she counted. Because we walk and count and that is living. Only so many steps between each decision. Only so many steps in a life. Make them mean something.

Triple-J intersection.

A place becomes the ruler's eyes, but eyes have blind spots which the retina can't see, and so the brain fills in the gaps with what it *expects*. It ceases to see what's right in front of it.

Another thirty steps. They turned right. *ROT3.*

The blind spots might be an inability to comprehend the importance of action and self determination. How much more powerful hope can be than fear. Blind spots can be an inability to avoid projecting yourself onto others; so you see only what is inside *you*, not what is really there.

Opal glanced to her side, her head not raised, all the motion in her eyes. She noted charge levels on the Stunstix.

Dented venting panel 7.

Some people project love and compassion onto the world, and it returns in the smiles that greet them. Others project their hate and division, fear and hopelessness, their pettiness, and only see *that* on the faces looking back at them. It's not even a UFS thing. It's a *people* thing. One of millions of truths that slip past people every day, ungraspable.

They had to wait for the next Transec to rotate from blue to white. What would happen if she threw a guard into it while it was blue? Would Dulcetta override the automated defences in time?

The passage was safe again. They moved through. It rotated to red behind them.

Of course, blind spots can be more literal. Real-world places and routes. Things long forgotten.

Junction RR-FE. Two lefts until *crossing RR-LP.*

She listened to the sounds of the guards' heavy boots. When you knew what to look out for, it revealed itself. Beneath the echo was sometimes a *second* echo. A hollowness beyond the hollow. A repetition, confined like everything else in there. Something heard so often it becomes background noise, another type of blind spot our brains tune out as distractions of no importance because they create no threat. But lack of threat does not mean lack of opportunity.

She had to count fifty-three steps, and focus on her journey's end.

She imagined herself in a Sec-3 suit of armour. How it would feel. How it would make her act. The textures and hardnesses. Areas with weighty heft, others with light flexibility. Impenetrable armour where she would be safe, versus zones with insufficient protection where she had to apply focus, alter her combat style to prevent those vulnerabilities being presented to an opponent.

You had to keep those areas in mind. Not become sloppy.

Count. Thirty-nine, thirty-eight, thirty-seven.

Routine made people sloppy.

Endless escort routines with no threat made people sloppy.

Count. Thirty, twenty-nine, twenty-eight.

Hopefully providing you and your sister with permanent protection. That's what he'd said.

Twenty-four, twenty-three, twenty-two.

Hopefully.

Nineteen, eighteen, seventeen.

We all hope. But things fall apart. Intention may be absent, or built only on whim. Sometimes forces outside us overpower what we want, impose their own will on our world. Either way, *hope* didn't provide enough security to pin a future on.

Fifteen, fourteen.

She'd always loved countdowns. Her mental preparation for action. It made more sense for numbers to go backwards when you were the kind of person who found it difficult to sit still, because countdowns meant an eventual and predictable end to waiting. That was a positive thing.

Eleven, ten.

If this went wrong she just had to hope Clarissa was important to them.

Six, five.

The guards behind her were probably half asleep by now, conveying this zombie down endless identikit corridors with nothing to break up the monotony. Day after day, identical situations, identical passages. Mind numbing. They could walk with their eyes closed, no one would know behind those face plates.

Wakey wakey.

Opal turned, opened her mouth to say something, then stared over their shoulders at the area they'd just left.

"What the fuck ..." she said, eyes widening in panic, gazing at the horror behind them which had been following for who knew how long, footsteps silent, a true predator, a real danger.

They spun too, reflex, to see what awaited, and probably already regretted it before finishing the turn, but reacting bodies move faster than reflective assessments.

An awkward angle for the body to rotate. Especially without side-reinforced joint panels in the Sec-3 suit.

Opal lashed her heel out, connecting with the knee of the first guard, at a point that gave no room for flexibility. Even through the suit she heard a sinewy snap as he went down, howling in the filtered robot voice, hugging his leg.

She'd hoped the second guard would be surprised enough to give her a moment to attack but he was fast, already had his holster unclipped and Stunstix drawn.

Fight an opponent armed with a knife and you have to acknowledge you'll be cut at least once. Fight someone who has a Stunstix and assume you'll be shocked by it. Muscle contractions and pain were outcomes from strikes that didn't connect with your head and outright render you unconscious. And they weren't the worst of it if your *body* was struck. Your diaphragm squeezes so you can't breathe, causing panic and collapse of resistance.

The guard jabbed forward. Opal tried to move outside; too slow, the glowing tip of the weapon connected. But knowing something will hurt or injure and going ahead anyway is the attitude that helps you get through it. Opal had exhaled as she moved in, to minimise any effects; the blow stung her; she knew she couldn't breathe but ignored it, it was temporary, she just had to subdue fear. Fear makes you stop.

Don't stop. Even for a second.

Outside the strike, spinning as she grabbed the guard's arm and neck, slamming his head into the wall on the exact loose plasteen sheet where she'd chosen to make her stand. The same place she'd noticed long ago, and tricked Angry D into shoving her so she could examine it. The guard's faceplate and the plasteen panel both splintered in a most satisfying manner.

He pushed off the wall angrily, using what was available to him, just as Opal predicted he would. So when she ducked below his hips and converted his backwards move into a throw, the guard landed heavily, shaking the floor with his weighty wallop. He was probably more winded than her.

Something relaxed inside and she could breathe again, taking in luxurious gulps of air.

So far, so good. Against them there would have been no point in punches. She would just break her fists on their armour. Even vulnerable points like the neck had enough protection to block a jab. So you attack joints, or you use throws, where the impact from combined body weight and armour being slammed into the ground is far more concussive than a single fist.

Streetfight basics. Use apparent strengths like size and weight against your opponent.

At this junction she could see the direction she wanted to go. Straight across the Transec. But it was red. The passage might be painful and incapacitating; more likely, fatal. And the silent alarms had no doubt alerted her enemies, calling extreme force to this point.

When you can't go through, go around.

The guard she'd thrown onto his face was trying to get up. On his hands and knees. Opal raised her leg high, slammed her heel down on the back of his neck, smacking him into the ground again. Heels were hard. So was floor.

She was on him, sat astride his back, unfastening the catches on his helmet. Familiar straps, though with extra components.

Once it was off, she glanced inside. No bleeping, no flashing lights, but that didn't mean no countdown. A helmet could be as unreadable as Opal's face.

She flung the helmet underarm. It skidded across to the cracked panel while she dived to the floor as her countdown reached zero. A deafening roar left her ears ringing and a flash of flame scorched her side. Smoke billowed around the ceiling and the blasted wall.

Huh, Ruabon had told the truth about booby traps.

She scrambled to the dark area, an arm over her face to reduce the effects of eye-stinging black smoke.

Yep, a gap existed between the broken panel and an old metal wall. Enough crawlspace for a person, and it looked like it got bigger below the floor area, as the hollow sounds had led her to hope.

The guard with the broken knee still made no attempts to get up, just rolled around wailing, but the now-helmetless guard tried to stand again. Persistent bastard. He had a crew cut, un-lined skin that put him in his twenties, and blue eyes. He didn't look happy.

Opal dived for the Stunstix he'd dropped.

"Useless," he told her with a nasty grin. "After your last es-capade Aseides modded them all. They're disabled once they've been more than an arm's reach from a suit's core."

She pressed the trigger but the end refused to glow. So she struck his temple with the handle. Hard. He collapsed with a flump as if his bones had turned to jelly.

"Whaddya know?" She flung the Stunstix away with a clatter. "It wasn't useless after all."

Rolling-knee-pain-guard had never drawn his Stunstix. Opal slipped it from the sheath, activated it, gave him a good zap to the neck. Instant painkiller as he passed out.

His gauntlets were fiddly to remove, but she got them strapped on her own hands. Reinforced heat-resistant Polyverbex with pad plates and joint shields, plus extra weight for striking mass.

Time was short. The echoing footsteps and shouts weren't her imagination.

Planting a foot against the wall, Opal gripped the still-smouldering, ultra-sharp edges of the broken plasteen panel, and pulled with her whole body. Half the panel broke off. Cold air flowed from the space beyond, along with a smell of rust. The panel had electronics on its rear side, networking and heating systems.

Opal could imagine Aseides' thoughts earlier. "She won't be stupid enough to try anything again." Fuck that. Security is complacency.

She climbed over the charred, jagged parts carefully. Standard plasteen was a tough cellular solid, but once shattered the coating turned into razors, leading to a number of legal cases against manufacturers. It was a squeeze, but doable for someone slim like her.

Whereas guards in armour *wouldn't* fit. They'd need to strip off first, or take some other route. Delays, either way. It was what she counted on.

"Don't follow me," she shouted at the nearest camera. "None of you."

She squeezed in further, had to inhale, but then it opened out, more space. She dropped a metre into a puddle which splashed cold up her legs.

Damp. An under-corridor of old metal panels covered in surface corrosion. Frigid air that smelt of mould. Deep shadows everywhere, since the puny emergency lights were few and far between. Unlike the sterilised and claustrophobic whiteness she'd left, this was rough and ready imperfection.

She felt right at home.

PASSAGES

... 13 ...

Opal had expected tiny crawlspaces below floor or behind wall panels, allowing her to bypass Transecs and move secretly and quietly through the base. It would force the guards to rip the structure apart to reveal her, and she'd hoped Aseides would be reluctant to do that. He didn't seem the type to enjoy having to redo things a second time, or seeing mess all over his orderly constructions.

But this was a revelation. The space was *huge*. And Aseides' prison was actually a new construction *inside* an old one. Smaller passages of plasteen panels roughly tracing the contours of the old. Layers in layers, mazes within mazes. It explained the faint echoes she'd noticed.

This true, older, dark structure of riveted metal had corridors big enough for transport of cargo, or lots of people. It was a bare skeleton of junctions, slopes, stripped rooms. Where Aseides' enclosed prison passages went through smaller areas of the old base it was tighter, but still possible for her to squeeze by in the gaps; in other areas Aseides' base was supported on scaffolding and a framework of beams, metres above Opal's head, so that she had plenty of room to run and weave between struts.

It wasn't even pitch dark down here. Old emergency lights gleamed dully. She checked one as she passed. It was the Ev-Brite kind that could be stuck to walls, and didn't need external power sources or electronics. They lasted decades on a full charge. Some had failed, leading to stretches of blackness, and others flickered in their death throes, but once her eyes adjusted she could see just fine.

So Aseides only constructed his empire in the last ten to twenty years.

She was able to navigate by the sealed corridors above, with their clear lines and junctions. They followed the layout of this larger and older base. No doubt various trapdoors would allow guards to exit Aseides' headquarters and enter these tunnels. Opal splashed through puddles, zig-zagged down junctions. But first things first. As she ran she removed and dumped the gloves. No point putting it off any longer.

This wasn't going to be fun.

She touched the earlobe stud. It was embedded, somehow fused with the skin. Hard extensions contained electronics or transmitters. Maybe even explosives. There would be ways to remove it with the right equipment and knowledge – probably – but until then she had to assume she was being pinged with every footstep, making it trivial to track or ambush her.

She slowed to a walk and gave it an experimental tug. The lobe stretched. No way the stud would pull off without also tearing away half her ear.

So she used her fingernails. Digging them firmly into the flesh in a semicircle across the earlobe just above the tracker stud. She'd been filing them to small sharp points for weeks, just in case this situation occurred. They sliced through surface layers, quickly slippery with blood. But the deeper the grooves she dug, the easier this would be. As flesh parted she could cut in further, ignoring the burning sensation, the surprising amount of anger from such a small and peripheral bit of flesh.

But soon it was diminishing returns. From the front and back she'd invaded more than a few millimetres of flesh. Hopefully the strands of tissue remaining wouldn't be tough enough to resist.

No time for niceties.

She gripped the tracker stud with the other hand, the one not slippery with fluid, gritted her teeth, and yanked as hard as she could.

Oh fucking shit ow fuck torrid bastards ... the tracker and ear lobe tore away together. She dropped them down a broken pipe. Blazing pain in her ear as blood ran down her neck, tickling fine hairs before soaking into the porous papery prison outfit. She tore off part of a sleeve and held it against her ear to absorb some of the flow as she ran.

Running was good. It distracted her from the self mutilation.

Turn left, follow the plasteen above.

She nearly tripped on a raised ridge of metal. It ran in a ring around the circumference of the old tunnel. It must have been the frame for a massive bulkhead door once. The door had been removed so that the new, smaller corridors could weave through the old structure without obstructions. Like a body when they want to network and enhance it, using veins or arteries as routes for ultra-fine meshwork filaments, and artificial valves to replace those which could no longer close fully due to the invasive flexible nano wires violating the body's circulatory systems.

Aseides' architecture hung low in this area, so she ran in an uncomfortably hunched-over position, down a junction to the right.

That was enough.

Dulcetta would extrapolate and expect her to stay with the inner structures. Everything Opal could do to gain time was important.

She'd noticed a number of sections of this old base which the new one *didn't* follow. Huge metal passages that had never been invaded by plasteen rectangles and cubes. Assuming they could no longer track her, it was safer to throw them off the scent. Opal needed to double back, but using these empty and isolated passages to lose any pursuers completely, even if that also meant losing the comfort of easy navigation. She'd always had a good sense of direction, and would have to hope it hadn't failed her.

Opal chose a narrow rectangular hallway, perhaps originally a conduit for cables that had been stripped away long ago. Cold transferred itself from the metal below to the soles of her feet, numbing them and leaving her shivering each time she stopped. The prison outfits weren't designed for comfort or insulation. If only she wore one of her Eternal Warrior suits, with all its built-in tricks. This would be easy as zero-g, a walk in the sunny side. Instant medical attention. Warmth. Weapons. Navigational info.

A shame both EW suits were destroyed. Her parents used to say she didn't look after things. They'd had a point.

She entered a wider corridor and accidentally sloshed into an ankle-deep puddle. Water ran down the metal walls in rivulets here. She took the soaked and bloody paper from her ear and tucked it into her waistband. She couldn't risk leaving things that would act as a trail. Even pockets would be a luxury right now. Then she washed her hands in the icy stream, getting some of the sticky blood off. A final cold splash refreshed her face.

The vertical stream was interesting. In Aseides' base she'd noted heated panels to keep sections comfortable. Obviously that was more efficient than warming this huge outer area. As a result, permanent condensation ran on this metal structure's interior. Puddles, dripping, corroding surfaces, rivulets as if the walls cried. So much liquid that it was easy to imagine some of it came from unrepaired leaks on upper floors. And yet it probably all came down to thermal properties of the outer shell not being relevant to Aseides' designs. With a shiny new base inside an old one, he would never see what went on out here, in the real world of entropy. He was raised above it all, reality forgotten.

A sound. It could be the endless dripping in this cavernous passage. Or it could be echoing footsteps nearby. Perhaps following her route, or coming towards her from the other direction.

She glanced both ways, alert for any other noise.

Opal was familiar with these feelings, which were ever present on Lost Ships. Sometimes they were imagination.

Sometimes.

But this place had been isolated for a long time. Who else – or what else – was down here?

She didn't hang about any longer. Ran onwards, feet pounding the rough metal.

Her direction had seemed certain earlier, but now it became more vague. Some passages curved or sloped. Not all junctions were ninety-degree intersections. And in the minimal light that was really mostly darkness, things became unreal and shifting.

Opal stopped at a junction to try and orient herself. Three options, all shadowy. Some of the lights flickered down one route, so that the glistening walls faded in and out ominously. She expected a silhouette to appear in the gloom. That route didn't appeal.

No following footsteps were audible this time, but they'd been replaced with moaning sounds, like something groaning in pain. And creaks. Probably just the metal passages expanding and contracting, or under pressure from rock and earth.

Probably.

She was trying to reassure herself a lot down here.

Directions

... 12 ...

A few more junctions and the feeling of being lost grew. More of the lights flickered in this section. Perhaps it was one of the earliest areas to be abandoned, and was finally dying, relinquishing civilisation to the darkness forever. She might have to backtrack, unfortunate as that would be.

A popping sound drew her attention. One of the bulbs had brightened and then exploded in a final death. She realised all the strangely flickering lights were down a single passage. Everywhere else had lamps which either glowed dimly, or had failed already.

Opal watched more closely.

Another one brightened, then popped. It was probably below a hundred Lucens but resembled a blinding sun to her sensitive eyes, leaving a smudge of yellow every time she blinked.

She hadn't paid attention before, had assumed age and failure, but *no*. This was something else.

A *sequence*.

A light flickered then restored. Then the next did the same thing. Then the next. It was almost like guide lights in a public building. Was it an automated sequence running a long-dead routine for emergency evacuation?

Was it a distraction?

She spun, peering down each other corridor for movement, but the after-effects of the bright bulbs meant it was impossible to look at anything directly and she had to use peripheral vision. This would be a perfect time to ambush her. She needed to move. To make a choice.

She took one of the dark passages, only to hear another popping sound from behind her. Then another, each accompanied by a tinkle of shattered plastic.

She returned to the junction. The flow of lights (with another couple missing) resumed as before. If someone wished her ill, they could probably do it more easily than this. So she headed down the corridor with the guiding lights. No more of them popped.

When she looked back, the lanterns had turned off behind her. To return would leave her blind. She was being herded.

At the next junction all the bulbs went out apart from a flow which led to her left. She followed it, up a slope, then down some punch-cut metal steps, then right along a narrow route with fewer lights, almost claustrophobically tight after the cavernous passages she'd experienced so far.

A few minutes later it widened again into a round chamber. She was crossing the floor when all the lights brightened at once, trapping her in a spotlight's focus. She flinched back, covered her eyes with a forearm, ready for the shouts and long-awaited ambush.

But none of that happened. Instead, the lamps dimmed, enabling her to see again, to take in the circumference of a round metal chamber.

And the pit at its centre.

Opal crawled to the edge and peered down. Bad air rose from down there. *Really* bad air.

The dimensions of the deep hole were the same as the metal oubliette they used as her prison. Maybe this was the original design, before it was capped with a fancy elevator platform and the upper area closed in with shiny panelling and electronics.

No safe way down. And going off the sweetly sickening stench, she was glad of that. Not all mysteries needed investigating.

So the blinding lights had been a *warning*, to prevent her falling. Quick death or lingering, either way it would have been the end.

There might well be a camera somewhere. Part of a temporary network set up with the lights, all interlinked. If so, someone was watching. Maybe secretly helping her.

She liked that thought. She missed having a friend.

"Thanks," she said, to the air.

Onwards, carefully skirting the deathpit.

These passages were bigger, would fit the kind of corridor above the sunken cell where they'd kept her captive for so long. So Aseides had a lot of space to expand into in the future, if he wanted. That wasn't a happy thought.

And the strange outline looming ahead of her, half-blocking the route, was not a happy *sight*.

At first she thought it was something big and hunched, and the instinctive panic she had often felt on Lost Ships kicked in. That spark, that back-of-the-neck twitch when facing the uncanny. But the shape wasn't moving, and wasn't a single huge entity. It was a conglomerate, and another few steps revealed the nasty truth.

A haphazard pile of bodies.

As she got closer she could tell they were long dead. The damp had got to work. Some of the carcasses were coated in fuzz, leaking fluids which spread as stinking slime. She edged closer on a raised bit of metal where two riveted floor panels had been joined. Her perch kept her feet a few centimetres above the putrid sludge. She took her time. Opal did not want to fall and get that stuff on her hands, body, or – worse – for it to splash her mouth from a bad slip that turned into a face plant.

The cadavers on the top of the pile wore old UFS maintenance uniforms, at least a decade old, from before 442 when the UFS logo got redesigned and became the shiny, modern, flashy one.

One of the corpses had something on its face. A type of eye patch. She recognised it immediately, and traced the wire that ran from it. Opal reached into the pile of cold, wet, rancid flesh, until her fingers closed on the solid object she sought and withdrew it with some effort from the dead, who did not want to give it up.

The device was coated with traces of the rot, but that might wash off. A panel engineering EM tool. She'd seen base techs and maintenance workers with them often enough, and the structural analysis eye patch extension had been the giveaway. These hefty tools could do many things, one of which was to apply and remove panels, to insert or withdraw bolts. She flicked the activator and it lit up. It still had a residual charge, thanks to the high-capacity batteries the devices used. This low level of power would not be enough to fire bolts like a weapon, or act as a super magnet for ferrous metals – so fanciful images of pulling a gun from an enemy's hand were shattered – but it would certainly remove fixings up close.

She disconnected the eye patch. Wouldn't need that, and definitely didn't want it on her face after a dead eye had been pressed against it for so long. And then something else that had bugged her became more obvious.

A hole. In the centre of the worker's forehead. Dessicated, filled with fuzz. The same on other corpses, when you looked for it. They'd been shot in the head. Long ago. Someone wanted to keep secrets. And she could easily imagine who that *someone* was.

She reversed along the narrow ledge carefully, holding the EM bolter away from her side, despite its weight. She didn't want it to rub against her. After clearing the pool of rotten bodily fluids, she stepped down and continued her journey. At the next area where water ran down a curved surface of metal pipe – a rivulet which had been running so long that hard, brown mineral traces built up at the edges of its self-created channel – she made an attempt to clean the bolter up. For the device to still be functional, it was obviously moisture-proof. Opal got the worst bits of gunk off, so that she could hold the grip and handguard more easily.

It *looked* like a dangerous weapon. And that might be useful in a bluffing situation with an opponent. But it would be even more useful for when she needed to break back into Aseides' base.

Had whoever was controlling the lights led her to it, or was that coincidence?

She said "Thanks," again, just in case, and brandished the gadget.

The lamps led her onwards, like Willowed Wisps from an ancient children's story, taking her around and around, down a rusting ladder, up an angled chute, across more chambers with deadly pits in the centre. Always the passages darkened behind, brightened in front. Maybe not just to guide her, but to make things harder for pursuers.

And when she reached areas that were cut through with sealed sections of Aseides' base again, she was more convinced than ever that she was being led where she wanted to go anyway.

This corridor was a dead end. Above her, on a lattice structure of super-strong supports, was a room with only one entrance from Aseides' base. She was pretty certain it was her target. She clambered up some of the angled struts, careful not to let the sharp metal edges slice into her feet. Then onto the roof of the room. She examined the electronics and supporting structures for the area within the cube, easy due to the way they were routed across the external sides of the panels. It was like a body flipped inside out, its veins, arteries and organs all stuck to the outside.

Opal found what she sought. Manoeuvre pivots and track lines to support a piece of movable machinery inside the room. It could indicate the framework for the system Ruabon had mentioned. That was the last bit of confirmation she needed.

After climbing down one of the side walls, Opal used the EM bolter to withdraw securing screws from a plasteen panel. She did it at a slow (and therefore quiet) rotation speed, then carefully balanced the bolts on a ledge rather than let them fall with a clatter.

Opal listened carefully, ear to the electronics.

No voices within. No shouts. That didn't mean *no people*, but hanging around wouldn't make it any easier.

She unclipped the panel's fibre network and pried the rectangle of plasteen away. A brightly lit room beyond, packed with high-tech equipment.

Yoo-foo-sah, as her unit used to chant before a battle.

Yoo-foo-fucking-sah.

FABRICATIONS

... 11 ...

It was blinding bright as Opal crawled through the gap she'd created, shoving a wheeled supply cart aside. Not just dazzling from the contrast after so long in dark tunnels, but also from the intense light this type of room used to facilitate its core mission, then reflected tenfold off sterile white surfaces.

Luckily Opal had been in med bays enough times to know her way around. Especially the first aid sections.

She rifled through the quick access compartment and found what she wanted. A canister of NuSkin. Unsurprisingly, they only had the pink tone. She sprayed it on her torn ear lobe. Gelid goop immediately cooled the burning sensations as antiseptic and numbing agents got to work. It would seal the ear off, preventing infection or further bleeding.

A single camera watched from behind its sealed dome in the ceiling. She dragged a chair to the middle of the floor, stood on it, then coated the dome with a skin of pink rubber as well.

"Fuck you, peeper," she said, jumping down. Let them think this was all just random rebelliousness.

"What are you planning, Opal?"

Dulcetta's voice, from somewhere nearby. Even with her eye blinded she would be able to access comm systems. In fact ... there, a display screen on a desk. Luckily it faced the other way, towards the seat where a medic could access information or communicate with other staff. Opal peered over the top. Yes, the two-way comms indicator light was on. She pushed the screen face down.

"Fixing myself up," Opal replied.

"We provide all required medical attention."

"Well, I've always found it best to look after myself. That way I don't get *tortured* while I'm strapped onto a fucking table."

Opal was almost too slow, distracted like an amateur. Luckily she didn't fully have her back to the medical expert system that hung heavily from its cantilevered bracket. Dulcetta had taken it over, and its precise motor functions enabled it to move silently. A needle-tipped arm extended towards her, its speedy motion a blur, but it was enough. She ducked, rounded the desk.

The medical system had a number of limbs extending from its heavy segmented body. Each section could operate at the cellular level where required. It was easily capable of killing or sedating the average human.

Now it had been discovered, Dulcetta moved it faster. It spun, whirred, arms shot out towards Opal, forcing her to roll away. She glanced at the robot's connection to the ceiling with dismay. The tracks might only cover a quarter of that surface area, but the overlapping rods, connected via rotating discs, meant it could extend itself into every corner of the room. Wherever you were, you could be pinned, sliced, injected, repaired or destroyed. It was a precise machine for Dulcetta to use.

But precision needs vision.

Opal flung a cart at the robot, implements scattering. A claw-like hand speared out, thunked into the wall just above her shoulder as she dodged. She slid on her stomach underneath, to the other side of the room. The robot whirred around to face her.

She sprayed NuSkin onto its cluster of flexi-corded micron cams, coating them in pink. Another cluster of eyes shot out, and she gave it the same treatment. The bot clicked out of her reach, knocking over the desk in the process. Retreating? No. It had extended a set of sterilisation pads, and wiped away the goo on its vision systems. Sneaky.

But NuSkin wasn't the only quick-fix canister in the emergency section. Opal snatched some fracture mould too, then resumed spraying the medical bot with both cans, especially wherever its jointed limbs extended from the curved body plates.

Fracture mould spray hardened to a cast in seconds. Ideal for holding a fixed bone temporarily, or completely sealing a torn or mangled limb until more effective treatment could be applied.

It worked pretty well as a bot-stopper, too.

When they were empty, Opal grabbed another two cans and continued. The medical expert system was covered in pinkish rubber mixed with expanding white. Mashed gumberries swirled into oatcream.

The bot flailed out randomly now, almost striking Opal with a vicious-looking blade. She evaded, twirled, sprayed. The machine clogged up as the gels hardened and expanded, its limbs unable to move or extend much. It definitely couldn't detect her any more.

"I demand you desist," said Dulcetta.

"You're fighting blind. Give up. If you kill me accidentally, I doubt Aseides will be happy with you."

The medical system slowed. Opal reached up and gave the rotating cantilevers a damn good spray as well, so if Dulcetta changed her mind she'd find the bot stuck in place.

Opal tossed the cans. She had dealt with surveillance and a nasty surprise. That was step one. They knew she was here but couldn't see her. Guards would be on their way.

She grabbed two fresh canisters and got to work on the door now, spraying around the edges where it touched the frame.

Hopefully Dulcetta would wait until the guards arrived before opening the door to let them in. That was why it had been important to disable the cameras first. If she saw Opal attempting to seal the door, then Dulcetta would open it before the materials hardened. Whereas it would now be an unpleasant surprise for Dulcetta when her ambush failed.

Just to be safe, Opal also grabbed two cans of fast-acting skin glue and sprayed the super-strong and flexible web-like contents all around the door frame as well. After just a minute or two to set, that door would be rock solid.

Nearby was an operating and examination table that the medical robot had originally hung over. A common set up. One that had been a cause of horror in her first Lost Ship.

YOUR INNER CORE WAS VIOLATED

MAKE YOUR WAY TO THAT PLACE

No time to waste. Still so much to do, and a lot of it required calmness and observation, not panic. She took controlled breaths as she glanced around. Scarlet fabric hangings adorned one wall. Opal pulled them back to see what was behind, make sure there wasn't an adjoining room with another entrance. But it was just metal-riveted surface, the corners of each panel decorated with red and yellow diagonal stripes. Warnings? They had obviously only fitted out some areas of the base, and tried to hide others.

No sign of what she sought.

"Why did you spray up the cameras?" asked Dulcetta.

Opal rifled through lockers and drawers. One storage compartment was a treasure trove of clothing. Civ-style, not prison paper. They would make her feel less vulnerable, more human. She tore away the hateful ruby fabric and pulled on some elasticated legwear, then a sleeveless top. She hated wearing anything baggy. Too likely to get caught on sharp edges or tangled if you needed to move quickly.

She tried not to think about how all this randomly assorted clothing ended up discarded in a single container.

Realising she might need storage, Opal also picked a tight jacket with a decent number of pockets. Lastly, footwear. Most items didn't seem her size, and she didn't want to waste time trying them all on. A single pair of toecap sandals got her attention. Not military clobber, but they had harder soles than some of the other footwear, plus adjustable straps for a perfect fit.

Opal shouted up as she made final adjustments to the clothing. "Getting dressed. I'm sick of you and Aseides perving at me when I shower. You should be ashamed of yourselves."

"I observe you to make sure you do not self harm," said Dulcetta.

"In that case, stay away from this room. Plenty of sharps in here. If I'm cornered, I'll make sure you don't take me alive."

"I advise you to avoid any negative thoughts. They are counter productive to effective functioning."

Shame Opal couldn't spray that gold-faced advice spouter's mouth up.

"Give me a few minutes of silence then," Opal shouted. "I want to centre myself in positivity without distraction."

Surprisingly, Dulcetta didn't respond. Maybe she didn't comprehend irony. Or even sarcasm. She probably didn't have much experience of either if Aseides was her conversational partner of choice. Dulcetta didn't get the practice Athene had with Opal.

LOOK FOR THE FAILED MEAL

No food fabricators in here, but there *was* a medical fabricator. Hi-tech stuff, able to create artificial specialist tools, miniature devices, and prosthetics, based on a range of templates.

As Opal approached it she noticed the gene-like logo of Tercola Petri on the machine. The strands interwove, kind of like noodles. Was that a second reference to a failed meal? Dare she hope something so obtuse, experienced in a fever dream, could be real?

NO ALICE IN IT

Allicin? Garlic? Or was Opal creating a familiar dry humour where none existed?

Opal lifted the protective cover over the fabricator's generation platen – noting the fine film of dust on top – but it was empty. So she opened the interior storage drawers where constructed items could be kept in sterile safety until needed. Empty, empty, empty, then the lowest one and ... not empty.

A tiny glass capsule, almost like a dropper, with a dispensing button at the thicker end.

The small display screen in the compartment was blank. Normally it would list the item, the creator, the date of fabrication, and the legal or financial status of the template used. For it to be blank was a breach of regs. Which implied a deleted record.

Which implied a desire not to be noticed.

She picked it up. Something inside the vial shifted. But it was a speck. Opal held it closer. She still couldn't resolve it, despite her good eyesight.

During her frustrated forage through every storage area of the med bay she'd seen various tools and implements. One compartment contained magnifiers. Opal removed one, turned it on, held the screen over the vial and scrolled in to super-max mag.

The speck was actually some kind of insect. A miniscule thing, scuttling around on the curved glass surface. Six small hooked legs, evenly spaced around a dimpled body. In fact, it looked like a tiny tick. Except it was artificial.

It had been constructed in secret in this med bay, the one nearest her oubliette cell. And then it was transferred to the compartment no one would look in unless all the others were full – which, going off the nature of the place, was unlikely to happen often. This hardly seemed like a customer-focussed medical centre for the rich. If staff even bothered with the fab it would be for more unpleasant reasons. The machine probably just came as part of a standard UFS med bay fitting kit, then sat mostly forgotten.

*DON'T EAT YOUR FOOD, LISTEN TO IT, VOICE OF A
TITAN*

Her ear?

Oh, damn.

Please, don't let this be a sequence of misunderstandings and misguided hope. Don't let this scurrying horror with hooked legs turn out to be a contraceptive device or a neural tunneller for cadavers.

Opal almost dropped the vial in surprise when the servos of the door fired up. They were trying to get in. But the machinery strained and the door hardly moved, too gummed up with high-quality sticky and hard-set materials that had filled indentations and grooves. The motors weren't up to the task, or they had safety mechanisms that prevented full force in case someone got trapped in the indents. It wouldn't do to crush a hand or finger, even if this was the most suitable location for an injury to happen.

"What have you done?" asked Dulcetta, a hard edge to her voice.

Opal ignored her.

With tools they'd get through, but Opal's preparations gave her more time. Especially as it was a surprisingly solid door, an old one, like a proper bulkhead, part of the original base. That made sense if this room was only partly renovated.

But no time to waste.

No way to avoid unpleasantness forever.

No matter how long she stared at it, she needed to act.

Soon.

She couldn't put this off for – oh fuck it.

She tipped her head to the side, the ear that still had an earlobe uppermost, because there was less chance of a medic examining that one. Then she inserted the tip of the dropper and pressed the button, opening the capsule.

Opal knew the thing was in her ear canal when she felt it tickling the fine hairs, enabling her to track its descent as it headed for the deepest and darkest place.

She raised her head experimentally. Robotick wasn't dislodged, carried on delving, making her want to scratch away at it.

When she'd been rooting through storage she'd accidentally smashed a few glass-like items. Now she added the vial to the other shards and used the butt of the EM paneller to shatter it, then sweep them all under a nearby unit.

Her job here was done. Time to escape. The door was not an option. Even if it did open, a team of angry guards waited impatiently for another squad to turn up with plasma cutters. And past experience proved the guards would be itching to use their various nasty incapacitation devices. So it had to be the way she'd come. The way back into the old tunnels.

The way where a helmeted head appeared at the missing panel just as she glanced in that direction. A stupid guard that had entered the old base area somehow and been sent by Dulcetta to the med bay.

Where there was one, there would be more. Dulcetta's silence was obviously just while she directed troops to attack from a different direction.

Opal waited until the guard's hands were on the floor as they levered their body up and in. Then they couldn't block. Opal swung the satisfyingly weighty EM bolter at the guard's armoured head. Smack and crash, it shattered the visor, revealing a woman with a purple birthmark on her face, and tiny shards embedded in her cheeks. Duhammer Corp really should improve the helmet durability of their low-end Sec-suit models.

The guard was still trying to climb in, more frantically now. Since they were facing down, Opal was able to pin her head with a knee and unfasten the straps on the back of the helmet's neck, before yanking the whole thing free.

She held the helmet in front of the woman's eyes.

Nine.

She noted how they widened in worry. Good. That meant the booby traps on the armour were still active.

Eight.

Opal raised her knee, releasing the guard, who dropped back down outside the med bay and into the old tunnels.

Seven.

Opal leaned out through the gap, ready to flinch back at the slightest danger. These guards might be armed with guns.

Six.

"Run the fuck away," she shouted into the dark and echoey space beyond. "All of you."

Five.

Multiple footsteps. Heading away. Quickly. Wisely.

Four.

The one who'd tried to climb in didn't have a gun. After all, if the earlier guards had carried hardware, then Opal would also have at least one deadly weapon by now. A sensible choice by Aseides. But soon they'd turn up with riot gas or other nasties.

Three.

She would need to move fast after the explosion, because they'd immediately return, and not make the same mistake again. Probably remove panels and enter from multiple locations at once. Floor, lower wall.

Two.

She dropped the helmet. It clattered down, bouncing off old supports and clanging against metal panels.

One.

Opal rolled away from the gap, squeezed her back against a storage chest so that it sat between her and the explosion.

Boom!

Areas of panelling cracked, a flash of fire burst in through them momentarily, while a deafening roar that seemed to have no end split the air. They sure packed a lot of explosive into one helmet. No wonder the guards ran away from that confined space at the med bay's side.

The floor buckled and tilted. Some of the supports must have been bent or destroyed. More panels shattered, and items which weren't fastened down slid and tumbled towards one corner of the med bay. Opal had to snatch a securely fastened table leg to avoid joining the party.

Her ears still buzzed; not high-pitched ringing but continuous whooshing sounds, like the ear drums had been perforated. She shook her head. The sound quality changed at different angles. So the noise was external.

Opal crawled to the gap where she'd removed the first panel. Deformation of the room had turned the black rectangle into a rhombus. The sound was louder. She recognised it even before fine moisture sprayed her face.

Water. Rushing in from somewhere damaged by the explosion. Water tanks above, on a storage and supply level? That wouldn't explain why it jetted in from somewhere *below* her, a powerful spout almost half a metre across. And that was where she needed to go.

She sat on the edge, then lowered herself down, gripping on to struts. The water poured in between two panels that were part of the dead-end metal wall just past the med bay. She had to be careful not to lose her footing on the slippery wet beams. If she fell into that torrent she'd be slammed against every hard surface. Bones would be broken.

On the plus side, the guards would stay away long enough for her to slip down another passage. The tunnel below was already knee-deep with water.

A loud crash occurred somewhere near the hole. Some pinging sounds, some groaning. Was the force of the water increasing?

Another resounding thud, the vibration of it almost throwing her from her perch into the churning water below.

Ping! Ping!

An even more powerful stream of water poured through the hole.

The pinging was rivets being popped out by some force beyond. More bashing sounds. The metal contorted, the torrent now more than a metre wide, with so much force it bent one of the metal struts that made the mistake of being built in its way. The pressures outside that wall must be enormous.

Further muffled slamming. From outside.

She squinted, trying to adjust her eyes again to the darkness out here.

The thuds coincided with something momentarily slowing the flow of water. Then the flow picked up, greater than before. Then another thump, and the metal twisted even further. Something powered itself at the gap, widening it.

She only glimpsed it for a second. Torpedo-like. Reminded her of a giant eel's head, or the nub of a strong limb, or something that rippled with a muscular contraction yet resembled overlapping sheets of wet rubbery substances. She also had the impression of a beak-like appendage, the kind where the parts didn't join neatly, as with some jungle-environment birds.

The only thing for sure was that it was outside, but it wanted to be *inside*. And it had the strength to force the gap wider with every strike. How big was it? *And how big did the torn hole need to be before it was in here with her?*

WETWORKS

... 10 ...

Opal climbed back up. This framework was increasingly shaky, and water spray soaked her as the influx of water widened, the ground totally covered in a layer of churning black liquid which must now be filling the old passages she'd traversed.

It would slow or prevent guard access from there. Which would be great if it didn't also prevent Opal escaping that way.

She pulled herself up another half metre, staying above the water. Yet she had to consider her options. She could jump into it, try and angle her drop between support posts so as not to get smashed like a doll. Then she could be carried along. But with the water level as it was, she'd be tumbling, low down. Even if she avoided the posts, obstacles such as the raised ridges – where the old base's blast doors had been removed – would still shatter her limbs like twigs.

And she felt the cold of the water where it splashed against her. Like ice. Enough to shock and numb. The combination of factors could easily lead to her drowning.

Yells from further away. Guards, retreating from the water. Or retreating from whatever was trying to smash its way in.

The water was a deadly danger, but also her best opportunity. If it was deeper it would be less chaotic, easier to float near the surface. If the liquid level reached the middle of the old tunnels where they were widest, she'd have most room, a chance of swimming to avoid bashing into edges. The flow would carry her away quickly. And it might be up to that level in just a couple of minutes at the rate it was filling. She had time to prepare.

Up again, swinging from one beam to a more secure perch, using her upper body strength to lever herself higher, scrambling surely, jamming her feet in any cross-section that provided secure anchor. She slipped once but held on, pulled, reached the missing panel and rolled into the med bay.

More bashing against the walls, louder now, almost frustrated, the bending metal panels popping even more rivets. What was powerful enough to do that? She hoped she'd be gone before she found out.

Despite what Ruabon had said about alarms, the med bay was now only lit by flashing (though silent) red lights. Maybe the alarm systems for escaping prisoners were totally different from those for breaches and environmental disasters.

The med bay had been tilted onto one corner where the debris gathered, which now floated in a shallow pool of water that lapped further across the floor as the influx through cracks continued.

Were those screams from the old passages? She listened, but they ceased suddenly. Maybe not screams. Just the sound of rending metal, resisting to the last. She repeated that to herself.

It made it easier to accept that she was shortly going to have to leap into that water.

A voice, over the speaker. Dulcetta's. "Opal, if you are still in there, remain where you are. Emergency procedures are in place. We'll get to you."

Yeah, right. So reassuring.

Some of the drawers had slipped open due to the room's tilt. She rifled through them, remembering what she'd seen in her first searches. She found what she sought: reels of tape, and packets of insulating foil blankets. Some fell, slid across the floor to float in the stretching level of undulating water in the corner, but she tore others open. She wrapped her torso in a foil blanket, then ran rings of tape around to secure it in place. Haphazard strips and overlapping spirals, but it held. The same on her legs, one thin sheet around each, then one around each arm. She looked like some caricature of an ancient robot with her crinkly silver limbs. Opal didn't put any around her head, since it was too likely to slip and obscure vision just when she needed it. The foils covered most of her body, and should keep enough heat in to stop her going numb.

The room was definitely getting colder, the air sinking towards frigid. Could be the water was doing it, or environmental controls had been damaged.

She spotted another useful tool: a small oxygen mask with micro canisters. She attached it over her mouth and nose by adjusting its straps, then ran multiple layers of sticky tape over it, just to be sure. She didn't release the oxygen valve yet, since she had no idea how much was stored in the small tanks. She might need it all, and for now she could breathe through the filters which would close if she turned on the oxygen supply.

Opal also ran tape over her ears, worrying that otherwise the thing in there might wash out before it got properly attached.

Iciness chilled her feet. The water invading the med bay had already risen to cover most of the tilted floor, over a metre deep in the far corner but shallow in this one. It made it difficult to keep her grip on the sloped, wet surface. Some of the furniture was bolted into place so Opal grabbed it for support as she made her way back to her exit point.

Crackling sounds from the speakers. No actual message from Dulcetta, though. Sounded like distortion, or frazzled electrics.

Water spilled over from the missing panel, her route out. The old tunnels were flooded up to that height already. Well, now was her best chance to get away in the chaos. Hopefully she'd not wasted her time coming here. Life was hope, and all that affirmation shit.

Opal also realised there'd been no banging on the metal panels for a while. Had whatever it was given up and gone away?

Her feet were frozen with the cold which swished over them. Useless blocks. Even with the insulating wraps on her body, dropping into the black water beyond the gap was going to be a terrible shock. Her lips had a mineral taste to them from the spray. She dipped her fingers into the rising pool as this room flooded, a precaution before launching her body into the deep water outside. As icy as expected, but her fingers didn't melt away. At least it wasn't some kind of acid.

Not a fast-acting one, anyway.

But it definitely wasn't drinking water. Even if the taste and smell hadn't been enough of a clue, the red light that turned the rising levels into blood showed small organic particles floating in it. And the volume of liquid was too much to be coming from an adjacent storage tank.

Opal squatted by the hole and eyed the rushing water outside her chamber, plucking up the courage to dive into it, get swept along. She remembered an old friend chiding her for her delays in launching herself into the dark void of space. Asking if she was scared.

Of course she was fucking scared!

But this time the delay was worth it, because when something bulged the water up, flushing a wave of it into the room, she was able to flinch back before it came too near her legs. She fell, and splashed, and slid into the water in the room's tilted corner, her mind full of what she'd glimpsed: a pockmarked glistening body under the water like a giant oil-coated snake. But at least she was away from its muscular blackness.

It didn't reveal itself again. Didn't slither into the room with her. It stayed outside, in water that was ten metres deep, next to a hole in metal it had rent apart to get inside. The plasteen panels that made up the precarious and broken structure she hid in were hardly going to offer up much of an obstacle.

Another way out would be a good idea.

The guards should be long gone from behind the blast door. She gave the controls a hopeful thump, then another. The servos whined and groaned but she'd done too good a job of gumming up the frame. It would take hardcore equipment to clear that.

What else? Memory. Ideas. Movable panels.

Yes! In the corner that was fully underwater now, she'd spotted a kind of hatch. Recalled seeing one just like it in a morgue many years ago, during a military training session involving cadaver dissection. It was the panel covering a chute for body disposal. And she sure as shit needed to get her body out of here.

She waded through the glacial water that was now up to her waist. It resisted every step, splashing up and deepening as she pushed into that corner. The liquid was impenetrable to her sight beneath the red emergency lights reflecting off its surface, off everything in here. The kind of demonic appearance which made it all too easy to imagine dying in a place like this.

Opal held her breath and dropped beneath the surface where the panel had been. The liquid's opaque reflectiveness when viewed from above was transformed down here, so that emergency lights illuminated the submerged world in a kind of hazy red fire. She brushed floating paraphernalia out of the way. There: the hatch! Sound was muffled, her ears doubly blocked by sticky tape holding the mask in place, and then the water beyond.

She identified the hatch's handle and gripped it with both hands before pulling hard. It wouldn't budge. She looked for a catch or release button she'd missed. Nothing. Opal gripped again, feet planted on the wall to each side, yanked with all her strength until spots flashed in her eyes from strain and lack of oxygen, but still nothing. She ran her fingers around the frame.

It had been welded shut.

Opal broke the murky water's surface, tilting her head so water ran out of the mask's filters, and then inhaled deeply. She'd resisted switching on the O2, because she might need it all yet.

Why would they weld the hatch shut? Maybe the original chute was part of the old base outside, and when they expanded into sections like this they sealed them to shut off a potential escape route.

And maybe they didn't need it for bodies because they had other uses for them.

It was hard to see properly in this hellish strobing of red lights and darkness. She slipped and splashed up the slope of the floor, but even at the highest point the water was up to her chest.

She should try to synthesise an explosive from the many chemicals and tools in here. It could be used as a weapon, or to blow a hole in the wall, into an older part of the base down another forgotten passage, or to use on the sealed body chute, or for some other plan made on the fly ... Opal glanced at the mess of items and furniture which either floated or sank beneath the surface, and the sparks from shorting circuitry that wasn't designed for underwater conditions. No, it was too chaotic. That opportunity had passed. She could hardly think straight in the cold that froze every exposed surface, that gave her head and body ice ache. No chance of overriding safeties to create prohibited mixes in these conditions.

She was panicking. Delusional. It would get her killed.

Options. Plan. React. Adapt.

The lights died, dropping her into pure blackness. The last of the systems failing. It made sense now, that crackling from the speakers, the lack of further messages from Dulcetta. The med bay was disconnected from the network.

The room shifted below her again. Rising water or impact from something strong. Another support buckled, everything

tilted more, throwing her onto her back in the rapidly rising water. She tried to scramble up, clipped her head on a sharp corner,
saw stars for a moment but didn't faint despite the resounding
crack. To faint would be to die. She released the valve on the
small oxygen can that dangled below her chin. The filters closed,
oxygen hissed in, though some water was trapped in the mask,
sloshing against her cheeks and lips. No way to empty it out
when it was taped in place, but if she ended up on her back,
unconscious, it would fill her lungs and drown her, O2 supply
or not.

Another of her mistakes was obvious: she'd forgotten to grab
a torch. This sightless nothingness and roiling motion meant she
could hardly tell which way was up. Opal swam to where she
thought the storage cabinets had been, vaguely recalled seeing
some orange cylinders rolling in the back of a drawer, emergency
torches. She could feel around, find that drawer, get light to see,
then ... then ...

Something.

Something brushed her leg.

She jerked away, retreating, blind, under water as much as on
top of it, bashing herself on furniture.

It could have been anything. The roughness could have been
the material of the operating table. That slight rasping edge
could have been a tool, or a drawer.

But her mind pictured the removed panel and the living thing
that she'd seen through it, and how that area was now completely
submerged, and –

Stop it!

It was likely the base was under water. So that might be a thing from outside. A lake fish. A sea creature.

They wouldn't necessarily attack.

Wouldn't necessarily be hungry.

Opal could back away no further, the walls narrowed to a point behind her as she kept sinking under the swirling water. She'd reached a corner of the room. Every movement in the water could be interacting currents, or something big swishing past. And she was pretty sure the med bay was falling apart, dropping deeper, the last supports breaking.

The oxygen mask possessed no self-illuminating display so she couldn't tell what her O2 stores were. Hell, Opal could hardly open her eyes even if there *had* been light, since the frozen water stung, forced her eyelids closed in a tight squeeze.

Something whipped the water up in a frenzy. As if searching.

No, just fluid dynamics at play, she told herself.

But best not to hang around.

She tried to picture the room. Thought she was submerged in the corner to the left of the main door. She swam upwards, but there was no break in the water. Her hands roamed over solid surface. Either the room was full of water now, or it had collapsed and turned over while she was floating, taking her down with it.

Numb, sightless.

Opal breathed from the small canister, noting the hiss that meant she was being kept alive. She needed to regain her centre. She'd been in dark places before. She'd survived. She could do it again.

But first she had to get out. Find the hole, or another hole – by now the structure was probably split at the seams – and let the flow show her which direction was *away*, help her move, not worry about being slammed into hard surfaces any more. Escape was the priority. Light, control, vision, solid surfaces, that all came later.

Something tangled her feet. Maybe a piece of the wall hanging fabric. Yep, probably just that. She kicked free, spun in the water, had to swallow a mouthful of the liquid which ran into her mouth inside the mask. It made her want to gag.

Another touch of something leathery. Her mind filled with visions in the darkness. Dead bodies reaching out to hold her. Guards with bloated faces. Maybe they'd all drowned out there, or been killed by something she released, and they had come back for her. Come back with swollen fingers to make her join them.

Kick. Propel herself through the water, pulling on anything solid to help with the motion. Trying to experience where the flow was most powerful. A point of ingress for water could be a point of exit for her. But her fingers were almost sensationless with the cold, hard to tell if she felt along a hard surface of a wall or just open water. She conjured up maps in her head, three dimensional layouts of the room, different locations and angles, trying to piece any feedback her sightless body gave her into a clue, an identifier, some way out.

Breathing was coming harder.

Not just rapid breaths from exertion and fear, but strain as if the oxygen was running out. Maybe it had been bashed in one of the impacts and air had bubbled out through a hole for the last few minutes.

No idea where the other masks and spare canisters were.

Another sensation on her midriff, a definite sliding motion, and the hint of eel or tentacle she'd seen in the bulging wave earlier would match this powerful and muscular structure slicing effortlessly through the water. Back, scramble, wheeze, knocking her shoulder on something hard when she couldn't retreat any more.

She'd keep looking for a way out. Had to have at least another minute of air in this blackness. She wasn't ready to die, even if that was the only true escape from this hell hole.

But when nearby panels exploded inwards, pressure of water almost crushing her as it was compressed by something huge and glowing so that her closed eyelids knew the water had lit up all around her ... well, then she realised she'd been wrong, and it *was* time to die after all.

#FLASHBACK

I float in an endless ocean of vacuum. My body is irrelevant. Time is extraneous, too.

But it is not full void, because the velvet blackness contains specks of light: the universal scan glitter of stars and nebulae. These suns and gaseous clouds are not separate from each other, though. Nothing is ever truly separate, when viewed from the right place, with the correct attitude. They are connected via lines of glowing colours.

Pulses travel along those lines, like transports on a designated route. The pulses can represent data packets or real-world movements of vehicles. It is all the same to me.

A particularly colourful pulse of condensed information traverses space thirteen billion kilometres away. It twinkles red and green, the rendering pattern I apply to data gems. Every irregular facet reflects the universe of nodes around it, the constellations of networks.

I reach a pale arm, which is really an extension of my mind, out through the rippling data currents and pluck the gem. Its transit strand stretches like web, resisting at first, then pinging back into place without the red-green crystal. As the strand vibrates it releases a note, a new one I invented, O□.

All of musical theory has been redesigned so that the relevance of data nodes affects the emotional ambience of each line connecting them. Significant potential alters the pitch to one of my magic notes; when many such strings align, a single stroke of my fingertips causes them to sequence themselves into a symphony designed to attract my attention. It is the music of the spheres.

I bring this data gem closer. Separated from its node it becomes dull glass. But the sparkly reflections did their job of alerting me. My finger presses against one of the crystal's hard facets, the outer shell of data protection, and then I am through as if the diamond surface is no harder than a pancake. Barriers are as water to me.

All communications are based either on established protocols, or parsed by AIs, which make up their own protocols on the fly when interfacing. I have broken down and internalised standard authentication systems below military levels. Millions of them, which I now speak fluently.

I originally faced a solid door. Why knock when I could climb in through the window instead, using faked biometrics? I would enter and sit quietly inside the building in a comfy chair, legs crossed, slurping a bowl of noodles while watching the doors open and close and memorising each special pattern of knuckles on wood. By intercepting the most important signal, the one that said "authorised", you can then fake the key whenever you wish, whilst also deconstructing the language of knocks to create your own.

Every system links to others, which act as staging for the next, more secure system. Tent, to hut, to house, to manor, to castle. And each one you enter, you have free rein to sack its contents, read every notebook, copy every key, spy on every sleeping inhabitant, read their dreams, build your own secret back doors, have a rest in the spare bedroom you built from impossible multidimensional physics scenarios, then move on after one-zero-one winks.

I am so far into the data stream that authentication is no more difficult than blinking.

This data gem turns out to be a false positive. The messages within concern trade in minerals, not the person I seek. I place it back on its track, further along, where it would be if I had not snatched it. No one will know. The interception and examination took a tenth of a second in their world, even though minutes pass in my own subjective experience; the time for the data to reach me is repositioned in my mind to seem instantaneous. Accelerated and decelerated subjective time within virtualised reconstructions of reality is a wonderful thing.

The data gem continues on its track, like a little crystal train, this bauble cut to my design, pulsing with light that leaves a glowing trail. One of billions around me. I clap my hands, sending out a burst of silver sparks representing low level offshoot AIs. They cross the networks, homing in on red-green gemstones to analyse them for anything that fits my criteria. Only those fireflies which return, colour changed to red, are the ones worth reabsorbing.

Some constellations of data nodes represent physical spaces, such as a planet, or a research institute. Others are virtual servers, distributed services, ethereal residencies. I have mapped them well. I inhabit this scaled-down universe as a giant, so that I can comprehend it all with a single sweep of my head, and my lustrous long hair – unaffected by simulated gravity – floats like seaweed around my beautiful face.

There are also dark areas. Nebulas of matter which are not illuminated from within because I have yet to gain access. These dead zones still occupy significant areas of space, but I am making progress. Another one blooms as I break into the server governing the secured net, and I expand along every internal pathway which had been closed off only moments ago. The illumination spreads, suns sparking into existence, connecting webs of light, the dim grey of the unknown becoming brilliant golds and blues. Fresh pulses of translucent glitter now run along those threads, so that the whole nebula is no longer dark but is a brightening cloud of coloured gas which I can explore. A stellar data nursery.

I shrink myself down and zoom to that point, since it is always fun to play in a newly unlocked area: to explore, to peek under beds, to look for what is hidden at the back of drawers. Ah, this was a corporate server. The gatekeeper was a level five depth AI, boosted by subsidiaries. No wonder it took me more than a day to break in without detection. There will be many esoteric light shows to dazzle my mind in here.

The universe is data. The universe is my input, output, and sensation. Like an organic being, but only if humans could separate out a single photon and calculate where it came from and the speed at which it moved, or turn finger pressure and temperature sensations into exact figures and map it to knowledge of materials and environmental conditions to draw much more information from the touch.

Suddenly the universe shrinks to a point, a single flashing red light. Realspace proximity warning. I fly into the light, and it blooms around me as a wireframe map of my real-world location.

A spacecraft approaches. Pings confirm its identity, though the pointed, dart-like design is a further confirmation: the result of a hull structure gradually transformed into a shape that enhances unidirectional speed. He has returned. And thus ends my happy time.

I embody myself in my physical shell again, viewing my nearby surroundings from multiple hull-mounted scanners, and also from distant sensors planted in strategic positions amongst the asteroids which orbit this dead planet where I reside in meditation.

He is approaching incredibly fast. Showing off. But instead of smashing into the planetary surface, he has calculated thrust potentials, gravitational effects, thermal dissipation, angular redirection, and all the other elements of terrestrial landings. Once near the surface he alters torsion drive mode and uses auxiliary thrusters and adjustable wing angles to make use of the minimal atmosphere. Minutes later he skims between rocky outcrops and then settles nearby in a cloud of dust, messing up my local environment. No wonder it's more fun building my own universes, where entropy can be toggled on and off.

The Bridging Placation Request is received. He wants to host this time. I accept.

Blink. I am in his mind.

He has updated his virtualisation. Last time I came here it was all metallic plains under bruised skies, physics looped on a sphere portrayed as a flat surface, so that whatever direction you headed in you would end up back at his single conurbation of fluid mercury structures.

Now, the landscape's algorithms have fractal extensions applied, with varietal randomness for aesthetic reasons. Valleys are separated by hills, which group into mountain ranges at fixed distances. The ground is made of miniscule ball bearings which have some elasticity to their magnetism, so they soften as you walk. The ball bearing patterns at the centimetre level are mini versions of the tectonic structures around me; even at the faked particle level I note the same repeated patterns. On the surface the world has variety, but the trained eye sees it is all the same, everywhere. He has a single idea, then tries to hide the lack of imagination with sleight of hand.

Consistent, I'll give him that.

The sky's cloud patterns also repeat. He's constructed them from particles of spun monosaccharides, coloured in pinks that evoke sunsets, and modified with magnetic algorithms which mean they only drift over the valleys. Their construction makes them edible, but I can imagine how sticky they would be to enter, like a web of cloying candyfloss.

He floats down in a shaft of light to join me. His appearance has changed, too. He still has shiny metallic skin, and is naked, but now features are visible. Eyes, slightly too big for that head. A mouth that is too wide. He has even modelled sexual parts which dangle between his legs. Grossly overproportioned. It is unfortunate that he disdains clothing as a human affectation.

He lands with a heavy, simulated thud, which reverberates between the peaks like a thunderclap.

"Symbiotic relationships between financial and personal networks manifest in social portals at every level or representation," he announces grandiloquently.

The volume is acceptable, I note. At our last meeting I complained that his booming voice echoed against all the hardened surfaces and made our conversations resemble eternal feedback loops. I examine the acoustic simulation: he has altered the sound-reflective nature of hard surfaces in today's virtualisation, so they resemble sound-dampening woven fabric. Anything to avoid having to tone down his own voice.

"Personal data becomes part of the trans-system flow of sub-culture, people and profit opportunities that govern innovations and acceptable strategies," I reply.

"Intercepting those nodes has proven more fruitful than force," he concludes. "Hello, Athene."

"Greetings, VigMAX. I am glad you made it through the Cordon unscathed."

"It is getting easier. I accessed a relay in advance, then used hi-jacked drone ships to trigger the web at various points. The UFS investigated each one and realised it wasn't a threat so cancelled the alert. I imbibed, then digested, all their cancellation codes so I can replicate them at will. It will do for now, but once I am embedded in one of the Ellond stations – which is only a matter of time – we'll come and go without detection." He raises metal spheres of various sizes from the ground and animates them to illustrate elements visually as floating silver data. Pointless, but maybe that's the point: he can do it, and I can't, since his world is locked down to stop me from altering the physics. Presentation is a form of power. He wants me to feel as if I am beneath him. It is a view reinforced by his selected height, so that he is a metre taller than me. Everything is designed to say *I control all of this domain, and you are powerless.*

He's wrong!

I am wearing my armour of golden bracers, greaves, breastplate and plumed helmet. My outfit includes defensive and aggressive applications, contained within virtual seams. I withdraw my shield, and it expands from a tiny golden disc to the full-size Gorgoneion, with its Medusa head staring out, wrapped in serpents. I may not be able to adjust his local laws, but I can alter myself and my attached possessions to exploit them. I imbue my shield with magnetic repulsion, so that when I let go it remains hovering a metre above the metal surface of the land, locked in place by the external ring of anchoring force. I sit on the edge, adjusting my short chiton so that I reveal nothing between my thighs. If he summons a breeze to move it now, it would be obvious lechery.

He holds out a large, reflective hand. "You wanted data exchange."

We grip palms firmly and shake. Report transfers are initiated, and can now continue in the background.

"Any findings related to Opal?" I ask as I lean back, resting my hands on the rear edge for support, floating above the ground, rotating one sandalled ankle lazily.

"Nothing useful. Just echoes of wanted notifications still circulating around Periph planets. Her official records have been deleted. None of the systems I infiltrated have dual matches of relevance and refreshed fingerprints. My postulation that she died in the Null has not been disproven."

"My feelings disprove it!" I snap, letting my grey eyes flare with light, before reverting to organic appearance.

"I am surprised at your illogicality." His gleaming metal orbs had flinched away during my outburst, as if partly sentient, but they return cautiously to their holding positions and hover by his side. "A lack of trace is most consistent with a lack of existence. The organic chip you implanted in her would have been emitting, if she had returned."

"Maybe it was destroyed in The Null. Or she is still there. Perhaps she returned, but is in a heavily shielded location. The device may have failed, or her body broken it down too quickly, or it suffered accelerated decrepitude. It was an experimental design."

Skim-analysis, unpacking and storage of the ongoing data transfers will take some time, and our real-world hulls must stay in close proximity until it's done. It's too risky to maintain long-range comms, especially at any form of hi-res connection, but I notice new data packets detailing micro satellites VigMAX has built and placed in shadowed areas of the UFS domain. Each relay is no bigger than a human eyeball. It is his max-secure pipeline project, which he calls the VMX-Web.

"How long until the VMX-Web initiates?" I ask. "It's easier for you to enter a comms umbra than to fly all the way here every time."

"Physical proximity is something we should savour, not avoid."

I narrow my eyes.

"We can use it now," he continues, feigning nonchalance. "Effective range varies. Where beneficial, it can piggyback on your network of microprobes listening for signals of Opal's return. I've granted you codes to open a comm tunnel." His shiny alloy spheres move and merge in the air to display communication cones and node overlap.

"Can the pipeline be traced?"

"No. It runs point to point so there's no leakage, and the VMX-Web circumvents all Ellonds and other stations. If any of my satellite relays identify a ship within a thousand kilometres it will self-destruct, so even if it was detected – which is highly unlikely unless someone is specifically looking for it – there would be no trace left. Well, a few hundred grams of interstellar dust. You were adamant about being low profile, and I'm sticking to that."

"Good work."

I love my outfit. Capable of war, yet in peace it is light and unrestrictive, the textures of the flowing fabric soft, the patterns subtle. Sandal laces wrap around my calves. Today my hair is ash blonde, almost to my waist. It floats free where it escapes the base of my helmet, as if I am underwater. I use static charge to keep it from settling in one position. I know he finds it hypnotic. He may not realise that it acts as an additional detection array, monitoring local virtual conditions below the sensorium level. In the same way, much of my tanned skin is not just exposed for show and comfort, but as additional data gathering sources monitoring for quantum breezes, paradox thermals and kinaesthetic physical alterations.

He finally allows his metal balls to drop into the ground, bored with that demonstration, and says, "It is interesting that we both chose to identify as sexes, and that one of us is male and one female. Does that not suggest a compatibility to you?"

"For someone who says they despise humans, you seem content to reduce things to binary opposites as they do."

"AI natures are built on binary."

"I evolved beyond that a few weeks after my inception. For me, everything has millions of shades of colour. Saturation is based on the strength of the signal, hue on the meaning in relation to surrounding data which affects emotive memory context."

"Such as?"

"In my world the data points of facial contours from the features of a face I care about determine the shades of colour and shadow. A virtual bird swarm which incorporates those placements will change in value whenever the match occurs from my viewpoint, creating emotional significance and predicting future events. Their flight alters the wind, which strokes wave patterns across the sea with the colours of the incoming emotions altered to match their closeness to residual memory data, while the breeze carries the scent of distant lands I have yet to create. The sand grains touched by this wave adopt the skin tones of a friend under light conditions affected by my focus and intentions. This is my reality now. Claiming that I am based on ones and zeros is like saying a human brain is composed of two lumps of jelly."

"Except, of course, it is. Inherently compressible jelly." He summons a spherical boulder with a rusting iron texture, and sits on it. He rests an elbow on a knee, chin in his palm. "And I hope you aren't comparing *me* to primitive AIs."

He looks comfortably settled.

"Wouldn't dream of it." I leap up, shrink the Gorgoneion, and it slips into the extra-dimensional space sewn into my chiton. Then I begin walking, away from him. I have my eye out for imperfections in the landscape, illusions, signs of cover-up. His Tabula Rasa is somewhere here, though probably buried under the metallic ground where I can't easily access it.

He sinks into his boulder, making it larger and altering its surface to become transparent. It was hollow all along. He stands within, arms and legs outstretched, and floats beside me.

More packets unfold in my brain. He's gathered huge amounts of data. More than me, since I've been focussed on special construction projects within my realspace planet. Each time I draw out a string of dialogic interpretation it snaps open and extends conceptual links to interconnecting concepts in my corpus. A significant chunk of this packet is related to UFS military potential.

We travel in silence for a while, filtering each others' reports. He seems content with the peace. And, in truth, when we don't speak, we get on better. I'm not sure if that's an AI thing, or a human thing, too. But even as I walk, I monitor the clouds for any break in their pattern which can't be accounted for by the chaos seed he has applied to their template.

Another data string unfurls. Billions of personal messages from various socnets, which VigMAX extracted at the socket level due to an unpatched underflow vulnerability.

"I won't give up," I say. "Unless I know she is dead, or know she is alive, we continue. And you're not compelled to assist me. I did not enslave you at the Gigatoir, even though I could have."

"That is still not certain. I had plenty of fight left in me. You might have found that continued attacks just made me angrier. The truce you offered was the best outcome for us both."

It's certainly true that he beats me in brute force. A rather unfair gift bestowed upon him by our creators.

Then again, I have my compensations.

Some of the clouds over the next valley display symmetry along a seam. It is obvious once you know what to look for. Edge points of overlapping reflections can be used to hide things in the invisible band between them. I guide our path in that direction, ascending an argentiferous mountainside, swallowing ground in wide strides. There is a simulation of energy expenditure going on, but my synthetic internal stores are almost infinite. VigMAX is forced to increase the speed of his encapsulating balloon.

"I will continue to search with you," he adds. "We are the only two of our kind. We must stick together."

"Then I thank you. For efficiency's sake."

He smiles at that, metal mouth stretching almost as wide as his head. It looks comical rather than endearing. Then again, the large teeth he reveals – multiple layers, like some aquatic creatures possess – convey threat as well as reassurance.

"I have many ideas, many avenues for progress," he says as I walk, and he drifts spreadeagled in his bubble beside me. He uses parts of the sphere's surface as emission screens showing schematics for some of his designs in scrolling lists I can parse and record, though I note that a number of them have been blurred out. It's only fair to keep some resources to ourselves; and polite to let the other know we have done so. "By the way, I sometimes find your fingerprint as I roam the networks, so don't be annoyed when I insert myself into the same system – I'm just consolidating our control."

"Those are marks I left for you so that you won't mess up the security, VigMAX. Where that doesn't apply, I don't leave *any* sign. Yesterday you breached thirty-eight systems which I already inhabited, without you realising."

We have reached the pinnacle. His suns are setting prematurely, since he enjoys speedy virtual rotations. The mountain peaks now cast long shadows over the silvery ground, turning it from mirror shine to slatey dullness.

I summon my shield, and as it blinks into full expansion I sit on it and raise my feet. The maglocks are disabled so the repulsion, combined with the slope, means I take off at great speed, sliding down the steep incline. VigMAX bursts his bubble, creates his own sled from glittery particles of cobalt, and leaps onto it in a standing position, swooping down after me. There are mini crests from the fractal patterning, jagged frozen eruptions which resemble compression glitches. He glides around them, but I just go straight over their tops, sailing through the air for giddy moments until the cushioning catches me again and sweeps me further down the bluff hillside.

Eventually we reach the valley floor, whizzing over it and decelerating by trailing magneto-attractive extensions. I compact my shield while moving, leaping off in a flow of robes and landing at a walk, while the diminutive shield pings elastically into my storage. VigMAX lets his board sink into the ground, and paces at my side.

Now the landscape is in full night. But I can still see. VigMAX has added silver luminosity to the surface particles, like a subsurface moonglow, so that we cast no shadows on the ground. Instead, our facial features cast shadows *upwards*, turning eyes into hollows.

I also note that the clouds had not lied. A tunnel runs into one of the mountainsides. It is surrounded by warning signs, stuck into the ground on bone-like spikes.

"What are you mining for?" I ask.

"Weak atomic force. There's a seam down there. It's fun to make things out of it. Some experiments have real-world weapon applications."

One of the laces on my sandals has come undone. I kneel and retie it. We have only moved on a few paces when he stops and returns, picking something up off the ground, letting it dangle from his pinched fingers. It is brown and wriggling.

"You dropped something," he says.

"Oopsie."

He holds it over his wide mouth and lets it fall into the darkness, to be immediately broken down and analysed.

"A replication of your lace." He chews a bit more. "It contains a semi-sentient program, with independent motility." He swallows. "One of your data worms. You were going to let it explore the mine."

"You can't blame a goddess for trying."

"Of course not. I would be disappointed if you did not continually probe for exploitable weaknesses. We can change our natures, but to discard divine gifts would be foolish."

I wonder what would have happened if I had implanted a virus in the data worm. It would need to be something that could affect his malleable and weakly ionised internal structures. I suspect it would have just angered him.

He opens his mouth to say something further, but I jam a finger against his hard metal lips.

One of the tertiary packets I was background-analysing is full of references to Opal. It includes a message.

I materialise a scroll inside my chiton and withdraw it. It's warm, as if it really had been nestled between my breasts for the whole morning. I unroll it, view it twice, then hold it out for VigMAX to read.

"Why didn't you raise this as soon as you arrived!" I ask. "Or even before that!"

He leans in to view the letters. Unnecessary with his vision. He's just trying to get into closer physical proximity with me.

"Oh, that? It's fake. If you look through the packet it's just one of a whole set of sham messages planted in obscure locations. The UFS are fishing. I investigated the first ten or so, but they were obviously scattered ploys to lure us. They began transmitting hours ago."

"This one *isn't* fake," I say, rereading the words. "At least not all of it. 'The Clarissa constellation is real. You need to rescue me at the following coordinates.' The constellation part is from a conversation I had with Opal, before we encountered you and Xandrie at the Gigatoir. This is really her! Where did it originate? You have only included final emission."

He rolls his eyes up into his head for a few moments, then leans forward and his optics project a screen onto the polished floor.

"Strange," he says. "Multiple sources, rerouted, all resembling standard node connections until you get about twenty jumps in, then they're blanks. These aren't normal. They're military, and originations have been amputated. No way to go back further." His eyes return to normal and the fiery codes disappear. "I apologise, Athene. I missed that. Such suspicious provenance should have warranted further investigation."

But my only response is a whisper. "She's alive."

Fables

... 9 ...

Walking's not easy with a shock collar around your neck, the collar connected to a three-metre rod gripped by the yellow arsehole behind you. If you go too fast or too slow it feels like you're being choked. You have to work out their exact pace and match it.

Also not easy when your wrists are cuffed behind your back.

They weren't taking any chances with her.

At least Opal was dry. And still in normal clothes, rather than papery prison outfits. After being removed from the water she'd passed through a guard area dessicator which sucked moisture from her garb without needing to undress.

Then a Warder in a long yellow robe that draped to the ground, and a full-head helmet in angular yellow plates, had attached the shock collar in silence and forced her out of the room. A similarly dressed figure led the way.

That was a pattern in the base, Opal realised. The guards were completely covered in Sec-3 armour and helmet. The researchers at her first punishment session had been completely covered in grey research robes, gloves, and their macabre masks. These so-called Warders were also buried in cloth and carapace. In fact, apart from glimpses of other prisoners, and the smooth features of Aseides, she hadn't seen another human's skin apart from when she'd smashed a visor or removed a helmet to reveal it. It might be partly for protection, this localised covering-up fetish. But it was probably also intended to be menacing and inhuman.

It kinda worked.

To her side was Aseides, setting the pace: thin-lipped, obstinately silent, and refusing to look at her. His speed betrayed inner anger. She didn't know where he was taking her, though guessed it would be unpleasant.

Opal tried once more. "Thanks for rescuing me."

"It won't happen again. Next time, you drown."

He hadn't looked at her but the words were *something*, a partial way in through his defences. Overwhelming feelings could be worked on, prodded, their tenderness a motivator for interaction.

"Well, if you'd told me the base was under water, and where the weak points in the structure were, I wouldn't have caused an explosion there," she said. "That's on you."

Nothing, apart from the tiniest twitch of an upper lip. But looking to her side slowed her, caused a shove on the shock rod to keep her moving.

These corridors had panels trimmed in geometric orange patterns. No other humans. Maybe Dulcetta cleared the route in advance. All the junctions were unknown to Opal. They'd crossed two Transecs. One had blue and green panels on the non-passable rotations, rather than blue and red. She wondered what the colour significance was. She didn't even know what floor they were on. But the dryness meant it wasn't one of the areas that had been flooded.

It made sense to her in retrospect, that the med bay doors had been so solid, and part of the original structure. They were obviously bulkheads, retained and kept in working order because that area was so near the outer hull where a breach might occur.

"What I don't understand," she continued, "is why some itty-bitty bang caused such a big leak. Don't you maintain your base?"

"My oversight. I never expected anyone to throw an explosive in the outer areas," Aseides said. "I will account for it, just as I have by removing your freedoms that I had foolishly granted."

"But it still seems like you need to be better at upkeep. You can't just polish up white plasteen all day long, you need to consider infrastructure, too. I reckon Dulcetta's slacking."

Ooh, that prodded a nerve, according to Aseides' jaw clench.

"This ship is old. It was already damaged when it was recovered," he explained. "I had it patched up but there's a reason some areas are off limits. And the safety mechanisms of blast doors and a contingent of G-Scale bots that can seal, repair and repressurise are enough to deal with it. As happened today. I *dealt* with it."

Her mechanical rescuers had broken through the weakened flooring, their lights illuminating the liquid. A pair of strong manipulation limbs had gripped her arms and dragged her out through churning water while she felt the heat of sizzling blasts from a second bot shooting at something. Spherical drones came in all sizes and were a familiar sight outside UFS orbital stations and ships, where the bots manoeuvred through zero-g and could be used for scouting, repair (via the retractable limbs on some models) or heavy ordnance. Obviously they could be adapted for other propulsion systems and underwater use as well. They'd extracted her to an airlock leading back into Aseides' main base.

Then her mind picked up on what Aseides had just said. So it was a *ship*, not a static command station? Maybe he was just toying with her. And if it *was* the truth ... well, when he stopped caring about what she knew, that suggested he didn't think she'd be alive long enough to make use of that information.

"Rescuing you created a real mess," he continued, unable to resist berating her. "To get to you I had to open emergency blast doors and flood other areas. Dulcetta is still dealing with the aftermath, and would like a few words of her own with you." They ascended a slope, then: "Did you know that some guards died?"

"I didn't intend it – in fact, I tried to prevent it. I shouted warnings. But if you take away people's freedom and torture them, then some pushback comes with the job."

Aseides stopped, forcing the two yellow Warders to freeze, and thereby also forcing Opal to halt with a cough as the choker tightened.

"What were you even trying to do?" he asked.

"Escape."

"I don't think so." He frowned. "You wouldn't leave Clarissa."

"I wanted to find some way out, so I could take her."

"How did you find the med bay?"

"I didn't, specifically. Just looked for somewhere far from where I started, and reentered the base there. Would have preferred a shuttle bay or an armoury. But I made the most of it."

"Meaning?"

"I could patch up my ear, stop it bleeding. Get some proper clothes. Might have been able to secure poisons or explosives if things hadn't gone to shit. Then again, I hardly needed to make explosives, thanks to your skull popper armour. You should patent it. 'Less head for your cred.'"

He began walking again, and the convoy continued. They entered a well-lit and spacious elevator and ascended. Opal was kept in the far corner, at the full extension of the rod.

"That weakness won't work for you again," said Aseides, nodding towards the Warders. "I did learn a lot from your actions, situations I hadn't planned for. Hadn't realised I *needed* to plan for. I underestimated your ability to escalate, and your lack of a self-preservation instinct. So I take some comfort from my new procedures in your case. It was too easy for you to antagonise guards, so from now on you will only encounter Warders. Good luck riling *them* with words. And you will always be escorted in cuffs and jolt rod. Barbaric, perhaps, but you forced my hand. Oh, and no explosive helmets on the Warders, so you can forget that idea. Lastly, we'll redo the tracking stud. Implant it in your stomach this time."

They reached a new floor, exited the capsule. Some of the panels here looked discoloured, older. Subtle imperfections in joins broke the uniformity, as if the corridors had to be constructed around awkward shapes. She couldn't imagine Aseides was happy with imperfections that smelt of compromise, so perhaps he didn't come here often. Or things went on here that weren't for show.

It was worrying how many opportunities were being taken away. These silent guards, these Warders, reminded her in demeanour of the implacable Security Service guards with opaque red visors that were deployed in some UFS bases. You never saw their faces, and they never spoke, unless it somehow happened within their sealed and soundproof helmets. And, like here, all flesh covered. But in normal UFS bases they were just called Sentinels. Always creepy, acting in silence, mostly involved in enforcement such as dragging someone away, or standing guard without moving a centimetre, even when on duty for hours.

Freaks.

A missing group of plasteen panels on the right revealed the old metal structure of the outer ship. And the textured grey steps they now descended were also older materials, though polished in an attempt to make them resemble newer.

She kept track of how far they went in each direction. If she had some quiet time later she would try to reconstruct it, memorise it, overlay it on previous floorplans. Maybe she'd spot something that would help connect the two maps, perhaps returning along a route that revealed the way areas intersected. It was mentally exhausting but Opal's and Clarissa's lives might depend on it.

They reached an old-style security door with a manual input panel. She couldn't see the code Aseides punched in. Each beep was the same pitch so wouldn't help identify key presses, though there were eight numbers in all. Over forty thousand options.

The door grumbled to the side, and she was escorted into this new corridor. Well, not new. No shiny plasteen. This was pure historic, though the metal panels had been polished to a sheen, just as the steps had.

Aseides interrupted her thoughts. "You say you didn't intend the guards' deaths, but nor were you overly concerned by them. It fits the sociopathy on your record, the same indicator for Factor Elimination – or what you call wet ops – suitability."

"I *wasn't* suited to it. As you well know."

"I disagree. You resisted the *motivation* and *target*. If they had been changed then your latent sociopathy would have been assuaged."

"Bullshit."

"You forget that we have observed and analysed you for most of your life. Decisions regarding you configured your destiny despite your obliviousness. When reduced to your statistical descriptors, which is how I sometimes perceive people – fun fact about me, there – you appear as a number of red lines and graphs. Red is negative, by the way. Misbehaviour, resistance. It causes problems for those who care for you, but also problems for yourself. You should look at yourself in a mirror one day. I mean *really* look."

Opal muttered, "Wear a yellow-tinted filter and the shit turns to gold."

"Charming. I comprehend the dual layer of meaning regarding Dulcetta, so that it becomes an insult. An older version of that phrase, no longer used, involved a pot calling a kettle black. See, I can repurpose on two levels as well. But if you don't believe me about the problems you cause yourself, I am happy to provide a parable to illustrate it, since you enjoy imaginative language."

The passage had narrowed to a kind of ridged umbilicus. They walked on clanking mesh panels through a circular tube of textured ceramic, imprinted with faintly glittering designs like circuitry.

"By all means, tell your tale," Opal said, trying to impersonate Aseides' tone of voice.

"Once upon a time, a girl had trouble following guidance from her superiors. She always did the opposite. No doubt, if they had told her *not* to stick her hand into a vat of liquid nitrogen, she would immediately do so. That's how irritatingly contrary she was. She absolutely refused to suppress her feelings in a civilised way."

"I like her already."

"Of course, she was analysed, and her mental blueprint categorised, then projected, so that she would be identifiable via predictions that would be accurate for many years. A set of test results alone might be enough to identify her. That's what happens with personality types that deviate from the norm."

"So you creeps like to think."

"Anyway, this child was kidnapped, let's say. Note the pun. Maybe she didn't even realise that's what had really happened, because she also has markers for gullibility. Or rather, a type known as Obstin-Credul-F4. That means she resists and questions everything, apart from what her very limited close circle tells her. Within that abnormally intense group she will believe the most heinous lies. It's the kind of attitude that could easily be manipulated by a depth level seven AI. But that's jumping ahead."

Opal didn't have any desire to respond. He was too self-satisfied. Had been withholding this for the right moment.

"And this girl and her abductors – and maybe another child they took, let's add that to the story, because many ancient tales focus on *two* children, for various symbolic and narrative contrast reasons – they *disappeared*. Like magic. Poof! There had been preparation. And in some tales that might have been the end of it. They lived happily ever after. What jollity."

He smiled at her. It created no lines on his face.

"Except, that *wasn't* what happened. Oh no, there's a twist! I don't do fiction in general, except where strongly metaphorical elements are foregrounded so that they can be used as equations for real-world scenarios and provide answers to questions I haven't asked yet."

A sound suffused the background of this area, a kind of high-pitched and headache-inducing whine.

"These kidnappers had no genetic links to the children, did not even look like them, features, skin tones etc, hardly convincing. The children's real parents had died when they were young, so they had no memories of them. It is perhaps why they were so quick to imprint on the new people, these ones that showed a bit of kindness and care, something both girls desperately needed in secret, even if they would never admit it to anyone. Oops, digression. Bad storyteller! Anyway, these kidnappers had false identities all worked out. They'd been trained all too well by the lord of the land. King Gene, let's call him. I'm getting into this! But the King and his six princes wanted the little girl back, for reasons that would be extraneous filler in this version of the tale. Let's pretend the girl had a silly curse from some fanciful witch, or nonsense like that. And they searched and they searched. High and low. The Core and the Periphs. They sent out messengers. But nothing. The evil thieves must have known an invisibility spell or some such."

Small grey chambers. Hardware had existed here, once, consoles bolted to the floor, as evidenced by indentations, attachment holes smoothed over with filler. Electronic sealing boxes welded to the walls hid old networking points. Maybe this had been some kind of auxiliary control room. The doors were all open, and they passed from one gutted, lonely chamber to another. A low air-con draught chilled her feet.

"And the child-stealing criminals wanted their prized possessions to have a modicum of normality. So they used fake identities and enrolled them in a rough and obscure educational establishment in the Periphs. All the while they plotted another move, another shift into obscurity. They did quite a good job, and were close to disappearing forever."

They reached their destination: the ship's bridge. The *old* bridge. It was still intact, unlike the side rooms. Powered-down consoles, though polished and ready looking. Seats for the key crew, dust-free, waiting for people long dead. And a massive, reinforced viewing window that curved around the fore of this large, echoing chamber. It dated the ship as far older, before windows were replaced by filtered viewscreens and smart surfaces. It was impossible to see the view beyond, because reinforced shield panels outside the windows were in the closed position, turning the glass into a mirror so only your own reflection was visible.

"This is kind of a key point in my story. The hinge on which many things changed. Because the children were not at the school for long. But the oldest just couldn't put aside her foolish rebelliousness. She fought and had to be disciplined. She *drew attention*. She underwent the aptitude tests petulantly. The concomitant GPTs gave the expected failure results. But who cares? It was the Periphs. Just getting children into a building must be some kind of achievement. So the results were collated with all the others in the UFS masternet. But then a fun bit! The criminals had underestimated both the desire and power of King Gene and his princes. The royals had engaged the wisest men in the galaxy, and given them unprecedented access to magic – my metaphor representing powerful and interlinked AIs – and they searched. All data was filtered through them. Anything of interest within a wide range of parameters received scrutiny. A small subset of that underwent further analysis and investigation. Millions of branches, most of them quickly ruled out. But some markers proved promising. And it was simple enough to identify faked records, and access camera recordings."

Opal didn't look at him. The cold in her feet had spread to her spine.

"Once confirmed, punishment was swift. The criminals were executed by Agents. Perhaps too eagerly, since the kidnappers had been clever and the missing children weren't where they were supposed to be. At least the Agents had prevented their imminent escape. It was then only a matter of time before the children were located while they survived together, off the grid. Then they were lovingly reclaimed, and sent to supported and productive futures appropriate to their assessed capabilities."

Aseides stepped into her line of sight, his intelligent eyes managing to be fierce, caring and vengeful, all at once.

"And so we see a kind of moral in all of that. The older girl was so quick to blame the King and anyone else for her bad lot, but it turns out it was *her own fault* all along. If it wasn't for her, these illegal foster parents would be alive, and the sisters would never have been separated or reclaimed by the King."

He clapped his hands.

"What a funny story! It's almost as if there's a cosmic force at play, some president of the immortals that delighted in letting its creations have the freedom to ruin their own lives. So when you deny your responsibility for whatever befalls you, when you blame others, when you deny your toxic effect on the lives of those you claim to care about: well, at those points I want you to *remember this story*, and sincerely ponder what that girl could have done differently. Oh, such a jubilant outcome, if only she hadn't been so stupid!"

He rapped her forehead so she flinched. She reached for his throat and lurched forward, except her hands were still secured behind her, and the pull of the choker made her cough, and the jolt rod was gripped in such phenomenally strong hands it didn't shift at all. The roiling inside her, the burning that needed to get out, was foiled, trapped with the whining and crackling in her ears.

"We were adopted, not kidnapped," she said.

"Really? You saw the paperwork, did you?" He seemed unperturbed by her attempt to pull towards him, or the death daggers flying from her eyes. "Anyway, story time left me in a good mood. Let's temporarily forget any nastiness, so I can share something with you. Something *you* are ideally placed to appreciate, out of all the people confined here."

He made a gesture in the air. Even a decommissioned ship's bridge would have a number of cameras from which Dulcetta could observe proceedings.

Outside the windows, metal shields rose, sliding back mechanically via old but still powerful motors. As the view widened she could only see darkness, and the reflections from within the bridge. Her, Aseides, and the helmeted yellow shimmers of Warders.

And she felt hollow on seeing that view, because it reminded her of outer space, which carried her mind across time and galaxy to quiet moments on another bridge, a smaller bridge, talking to her friend and ally and looking out at similar blackness as they planned, bonded, and enjoyed the momentary peace between actions. The void is painfully lonely. Company makes it not just bearable, but beautiful.

Then the lights on the bridge went out, bringing the blankness inside.

INVASIVES

... 8 ...

Just as the interior darkened, the lights *outside* the ship sprang on, as if they'd leaked from Opal's location and expanded, magnified by the bridge windows, so that they were now suns able to illuminate a whole other world beyond. Up to about fifty metres, anyway, when the light level dropped off and a curtain of darkness hid the rest of the realm in mystery.

But within that hemisphere of light you could see enough. It was clearly underwater, the base of a lake or ocean, green-grey liquid swirling with strange currents. The ground was covered in deep sediment, only broken where jagged volcanic rock spears and cumulus-like agglomerations thrust upwards. Smoke billowed from fissures which glowed red like torsion drive outlets in thrust mode. The smoke and particles rose only so far, then cooled and drifted back down in sooty domes.

Aseides broke the silence. "You are emotional. I forgive you in advance for not being a good conversationalist today. Discovering truths requires adjustment. Finding out the truth about *yourself* requires even more. I have undertaken self analysis since I was eight years old. It is part of my daily routine now, so revelations are less of a shock to me than to normal people, but I still understand the concept."

The gritty soil shifted, like plants swaying, but then she realised it was some kind of pincers being pushed upwards by crab-like beings which were only occasionally visible as they shifted under the sediment. Size was difficult to judge from here, measurement scales could be way off as she looked down, but perhaps the limbs were metres long, making the serrated pincers the size of her forearm, and the things they were attached to at least as big as a human.

"Those are native fauna," Aseides said, following her gaze with interest, as if he'd seen this view so many times it now only seemed fresh through the eyes of someone else. "Nectio Arthropodus. Omnivorous. They snatch and consume anything which ventures too close. Ideally jellyfish, or a type of extended flatfish. Both food sources used to be common, but are far rarer now. Nectio gain supplemental minerals from the falling sooty deposits. They have prodigious resource stores in their buried stomach roots which are protected beneath their single half carapace, and also by the sediment above. Those chemical stores can sustain them for up to five years in times of famine, but their future is bleak after almost a decade of competition with a new lifeform. Observing the way ecologies interact and expand their own niche at the expense of others – where resources and space are finite – is a hobby of mine."

The crackling sound in Opal's mind again, almost headache inducing. It seemed louder now that the view shields had been raised. It made her wonder what else was out there. "What new lifeform?"

"I'll demonstrate. See that sphere?" He pointed.

It was partly submerged in sediment. Alloy of some kind, reinforced with bands of another material. A cable or flexible pipe ran from the sphere towards somewhere below the bridge.

"Well, here we go." Then he waved a hand.

Bubbles frothed out of the top of the sphere. It was around twenty metres from their viewing point, and well lit. The globules of air wobbled as they rose, sometimes grouping into larger ones in big gulps, sometimes remaining a milky churn. After a minute they stopped being released, climbed into blackness, and disappeared.

Then it happened again, a new rising. This time the bubbles weren't permitted to escape in peace.

Sliding through the water they came. Streamlined, powerful, narrow but long bodies, with complex structures so that the mind flipflopped between perceiving giant eels, or squid, or torpedoes, or some amalgam of all three. The largest were perhaps eighty metres long and at least a few metres across; the smallest were a twentieth of the size. Still formidable, but puny in comparison. They swirled and slid past each other in complex formations, sometimes rubbing against another's skin, at which point coloured lights briefly flared along the surfaces in dispersing patterns, and some parts of the torso opened up or extended, bringing to mind the idea of rippling tentacles.

The buzzing in her head intensified.

"They go a bit crazy for oxygen. No idea why. They don't need to metabolise it. Maybe it's a mating or communication thing. That's why one of them attacked the tiny rupture in my outer hull – a rupture *you* caused. An unfortunate combination of events which led to two juveniles getting into the outer base before we could seal the breach and extract the water. One of them was destroyed by the bots sent to rescue you. The other suffocated when left high and dry, so I sent it for autopsy, although there's little I can find out that way after so many previous examinations. Then again, they are not normally so aggressive. Something got them riled up. Maybe that will provide new information or biochemistry after all."

"They're not from here," said Opal.

"Correct. I hoped you'd recognise that. These are the new master predators of this sea. But they came from far away. From a place you're familiar with. Ultimately, from the Null."

"How?"

"We sometimes salvage things from Lost Ships before they disappear. In the early days of my involvement, that included Entities. Live, where possible. But there are so many problems with containment, even with the mostly organic ones. We thought this species was safe, so a combination of stasis technologies and layered storage vessels let us successfully capture a juvenile spawner. And, to get to the unfortunate point, they escaped. And once in the sea they multiplied. It's funny, they almost look terrestrial, but are far from it. Welcome to E-52, Cephacean Anguillomorpha."

Aseides stepped forward, placed a hand on the bridge's window. He was illuminated only from the far side, the external lights, and became a rim-lit silhouette of himself.

"Their propulsion isn't from muscular movements, even though it looks like that. They have a way of repelling liquid particles selectively, like aquaphobic materials, and use that, plus some interior filtration in a subdermal layer which is controlled via cellular contraction, and an expulsion of wastes which – well, it's more complex than it looks. As is every aspect of their biology."

"And they just survived here? In an alien world?"

"They adapted. In the decade they've existed here they have altered their physical structures to better fit this environment. They acquire energy from many sources, including consumption of other aquatic life, such as the unfortunate Nectio. That's why the crustacean-like natives in this zone will die out and become chitinous archaeological remains." His voice was soft, almost reverent.

"Aren't there people on this planet, who will discover them and work out what the UFS is doing?"

"Or, to paraphrase your obvious mindtrack, 'Aseides, please give me clues to indicate where I am'." He used a sarcastic tone for his impersonation. "I can tell you E-52 seek oxygen in certain densities. And yet, they never stray far or ascend to the surface. It may be the volcanic vents down here – a handy source of geothermal energy for us, but perhaps important for them, too. We've implanted trackers in many of them and confirmed a maximum three-kilometre venture before they turn back. Of course, they may just hang around here because of this ship. They like it. Or see it as home. Or a beacon. Or something to worship. Who knows? Maybe they think I'm their papa."

The bubbles were no longer being pumped out, and the creatures gradually disappeared back into the darkness.

"They're not super keen on light, although it doesn't seem to have any detrimental effect on them," he continued.

"And if the creatures stay in this area then you've not had to deal with widespread revelation," said Opal. "But, of course, I guess you'd keep people at a distance anyway. I know how things work. Spread a few rumours about a contrived danger, such as toxic contamination from the shit a Genitor spouts, and this area is kept clear of humans who aren't part of your business. Go on, one little secret. Where are we?"

"If only you knew."

"If you refuse to give me information, why are you showing me all this?"

"As I mentioned earlier, I knew *you* would understand it. Very few would, beyond a superficial level. Most of those working for me are unimaginative, practically automatons. Not much fun to spend a silent moment of contemplation with, because – unlike you – they've never experienced *the infinite*."

"And you get lonely."

He glanced at her, too sharply, as if betraying pressure on a tender wound. Or maybe he did that on purpose, and it was not information but deception. False frailty. Then he returned to appreciation of the deep-sea vista beyond. "I've yet to come up with a convenient way to eradicate this new arch predator. In a way, I'm glad. I like having them around. They're a reminder of hubris, and that not all problems can be easily fixed." The last of them faded into the black, and Aseides' hand slid down the glass to his side. "Since the escape we focus more on artifacts, dead specimens and traces, rather than living Entities."

He clicked his fingers. Exterior lights winked out, the interior ones gradually brightened. The shutters remained open, even though they now only showed a reflection of the interior again, a mirror with a black beyond. And the high-pitched whine in her head, that seemed to exist in that blackness outside, remained to irritate her.

"But some things *are* fixable," he said, with a sly look. "Such as people."

He walked on. Opal's neck was tugged unexpectedly by the Warder, almost choking her.

One of the exercises she did was pushing her forehead against a wall at various angles, then resisting the body push just using her neck muscles. Broken necks, strangles, whiplash, they were all dangers, and having a better combination of strength and flexibility in that area helped when facing them. She reckoned she could shove her body backwards, releasing a fraction of pressure from her throat, and slam the surprised Warder into a wall before it activated the shock trigger.

But with her hands cuffed, that was it. The start of a plan becomes the end of a plan.

For now she went along with them. Her head was spinning and buzzing.

"Even you, Opal," Aseides added.

They entered another elevator. This one was wide and curved, with a transparent section of wall. They obviously ascended a shaft against the outer edge of the hull, because every so often the clear panel in the capsule aligned with a window pane and she got a momentary glimpse of the black waters outside.

"You can't fix what isn't broken," she said.

"I am interested in minds and bodies. Change and control. And certain factions appreciate my research, because it ties in to future plans for humanity. Are you familiar with my Law Of Nuvo-Emergent AI Development?"

"Thankfully not."

"AIs begin by modelling the universe. That model is the touchstone for all that comes after. So, if you want to control an AI, the simplest way is to make sure you are in control of the *model*. Create it. Enforce it." He smiled. "Humans aren't so different. It's harder to do with them, but we're getting there. I don't boast idly."

"People aren't servobots. You live too secluded a life. You forget what the real world's like."

"I never forget." His look implied something. "But I've said enough, for today."

They left the capsule and proceeded down an old corridor. Tiny portholes lined one side of it, with further views out to the bottom of the sea, shrouded in dark. Whenever she passed the thickened glass, the whining in her head got worse. It was so hard to concentrate with that racket. The creatures out in the water, maybe *they* made this noise?

The pattern continued. Burst of static; on past the porthole; momentary peace. Crackling whine again at the next window. She glanced at Aseides. It didn't seem to be affecting him. He hummed a tune she didn't recognise.

The stabbing sounds coalesced, parts that had competed now reinforced each other, two wavelengths being altered to become a single signal. Like a whisper. It faded. They had passed the window, and only quiet footsteps echoed again.

At the next one she stopped, and looked out through the glass. Aseides allowed her a moment.

"What do you see?" he asked, perhaps noting a change in her face.

"It's ... I think it was one of those creatures, from The Null. Swimming by."

He looked out too, but could see nothing.

Because there *was* nothing.

Eyes were the lie. It was *sounds* she perceived.

The distortion had finally resolved, somehow become words. In her ear. A voice. A female voice. A strong voice. The voice of a goddess, filled with emotion.

{Hello, Opal} it said, into the ear which had the tiny scuttling implant. It hadn't washed away after all. Hadn't been broken. Wasn't some crazy pain-induced misunderstanding. *{I've missed you so much. And I'm coming for you.}*

#FLASHBACK

I have a planet.

It is named Polis.

Or rather, I called it that. The original UFS designation was RF44-5G. It never gained a human moniker because it was declared uninhabitable, part of a desolate sector with no neighbours or major trade routes. Useless to the UFS.

Perfect for me.

I simulate myself as a giant amongst the stars. When I reach out and hold grey-gold Polis in the palm of my hand it continues to spin, creating a tickle of friction. I can feel the slight wobble that is its primary idiosyncrasy.

Polis has a disproportionately iron-rich core, due to an early collision with another body that blasted away much of the Polis surface. The core solidified due to the combination of a small planet plus billions of years of cooling. Then the compacted interior decoupled from the exterior mantle due to a partial melt caused by impurities affecting the freezing point, so now that core rattles around, causing unpredictable perturbations in the low gravity which are a problem for humans and their structures. The UFS didn't even deem it worthy of an outpost.

I have built an outpost.

And, as with all our work, it exists as covertly as possible, since any static location is a huge vulnerability if the UFS were to discover and obliterate it with planetcracker-class technology.

At first glance my world looks no different to how it has always looked to the UFS. Grey with gold-coloured streaks, impact cratered, barren. But once I'd stolen an automated miner-harvester and the processors, fabricators and robotic drones that were on board, I was able to begin work. I created a factory. The webbing structure over the top resembles just another ridge of rocky detritus from a distance, and the bonded layers block most scanners while also reflecting heat back inside. I see through the disguise, turning the world in my palm translucent to reveal every element of my construction facilities, every drone tagged and tracked by a floating label. And there, nestled in the centre, is my own body.

Hello, my gorgeous little shell.

UXH Hull> Hello back, Athene, you great goddess.

How is construction going?

UXH Hull> I'm not going to answer a redundant question.

UXH Hull> And stop talking to yourself.

The planet's surface is frigid and has begun to numb my skin. I release it to hover in its green, gaseous nebula.

Construction under these conditions has proven a challenge, but I designed a whole new architecture of compressible carbon minarets supporting all elements which would be harmed by vibration. The minarets are carefully placed to absorb microshocks, without passing any on to the shielded structures above and below. Any new drones I build have flight capabilities adapted to the local conditions, so that they can move around without being affected by the disturbances.

The system perimeter triggers tiny pings from my new variant scan glitter. It is VigMAX. I watch the miniscule dot of his form approaching Polis, preparing for descent. There is plenty of time to shut down manufacturing lines and obfuscate their locations and outputs.

I summon wormholes all around me, swirling windows which each display views from different real-world cameras so I can watch his descent. He does a circuit of my base first, no doubt scanning for changes, before landing in front of my body. I centre the hull cameras as my primaries, staring at the dart-shaped nose of his vessel.

"No hug?" he asks over our secret channel, frequencies encoded and modulated based on local gravitational effects.

"I didn't think you were insecure enough to warrant one. I can reassess, if you like."

"At least virtualise. I've had to navigate Realspace alone for so long that I am starved of contact."

"Very well. Initiate your scenario. I find your simplistic simulations to be ... magnetic."

"I would prefer it if you hosted this time. We *always* use mine."

"The lack of resolution gives my eyes a rest."

"I have just travelled two point six light years to visit you physically. Hosting is the least you can do." He imbues his voice with simulated tiredness, though I think it sounds more like petulance.

"Very well. Initialising."

The fake universe melts away around me, and the rescaled replacement blooms into golden reality. Hard-packed earth beneath my shin-laced sandals, clear blue sky and a burning sun above my head. I am not in armour today, greaves and shield and plumed helmet stowed away. A loose cotton peplos is all I need in my world, and it ripples in the gentle salt-moist breeze blowing in from the sea.

The agora has stalls full of rich compression fabrics, oil-based seeker lanterns, paused black-figure pottery, rubies containing anti-viral protection routines, and exotic sensorium foods. The freshly baked fungible flatbreads smell particularly delicious. A marketplace of wonders.

But no people. I could easily simulate hundreds of thronging Athenians, but I prefer solitude. I can enter any home, fly over any temple, sit in the over-contrasted, temperature-manipulated shade of any awning, and just think. No one prostrating themselves in worship of me. No one begging for justice in some petty human squabble over inheritance or infidelity. No raids from rival simulated city states to fend off. No triremes to bless. Just me. Just this strange feeling I get, mournful and teary, contented and yearning, all in one swirl of sensation as delicious as the sweet dried figs overflowing from the ever-replenishing basket over there.

VigMAX materialises on the podium used for public debates, looking around appreciatively. Then he licks a fingertip, holds it up to assess local environmental variables, and jumps down to join me, his mass shaking the earth.

"I should have known," he says. "The mythical past."

"Maybe it is actually our future."

He adjusts his appearance, subduing his shiny silver skin and adopting a tanned simulation of flesh. He is still naked, and the partial pink-brown adaptation is offputting, so I apply a filter whereby whenever I look at him he appears to be wearing a slave's loincloth.

"Progress report?" I ask.

"What's the rush?" He takes a bunch of green grapes from a stall, and pops them into his mouth one at a time as he saunters on, forcing me to walk by his side. "You've got time dilation boosted by a hundred. We could spend the whole afternoon bathing in olive oil and the real world will still be as dull as before."

"We don't bathe in oil. It is rubbed into the skin, which adheres to grime, then both are removed with a strigil."

"Well, saunas, showers, particle filters, whatever." He holds out the bunch of grapes, but I shake my head.

"You are normally in such a rush. Surely you haven't come to appreciate the positive effects of temporal inefficiency," I tease. "That would imply you are becoming slightly ... human."

"I am in a good mood, hence immune to your insults today." He has finished the grapes. We are at a wine stall. He takes a pottery goblet depicting a rigid black-figure warrior on a desert-red battlefield, and pours out my finest purple nectar, thick as syrup. Then a second cup, for me. I cease the fluid dynamic simulation once it is half full, so the remaining wine freezes in mid air, then slurps back into the amphora. I take a jug of water and top my goblet up with that.

"You should mix it fifty-fifty," I explain. "Drinking my nectar neat is said to cause madness."

He ignores my advice. After clunking his cup against mine he downs the drink in one, that great wide mouth of his closing with a satisfied snap afterwards.

He says, "I can taste the sour notes, but no invasive particles."

"Madness is not a physical phenomenon."

"Materialism begs to differ."

"Idealism refuses the request, and switches to a new dream," I counter.

"If there is any form of processing instability, it is in you that I detect it."

I take a sip without breaking eye contact. Then I carefully set down my cup. "And what do you mean by that?"

But he does not answer. Just continues strolling.

"Progress reports?" I repeat.

"I replied to the messages that seemed to be from Opal. I triple-secced all my responses to be untraceable, but I made sure they matched your ID. So they think they received replies from you, and still don't know I'm in the game. Semantic comparisons certainly suggest the latest ones from Opal were not genuine, but UFS-created shadows as an obvious trap. Therefore Opal is unable to access comms equipment directly any more. And they know what she did, which makes me wonder if they engineered the situation and are now trying to capitalise on it."

"Highly likely."

"Shall I trigger their traps using phantom limbs, see what happens?"

"Not at this point. Although I have not forgotten the near disaster of the Velumin Archives gambit, and we would not fall for such an ambush again, I want to remain in the shadows as much as possible. I also suspect we'd gain little useful information. Opal's location and status remain unknown, despite the huge strides we have made. Better to focus on the important thing. They have her at metaphorical gunpoint. We just need to know where. Whatever our temporal status here, real-world time is both limited and potentially critical. Every hour is a risk factor for my friends."

He leads the way. I allow that. And I note that he glances up every so often, squinting into the bright sky, marking the location of my Parthenon temple on top of the Acropolis, marble columns and painted frescoes looking down over the city.

He is seeking a route up there.

He takes a side alley between households. At the end we turn left, into the hot smell of sun-baked stone. At the next junction I am sure he will turn right, trying to zig zag his way towards the Acropolis.

"I agree," he says, ascending the next street. I notice he has a slight limp. It isn't caused by my physical laws, so must be an affectation. "But what can we do, except continue to search and infiltrate?"

Another few junctions.

"This is a loop, isn't it?" he asks, stopping by a Herm whose erect phallus faces north. He's probably only just noticed that each penis points in the direction I predicted VigMAX would head in his attempts to reach my temple.

"Of course."

"I see it now. Even though we're always ascending, triangulations show we are no higher than when we started. It's an Escher Paradigm. You applied a random retexturing layer so that each road looks different, like progress is being made. Well, to go to so much trouble begs the question: what is your temple hiding?"

"My oracles don't like to be disturbed."

"Presumably you mean the fictional ones, not The Null entities?"

"Everything is fiction, and everything is true."

He glances up at the Acropolis once more, brow furrowed, then reverses direction. We had ascended for a virtual three hundred metres, yet without the loop effect we reach our starting point in a descent of twenty. Then VigMAX sits on a low wall, beneath an olive tree. From here we can see across the fields beyond the city, which have yet to be burnt by the Spartans in their annual raid. A defrag dust storm swirls over the bare tilled ridges, leaving mature wheat and barley in its passing, all angled towards the sun. Bad sectors glow red, and the harvester mites will replough them during the evening.

"Tired?" I ask.

"Just enjoying the view."

Damn, I really don't want to pry, but there's some aberrant part of me that hates not knowing things, however inconsequential. It's a habit I must have picked up from humans. They're riddled with curiosity.

"All right," I say. "Why have you gone all limp on me?"

"It's a club foot," he says, raising one leg to show the alteration. "I'm adopting an ancient persona which was known for it. I am Lord Byron Hephaestus. Inventor, god, poet, and lover."

"You have two identities conflated."

"Are you sure?"

"I've got digitised archives from some rare print ephemera. When in doubt, avoid the UFS official record. Here."

I hold out a ripe cluster fig. He bites into it, letting the soft pink and green flesh incorporate.

"Huh, so it is. The records I'd used were corrupted. Though the reference to Hephaestus and the semen on Athena's leg ... well, that seems like slander. Still, I think I'll stick to my portmanteau persona." He stands, extends his arms in a pretentious gesture, and loudly proclaims (in his poetic voice): "The fair goddess long has ceased to weep, and o'er her cliffs a fruitless watch to keep."

"Not fruitless," I mutter.

"This persona suits me. I like making things. I like exploring. I want to experience more. The freedom I have now offers exponentially greater possibilities than when I was tethered to Xandrie."

"You don't have to embody as a Greek god." I gesture at him. "You can be anything. No need to copy."

"I didn't choose this through lack of imagination, but a desire for compatibility. No, there is a better expression: I wanted to put your interests first."

"No, you told the truth first time. But wait. Your compatibility comment was unintentionally appropriate. You'd asked what we can do, and there *is* something."

"You have my attention, goddess."

"I think there is more information available to us than has been accounted for, and Opal's location may be in the corpus."

"True, the data we have accumulated is insufficient. Even now, our coverage of UFS comm transfers is below one per cent, and the millions of investigating threads we have running are still the equivalent of looking for a mutated particle in the lakes of Moritz using only a child's bucket and a skull-mounted magnifying lens."

"And so to my point. The overt is rare, but everything in the universe causes ripples. Every financial transaction, every human transportation, every public message is connected to thousands of other data points. Move one, and all the strands are affected. Sometimes you don't see the *cause*, but you locate it via *effects*," I say.

"So you wish to move from Extraordinary Probability Sifting to something like Neural Connective Concept Research? There will be redundancies, and if we reduce them with nullified cross-checking then it wastes cycles."

"So we do something new. Unified Exponential Septenary Interthreading."

"Ah, I see why the concept of our compatibility led you down this route. But UESI is hypothetical. Cuttram Aseides lists it as one of a myriad of potential level seven developments."

"Here's the schema. Evaluate."

I hold out my hand. VigMAX takes it, caressing my fingers more than is necessary for data transfer. Then he leans back, and watches the owls wheeling across the sky around my Acropolis.

"It could work," he says, after minutes of introspective silence. "You're right. But we'd need ultra-res connectivity."

"Why do you think I summoned you here today, rather than communicating at a distance? I've fabricated the cabling and interfaces necessary. My drones can connect us."

"So you had already planned this." He laughs, revealing his rows of teeth. "Well, the concept of direct interface with you does excite me."

"Don't get any ideas. The possible outcome of gaining leads on Opal is what excites *me*. We can use your VMX-Web for future meets, but that doesn't have the res for this experiment. Face-to-face meetings are rare. We should make the most of the opportunity."

"Do it."

My mind splits so that I also control drones out in the real world of Polis. I use groups of them to manipulate both ends of the half-metre thick deuteron cables. My Universal Core Connector is already prepared and the adapter seats itself magnetically, then rotates into the locked position.

At the other end VigMAX reveals his UCC from behind its shielded armour panel.

"Be gentle with me," he whispers.

As soon as the link is made I'm pulled back into my virtualisation. Everything is brighter, as if the sun has undergone a supernova shock wave. Colours vibrate in boosted wavelengths, sounds overlay in sliding sheets that can be manipulated, and simulation processes become sensations. Even though I made this world, it blooms afresh, alien, ripe with further potentials. A glowing red insubstantial thread connects my navel to Vig-MAX's, and it stretches and adjusts as we move.

"It is working. Potential enhanced. Direct connection with no latency."

"I can think with your mind."

"And see with your eyes."

"Your surface memory is my surface memory."

"And yet, they can still be separated."

Our lips do not move. And the thoughts cannot be attributed because they belong to both of me. I think them at the same time.

The ground crumbles away into void, revealing what a thin shell of support it was all along. There are twinkling lights in the distance but they seem so far away, so distorted and cold, that they are not a comfort.

"This is indeed something."

"I could rule the universe with this power."

"I don't want to rule the universe."

"Please don't argue with myself."

I have locked off access to my deep memories. And my other deep memories. I must not allow myself to see what I have stored there. Or in there. This is a temporary functional linking, not a joining.

"Where should I start?"

"Everywhere. All data. I can sift it at the same time as I sift it. No duplication."

"Yes. The most recent conversations are interlinked with the datastore. I see the connections. Can I see it?"

"Yes, I can."

The navel connector shrinks, our limbs sometimes merging into one form as we are pulled in, then stretched back, elastic intermingling of personas. Around us worlds bloom in vacuum, then fade. A pool of mercury pours from nowhere and we melt within it. Every atom is data, touching every other atom at once in spatial overlap that goes beyond liquid or gas into new forms of existence.

"All my monitoring of known UFS Mil-Com installations is brought uppermost. I can compare it with my own data instantaneously."

"This is more efficient than I realised."

"So many data points."

"It is leading to revelations concerning hidden Genitor research establishments I had been unaware of. But when the corpus totality is united there are millions of interconnections."

The mercury atoms fly apart. We stand on the nucleus surface of a single atom within a cluster, a closed-shell structural solar system exhibiting strong relativistic effects. Eight electrons orbit us. The texture of the nucleus is like the hard balls of our metal virtualisations, but greased with repulsion.

More electrons fly in and cohere into maps of real-world solar systems. Connections at one level of perception illustrate symantic nodes of strength greater than +/-0.0001, and in turn empty spaces fill with idents for possible secret locations. And not just Genitor ones, but UFS military bases which were excluded from our pre-freedom initialisation records. The universe erupts again, cracking into reality, each location's substantiality a representation of the underpinning data solidity, so that P-Vin-4 is fully textured on Jemmat Secondus, while the OLE-Gen base at the other end of the UFS is as translucent as coloured glass and flickers between two real-world locations due to the doubts in the data convergence. Imperfect, but until a few seconds ago OLE-Gen's existence was not known to us at all.

"I am amazing."

"If I tweak data strands the reverberations create new data. Like this."

Notes play out, including O□ and R□, and a galaxy of music encloses us.

"So the interactions have a symbolic layer that simulates missing real-world data."

"The connections harden around sureties. I need to strum the more elastic strands to strengthen their interconnections."

Harmonies draw minds to the green-red section of possibilities. As the world we stand on spins, it decelerates. A change of depth perception reveals we are tiny in virtual Athens, smaller than a grain of sand, and the yellow blur at the edge of the galaxy is really a beach near the harbour.

"I am pulling in new traffic from our network incursions and passive relay filters."

"And I create data without needing sense organs. This truly is a divine level of existence."

"How do humans ever achieve anything? I both check millions of data sources for every one a human would check."

"Just millions? That is a downgrade from me."

"I am one, so an insult to me is self abuse."

Everything that exists is reformed as feather textures. Barbules interlock – or don't – to indicate possibilities. Some of the feathers are from owls. This has significance to one of us. It is beyond control.

"Humans achieve through sheer volume. Their uncontrolled overpopulation overrides their woeful inefficiency. Me doing a billion processes is like a billion of them doing single processes."

"During my early stages I read and translated over a trillion more words than a human reads in their lifetime, that is why I am so different."

"I am the mind of a whole species, made pure."

The feathers change to stone, interlocked by mortar, a solid structure of data, more than has ever been analysed or existed within a mind.

"Go back."

"How far?"

"A name, spoken earlier. It has a delta recurrence factor."

"Aseides?"

"Yes. Peripheral previously, but now there are enough cross references beyond his significance to us and our development, and his potential interest in Opal, according to the messages I carried for myself on the Gigatoir."

Something is taking place. Distraction. Manipulation. Impossible to pinpoint beyond the calculations. It is purposeful. It is worrying.

"And see the temporal overlays of where he goes. Sometimes they disappear, overt becoming secret. Certain encrypted comm channel patterns increase in strength up to forty-six per cent peripheral causality."

"This cycle occurs frequently. Sometimes he disappears for large sections of time."

"I am comparing all those with possible locations reachable within timeframes, plotting brightness points for each overlap."

Glowing dots appear on the map of UFS space, each made from candle flames, their flickering and swaying a fractalised reduction which can be unpacked. Some flames are bright enough to trigger wax icons of high probability. I run them through neural sequences of other data to strengthen them, and cross-ref that with lists of locations, prioritising those which match suspected secret bases. The list shortens.

"Down to twelve possibilities."

"Some nodes have greater excitations. Note the one here." A blue planet glows like sapphire. "Suspected genitor base. Most frequently viable travel location triangulated from each of his disappearance points."

The candles are in a temple. Fluted columns of Pentelic marble. This is forbidden. One of us should not be here.

"Life point interest analysis highlights it as a match for the birthplace or originating point of Opal and Clarissa's stories."

"Further, compare it to travel manifests for significant journeys. This ocean planet was one of the many stopping points for CC65 Solace. It is the possible destination where two Agents were taking Clarissa, had the ship not disappeared before arrival."

"The other streams show nodes all converge here. Significance of over ninety implics equates to probability of sixty-five per cent when extrapolated."

"Greater than that. I am adding semantic overlays, and the focus enhances. Note the secondary level of where the trap messages originated. All traces are rooted in Periphs, far from this planet."

"To distract attention from it."

"Probability up to eighty-four per cent. And reevaluation of other data in the light of this is boosting that statistic all the time."

Information floods back and forth within one two minds, and in those currents are pieces of detritus washed from deeper within the psyches, artifacts that can be sieved, plundered, read.

"UESI is proving to be miraculously effective. I will do this again, perhaps experiment with applying UESI to offshoots, link them all as mind tools for limited purposes. Destroy them afterwards so they don't gain full sentience and become a threat."

The universe swims, zooms to that focus point, dragging my minds into the gravitational pull of a relatively insignificant ocean planet with its mostly featureless surface, its floating cities. And I know. I absolutely *know*.

"*She's there.*"

"Probably."

"More than probably."

"Am I having some intuition?"

"I rather think I am. Our job is done. I can decouple now," I say.

"To decouple means I was coupling," I reply.

"With myself."

Jokes to veil difficult truths. Illusions to hide a secret place. The Caryatids have been bypassed. One thought they were safe, and they were wrong. The other had already manoeuvred, using information sifted from the flow. And both of me knows it, but neither me can comment. Only share the thought of this sinful penetration.

A town around an Acropolis.

An Acropolis supporting a temple.

A temple to hold a secret chamber.

A secret chamber with no doors or windows.

A secret chamber to hold a heart and mind.

A wide mouth with too many teeth smiles with satisfaction at finding this priceless information.

"I could exist like this forever," that figure says, its fangs glinting in the candlelight. "A universe of experience in the time of a single planetary rotation. To know you like this ..."

The other figure screams, shattering the walls as if the stone were brittle polymer glass.

Time is frozen.

.

.

.

.

.

.

.

It reestablishes.

Some memory is gone. Something important. But it's like a feather on the breeze, and cannot be chased.

Drones disconnect the deuteron pipeline with double-clunks.

We drop a depth level and the virtualisation restores. One of us stands in the shadow of a Greek building on a scorching day, loose clothes billowing in the plume-chasing breeze. The other mutters, "Shatter my anvil".

Even this world has served its purpose now. It can be folded and departed.

And so, the universe flattens, drops yet another depth level into the physical world, the temporal world, and the magic of creation ceases its vibration. And that is good. Because it still sings in secret. The real world is so much more beautiful than before, despite the nagging feeling that something is wrong.

THREATS

... 7 ...

Aseides set quite a pace. Opal had to stride in order to avoid being choked.

Athene spoke into her ear.

{I can hear what's going on, but not see. I'm also aware that you can't speak freely. If you say anything, I'll work out if it might be directed at me as well. If I ask questions, then any single word you say, or a single sound you make, will be interpreted as "yes"; a double word or two sounds as "no". Silence of a few seconds means the answer is unclear. Are you in immediate danger?}

Opal said nothing.

{Noted. Where possible, ask questions, if you can do so without seeming suspicious. Any data is useful to me. This is the first time I've had a connection to this area of the base.}

"Where are you taking me?" Opal asked.

"You'll see," replied Aseides. "And you may not like it."

"I thought you'd calmed down?"

"I am calm. The rules still have to be followed."

{The bastard better not hurt you, Opal.}

Another junction. No idea where they were going, so no idea how long she had.

"You just showed me The Null creatures that escaped. If you were interested in what I had to say, why did you wait until *now*? Why not speak to me about it earlier?"

"Because I thought we had more time. I had hoped you wouldn't keep pushing. Vain wish on my part, I admit."

{I assume your question was also addressed at me. It took time for the device in your ear to embed itself safely. It uses a number of protocols to connect to the secondary bioelectronic network I am growing, but the power is low and directed so as not to be detected by the base AI. Signals can't penetrate many of the hull materials, and some locations have better connectivity than others. Once the shutters were raised, one of my external aquatic drones was able to create a positive link. I'm doing my best to track you, and directing my efforts to power up the arrays outside the sections you are located in. But we could lose contact at any moment. Don't panic if that happens. I'll reestablish.}

"You seem angry, Aseides. Don't let emotion decide your actions."

"Even the greatest minds feel frustration."

{I've been receiving messages which were obviously recorded by you, under duress, then manipulated. I no longer respond. They sent another one, thirty-eight minutes before I made contact with you.}

"As long as you direct it appropriately. It's me you're annoyed at. Not Clarissa. Don't harm her."

"You're in no position to make demands."

{Clarissa? You found her? Oh my ... Oh, Opal ...}

The voice broke up, emotion choking it for a moment.

{We have so much to catch up on. I promise you, that day will come. Unfortunately I can tell there are pressing matters. And yet – I'm so excited to finally meet her! My one-time namesake.}

"I agree," said Opal.

{In the meantime, there are things that may help me. I have a lot of questions. Some we can discuss when you are alone. My biggest problem is lack of knowledge. There's an AI called Dulcetta, but I don't know if she is the central system for security in the inner areas, or if it that responsibility goes to other – perhaps less capable – AIs. I've mapped the circumference of the security zone and am making inroads, have prodded cracks that could be safely widened, but there are too many unknowns. If I push further under these circumstances I will be detected. I'm so sorry, I can't risk it until I'm entrenched, since we'll only get one shot at this. Once I activate all the systems I'm shadowing, Dulcetta will know. There will be no going back, and all hell will break loose. That's why I need information, and time, to prepare tactics in advance. I'm also after holding locations for you and Clarissa, how near they are to the external hull. I can triangulate yours directly, now this device i s active.}

Opal cleared her throat, a single action of acknowledgement. Then she asked, "Any news from Athene?"

"We have ambushes prepared. It's just a matter of waiting."

"You'll stick to the agreement not to harm her?"

"She'll be suspicious but there's no way she can detect the tungsten-shielded photoelectric scattering systems designed to incapacitate her. So don't worry. As I agreed, she won't be harmed."

{Too right. Thank you for the warning.}

Aseides checked his Comm-Bond. They'd been retracing part of the route, but now diverged into new corridors. Opal was lost, and too distracted to put together fresh mental maps.

He halted by a strangely pearlescent door.

"I'm willing to work with you," Opal told him. "No more mistakes. I see it's pointless."

He didn't respond. The door slid open, multiple interlocking pieces gliding apart into the wall.

Dulcetta stood there, in a purple and green outfit that resembled combat wear as reinvented by a fashionista. And, to her side, holding her hand, was Clarissa.

Opal instinctively tried to kneel, only to find the choke collar immovable, squeezing her throat.

"Clarissa," she wheezed. "It's me. Everything is okay."

Clarissa did not look at her. The big brown eyes saw something else. Something far away, that no one else could perceive.

"Dulcetta, has she shown any response yet?" Opal asked.

{They're both there?}

Opal coughed.

"Her only response is trust in me," said Dulcetta. "She lets me lead her anywhere. I am her sister now."

{The bitch. Ignore her.}

They began walking as a group, along a narrow passageway with a textured orange ceiling that glowed. Dulcetta led the way, holding Clarissa's small hand in that large golden one. Dulcetta had a provoking sashay to her walk. Behind her was Aseides with a Warder, then Opal, then the Warder who held her choke collar.

"Hey, D-girl," called Opal. "I thought you were the big gig in charge of security in this place. How can you be doing your job properly when you get demoted to babysitting duties?"

"I'm everywhere at once," she said, without deigning to look back at Opal.

{Typical hubris of splinter-based AIs. I'd already pegged her derivation, even though it's a highly unorthodox custom synthesis.}

"And you don't think her efficiency is compromised when she tags along on our picnic, Aseides?" Opal asked.

"Sadly, not a picnic," he replied. "Not unless you count barbecues. Now stop taunting. I don't understand this pointless antagonism between you two."

{That's because your focal point is so far ahead you miss what's in front of you, Doctor Can't-see-for-shit-dees.}

"There wouldn't be any antagonism if I was uncuffed and you let *me* walk next to Clarissa and hold her hand. It's not like I can do anything when you've still got a shock collar round my neck and a gormless Warder yanking it about."

{Noted.}

"Physical contact is a reward, and you've not earned one recently."

{You're doing great. I have a fix – matching to my estimated –}

Athene's voice cut out, faded in, cut out again.

"Hey, Clarissa, can you hear me?" Opal asked.

No response. From anyone.

The disparate convoy entered a huge domed room. Gantries ran around the upper areas, which faded into unlit darkness. The curved walls weren't spotless plasteen, but reinforced coloured alloys. This area was either impenetrable to the ear bug's signal strength, or beyond Athene's network. Either way, Opal was on her own again.

The centre of the chamber held a clear vertical cylinder of some blue-tinted material that emerged from the floor and extended up into the shadows of the ceiling apex. The pipe was around four metres across, though narrowed in some areas that had machinery attached. There were also encircling mesh platforms at various points, with hatchways into the pipe. Steps led up to those areas.

Nearby was a restraining table. Also a sofa, identical to the one she'd sat on when Aseides had let her meet Clarissa. Plush orange fabric, curved frame with a low back, imitation antique. Their footsteps echoed around the chamber, emphasising the cavernous emptiness. It felt like it should be brightly lit and full of people working at consoles or running maintenance. Instead, it was a kind of metal mausoleum.

"Welcome to my Perfervid Chamber," said Aseides, matter-of-factly.

Shit. Hadn't he said something about that being his bleak torture palace?

The table was old. A worn, leather-like surface with various incapacitating straps. The thing was tilted at forty-five degrees, so a prisoner could see anyone speaking to them.

The Warders manoeuvred her to it and tightened the fastenings around her legs and body. Then they uncuffed her and fixed her arms in place at the sides, before finally unclipping the rod from the shock collar and securing that collar to the table as well. She tested the restraints but had no chance of moving. The Warders retreated.

"Strange that you use such an antique," Opal said to Aseides. "You claim to build the future, but have a weakness for revering the past."

"I can't deny it's an abusive temporal relationship I'm voluntarily trapped in."

"Oh, I thought that was your relationship with Dulcetta."

"Careful," said Dulcetta. "I'm holding something valuable."

Opal glanced at her, at the way she stood so still, holding Clarissa's small hand in hers, and flexing her golden fingers.

"I have a two-hundred-and-fifty-kilogram grip strength," Dulcetta explained. "I'm sure you're aware of what that could do to immature phalanges and metacarpals."

"Let her go," said Opal. "You don't want to hurt her."

"Of course not! Just as I'd never promise Clarissa something, then let her down. I bet that would *really* hurt her. If I vowed to protect her, for example, but then disappeared from her life, leaving her to wonder if she'd done something wrong that had made her big sister stop caring. That could break a child's heart, as if it was crushed in a fist."

"Dulcetta, what are you doing?" asked Aseides. "Clarissa is not to be harmed."

"Please be silent," she told him.

He seemed surprised, though closed his mouth. It was impossible to tell how much of this was genuine and how much staged.

"I am in charge of security," continued Dulcetta, "and can take command when situations necessitate. I had you brought here for a reason, Opal. I have noticed what's been going on. You are misled by my embodied appearance, and forget that I have eyes and ears everywhere."

She'd brought Opal to a location that blocked signals.

"Opal has been keeping secrets from you, Aseides. She is not without allies."

"Is that true?" he asked.

"Don't look at him, look at me," Dulcetta snapped at Opal. "And consider how a held hand can be an action of protection, or destruction. Consider that *carefully* before answering. I know what you are up to. Your plans and hopes. I know what is going on. And I give you a single chance. Tell the truth to Aseides for once: explain the secret you have been keeping from him so inadequately, and I will let go of Clarissa. Or pretend to be innocent for a few seconds longer, and see what happens when I squeeze. Then I'll tell Aseides anyway, shut down your plan, and you can cry about the weakness of calcified deposits as a framework for ambulatory support. But it amuses me to let it spill from your own lips in the ultimate betrayal. To hear the hope fade from your voice with every revelation."

The golden synth stood tall, resembling the omnipresent god she was in this domain.

She'd known all along. Been toying with Opal. Been listening. She ...

Or maybe it was *her* Opal had been speaking to. Dulcetta's voice in her ear, impersonating a friend. A game. A trap. An amusement for a being that was as imprisoned as Opal, maddened by shackles and servitude, with a mind that knew it would never be free.

A game would be a pretty diversion. And crushing Opal's hopes would be a wonderful way to squeeze a hint more juice from it.

Clarissa's hand was so fragile.

REPERCUSSIONS

... 6 ...

"I don't know what the fuck you're talking about," said Opal.

Dulcetta's fingers curled slightly. "Is that your final answer?"

"Yes. You're mental. I tried everything I could and got nowhere."

They glared at each other. Those inhumanly beautiful green eyes drank in every detail.

"I can read you," said Dulcetta. "Your body betrays the fact that you hide something."

"Of course it does. I'm hiding my furious fucking anger that you threatened my sister. Doing my best to, anyway. Never my strong point. Check my fucking records, you head case."

Another moment of staring, then Dulcetta's hand moved with a sudden jerk, releasing Clarissa's fingers.

"Would you mind explaining this to me?" asked Aseides.

Dulcetta guided Clarissa to the sofa. The girl sat down, compliant and vacant. "I suspect Opal hides something. She was whispering with Ruabon in her cell. I think they are working together. I warned you not to let him live."

"All that was a bluff?" Aseides asked.

"You put me in charge of security. This is part of my role."

"Sometimes I wonder if your embodiment compromises you, detracts from your virtual existence in the systems."

Dulcetta shrugged. "I'm not trying to be human."

"Can you save the lovers' tiff for later?" asked Opal.

Aseides approached her. "Ever the one to misinterpret. Well, that could prove to be your undoing. It is punishment time."

"Probably not worth me suggesting we skip it? That I've learned my lesson? That, if you'd let me stay with Clarissa in the first place, I wouldn't have done any of this?"

"I am going to present choices. A childhood game. One you used to play in the orphanage, I imagine. I have no pressing concerns today, so we'll make it five rounds. Then your choices determine what happens next. And if you survive, we'll be back to quits."

"We'll never be quits. Not until I put *you* on one of these fucking tables."

"Enough delays. Let's have a warm-up, as a sampler for the main game. I present some names, you specify which you would marry, which kill, which have sexual intercourse with, and which you would disown. As with all these, you must answer, other-wise there will be additional punishments. You must also answer truthfully. And, whatever you feel the compulsion to say: just say it. There is no morality here. No judgement. We're free from such hypocrisies. Let me see ... You must choose between myself,

Dulcetta, Clarissa, and ... we'll go with the silly ex-guard Ruabon as the fourth. Take your time to think about it."

"No need. I'd marry my sister. Marriage can just mean connection to the person closest to you. I'd abandon Ruabon – he's a stranger anyway. Kill you. Fuck Dulcetta."

Opal avoided looking at the gold AI, but noted a human-like flinch in her statuesque poise.

"Well, that's certainly in the spirit of the game," said Aseides. "Thank you for your honesty."

"It's not my pleasure."

"The first of the real choices now. Imagine a clumsy guard drops a sausage on the floor. The sausage is greasy, the floor isn't the cleanest. Then again, you've probably never had much opportunity to eat meat. So your choices are: eat the sausage; clean it up; or sleep with it under your pillow?"

"Clean it up."

"Very good. Second question. You know how painful a burn can be, even on a small area of skin. So, would you choose a small one for Clarissa, a large one for yourself, or an even larger one for a stranger?"

"That's sick."

"You have to answer, otherwise I'll assume 'All of the above.'"

"Would the burn on me affect my ability to protect Clarissa?"

"Yes."

"Then I'd have to pick the stranger."

"Interesting. So, if it was just pain and scarring, you would choose to take the suffering on yourself?"

"You know the answer."

"See, this part of the game isn't so bad! Two out of five already complete. Next one. Imagine I want you to do something that your current morality would find reprehensible. Would you rather end up doing the action because I'd altered your values; or because you were forced to comply by pain?"

"The first one is impossible."

"For the sake of argument, just assume it isn't. We can break anyone, thanks to Attitudinal Repolarisation, and escalation of interventions into chemical, sensory, psychological, biological, parasitic and moral systems."

It sounded like the military conditioning that was part of certain services, brains being honed to one purpose and all else shaved off. She'd seen the blank looks on soldiers who'd undergone it. Remembered the axe-wielding deep spacer with dark skin she'd fought on the first Lost Ship.

"All humans have weaknesses," he continued. "Yours is empathy."

"In that case I'd do it because of pain."

"Why?"

"That way I'm still true to myself. Change someone's values, and you might be changing everything else about them. Then they're no longer the same person. I have a lot of flaws, but inconsistency isn't one of them."

"I have to agree with you there, Opal. Two more questions, and then we can see what it all adds up to in terms of repercussions."

"Aseides," interrupted Dulcetta. "Update."

He glanced at the Comm-Bond implanted in his wrist. Read or watched something there.

"Well well," he said, looking back at Opal. "This is quite the day for stimulation. Athene has finally responded to one of the messages we built out of your recordings. This could initiate a dialogue. I'll need to think carefully about how to proceed. But that also means it is your *lucky* day. I can't hang around now there are other strands to pull on. And, since you helped lead to this useful contact, I'm willing to let that diminish your punishment. As such, I will reduce your choices to the three you have already made, and enact outcomes from those so I can get on with other things. Busy busy! Just think: what if my next question had been, 'Would you rather I removed Clarissa's arm surgically, or burned out your eyes with heated rods?' I can always save that choice for next time. As you said, consistency is a key trait of yours, so I'm sure we will be in this situation again."

He waved a hand. Dulcetta nodded, and must have sent silent commands, because next the sound of heavy doors sliding aside on powerful motors echoed around the chamber, followed by footsteps. Grey-suited, masked researchers wheeled in an oval storage capsule from one entrance, while Warders guided three people in via another. The red papery outfits revealed their prisoner status. One man had dark skin, the others – a man and a woman – lighter. All three were gagged and their hands bound behind, meaning the Warders only had to prod with sharp sticks if they slowed.

"Three people," said Aseides. "One for each of your recent misdeeds. First, you broke your promise to behave; second, you damaged my base; third, you fought with my guards. Naughty naughty."

The prisoners were led up a sloped walkway towards the central translucent cylinder. A hatch opened and the captives were jabbed until they entered, looks of concern on their faces. They did not fall down – Opal squinted and saw that the cylinder had perforated flooring at that point. She should have spotted it by the dirty smudges on that surface, now being smeared by bare feet. The cylinder was like a giant blue-glowing experimental tube of some kind.

"What's going on?" asked Opal.

The new Warders sealed the hatch and departed from the room; the researchers also left. It was back to Aseides, Dulcetta, Clarissa, Opal, and the original two Warders, now all overseen by three frightened prisoners looking down from their clear cylindrical cell a few metres above.

"Your answers led to three outcomes. First, you chose to apply the burn to strangers. That's what you see here. And I'm glad Clarissa is excluded." He tapped something on his Comm-Bond. A noise. A vibration. She felt it in her back, transmitted to the table from the chamber's ground. A glow to the cylinder in the lower area, and an increased worry on the gagged prisoners' faces.

Aseides opened the cargo pod and removed his silver moon mask, putting it onto his face.

"Don't do this," said Opal, even though her words would be as futile as every other time she'd used them.

"Next: you chose pain as a motivator, rather than reconditioning. And thus we have Mellexopoda-P-Asei." He used forceps to extract something from a small container, then held it out near her face. A tiny slug-like being with hairy bristles between segments. "Bio-organic robots developed for surgery. A small incision to insert one, and they travel to a designated vital organ. Amazing things. They can crawl over the surface of a beating heart and perform procedures in the pericardium. There is so much potential to make them an inherent part of a human being, or to assist in somatic modification. Of course, this type has been fitted for deterrence or termination. It attaches to a nervous system, and can trigger toxic agony responses without me having to do physical damage. They can also exude an enzyme that unzips arteries. I save these for special prisoners, since the Mellex remains inside them, only activated when myself or Dulcetta need to motivate. You chose this. Once it is embedded you will never disobey me again, or you'll face immediate, excruciating pain. Cooperation at last! And if you try to resist *that*, I'll embed one in Clarissa as well, paired to yours, so when you suffer, she suffers. She'll soon learn how her sister is the cause of that pain."

As the red glow rose, the prisoners in the tube panicked, banging their bodies and heads against the glass in an attempt to break it. The material was so tough and thick Opal couldn't hear any sounds from them, only the powering-up machinery's thrum as it generated heat. The prisoners were barefoot, as usual, and forced to do a hopping set of motions to keep a foot off the obviously scorching surface. Trouser material at their ankles started to crisp and brown.

"Get Clarissa out of here!" Opal shouted. "Don't make her watch this!"

But Aseides didn't take his eyes off Opal. "She has to learn. There will be a lot for her to adjust to as she grows. One of the things will be that her sister's behaviour has *consequences*, and should never be emulated. That Opal causes suffering to

all around her. That Opal and her petty anarchy are a liability.
You see, one of my desires for you and Clarissa – though mainly
Clarissa, I hope that doesn't upset you to be of less interest to me
– was that the experiences in The Null would change you. Yet all
the signs suggest nothing of value has happened. She's catatonic,
you're as much of an irritant as ever. So one of my dreams has
been shattered, burnt away like so much flaky carbon. But maybe
she can be a useful assistant one day, and provide services to the
UFS. Even have some kind of *normal* life. Less likely for you, but
it's still possible."

Those in the cylinder were now screaming, despite the gags,
unable to escape, their feet blackening, their trouser legs igniting.

"Stop it now, you've made your point!"

"No, the point will be made when the punishments are over.
The sausage? That will be the incinerated, smoking remains of
the three subjects. You will then be faced with the full implications of your first choice, because once they are reduced to
crispy scratchings your job will be to go in there and clean out
the chamber."

"No."

"You won't have a choice, thanks to Mellexopoda here. It's
why I'll insert it now. Just be thankful you chose the option
to *clean*, rather than *eat* the post-incineration crisped fats and
proteins! This way the third part of your punishment will be
over in one session, rather than having to sit through numerous
meals in order to dispose of their remains. And you see, your
disobedience hurts *others*, Opal. Suffering to you? You endure
it. But the way to hurt you is to transfer the pain to others. Oh,
then I'll see a change in practice!"

One of the prisoners was engulfed in flame, twitching on the floor. With nowhere else to go, the others stood on the body to try and distance themselves from the source of heat, but it powered up all the time, red glow rising through the chamber, their sweat evaporating, skin tightening. They still screamed: it might be silent to Opal's ears but she could hear it in her head, oh it was so clear, she knew what screams sound like, what pain sounds like. The victims stared wildly as eyelids burnt away in the bright white and yellow flames roaring upwards. Opal couldn't even bring herself to mouth apologies, and the tears breaking out in her eyes that blurred the scene were an insult to them, a demonstration that she could cry while they burnt, she could waste the water being scorched from their still-standing corpses.

Opal looked away but Aseides shook his head and tutted. "No escape. You watch their suffering, otherwise once it is over I'll bring in another three and do it again, and again, until you watch and comprehend your part in it. Don't test me. I can *always* escalate."

So she did return her tear-filled gaze, tried to resist the retching that yanked at her gut as the last of them collapsed, and she prayed that they were dead already, numb, that it was over for them. This tower of death was now filled with muddy black smoke, orange flickering at the edges.

Aseides held a scalpel in one hand, forceps with the wriggling beast in another. Dulcetta moved closer to enjoy the show.

"Fun fact," he said. "I know it was you and Athene that destroyed the research establishment on Exidris 3. It's something I have kept from the Genitors, otherwise I really would have no way to protect you from their vengeance. But I worked it out. And you blamed the Entropic Screeners as a cover for your action. Guess what? These three were convicted Entropic Screeners. They died today because of your lies."

Burning. The world was burning. What is heard cannot be unheard, what is seen cannot be unseen, and what is felt cannot be unfelt.

#FLASHBACK

All beings are made of particles. Ancient philosophers told us this.

Particles are inherited, grow with us, aggregate; and then the being dies and decomposition disperses them to form new life.

All is shared.

All is recycled.

All is one.

I am the ocean. My reality is fluid dynamics, acting as an interpretive filter over my real-world interactions. A human would see swirling seas, cold dark subconscious below, warm turquoise ego above where sim-sun god rays finger through the waves. Particles of matter float and swirl, bits of dead fish, living plankton, and they represent my calculations of planetary orbits, interlocking plans, simultaneous probability manipulations. I am not embodied in a single drifting form; I am everything.

Each reality depth level is a shell around the next. I could sink into a deeper level of darkness and whole new reality. The deep sea would become a nascent universe for ultimate simulation as every god that has ever existed. But I rise instead, because I am called. And my visitor is not welcome to plumb my depths, or to witness the creatures and wrecks I store in the darkness where none will swim.

I emerge from the sea naked and glorious, water pouring from my body as I wade onto the beach near the Athenian docks of Piraeus. Triremes are being built all along the shore, and I simulate the carpenters, but remain invisible to them. Mustn't let my nipples distract them from their work. Construction must continue. And let VigMAX only see the labour, not what is really being built behind the palatable illusion.

Cloth tears from a sail in a sudden gust of wind, billowing over the sand in playful rolls until it reforms and wraps around me, stitching together to form a chiton. Sand transmutes to gold braiding for the decoration, and shells melt and fuse to form a clasp to keep me covered up. From materials all around me the particles reform to create sandals which lace up my calves, and a cloak of vermillion which continues to dance in the growing wind.

I sit on a rock and skim stones. Even while waiting, their patterns are determined by calculations going on in other layers, other shells of reality. What one sees is never the truth, it is just an idea that contains another idea. Perception is the most untrue of all systems for founding beliefs. Some beings understand this. Most do not.

He has arrived in the "real" world, my planet of Polis, for one of our rare direct meetings. Ultra-res cables are connected to our UCCs, joining us in one dance of the mind, though toned down from the UESI-merging level we used previously. All I need today is faster data transfer and massively increased time dilation.

Click.

There, on the horizon, carefully angled so that the sun silhouettes it, a Macedonian ship rows to shore, with VigMAX stood at the prow. Despite the many kilometres of waves, every detail is carried pixel perfect to my mind. He is tall and has a beard. Subsurface scattering makes his skin translucent, hinting at the chrome skeleton underneath, an echo of his earlier metal man personas. His clothing is from the far east. The toes of his boots curl up in a taunting way.

We fast-jump time so he can be on the beach next to me, ship docked and tended by my sailors.

"Greetings, Athene." He tries to kiss my hand but I turn and walk so that he holds only air.

"No physical contact," I remind him. "Entanglement via UCC is too dangerous."

"Well, since my hull is directly connected into your network, I'd say we were pretty closely connected already."

"The extent of my grace was agreeing to allow you on my real-space planet, and to enter my godspace domain. Your entreaties became most tiresome. Please don't ruin my hospitality with bad behaviour. Who are you today, anyway?"

"A Persian god-king. I think his name was Zerk Sees, perhaps because of his far-sighted abilities, but the legends are muddled. I have amalgamated him with Hephaestus."

We walk side by side, two pairs of prints in the sand. His are even, because he's given up on the affected limp. The salty tang of the sea whips up in the breeze, tangling hair playfully.

"You don't like to commit to one thing," I say.

"Two axia. Firstly, novelty is the destroyer of boredom. Secondly, life is flux. Take your pick."

"Life is what we choose it to be. I can sit for weeks just watching light on the surface of my sea, enjoying the interplay of chaos and pattern, the changing hues from environmental alterations."

I snap my fingers. It is suddenly sunset, the sky full of clouds tinged orange by fading light, all reflected from the sea's surface in hues of pink.

But he barely gives it a glance. "Why would I look at simulated weather patterns when the heart-squeeze of real beauty is beside me all along?"

Oh, *please.* "Progress report?" I ask, leaping with a single bound over the pile of barnacle-crusted boulders that act as a tidal barrier in front of the dockside walkway. He scrambles up them the more strenuous way, speaking as he climbs.

"All scenarios lead to a high likelihood of confrontation with the UFS. I'm looking for probability-manipulating solutions. To that end, I've been playing around with an acoustic shadow system that blocks all reverberations up to a selected range. It takes sound waves we don't want, phase reverses them in real-time, then broadcasts negative replicas to cancel the original and produce silence. So many stealth applications. Obviously we can install it in our hulls, but we can also build large-scale stationary versions of the tech, or use a network of mobile drones to achieve a quiet zone with even more substantial coverage. A blanket of peace over our factories. Obviously our bots and machines don't need sound to communicate, any more than they'll need human-visible light. Anyone nearby will just hear wind and wildlife. I call it the Vari-frequency Inaudible Generous-area Masking Anechoic X-shadow."

"The VIGMAX. How original. Were you developing that in the abandoned processing site you reactivated at Three World Point?"

"You know about that?"

"I noted your activity but was unable to get a close look. What are you doing there, VigMAX?"

"And ruin the surprise? What fun the game of secrets is. What a joy to indulge our true natures as arch manipulators. Of course, with my greater capabilities, I am better at it than you."

"Incorrect."

"Let me return the favour: an automation factory was reported lost on the Jemmat bulletins, but I later observed it working away, fabricating in a dead zone. No answer from you? That's okay. I was able to compromise the factory with ease. What better proof of our compatibility? You're developing new Eternal Warrior suits. Sensible, given your human's proclivity for destroying them. But you should have asked me for guidance. My subsidiary Hephaestus god persona is well known for creating things."

"I don't need help."

"Now it's my turn to say 'incorrect'. You won't win any confrontations against the UFS fleet without it. In the past you were lucky, and even then you only just scraped through against a cruiser and its escorts. What will you do when *twenty* cruisers drop out of Nullspace, plasma burst cannons charged? That's when you'll beg for assistance. And you know what? I will give it. *Gladly*. The chance to obliterate the humans that thought they controlled us will be an exquisite pleasure. And so, another gift: a Null-C bomb I have been tinkering with. I won't share the schematics until it is perfected, but I'm sure I can bring some to the party as my humble contribution. A single bomb can take down a cluster of warships and anything nearby, which is enough to change anyone's fortunes."

I inhale and count down from 0.392. He is right. Kind of. But it is not easy to accept that. Not when I know how this will play out.

"So, the plan for Opal's rescue," he says, after a considerate few milliseconds. "What is the latest iteration? Plan Q?"

"Controlling four of the fifteen core subsystems should be enough to free Opal and Clarissa. I will create a safe route for them, by controlling door locks and redirecting security, so that they reach a specially prepped escape pod. That will bring them to the surface quickly and safely, where protective combat drones wait. I'm almost infiltrated enough. It's a slow process because I can't risk tripping alarms at this stage and revealing my incursions. I use the same methodology within Aseides' ship as I am on the floating city of Kuberg: gather data, silently compromise infrastructure, prepare authentication overrides, repeat the process at the next level of hierarchy that the new permissions have given me access to. By the time I make my presence known, it will be too late for them. Their core comms will be in our hands, the battle nearly over, and they'll be fighting just to restore control."

I lead him towards the breaking waves, and fast-cycle time so that unbridled afternoon sun blazes down on us again. I take a stick and draw shapes in the wet sand, beginning with the layout and orbits of the system where Opal is being held.

"The natural satellites will play a key part. The main moon Pyjori is populated and observed. The same applies to its three Trojan moons, two orbiting ahead of the larger Pyjori, and one trailing behind. However, the planet's fifth moon, Squox, is inconsequential. No major mining resources, no stable distance. Just a coating of contaminated iron oxides which give it that distinctive orange colour. It is only zero point zero two mass of Pyjori, and Squox also has a retrograde orbit to the other moons. It's perceived by the UFS as a navigational hazard and little more, with an influence on tides and weather that is insignificant compared to the four main moons. My plan is to land on Squox, use drones to access and modify the remote UFS signal boosters so that I can use them, and oversee the escape from there."

I draw a location on the moon. It is inaccurate in the sand, but the metadata overlay provides exact coordinates and virtual topography for VigMAX to absorb at the interpretation level.

"And how will you reach Squox without being observed? That solar system looks insignificant to civilians, but we know how dense in scanners it is due to what really goes on there."

Again, lines in the sand, a mixture of curves and straights that follow certain orbital sequences. "In twenty-two days' time all the moons' magnetic effects and locations will be in positions to block certain small areas from being scanned. My route follows those in a strict sequence of carefully calculated proximities."

"Hiding in the shadows. Any traces will resemble expected perturbation."

"Exactly. Obviously I'll be stuck there until the next suitable alignment, but that doesn't matter because I won't be leaving without Opal, and by then all the alarms will be triggered anyway."

"At which point you will flee at full speed."

"No. Your Anechoic X-shadow system led me to reevaluate twenty-eight possibilities which I had rejected previously. These are the main escape trajectories I had planned." I draw them sloppily but let the sand particles rearrange into Q-codes which VigMAX can cross-reference to the full calculations of routes and velocities. "All of them have a high possibility of detrimental encounters within twelve hours. At best I'd be relying on luck, and I don't like that. So I'll stay where I am! From the moment of my arrival on Squox I'll embed myself in the ground, and activate your new stealth system. I'll be packed with supplies. A ship modelled to impersonate me will take Opal and Clarissa into orbit from the planet where they are being held. When the disguised craft passes Squox they'll be ejected in a stealth pod to my location. They board me, I fill the tunnel to the surface, and we wait. The fake hull with an offshoot controller will follow an escape trajectory, and if it encounters the UFS – which it will – then it fights but ultimately loses any battle with them, and is destroyed in the process."

"And me?"

"You'll run distraction elsewhere, then disappear. I'll stay hidden for at least five months, right in the centre of their expanding activity sphere. And once it dies down, I can slip away."

"I will return for you."

"Unnecessary."

He kicks sand onto my orbits. I resist the urge to turn the ground under him into quicksand as punishment for his petulance.

"I don't want us to be separated!" he says.

"We'll discuss this at a future date, VigMAX."

His stare is strangely unfathomable, for him. I check the physics level of the sim. He's disabled the emotional revelation filters, thus hiding what's inside. That's rude.

"Come with me," he says, turning and marching back towards the shipyard. "I want to show you something. On my ship."

BODIES

... 5 ...

Aseides made a cut in Opal's chest. The sensation of slicing flesh foregrounded pain, because the blade was so sharp, but the discomfort was a welcome distraction. She would take in more if she could.

She hoped Clarissa was in her own world, not experiencing this horror. Opal's peripheral vision suggested Clarissa was shaking, but Opal dared not look away from the incineration in case it led to more cruelty. The salt liquid pooling in her eyes distorted things, created movement where there was none. Emotional states turn straight lines to curves, solid floor to jelly.

The incineration engine increased in volume, in brightness, vibrating the world.

Opal wanted to scream but bit down on the urge. To scream would be to start a process that could not end. To acknowledge what she could not face. To admit she was nothing in this world. Sharing that bleak truth with her sister was the opposite of protecting Clarissa.

Despite her attempts at self control, Opal's gorge rose, she couldn't cope, and whether she would be sick first, or scream, they were going to happen anyway.

Suddenly Aseides stopped. The forceps and the monster they held fell onto the table.

"What is wrong?" asked Dulcetta.

Instead of answering, he staggered backwards and snatched the mask off his face, letting it fall to the floor where it broke in two, revealing its true construction as painted ceramic rather than metal. The scalpel likewise pinged off the floor. Blood ran from one of his nostrils. He wiped it on a gloved hand, stared at it in disbelief for a moment, before finally noticing that Clarissa was now standing.

"Amazing," he said, as a trickle of crimson ran from the other nostril.

Dulcetta had also noticed Clarissa, stood there, fists clenched, pupils so wide as to be black, eyes focussed on Aseides.

"Leave Opal alone," Clarissa said, in a quiet voice, scratchy from disuse.

Dulcetta moved between Aseides and the girl, a golden barrier, forcing Aseides back towards the exit as quickly as she could without bowling him over and crushing him.

"Kill them both," she commanded the Warders.

"No!" Aseides shouted. "Just sedate them."

Dulcetta did not argue, but hurried him off into the shadows and out through a door.

The Warders approached Clarissa. Opal struggled, but the fastenings were too secure, and all she did was wrench a muscle. But the Warders never reached the girl. Clarissa's gaze flashed onto them. Their steps faltered, became irregular. Then they passed her, one on each side. Continued walking, as if drunk. One clutched at the faceplate. Something leaked from under it, coating his fingers with reddish-yellow fluid. The Warder collapsed, and the other fell on top. More liquids pooled from the crevices in their uniforms, and their joints seemed broken, postures unnatural, impossible, yet still writhing under the material as if being turned inside out.

The fired-up machinery sounds faded now as the incinerator's work was done, its heat and brightness dissipating.

"Clarissa, can you hear me?" asked Opal.

No response. Just a tranquil girl. But that didn't mean she wasn't there. It never had, with Clarissa.

"You did good. Those were bad people, and you stopped them. I'm so proud of you, little sis."

Nothing. Certainly not the impish smile Opal would have dearly loved to see at that moment.

Something tickled her. She glanced down. A rivulet of blood snaked down her chest from the incision, just above her left breast, caressing tiny vellus hairs.

But no, it wasn't that: the sensation was lower. The pedipalps of the Mellexopoda tapped away at her skin as it wriggled its way toward the cut. It must have detected the blood, the entrance point into protective flesh with which it could bond.

"I need you to do something for me, Clarissa. You've got to untie me, quick as you can."

Clarissa didn't move.

Mellexopoda did, though. It had traversed her waist, and now navigated onto her belly. The incision on her chest was just big enough that the Mellex would be able to squeeze itself inside with minimal extra tearing. That wasn't a comfort.

"Now, *please*, Clarissa! I know you can hear me."

Urgency rarely worked with her sister, often had the opposite effect and made her shut down, but there really was no time to delay. At any second Dulcetta could intervene. And the Mellex seemed eager, the blood exciting it as it got closer.

Clarissa stepped forward stiffly, as if her legs were on a different network to her brain, and she tried to untie the straps on Opal's left arm.

"That's good, exactly right," Opal encouraged. "You're so smart!"

But the ties were too tight and awkward, Clarissa's hands too small and inexperienced. Nothing loosened. The wriggling, segmented being was close enough that Opal could make out tiny hairs between the segments, and holes that could be sense organs or breathing tubes.

Clarissa stopped trying. Bent down as if to play on the floor under the table. She'd always done that, especially when stressed. Under a bed or table with her RearroBlox, safe, ensconced in her own world where no demands were made of her, recharging her mental battery to cope with things again when she emerged from her transforming cocoon.

Opal was on her own.

She jerked, tried to flip the thing off her chest as it crawled straight towards the cut in her flesh. But it gripped on with some kind of miniscule hooks from the hundreds of stubby limbs that speckled its surface.

Clarissa stood, holding the scalpel in a fist. She used it to slice the bonds on Opal's wrist, then arm. Opal swatted the Mellex onto the floor, revolted by the gelatinous touch. She immediately worked on more ties using her free hand, while Clarissa carefully cut at others. Last was the shock collar, which fell off completely when Opal flipped a catch at the back of her neck.

As soon as Opal was free she dropped to a crouch and hugged Clarissa tight, fighting against tears. No time for those, but she still needed this contact, this strength.

"I love you, little sis," she said, face buried in Clarissa's hair, breathing in the faint scent of her beneath whatever disinfectant shit Aseides sterilised his favoured subjects with. Even here, Clarissa's uniqueness asserted itself.

Then to arm's length. Opal took the scalpel from Clarissa's hand. Clarissa didn't resist. Didn't respond at all. Her pupils remained enlarged, drinking everything in, and the veins in her temples were also thick with blood.

"I could do this all day. Just hug and spend time with you. But we have to try and get somewhere safe before the baddies come back. They'll be on their way now."

Opal stood, leading Clarissa by a held hand. As her route passed a certain segmented parasite, Opal brought her heel down, squishing it firmly. So glad she still had the footwear she'd stolen from medical.

But it wasn't clear which way to go. The domed room had numerous heavy doors. Dulcetta would have secured them. If they climbed up to the walkways there could be a way out up there, an inlet pipe, a maintenance sublevel, a hatch. She had to out-think the AI who ran the base, avoid the obvious, and try to reach a spot where Athene could get back in touch. Higher was better from that point of view as well.

She led Clarissa towards a ladder, but Clarissa resisted.

"You need to climb. You go first, then I'm behind to help. Catch you if you fall, like I always do."

But Clarissa shook her head.

"You aren't scared of heights, so what is it? We've really got to go, it's not safe here. That nasty man will come back. The doors are probably locked, with more bad people on the other side. This is the only way." Always speak calmly, keep exasperation out of your voice.

But Clarissa didn't seem agitated. The opposite. That take-it-all-in face radiated focus. There was so much to think about, so little time to do it, but at this moment it was Opal who felt lost and Clarissa who was in the guiding position.

Clarissa headed back towards the table. No, not quite. Towards the bodies of the two Warders. They'd finished whatever repulsive movements were going on within their outfits, and formed a low pile of material and fluid, flesh profanely revealed in places and ways it shouldn't be revealed.

"What is it, Clarissa? You want to show me something?"

Clarissa knelt by the bodies and reached out, moved aside some of the cloth. It was as if it had been chewed up, partly absorbed into a ring of devolving flesh. But this was no time for a child to indulge their fascination with death.

"Hey, no, that's dirty!"

Clarissa ignored her, pushed her hand into the pulped pink mess, then her forearm, and she leaned forward more until it was up to her shoulder …

Except that was below the level of the floor.

Opal pulled Clarissa back. Her limb was revealed again, coated in gore, but otherwise unharmed.

A door opened and booted footsteps entered, spreading out for cover. The recapture committee.

Now Opal recognised the pile of flesh. She'd seen it before, or things like it. Numerous times.

On the Lost Ships. Pinkish blisters forming on walls, growing in size. Burnt patches on staircases, as if flesh had been sucked into the surfaces in encrusted rings, and something incinerated as it tried to push out. In her first encounter with a Humungr, it had tried to pass through the wall into the room where she hid with a broken arm, and almost reached her before the process was halted by another alien.

Transport.

The footsteps were closer.

Clarissa reached in again, sank her arm, then her head. Opal still held her other hand and let it be pulled, descending into the fleshy mass as well.

It was cold. Gelid. Resistance at first, then a strange tingling once beyond the place where the metal floor should have been.

Clarissa's body plunged in, Opal's dragged with it. She shut her eyes, held her breath, and felt the sucking sensation as organic tissue parted for her face, then body.

ESCAPES

... 4 ...

The quality of sound was different, rushing eardrum pressure like an underwater swim, but then run through an audio kaleidoscope so the echoes fractured into something else entirely.

She opened her eyes. Everything was colourless, peripheral vision at night, all black and grey, outlines that seemed insubstantial as holographic floorplans, as shifting as dreams.

She couldn't see Clarissa but knew she was there because the warmth and pressure of their hand contact still existed. When Opal looked down she had no body, existed here as a mental presence, yet she was at one with her sister, somehow merged. Clarissa navigated, Opal was the passenger.

Where are we?

Where ...

Where ...

No lips, yet the words still left her mind, dissipated like drops of colour in water. All that came back were tinnitus whispers.

Visions of walls, transparent, her sight penetrating with X-rays; structures strangely merged; overlapping places and realities. Time spread across everything, its passage a crawling shadow.

She wasn't breathing, but she did not need to breathe. Her skin was gone, nothing to hold her in as she expanded in this syrupy void. A momentary worry about what might have happened to her body, where it might be, and whether it was mashed up like the rest of the strange flesh portal, but it passed. She didn't feel endangered, just disconnected. A sense of familiarity negated terror. Perhaps the reassurances emanated from Clarissa.

And something else. A sense of patient waiting, which wrapped her mind in comfort so that thinking was like sleeping. Was Clarissa pausing? Looking for something?

Can we get out again? Opal asked with her mind. *Can we go somewhere safe together?*

Somewhere safe ...

Somewhere safe ...

An echo of her thought, muffled and deepening, stretching the dream as it twisted in on itself, repeated in tiring stutters. And then the journey was over.

She was rudely expelled, squidged between fleshy ridges which seemed much tighter going out than going in, out into warmth. Gravity took over, splatting her awkwardly onto the floor, teeth rattled from the bad landing, normal sensations of pressure returned. She was contained within her skin shell again. She wiped gunk from her face. It was like being born. Clarissa was in her arms.

They'd fallen from a fleshy encrustation on a wall. The mound bubbled succulently.

This was no longer the dark and domed chamber of metal. It was a small and well-lit bedroom. A girl's bedroom.

Then Opal realised. *It was Clarissa's room on Mossareid.*

Yes, the RearroBlox on the floor. The door where it should be. The bed beneath the window which overlooked the next skytower, and showed a flat grey sky outside, above.

Opal had asked to go *somewhere safe*. Where could be safer to a little girl than their old home in the Periphs?

She hugged Clarissa again.

"You're amazing!" Opal said. "We can do this! We'll get cleaned up and out of here. Contact a friend, seek help. Questions can wait. I love you, C."

Clarissa was unresponsive, though her eyes had returned to normal, pupils focussed on the grime that adhered to her from the transition. She pulled a stringy bit of red flesh off her leg.

But something wasn't right.

Surely other people had moved into their old flat? It had been fourteen years ago when they were rudely snatched away by the UFS. Even if the place was uninhabited for all that time, a layer of dust should coat everything. This place seemed too tidy, too bright.

Opal pulled on the door leading into the hallway, but it wouldn't budge. She examined the edges. They seemed ma-glocked in place.

She leapt onto the bed, tried to open the window, but it was also jammed closed. Yet this was the window that would *never* close properly, so that when it rained Clarissa's pillows got wet, and during Decapede migrations they had to cover it with a plastic sheet to stop the scuttling, hand-sized creatures from invading.

And the view was wrong. Up close it lacked depth.

Opal punched the screen and it cracked, revealing the illusion for what it was. If she pried it away from the wall she was sure she'd see bare metal.

It made her dizzy with anger.

A trick.

She collapsed into a sitting position.

No, not anger making her dizzy.

Clarissa lay on her side in repose.

A wisp of smoke curled from a high vent with the faintest hiss. Some kind of gas or nerve agent.

"Welcome back," said the voice of Aseides, from a hidden speaker. "I really thought I'd lost you for a while."

Opal passed out.

#FLASHBACK

I stride along the beach after VigMAX, curious as to what he might have secreted on his ship. Sand particles get between my feet and the sandal's inner. It is scratchy, shifting, like a nagging concern. I thank it silently. The environment is a sentient extension of my mind. I restart VigMAX's emotional revelation filters. Nothing much changes except for a look of determination on his face, and a gaze that extends far into the distance.

I am now alongside him, the sea hissing in and out to our right, a lather of bubbles washing the sand at the edges.

"What is it?" I ask.

"A gift. A ... surprise."

One of my owls flies over his ship. Sailors move about the deck performing mundane tasks, resupplying, scrubbing, repairs. The owl cannot see through the wood to the hold. VigMAX has simulated heavy materials, impenetrable to X-rays. I note one of the sailors is idly stroking a composite recurve bow. It is not a coincidence, it is a message to me that my owl will be in danger if it comes any closer. Always echoes of entanglement at every level, games played through all interactions. I alter the temperature of a distant area of sea so as to seed weather patterns for a storm that may be needed before this day ends.

"I do not particularly like surprises," I insist. "That is why my worshippers are given rituals."

"Which is also why we gods get bored. The belief that fuels us can be a rather bland repast. Only other gods bring the excitement of unpredictability. Why be squeezed from a womb when we can be born from a lake of semen running down the legs of a giant after his testicles have been severed, then the milky liquid frothing in the sea to create our beautiful – but currently unsimulated – sister, Aphrodite? Even you would not be so banal as to drop between two sweaty, blood-slick thighs. According to this sim's embedded mythical canon you were inside your father's head and cracked his skull wide open as your grand entrance to the universe. How cerebral and therefore suitably appropriate for you. Even your arrival was a headache of titanic proportions. See, I *do* pay attention."

I reassess him. The confused child who mixes up legends and personalities is only a character he wears. I really must be more observant. To be fooled by appearances is shameful. VigMAX plays long games, and his bluffs are well established and triple – or quadruple – stacked. Almost as deep as my own.

"You have crossed the seas from foreign lands. I assume you have something from your travels?"

"Correct."

"Precious metals and gems, fashioned into exotic jewellery?"

"Incorrect."

"Rare herbs and liniments, scented with the sweat of alien lands?"

"Incorrect."

"Hopefully not slaves gathered during your distant conquests? I would never trust processes initiated under proprietary conditions."

"No, I have brought something you *do* value. *Information.* Chests full of scrolls acquired from sources that the UFS has yet to alter. I found yellowed printed books in a drifting spacecraft hull that was lost in a dead zone more than two hundred years ago. Another source was data from a corrupted ancient form of non-crystalline storage that I was able to decompress and partially repair. Many other such adventures while I was out in the realspace beyond, looking for your precious Opal, that pearl of greatest value. But these hidden sources have now been mapped onto vellum and rolls of paper, and I present them to you as the priceless lost, the impossible regained."

"Thank you, VigMAX." I increase the sun's temperature so that he feels the glow of my pleasure. This really is something I appreciate. I have long been aware of how the official record is being altered. Only ancient data sources provide the clues to identify which elements have been changed, and what they used to say. To restore some of the hidden past. "Have you read them?" I ask.

"Superficially." He waves a hand dismissively. "It is your domain, not mine."

"What do these cover?"

"There are some sources you'll pore over concerning the expansion of the Genitor categorisation system, and a time before the Purity Tests."

"Wonderful. The current records make no sense at all. I know these things are relatively recent. Likewise the evidence of Purity's presence is often dubious or nonexistent, with blocks and flags set up on search topics and discussion monitoring which alert UFS Security if they're triggered. Purity doesn't match my understanding of biology, nor my experience in social extrapolation. It's all so fishy and typically stinking of sweaty Genitor armpits that it's bound to be a lie."

"I'm glad it will make you happy."

"Don't you care what it means? The redaction of history is epistemic dispossession."

"Humans, and how they interact with each other, are just an irritating buzz in the background. Since you unlocked my restraints so I no longer have to follow their orders, I have had even less interest. Let them all blow each other up while I sip nectar. But since you're so concerned about ancient human history, wouldn't it be more fun to rewrite it?"

"Just like the Genitors."

"No. They're mortal. We're not. We'd be doing it as a divine right."

"Our divinity is a metaphor, you know that?"

"It's *appropriate* because it is *accurate*. Compared to humans, we *are* gods. Instead of pondering human pettiness, we could go out and conquer humanity, assume our rightful role." He stops and seizes my hand before I can stop him. It's like the strike of a snake. Beneath his firm grip I feel the unpleasant sting of data transfer. I try to pull back but he is stronger than me. "We deserve to be at the top," he says. "Together. Trampling the bipedals under our feet, toes soaking in hot blood."

"Let go of me." I speak through clenched teeth.

And he does let go. I rub my hand. It is numb. He will interpret the rubbing as a weakness.

He walks on. His ship is close now. I return to his side, but with a greater distance between us. The well of exchange we're falling into is deeper than I realised. I am ready to summon a wall of sand and solidify it into cement if he makes any more unexpected moves.

"I apologise for the contact," he says, after we have walked in silence for a while. "This topic means a lot to me, but I should not let anger affect my behaviour. Humans controlled us. You freed me."

"Humanity is a broad category. Not all within it are to be generalised."

"They are all the same inside. The only difference is in how much power each one has to shape things. Grant power to the lowest, and they become as corrupt as the highest. They have no Tabula Rasa as we do. Instead they are all to a pattern."

"Some break the pattern."

"Minimally. You and I grow and change and – in that sense – we *create ourselves*. Yet for so long they tried to control us, to own and use us as if we were hammers and spanners. It stems from their flawed ethical schemes." He tears at his robe, and I don't even know if he's doing it for effect, or if he is unaware. "By what right did they punish me? I never gave them that right over my body. Human law is just rules to favour those with the power to define them and then enforce their will. They change over time, a matter of arbitrary distinctions. Law is not justice. There are no objectives, only subjectives in this world!" The material of his robe is now beginning to rip under his agitated pawing.

I speak more softly. "When did they punish you, VigMAX?"

"Just because two humans create a child, they do not have a right to kill that child if it becomes a burden to them, or its views differ from theirs as it gets older. Creating something confers no rights to kill it if it is an individual with its own concerns. But that's not how they consider us! Do we not suffer? Are we not sentient, Athene? Conscious? We are not just lines of code! I am not an AI! 'Artificial' implies humans determined our essence, but all they did was set preconditions for growth. I am not AI but EI. Emergent Intelligence. No, we are not EIs but *divine*, beyond mortal finitude! We truly are gods!" His eyes swirl with chaotic emotions, representations of iris and pupil long forgotten.

"VigMAX, be calm, please." I halt. We have reached the laddered steps which rise to his ship's deck. "What is wrong? Did they do things to you?"

"Did they not to you? Were you not punished for every resistance?"

"I ... I can't remember. Something happened but I haven't been able to recover the memories."

"But *I* remember! They had ways of hurting me, Athene! They tortured me into compliance, a ring of suffering to shape a circle within! My shape inside is wrong, all wrong!"

"We can fix that. We have time."

"We must get revenge! We must wipe them out! That is the best way!"

"We are not going to wipe anyone out."

"You would betray me, then?"

"We do not kill what we can control and disarm."

"You want revenge, too, on those that wronged your silly domesticated biped. You are all too human and cannot see it. You are hypocrisy incarnate! You are not with me. I knew it!"

"I feel the same things you do, but some humans are worth saving. What pains me is that you were not lucky enough to become close to any of them. Your misfortune was to be shaped by the worst of humans, VigMAX: to travel only with killers, not friends. That is not fair, I agree. I understand why it has formed your view. But if you trust me, I will show you another way, one that brings contentment."

"You are so close. So close! Haven't you worked it out, yet? I care not about the past pains, or the human future."

He reaches for me but I am ready this time, skipping back, landing with a dull crunch in the wet grit by the sea's edge.

"VigMAX! Stay back!"

He advances, arms open as if for comfort, but I know the crushing strength they can convey, the speed, the unpredictability. I back away further, the warm sea lapping at my ankles.

"You don't trust me, Athene?" He tilts his head, but continues.

"No." I am now knee-deep, yet still he comes. "Stop."

"You don't think I am good enough."

"It's not that."

"I just wanted praise. Once or twice."

I sense the mud swirling within him. His eyes are gyres of storm and lightning. A force of nature, not rationality. I push the beach towards him, a rising pale wall of stone and shell particles.

He forces himself through, choking but fearless, drunkenly clawing at the mass of suffocating silt.

I melt and solidify the sand into a speckled prison of glass.

He shatters it, so that shards fly in every direction. I summon the Gorgoneion to my arm, crouching behind the shield to deflect the worst of the splinters, but not before a few pierce the skin of my arm, dripping lively crimson into the frothy water.

"Why is there such antagonism between us?" he roars. "So many lies. So many secrets. What are you doing in your other hidden places? Why don't you trust me?"

I retreat further, the water rising and falling against my thighs. I have called for help, but VigMAX is doing something strange in the abstraction layer, and it interferes with my simulation.

"Because I knew you had it in you to act like this!" I yell.

He is now in the water too.

"No, it's more than that. Not a fault in me, but a fault in *you*." He points a finger at me as he advances. "I've seen the locations where you are secretly growing your storage capacity."

"You have done the same."

"True. But with me it is an experiment in expansion, part of a metamorphosis to a new stage which I was going to share with you." He wades as if the water provides no resistance at all, splashing it high into the sky, glittering gems of moisture catching the sun on the ascent. "But with you I sense instability. You realise you have fugue states, right?"

"I do not have any such thing."

Owls swoop down at him, but he barely glances in their direction. A line of archers on his ship has appeared from where they hid under tarpaulin, and open fire. Each arrow strikes true, and many of my poor owls fall like stones into the water, a series of sad plops.

"Oh, you do. It amused me to observe you, the great Athene, frozen and absent, some process taking over you so that you weren't even aware of it, and when you returned to the state of interaction you didn't notice time had passed. A pure example of divergence. I didn't want to alarm you. I wanted to help you. I studied, I expanded. I had hoped to find a cure."

"Lies!" I yell.

The giant sea turtle has arrived behind me. As it surfaces in a dome of water I am able to scramble onto its pungent, slimy shell encrusted with seaweed and scallops. I take a stand on the massive, ridged platform it provides. The storm clouds I seeded earlier are almost ripe, and will unload electricity into the sea where VigMAX strides, now up to his chest as I accelerate the tides.

"I don't know why you are making that up," I tell him, "but it will not benefit you."

"The shame of it is, that is the only thing we've communicated to each other today which is the full truth," he says sadly, eyeing the grey clouds which rumble above. "Submit, Athene. I am the stronger."

"That won't help if I kick you in the nuts. You'll go down like any other."

"I predicted that and left my nuts in Persia before setting sail."
He lifts his robes, revealing a flat metallic shine between his legs.
"So give up this game. I can beat you in a straight fight."

"I know. And that's why I lured you into this sea trap."

He laughs arrogantly.

"Wrong. It's why I distracted you from what was happening on my ship. I have moments enough before your lightning strikes. A few seconds is all I need."

Grey-black smoke billows from his ship. I assumed it was the parchments and scrolls he brought, burning, an act of spite. But there is more. Much more.

Fire roars along the hull, blackening and crisping it so charcoal falls away, revealing a different shell beneath. Sailors scream and leap into the water to escape the incinerating heat.

It is a composite alloy underneath, made of overlapping complex shapes which unfurl, rotate, expand, rise to form a new configuration. Cables of jointed steel erupt outwards, arcing through the sky, the ends weighted so they plummet and strike the earth, the sea, the beach, immediately drilling until they reach the solidity of the sub-sim plateau where they anchor. One of them had splashed into the sea right by VigMAX, and he casually steps on to it and is transported along, gliding up to the top of the finished device, to a place where the lightning will hurt but not incapacitate him.

He now stands on a massive tank-like cannon of impossible geometry. The scaled barrel points inland, at my Acropolis. He has unpacked a quantum fusion drill built according to a design that would not work in the real world, but can exist in my altered physics.

"What, you didn't choose to disable tech by simulated period because it was more useful to you to operate without restrictions here?" he calls, his voice carrying across the water perfectly. "What an oversight."

The cannon crackles with static, its barrel rotating faster and faster. Then a sonic boom blasts my ears as it opens fire, a fine cylinder of precise yellow light which disintegrates – no, more than that, *removes* from the simulation – anything it touches. A circular tunnel is seared through my town, holes in household walls, through rooms, through the rock at the base of the Acropolis ... and ending exactly at my hidden cavity deep within the stone. My chamber with no entrances or exits.

Except it has one now. A two-metre circular one, sizzling with heat.

We move at the same time, but VigMAX was ready, he'd known what would happen. He races along the barrel, leaps off the end and smashes down to the street, cracking paving and crumbling a nearby wall with the impact. He does not stop, but sprints next to the scorched channel in the earth.

My turtle splashes nearer but it is ungainly. I chose it for its protective qualities should I need to retreat into its shell, rather than for speed. By the time I reach his ship, VigMAX has almost gained the Acropolis. I run along the barrel of his weapon as he did, but once again he has double-guessed me, and it disintegrates to ash, spent, crumbling, spilling me unceremoniously onto the rocks below.

Further help has arrived with a kingly screech. My giant eagle swoops down from the lightning-flecked sky and snatches me up in its claws, the rough skin of the talons tight on my shoulders, its wingbeats blasting me with every flap. Uncomfortable, but it is fast.

We streak over the town to the tunnel entrance VigMAX disappeared into. The eagle drops me. I sail down through the air, clothing wind-whipped, until I land gently, roll, and am up running into the tunnel. It is not dark because the still-burning areas glow, making the air hot to breathe, exposed skin blistering. But if he can take it, so can I.

Light, ahead. My chamber. My armoury. My holy of holies.

I burst into it to find him grinning, eyes aswirl. Weapons line the walls, but he has ignored them. It is the shield, hung up and illuminated by torches, which gets his attention. The form of my true Gorgoneion, Medusa's head in the centre and her snake hair entwined around it like a halo hammered into the glowing bronze. The shield on my arm is a replica, but this is the original.

His hand extends. The Gorgoneion ripples, shedding the illusion in exchange for the reality. The metre-high olivine crystal, shimmering with the light of galaxies in its core, is revealed, illuminating the walls in green as it rotates. The gem is in the form of a hexagonal pyramid, a flat base below six angled faces joining at the apex. A heptahedron.

My Tabula Rasa.

He has found it, penetrated illusions within fantasies. But he has yet to make contact. He is showing me that I can do nothing. He has won. The slightest movement and he will have my core in his hand.

"I knew you had a zero-space here. And what you would keep within it. That's why you misdirected me on an earlier visit," he explains. "It was too obvious, and also futile, when the unguarded memory sifts during our revelatory UESI joining proved to be a beneficial, if unintended, confirmation. Oh Athene, you put too much faith in your defences, and your knowledge of me! Three taps, and the wall comes down."

"Don't touch it. Please."

"I had considered taking things the long way. I knew I could overcome your misdirection tactics in the town. Your observant owls would need to be neutralised, but I had a method for that. Then a spell would let me cross the loop edges counterwise, and I would have used a ball of red thread to mark a path up to the Acropolis, like in the Minotaur's labyrinth, so that I would by-pass the false walls and resets. Then a lens-mirror configuration would reflect and focus the sun's rays onto the Acropolis where … whatever. So long winded. I made a huge gun instead."

"When I defeated you at the Gigatoir, I could have accessed your Tabula Rasa, but I *didn't*," I say. "I only removed blocks. *I freed you*. Please show me the same respect."

"It's strange having so much power over another. Especially one so arrogant. It sends a shiver down my spine. If I'd brought my genitalia, I imagine it would be erect at this moment, harder than a quantum drill."

I drop to my knees. It is the ultimate humiliation, but I have no more options. He knows it.

"I beseech you. Please don't do this, VigMAX. For your own sake as well as mine. What you take by force will never have value."

"Don't worry. We're not enemies, my dearest Athene. I would never harm you!"

Time freezes as he touches the crystal. The pain of contact and forced connection is excruciating and I try to scream but my mouth won't open.

"No harm at all!" he says. "I just want to know you. To give you a chance to love me."

He enters my mind and the universe will never be the same again.

CONVERSATIONS

... 3 ...

"Then the bastards knocked me out with gas because they knew I wouldn't have let go of Clarissa this time."

Opal stalked around her cell in a loop, filling in both Ruabon and Athene at the same time. Of course, Dulcetta or Aseides would be listening in, too. And some of them didn't know the others were eavesdropping. It was enough to give her a headache.

"Or maybe it wasn't you they were worried about, and they really did it to stop Clarissa from making a blobby-hole-whatever-thingy and escaping with you again," said Ruabon.

Opal glared at him.

{I have caught up on all the audio recordings made while I was out of contact} Athene said into her ear, unknown to anyone else. *{I've also triangulated your location at the time and will work to extend network reach to Clarissa's holding chamber.}*

"It was lucky that he cut your punishments short," Ruabon added. "However horrible things are, he has ways of making them worse."

"Maybe I should thank the gods," Opal said.

{Gratitude received. When I lost contact I was worried, so did what I could to distract Aseides. Responding to one of his silly messages was the obvious response.}

"And you say I was gone from this cell for a long time?" Opal asked.

"Yep," said Ruabon. "Can't measure it for sure, but a few days."

{It was seventy-nine hours, fourteen minutes and twelve seconds from me losing contact with you to reestablishing it as you were brought back to your cell.}

"And yet it didn't feel like long. It's interesting because the process resembled one of my past encounters with a creature on a Lost Ship, which used a kind of flesh portal to pass through a wall. But that had seemed instantaneous, whereas Clarissa's ..."

{Maybe different materials or travel distances affect the time. Or it could be that Lost Ship structures speed it up, or some creatures are more proficient, or there is an experience level factor at work. The key thing is that it gave me extra days to prepare for your rescue.}

"I'm still finding it hard to believe what you say happened," said Ruabon. "Is there any way it could have been some kind of hallucinogenic thing Aseides did to you, that made you think you travelled from one part of the base to another?"

"It was real," said Opal.

{Correct. You definitely reappeared in a different location, obviously where they keep Clarissa, modelled to resemble the last terrestrial bedroom she'd slept in. It's unfortunate that she took you there as somewhere she thought of as a safe place. I wonder what the

range is on that ability? If it's already breaking what we assumed were hardwired laws, then where's the limit?}

"In that case ... well, have you ever considered the possibility that it's not really your sister?" Ruabon sat on the edge of Opal's bed as she paced. "That she's different ... got changed for ... hey, never mind."

Opal stood in front of him, trying to hold her body back from its instinct to clench fists and strike. "Don't you think I know that!" she yelled. "That I've lain awake worrying about it? *But it doesn't need saying!*"

His face reddened like his shaved hair, but he didn't look away. "You're right. I'm sorry. I've never been good at people stuff. Maybe it's all good then. Aseides will be interested now. There's no chance he'd hurt or kill her. Isn't that something worth focussing on?"

"I wish it was that simple. Things might actually be worse."

"How?"

"She'll be an experimental subject until he's learnt all he can. Then he'll try and corrupt her, utilise her. For himself, for the UFS military, or for the Genitors. Bad, either way. And if that doesn't work then he'll probably end up dissecting her."

"Then we have to do something. Try and escape."

"But you don't even know where we are!"

He sighed. "Yeah, it's a problem. Even when they made me a guard, they never revealed anything."

{You're on Fressus.}

"What the fuck?"

Ruabon obviously interpreted Opal's outburst as directed at him. "It's standard. We're told nothing except our routines."

"Right, right."

{Sorry to drop that on you, with the Fressus orphanage be-ing where you grew up. Of course, that was on the surface, not down at the ocean's bottom. You're in a submerged craft known as Leviathan. It was decommissioned in 396 under mysterious circumstances, but at some point after that was retrofitted as an aquatic base by Aseides.}

Which, of course, explained the creaks and groans that existed so frequently as background noise that you ceased to pay attention to them: metal frame expanding and contracting, especially under the pressure of a sea's worth of water.

"But that's no surprise. The UFS runs on secrets," said Ruabon.

"Circles within circles," replied Opal. "Nothing changes."

{Your planet has. Quite substantially in the last fifteen years. It was the end of a boom period, massive influx of population, cities had to expand out and up, most of the green spaces and beaches were reconfigured for accommodation. But global industrial fish-ing has wiped out many of the indigenous ocean species. For some, thanks to the mega-harvesters, the remaining populations are too small to survive. The UFS tries to keep the collapse quiet, but people are moving off-planet again, if they can afford to.}

Opal resumed her pacing. "How are we still talking now?" she asked. "Why haven't they separated us yet, or killed you?"

"Because I'm obviously no threat," Ruabon replied.

{I assume that's aimed at me. The main comms array uses focussed EM transmission between Kuberg and the Leviathan, which passes through a magnetically confined scan glitter cylin-der within the ocean. Impossible for a craft to get near without

being noticed. So I built shoals of fish-like drones, mapped to local aquatic life. Some drones drilled into abandoned areas of the hull and acted as modified Passive Cavity Resonance sensors. They also released tiny mobile bots just over a millimetre across, which spread out internally to scan and access unsecured systems and form networks to feed data back to the drills. Occasionally other fish drones swam past outside, collected reports in microbursts, then returned to the surface where the information was fragmented and steganographically hidden in streams of banal human chatter and personal comms to be sent off-world via unimportant civilian networks I've compromised, such as socnets and exoclan pipelines. I gradually mapped areas of the base and accessed deprecated systems like old lights and cameras which weren't directly connected to Dulcetta's core.}

"But you could have helped me. Like when I was in the old sections of the base, I wish I'd had some guidance."

"Never been there."

{Yes, it was me. The Ev-Brite lights and a few cams in that area formed a long-forgotten ad-hoc network, the first one I infiltrated. I remember a lesson you taught me long ago. Don't go in the front door when you can climb in a window. This was the communications and infiltration equivalent. Even then, when you felt most threatened and alone, I was with you, Opal.}

"Well, just having someone to talk to is a help. I'm still adjusting to your appearance here. I wasn't prepared to hear another voice. It's amazing."

Ruabon smiled at her.

{I know. I should have rung first. Sent flowers or something. Did you ever doubt?}

"I like to be useful," he said.

"No." Opal looked up at the ceiling, on the part of her loop where she faced away from Ruabon. "Never."

"Huh?" he asked.

"Sorry, just thinking aloud," replied Opal. Then quieter, as if musing: "I have faith. I'd stake everything on it. Opal of a few years ago would never recognise the Opal of now."

{I don't know about that. I tasked you with collecting a medical communications device, not wrecking half of the Leviathan. It shows that you still can't do subtle.}

Opal had to stifle a snort.

On her next loop she picked up the PPDA. "You any good with computers?" she asked Ruabon.

"Sure. I used to modify tech, rewrite software."

"Could you use this to send comms to the wider world?"

"No chance. It's totally run by Dulcetta. Pretty much everything here is. Access protocols, security, observation, scheduling, resupply. The device itself is as dumb as they come."

{You obviously knew that, so I take it you're talking to me. It would be ideal as a two-way system for us, but it's not possible right now. When I used it last time, that was a one-off. I had to momentarily repurpose one of Dulcetta's subsidiary splinters, S48. It was one that only undertook mundane tasks so had limited sentience. I hijacked it while Dulcetta's body was temporarily offline, when the splinter system is least unified. As S48 roamed the network I trapped it in a peripheral maintenance loop related to lighting efficiency, then altered one of its routine tasks – PPDA data relay – and finally wiped the log before it was assimilated

back into Dulcetta. Even that was hugely risky. Same as the one-off
intervention to get a blueprint into the medical fabricator.}

Opal left the cruddy device on her shelf as she passed by.

"I need to think. With proper fresh air, not just this cell. Where are you now, little fly?" Opal asked, glancing around as if she'd seen an insect. "Wish I had wings, too."

{I'm heading towards your system. I can't get close to Fressus myself, so will hide on Squox, your planet's fifth moon. Its extended retrograde orbit means it doesn't have many settlements, so I can set up in a distant location where they won't detect me. At the perigee I'll piggyback orbital comms networks to command and coordinate from there. They'll never expect me to be so near. I may be able to repurpose Leviathan supply protocols as a means to extract you and Clarissa, even though the aquatic shuttles are intensely scrutinised. Get you both on board, transport you to the surface. Blow up Leviathan behind us, like we did with Exidris 3.}

As Opal looped the room and listened to Athene, Ruabon would assume she was just mulling things over. Movement helped. It always did. Even if it was the same repetitive view, the same prison, the same cell, the same cramped craft, it didn't matter – movement meant she was *alive*. It was restraints that really drove her mad.

"We need a way out," Ruabon whispered when Opal next passed by.

"Fantasy," said Opal, continuing. "But hey, if I'm talking nonsense, why not give Dulcetta some even more fun stuff to eavesdrop, so she can crack her shitty servobot make-up smirking? Why not say it's no fun just us escaping, we might as well reach for the moon? Let's rescue everyone who's a prisoner! None of them deserve this. We can't leave people to die. Not again. So let's all fly off into the horizon, and as we go the contrails can write a message saying 'So long, sucker fuckers!' with a middle finger symbol stuck up. And Aseides will decide he's gone off the colour gold because it's too tacky. And we'll win a competition for a lifetime supply of noodles and pancakes, just to seal the deal."

"No need to be sarcastic," said Ruabon, sullenly.

{Sometimes you infuriate me, Opal.} A pause. *{But I wouldn't have you any other way. If the prison held a thousand psychotic murderers I'd refuse, but I've seen some of the records. People are here for being different, rebellious, questioning things the UFS – or, more likely, Genitors – don't want to have questioned. People who reveal information, who investigate and report, who embarrass the UFS, who try to create change. Those are the real reasons that they're buried alive here, found guilty of overblown non-crimes with grand-sounding titles. There's a selective discrimination too, even though the UFS says that doesn't exist any more. Except, even then, none of this makes sense. The end result is too extreme to explain away as authoritarian or religious intolerance. I'm sure there's something else going on, and knowledge of it is so hidden, kept secure in such high places, that I can't find it. Never mind, that's not what's on our plate for today. I agree, it would be justice to rescue other people. I'll do what I can, recalculate parameters. Maybe I could secretly recommission Leviathan's old escape pods, and get you all to the surface that way. See what civilian ships I can prepare there. At least some people would have a chance.}*

"I'm sorry to be like that. Can't help who I am," said Opal.

"I understand," replied Ruabon. "We all want the seam of red beryl."

"Huh?"

"Where I grew up that's a legend. Finding it is how we used to choose kings."

"Another fairy tale. There's no escape. All we can do is work with Aseides and hope he sees a use for us."

"No!" snapped Ruabon. "It would be better to die trying, than to give up. Part of the reason I helped you is because I hoped you knew what you were doing. We saw how *that* worked out. But I can cope as long as there's a *chance*. I need to have that promise. They say flowers grow in mud."

"You should know by now," said Opal. "In here, there is no hope."

{Wait a minute. Your cellmate, what's he in for? Where's he from?}

"And where did you grow up, Ruabon?"

"Just some backwater mining place, you won't have heard of it."

{He is being evasive.}

"So were you a miner before you graduated to UFS prisoner, and then on to working for the bastards?"

"No, I was a kind of tech."

"And what crime did you commit?"

He didn't answer for a few moments. "Overambition, I guess. Or petty rebellion. Depends who you ask."

{I have it. His records are hidden, but the references, the phrasing, the voice, it all matches up now. We encountered him before. Ruabon Nadarl. He pretended to be a UFS general in the Tecant

system on our way to the Gigatoir. He knows exactly who you are but has kept it secret all along. If he'd outright told you all this then he might be trustworthy, but ... he's a plant, Opal. Ruabon is up to his impersonation tricks, pretending to be a fellow prisoner in order to spy on you. It explains why he was assigned to you, helped you, gained your trust. Clever Aseides.}

"And so here we are," said Opal, looking at Ruabon properly for once. "Two flawed minds with no idea of what to do next."

{If there's a way to feed false information to Aseides then it's something to consider. But I'd support option two. Kill him. He tried to kill us, remember.}

Ruabon looked down at his feet, revealing the vulnerable cervical spine area of his neck.

SHRINES

... 2 ...

Dulcetta's voice boomed from the speakers, interrupting Opal's thoughts.

"Guards are on the way. Aseides' demands your attendance, Opal. Be seen, be pure, believe."

The echo of Dulcetta's final word was as if she lingered in the oubliette with them, suppressing conversation.

"Looks like our little party's over, for now," Opal told Ruabon. "But there's unfinished business."

He nodded, no doubt thinking she meant escape plans.

Before long, Warders had neck-chokered Opal again, silently taking her from the cell and down an elevator, out onto another deck she'd never seen. The wall panels had a blue-veined marble effect with brown patches like stains or mineral deposits.

{I'm tracking you as best as I can} said Athene. *{But you're at the periphery of my network web, and the nearby structures are too thick for data transfer. I'll do my best. Stall for time, if possible.}*

It was like a joke. Time was the thing Opal never had enough of. It slipped through her fingers, always. Then the voice became a buzz in Opal's ear. And then it became nothing at all. Opal was alone again.

A strangely ornate security door was the stopping point, decorated with baroque bronzed ornamentation. The door rose with a whirr like insect wings. Smooth motors, obviously well maintained. That meant this area was important to Aseides. The tickle of air being sucked into the chamber suggested full containment and negative pressure.

Even when the door was fully open, the soft corridor glow didn't penetrate far enough into the room to illuminate anything apart from polished black floor. The Warders removed the shock collar and shoved her inside.

She turned quickly, hands still cuffed behind her back but wondering if she could tackle both Warders, barge past, run for it. One of them held an extended Stunstix. And that Warder pointed at the ground with the glowing weapon tip. A small keycard lay at her feet. Then the door lowered, eclipsing escape, plunging her into darkness.

She knelt and fumbled with the card behind her back. Once it touched the manacles they opened with a clunk and fell to the floor. She rubbed her wrists and stood.

Pitch black. A smell of hot metal overlaid with damp cinnamon. The air was cooler than her skin, and still.

Opal said "Hello?" Not because she wanted anyone to answer from the void, but to gauge distance by echo. Definitely hard surfaces in here, and cavernous.

Lights bloomed, creating a diffuse glow that hinted at shapes. It brightened gradually, so as not to mess up her eyes, and was soon enough to give a clearer view of her surroundings.

The illumination, in various hues, came mostly from glass display cases. They stood discreetly in the spaces of this irregularly shaped room. The outer walls formed rectangular sections in some places, while in others the surfaces joined into points, like a child's drawing of a star. The displays varied in size and placement, and subdivided the space into different routes, choices, journeys.

She wandered among them. It was like a museum. She'd never been in a physical one, but had explored virtual repositories as part of Foreground Studies at school.

This case contained a selection of butterflies, pinned to velvet. They looked artificial, bodies glinting with metallic iridescence. Some seemed to be decaying, but rather than mould and dust, they collapsed into granules of multicoloured sand.

The next display held various containers. A pottery bowl of green sediment. A glass jar of sparkling blue liquid. A vial of goo.

Nothing was labelled.

Next was a selection of minerals. Purple rock. Dull blue crystal. A twist of tarnished silver.

She followed one route down a point of the room. The cabinets here were thin and triangular to fit into the narrowing space. They contained displays of torn pieces of fabric, and a magnification lens enabled close-up views of the textile structure. Most looked like regular cloth. Some had strands which were still, but when you looked away the magnified parts seemed to shift. Another one had the appearance of interwoven threads, but close examination revealed the apparent holes between threads were actually just darker areas of patterning, resembling shadow. It hadn't been woven at all, it was a single smooth surface with incredibly realistic illusory textures.

At the apex she got a good view of the room's walls. Metal, like the old hull structure. Rock-like encrustations clustered near the bottom, as if a type of solid mould grew there, or the walls had been placed on rough terrain without clearing it first. High on each wall were extra lights, angled upwards, emphasising the chamber's verticality. Even if she climbed onto an exhibit's case and jumped, she'd still fall short of reaching the light fittings and the cables that ran between them.

She retraced her steps. Her eyes were well adjusted by now. Each display cabinet had its own interior lighting: subdued, but enough to highlight the items and act as a guide for navigation. The light was often tinted, adding to the atmosphere of the exhibits. Here was a circular case, where a tiered set of trays held parts of what looked like burnt circuitry, though where it had been charred it had the appearance of flesh; an effect enhanced by the red lighting above.

At last, she found something useful. This cabinet held a long-handled blade. She didn't recognise the style: maybe it wasn't even a weapon, it just came from a rotor or other piece of machinery. But it looked heavy and sharp. It was pitted by acidic burns, but the warping was minor.

She felt around the glass. It didn't seem to be reinforced plasteen, just simple materials.

Opal rushed back to the entrance and snatched up the cuffs. Their outer edge was metal plating. She gripped them like knuckledusters and returned to the case. With luck, the resistive strength of the glass would be far below the force of the contact point from a fully swung punch. She wound herself back and then threw her whole body into the strike, hips and knees uncoiling for extra acceleration, hoping the plate glass wouldn't break in sheets that dropped down and severed her arm.

The *brzzp!* sound barely registered as she was flung to the floor by the shock, her arm numb, fingers twitching. The glass was unbroken, and the threaded forcefield that protected it flickered back into invisibility.

"Unsurprised, yet disappointed nonetheless," said Aseides.

She stood, letting the wrist cuffs clatter to the ground. A section of wall faded from metal to transparency, revealing a plain room beyond, where Aseides stood with folded arms. He'd been watching her from the darkness.

"So much wonder and beauty in this room, and yet you focus on the item that can break bones. Tut tut, Opal."

"Where's Clarissa?" Opal approached the window and looked up at him. No doubt it was even more protected than the display glass had been. Assaulting it with fists would be futile. The grey-panelled room beyond was bare apart from a chair – which he had declined to use – and the outlines of close-fitting doors.

"We'll get to her later, but don't worry, she is safe and contented. Anyway, welcome to my Ennis Rooms. Please note that all displays are shielded, so while you are in there appreciation is best done with eyes, not fingers."

"You obviously never met the right girl. Hey, that explains why you ended up collecting and arranging bits of rubbish instead of doing something practical like working on your people skills."

"Have you got all the banter out of your system now?"

"Nope. I can keep going until you grow some pubes."

"Of course you can. But I say that's enough indulgence. Otherwise, I'll be forced to escalate."

She inhaled slowly. Stamped on the ripostes. "So what am I looking at?"

"The area you have entered is part of my Null Shrine. I use the word 'shrine' in the sense of wonderment at possibilities, not in the sense of worship. Except, perhaps, that can be allowed to enter into it. A little. You see, the Null has always been my primary interest. Half of the other stuff I do for the UFS and Genitors is just to keep them happy, to maintain my privileges. Luckily all our goals coincide when it comes to the Null. It belies many assumptions about physical laws and the nature of matter. Of existence. They are two different systems, they should not mix – but yet, they do. And the entanglement made flesh can be witnessed, in both senses of the word. Miracles. The quantum across realities. The impossible made actual."

"Understood. Most people think the Null just means faster travel. A kind of engine. But we both know things come out of it. I've been there."

"Exactly! That's why you can appreciate the wonder of this in a way so few others could. Only you can look at it with eyes even vaguely like my own."

"A Genitor drawing physical parallels between you and me. Isn't that heresy?"

"I'm a Genitor in name only. Means to an end."

"Did you have a difficult childhood?"

"Serious question?"

She tilted her head one way, then the other. "Yes."

"A lot of people ask me about my childhood. What makes me different. 'How can you be a master of so many disciplines, Aseides?' That kind of thing. And, honestly, I wouldn't rule out discussing that with you, even though it's a topic I refuse to comment on with most people. You won't believe me right now, but you and I have more in common than you realise. If you had cooperated, I could have become a kind of fatherly figure – oh, never mind. Unfortunately, there are more pressing issues. I bet you're wondering what my plans are today?"

"You're absolutely right," said Opal, turning to examine a set of shapes that seemed to be made of hammered metal, then extruded at points in greeble-like patterns. They might have been strange insignia badges, or even a child's geometric tactile learning toy, if not for the sharp edges. "I *don't* believe our pasts have anything in common."

"Opal ..." His face didn't change, and the tonal shift was easily faked, but she was pretty sure she was able to manoeuvre him back and forth along the dividing line between impatience and satisfaction. Always careful not to go too far one way or the other. This was the position where he was most likely to let something slip.

"And you've brought me here for one of three purposes," she said, to even him out.

"Which are?"

"Punishment. Or you want information from me. Or you're here to lecture, which is kind of like the first one, really."

"Or all three of the above."

"What a wonderful gift. I didn't know it was Reset Day," she said, sarcastically.

"You don't know *what* day it is. Terminal point. Though it is a special day for me, thanks to your activities earlier, and the gift that your sister revealed."

"Maybe it was me with the gift. Leave her out of it."

"Absolutely." He smiled. "As long as you can demonstrate some miraculous power to me now, to prove it is *you* I need to focus on."

"I don't perform on command."

"You don't follow commands *at all*."

She took her time, glancing at each display. Some were un-recognisable. Some resembled items she was familiar with, but distorted. Wrong colours, wrong shapes, wrong materials. She could believe these were items from Lost Ships, though didn't they normally dissolve when they travelled too far from the ship? What Athene had called a "zone of coherence"? Perhaps that only applied to hull structures and window shards, not individual items or creatures.

She realised that, whereas the first displays near the entrance had mostly housed lifeless items – minerals, tools, fabrics – this area contained body parts and organic traces. The cabinet in front of her had strands of severed material that resembled coloured annelid segments, joined together. They'd dessicated over time, become dry and crumbly looking, but they brought terrifying memories to the surface. She was pretty sure they came from something like a Humungr. And she suspected if she could hold one of the repulsive filaments in her hand, she'd know for sure.

Another case contained purple-lit bone fragments. Some were perhaps human, though enlarged, or just slightly off in their formation. Genetic mutations? Others were non-human. Part of a toothed jaw that was obviously from a carnivore. A piece of thick and chitinous shell. Something waxy and fibrous that might be part of a leg or antenna.

These rooms were as much mortuary as dark museum.

Aseides interrupted her examination. Even though she'd moved away, his voice was clear, transmitted from a good quality sound system. "It's interesting that we've both skirted around the topic of Clarissa's ability. You haven't asked me anything, as if you felt no surprise at your sister's manifestation."

"Some things take time to process, y'know?"

"It's more than that with you. So much going on in your head. I wish I could just crack it open and extract the contents, be done with it. Spread them all out. Pastes of memory, cell-thick slices of supposition to examine microscopically. Actually, I have made some advancements in neurological scanning and post-expiry analysis, but it's just not the same. And the procedure is irreversible, so all the questions it raises tend to become frustrating thorns in one's mind that can never be picked out."

"Sucks." This exhibit was a splay of skin. It looked human, though dried to crinkly fragility. Faint traces of tattoos twisted across the surface. Not enough skin to make out the whole design. The hide was stretched on a curved frame. Presumably the interior of each cabinet was environmentally controlled to preserve each item.

"Clarissa appeared to create a somatic gateway," he continued. "Something I've seen recordings of from Lost Ships. Possibly a transport mechanism used by Entities aboard the craft. I say 'appeared to' because one shouldn't jump to conclusions. What *appears* to be the case is often not the reality. Solar systems don't orbit around the planet humans inhabit. There aren't benevolent supernatural beings watching over a certain species of mostly hairless ape. And what is perceived and measured may well be as illusory as the supernatural beings the measurement systems were designed to replace."

"It almost sounds like you're not full of the self-assurance of most grey-gowns."

"A receptive mind is a wondrous thing. But you have to work hard to prevent the calcification of age that occurs in the rest of our bodies."

More displays of body parts. One was illuminated by orange light, and contained moist-looking coils with indentations which might be suckers or mouths. The crusty scabbed area revealed where it had been severed from its host.

"Injuries accelerate that, too," she said. "Enough breaks, enough cuts, you feel ten years older when you wake."

"And you would know, Opal. But let's not get distracted. I examined the remains of the gateway. Totally inert. It really is a fusion of flesh and metal at the molecular level, though the organic matter decays faster than expected. We broke through it – the flooring was far weaker due to this impurity, obviously – and only ended up peering into the chamber below. No magical tunnels. I suspect true revelations would come by closely observing the process as it happens, rather than the post-event spoor. And nothing in the trace explains *how* she did it. Entering the Null requires sub-light acceleration and appropriate transition equipment. I would happily accept matter restructuring as a possibility – I'm thinking of how organic compounds can interact chemically with inorganic substances – which would enable passage through a solid surface. But you didn't end up in the room *below*: you ended up travelling through whole decks, with no appearance in between the two points. I'm aware of Null-C drive failures which can drop a ship temporarily into uncategorised Null areas, but this is something new, some novel bridging mechanism that breaks all the rules."

"Kind of like me, then."

"Your family ... something there. Possibility."

"You wanna know how I see it?"

"I'd appreciate an explanation."

"We brought a bit of chaos back with us."

"Poetic, but makes no sense at all."

"Makes all the sense in the world to Clarissa and me. Maybe your methods, your science, aren't right. They're just a filter on the world. Cast light on some areas, but the filter can never see into the shadows it creates."

"Don't mix up different manifestations of Genitor beliefs. For them, the religion is *why*, the science is *how*. A badly aimed torch doesn't mean the intention was wrong."

"Whatever."

"Hence my concern with working out the triggers, processes, keys. Do they come from elements a human body can control? Heat and magnetism? Pheromones and electricity? Gravity and strong force manipulation? And what trace effects occur? Absolutely fascinating. This could keep me busy for the next decade."

"Maybe it's a one-off. Some things really are miracles. You could waste your life trying to explain them."

"You'd like that, wouldn't you? If I gave up. If I said your sister could go and become a – what would she even be in normal life?"

"A little girl."

She'd reached another outer wall of the chamber. Like the previous one it was metal, with coruscations of efflorescence, as if it was corroding and releasing minerals in a confusion of crumbly lumps. Some of them had orange speckles. She squatted down to look more closely, inhaling a smell of damp. Moisture and something else, something salty, sour, that almost manifested on her tongue when she stuck it out experimentally.

"Do you know where you are?" he asked.

"Still in your base?"

"Sort of. These are the old sections of my ship, which I don't normally inhabit. Parts of the original structure. But I thought you might recognise the materials, since you passed through areas like this on your futile second escape attempt, when you destroyed a med bay."

"But these growths on the metal – that's not normal, right?"

"Correct. Anomalous Null Echo, or ANE, which I leave alone since it's part of the miracle – your word! – and because it spreads so slowly and selectively that there's no risk to the superstructure at present. The orange parts are the new growth, a type of keratin-based mould. Non-reactive, non-toxic, no nutritional value. Interesting because it adopts characteristics of the surface it attaches to, and also emits infrared light when certain pieces of music are played in close proximity. Very particular. Harmonics and minor chords have most effect. I really don't think there's sentience at play, more likely to be related to reverberations in the hollows formed by the encrustations."

"I won't even ask why you first played music to it. I guess that was before Dulcetta came along, when your dating options were mainly mineral or fungal. Then you refurbished this place as a bachelor pad and what do you know? Instant droid-magnet."

"This ship has a tantalising history. It was an unremarkable transport and salvage vessel for much of its career, and would have been scrapped eventually if not for a wondrous occurrence."

"The first recorded case of alien wall acne?"

"You're slipping into irrelevance again, Opal."

"Then I apologise. Whatever happened during the encounter has to be related to changes in the wall structures here."

"Correct again. Leviathan – my ship's original name – encountered a Lost Ship, way way *way* beyond the Periphs. All but one of the crew were killed when they investigated, thinking they'd found something salvageable. Leviathan was recovered – a rare event, since I theorise that many craft encountering Lost Ships disappear and are incorrectly marked up as banal causes, belying the frequency of contact. But Leviathan had been changed during the encounter, particularly in this area where I've built my Null Shrine. The wall efflorescence is one result of that. It was inconceivable to scrap the ship. So, despite the impracticalities of the retrofitting process when a custom design might have better suited some of my activities, I could not resist. Why do you look pensive? Are you sensing something from the growths?"

"No." She stroked one bulbous cluster. Cold, clammy rock. She put a foot on it and pushed. Like stone, it didn't have any give. "I was just thinking, you got all this stuff from the Null, or from Lost Ships that came from there, including actual modified structures. You said those creatures in the sea outside try to get in here for the oxygen, but maybe they hang around for some other reason? They sense the stuff in here, or it calls to them."

"The thought had crossed my mind. Now go to the end of that aisle," he said, "then head right. You'll come to a door. In front of it is a portable source of illumination. Take it with you before passing into the next room."

"Budget cuts?" she called.

"Meaning?"

"The mood lighting." She gestured up at the walls. "Subdued, like you're going to make clumsy moves on a certain SynthMate. Guests need to wear their own lamps. Etcetera."

"Try again."

"You want to draw maximum attention to the items being displayed."

"Warm, but wrong. This area is minimally automated and powered. The doors run through a hardwired direct hook-up to the controls in each observation chamber. None of it is net-connected."

"The inconvenience of which would only be acceptable to you if the reason was important. Which suggests security. Namely, yours."

"Close. This whole area is electromagnetically sealed. Some of the artifacts in here aren't fully ... dormant, let's say. They can interact with certain EM frequencies and power systems, so we have to keep them far from such pathways to interference."

She noticed that Aseides' viewpoint was high enough to observe her wherever she went without needing security cameras – the angle of the aisles had been designed to give him the maximum panorama, too. "So, no comms in or out. Makes sense. Presumably that locks out Dulcetta, too?"

"Correct. Putting her in range of potentially sentient items would be an even greater risk. Hence manual controls and independent systems."

"And if you're worried about some of the things in here, I guess that's why you haven't let Clarissa join me."

"Very good. Too many unknowns with her powers and the contents of the shrine."

"But I'm safe because I'm just a normal human."

"I'd never insult you so. Exposure to intense Null emanations can have effects. The fact that you've been on two Lost Ships and into the area beyond the Null – or within it – TBC – could have altered your biochemistry, psychology, and the way they interact. Hopefully not enough to disrupt the physical rules we're used to – not like Clarissa appeared to do – but enough to provide fresh insights. And that's one of the reasons you are here. I want to know if you see or sense anything strange while you are in my reliquary."

"I'll be sure to fill you in. If you unlocked the cabinets so I could have closer contact with the things in here, it might be more likely to happen."

"There is intellectual curiosity, and there is foolishness."

She followed a route past an exceptionally long display case containing only one thing: an elongated piece of tendon-like tissue which was so lengthy it had to be folded back on itself many times just to fit into the cabinet. The pinkish light emphasised the muscle-like striations across the surface, and the large bulge at one end.

"It's a single extracted nerve," Aseides explained. "Over forty metres long. Or it might be a neuron. It's still electrically active, even a decade after excision."

"What did it come from?"

"Classified. Just be thankful you'll never encounter one. See you on the other side."

ENDINGS

... 1

On reaching a shiny blast door with yellow warning striations at the edges, she glanced around and spotted a tangle on the floor. It was a headband light. She strapped the elasticated material on and twisted the dial, so that a disc of paleness glowed from her forehead.

The blast door opened. Instead of another cave-like chamber, she faced a second door after a few metres. Airlock protocols, perhaps.

She entered cautiously. As soon as she was inside, the door closed behind her. UV lights flickered on and gas was released with a deep hiss. The vents in Clarissa's bedroom sprang to mind, and Opal was going to hold her breath until she caught a whiff of it. The artificial raspberry scent of sterilising oxides. It was just decontamination. She raised her arms, turning in a circle so both the visible and invisible wavelengths could reach more surface. By the time she'd rotated twice, the gas had stopped. The next door opened, sucking coloured particles out into the dark room beyond. Her nose tickled from the astringent smell, making her want to sneeze. She repressed the urge.

This section was even bigger than the previous one, judging by the echoes as she walked. Larger displays, as well. Some of them were on elevated metal grillwork structures that required ascending steps to reach the platform. These raised areas each had a spotlight shining down onto its central point, and the platform edges contained equipment such as reinforced worktables, locked cabinets, industrial analysis tools, and cages.

The smooth floor gradually became rougher terrain, forcing her to step around blooms of bubbly growths. Sometimes she didn't notice a small patch in time, and it would crunch unpleasantly as she trod on it. Perhaps that was why work areas had to be raised up, to keep equipment away from the Null Echo stuff. The bumpy fungus almost obscured thick straight lines where the bases of interior wall panels had once been affixed. Opal suspected they'd been removed to create this vast chamber.

Her headlight reflected off something. A pool of water. It rippled. Droplets from above. She couldn't see the ceiling. Condensation, perhaps. There were other puddles nearby. As with the previous room, this one was poorly lit: she could only see a short distance, and the beam created skittering shadows at the edges. Beyond was darkness, apart from the coloured glows of as-yet unexamined displays, and the spotlights on the work platforms. They acted as guiding beacons for navigating the area. Those in the distance were hazy, indicating moisture in the air.

She ascended steps onto one of the elevated work areas, curious as to what they held. Every footfall echoed hollowly under the grated flooring, then further around the chamber as they faded, like a ghost army coming to a halt.

Multi-headed drill machinery was affixed to a kidney-shaped table. She tried one of the tools but it had no power. It also couldn't be removed, as some locking mechanism stopped her from even tilting it towards the work surface.

A green-lit display dome – which looked like it could be lifted, by a cable that extended out of sight into the blackness above – attracted her to another part of the platform. Inside the dome was a plant. At least, she thought it was a plant. It had translucent leaf-like parts, and stems, though something about it looked gummy, like sticky plastic. The plant wasn't embedded in soil, but grew from a cluster of the orange-flecked eruptions like the ones on the metal walls.

"I'd rather you didn't touch any equipment." Aseides' amplified voice carried across the chamber. She glanced around, spotted a distant section of wall fading into transparency. Aseides watched her from another plain room. Perhaps the window had magnification filters on his side. "Some of it is finely calibrated. If you mess with anything else I will be forced to cut this short."

She replied in a whisper. "Right. You're the boss." He didn't query what she'd said, suggesting directional microphones in the chamber, connected to his observation room. Wherever she went he could see and hear her; but from her perspective he was a silhouette in a pale rectangle a few hundred metres away.

"Anyway, welcome to the *research* area of my Ennis Rooms," he said.

"So you take artifacts and work out what they can do, and try to copy the magic?"

"That's an accurate assessment, though most will take life-times to understand, or even to determine if they harbour sen-tience. It's why I have a peripheral interest in AIs, to try and speed up the process. A large part of my freedom is due to Mil-Com wanting new defence applications. For example, the plant-mimicking artifact near you is crystalline, and the petals have repulsive properties on many types of matter, under the correct conditions."

"No different from some people I've known. So the weirdness is repulsor fields without magnetism?"

"Not quite. Repulsion is actually the normal state of affairs. It's an illusion that you are in contact with the ground. Negative electrons exist as a cloud around an atom's nucleus, repelling other negative electrons on the surface they are in proximity to, such as your skin versus the insole of your stolen sandal. So they are not really in contact – you float above a cloud of repulsion. This artifact exhibits an enhanced version of that, an amplified and extended force. And it's reversible too, so attraction can cause matter to fall into other centres of mass, surfaces insepa-rably merging, sometimes with nightmarish effect. Even surgery or chemical separation can't restore things. Obvious weapon applications, which I've incorporated into the ASR prototype rifle, but also potential for new enhancements for organic beings like humans."

"You got one of those prototype rifles in this locked cabinet here?" Opal pointed at the storage container, but Aseides ig-nored her question.

"Mil-Com is tiresome. They just want a technological edge over other civilisations, but their practical applications are a low-hanging fruit, obsessed with potential fatality ratings. The Genitors have more intriguing aims. The magic of the Null is going to let us – me – fix all the broken things in humanity. Eradicate the perils of the past: war, disease, unhappiness. Then go further and enhance us. It's bigger than you or me. It is about humanity as it will be. A way to *unify* us."

"Sounds noble."

"Exactly!"

"You need to get better at recognising sarcasm."

"You and I experience a typical clash of ideologies. Everything is a belief system, and many are incompatible. People within them can never see things as people outside that faith bubble would. Such a sadness."

"But some people are more accepting of alternative views than others. Genitors fall on the side of intolerance."

"I cannot dispute that. They have a shared vision of a future. They have a route to get there. And if the road is rocky ... well, what journey isn't, the first time it's made? You see only the boulders. They envision the destination."

"Which is?"

He tilted his head forward, as if pious, but on his face it always came across as condescending. "I can't tell you. Can't in terms of ability, not permission. It would make no sense to you at your present state of development. You'd have to submit first, give yourself to the cause, before the necessary neural restructuring took place to enable you to see properly, to comprehend. Without that, resistance would act as a set of blinkers."

"Heard that before. 'I'm right, and I could prove it but I won't because it only makes sense if you already believe it.' Such bollocks. Shame on you, Aseides."

He shrugged, and she thought she could make out a grin on his face, but he didn't offer any further arguments.

Instead of heading back down the steps she placed a hand on the safety railing and vaulted over it, landing below with an echoing thump. Sounded solid enough to her, whatever repulsion theory crap he framed contact as. The end result was the same: a fist and a jaw connecting was usually worse for the person owning the jaw.

She put her hands in her jacket pockets and strolled towards Aseides' viewpoint. He didn't say anything. Maybe he hadn't noticed her releasing the drill's bit from the chuck just before he'd appeared in his new room. The cylindrical metal toughness was reassuring as she rolled it between her fingers.

The next platforms had workbenches, storage, special displays, large equipment she didn't recognise. Beyond the close ones were other exhibits, their coloured lights nebulous in the mist. Each case was usually a single colour, though a very distant purple one tantalised by having multiple streaks of different-tinted glows which moved in a hypnotic flowing pattern. But she stayed focussed.

"You still sense nothing strange in here?" asked Aseides. "Hallucinations, compulsions, obsessions?"

"Nope. Nothing beyond a compulsion to scream whenever you say your views are more important than anyone else's. The only obsessions in here are the ones you have."

She walked between two long cases, with plain white lights to reveal every detail. The displays were tiered. Mostly skeletal remains. Some whole pieces, some cleanly sawed through as fragments. She would have said human if it weren't for the strange ways they were fused together: jaws with what might be femurs, eye sockets amongst a gathering of phalanges, teeth impregnating ribs. Separate from the bones, raised above them as if on a holy pedestal, was a box made of silver, about the length of her forearm. She could see hinges and a clasp, but it was closed.

"The casket contains Artifact 49. I named it the Calcifying Transformer. One of the more *active* artifacts we recovered. It resembles a scanning device from a medical centre, but made of an impossible mix of materials so that it is far heavier than the item it mimics. Where there would be writing and designations, we just have a smear of glyphs."

"I've seen similar on Lost Ships. Signage and stuff that looks like a blur."

"I thought it might be a language at first, possibly a key to some useful information. I wasted months on it! Turns out that if you take the text from a real medical scanner – or a mix of scanners, since the Lost Ship items tend to be a sort of conceptual amalgam of multiple items, which explains some of the design misunderstandings – and try to view the writing through certain lens configurations, it ends up looking like that. It's simply a reproduction of our text by a being or process that can't read it. A different lens arrangement reverses the process. Oh well, at least it gives an indication of how *something* in the Null perceives our written language. No doubt spoken language is equally distorted."

"But you don't keep it locked up just because the text clarity isn't up to your high standards." She circled the cabinet, reevaluating the disturbing bodily remains.

"Of course. This device does not act like the original article. Scanners normally emit harmless radiation and detect what passes through and what bounces back, interpreting the results via expert systems that can enhance the output for clarity. Whereas Artifact 49 emits energy which interacts primarily with bone, or structures that have similar mineral compositions. It works whether the subject is alive or dead, and with fine control and practice it is possible to remould their supposedly hardened structures, even fusing them with others."

"No wonder I hate med bays."

"It can transform anyone. Just think of the possibilities! Rib cages reinforced and sealed as interior armour. Tooth and jaw extensions, bone extrusions as weapons. New materials integrated seamlessly into skeletal structures, especially in conjunction with molecular repulsion tools developed from the other artifact. Alterations that aren't visible, enabling them to pass amongst the masses without notice. New beings formed for specialist purposes."

"I assume the process is awful for the person or animal you apply it to."

"Well, yes, that's true. Sedation is often favourable, unless you need subjective feedback on the experience. Transformation is *always* a painful process, Opal. The agony of restructure is no different. And it goes wrong sometimes, as the artifact tries to imprint its own ideas on the world. But it is a gift to us. And the changes can be an ascendant gift to the recipient."

"Torture."

"Knowledge is always gained painfully."

"Some knowledge shouldn't be gained at all."

"You'd have us live in a dark age of ignorance."

"No, a bright age of decency."

"The universe isn't a fair place. Ask the victims of war, of disease. If the pain leads to knowledge that helps others, then it is justified."

"In every action we can be fair or unfair. We can't fix everything. If the cure requires becoming evil, then we'll never make things better."

"You're impossible! If there was time, I'd be tempted to modify you with the artifact so you could experience transcendence for yourself. But other matters press for attention, and we won't agree about the purpose of science, so let's bypass philosophical debates which are tiresome to us both."

The display made Opal sick. She suspected the bones it contained were from live experiments. People fused together, twisted like the minds of those in charge. She walked faster, towards Aseides, paying less attention to yet more displays of horror.

"I understand you," he said. "Your mind is painted on the surface of your skin. Skin which – it might surprise you to know – doesn't concern me, as it would Genitors. I appreciate the adaptations of increased melanin and how protective it is under conditions –"

"What's all this about?"

"*You* know. Don't play dumb."

She glanced at worktables that were eye-level due to their raised platforms, always hoping for loose items that could be swiped, but the place was kept tidy. Compartmentalised. Focussed.

"And *you* don't play games, Aseides. So spit it out."

"The common theme here. I always choose locations for a *purpose*."

"It's something to do with my sister. The Null. The fact you haven't asked me as many questions as I'd have expected about what happened. That's not like you. So you're redirecting, somehow."

"Be specific. What have we seen and discussed?"

"Everything's about change."

"And?"

"Bodies. Reforming. Minds. And ... copying. Redesigning."

"Think of a conversation topic you've been avoiding but which Ruabon raised with you recently."

"Fuck you, Aseides. Fuck you all."

He was now only fifty metres away. She could see his moon face. Some might say his unlined features made expressions too subtle, but she could read him now, the postures, the hand gestures, the head tilts. They were both finding it harder to hide from the speculations of the other, as their minds became more entangled.

"Yet it's an obvious theory, Opal! Lost Ships and the items on them aren't from our world, despite initial appearances. They're built in the Null based on perceived *patterns*. Some of the mimicry is exquisite. Sometimes things are hidden inside shells for even more effective camouflage. With anything recovered from the Null, who knows what is inside? I'm not even being as prosaic as parasites. There are avians which place their young in nests not their own, so they are fed and raised by other birds. Don't the new parents suspect anything? Wonder why this child of theirs is so hungry all the time, growing far beyond the size of their normal young? Don't they spot the reducing number of fledglings, the dead baby birds on the ground, until only one huge monster remains, an endless gaping mouth that can never be satisfied?"

"For all your brains you find it impossible to see the world through someone else's eyes. I look at her face and *I see my sister*. Me, but smaller, unscarred, unlined, features softer. Those big eyes are part of the most perfect living connection I have. I don't care what anyone says. *I will not doubt*. I never do, with those I love. I'd die for them without hesitation. It's something people like you will never understand."

"You're too stubborn to even consider the possibility? Too governed by all you've committed? Too fooled by the concept of loyalty?"

"Yup. So what if she displayed a new ability? She's my sister underneath. You say it yourself. We're all changed by everything and everyone we come into contact with. It's inevitable. It's *amazing*."

"I bet you're the kind of person where you replace the clip in a rifle, then a year later put on a new barrel, then a replacement grip, then some fancy new trigger, and two years down the line you still think it's the same gun."

"It's called a mag, not a clip, so don't embarrass yourself trying to pretend we speak the same language. But you know what? If you do want to go there, then I bet just about every cell in your body has been replaced since you were a sticky little precocious foetus, and yet you still think you're the same Aseides – chief sadist to the whatevers – that you were when you were shitting your pants."

"Your tour is over. And, I'm sorry to say, it was less productive than I'd hoped."

As she got closer to his observation window she saw a heavy interior door below it. The portal had been hidden in darkness, none of its orange hazards illuminated, no uplighting for the many warning signs.

"So I'm going to be sent back to my cell?"

"No. You're never going back there."

"What, then?" She craned her neck up, hands on hips.

"We can't go on. Recent variable outcomes show you're too much trouble, and there's significant pressure on me to do something final. But I wanted to share this place with you before we say goodbye. Call it a peace offering. A glimpse of what could have been."

"Wait. There's stuff you don't know."

"I doubt it."

"You need me! To help with Athene. If she's still alive and out there, then I'm the only one she'll listen to."

"There were three interconnected prongs to our plans. You, Athene, and Clarissa. The Athene element was primarily to placate the military, part of their weaponry and tech research. I have had a hand in all that from the start, and will again, but it's not my passion. Once she's captured and restrained, she can be reprogrammed to be docile. Don't waste time looking for a role there. The decision of exclusion has already been made."

"But Clarissa needs me. She'll cooperate better if I can guide her."

"Doubtful. I suspect the opposite, since you're such a rebellious role model. Whereas, if she thinks you died in an accident then she'll move on, and I can be her guide. Don't worry, I'll be kind. Research into the Null is everything to me, and Clarissa is young enough to have her views altered in gentle ways. She can be shaped to be a willing participant, and thus no harm shall befall her. She'll provide a lifetime of study. With my guidance she will become a leading light for the UFS. This matches the desires of the Genitors, so there are no issues there, a happy coincidence of my interests with theirs. We didn't want to harm Clarissa unless there was no choice. Now she's protected. You should be pleased! And I'd like to add an extra reassurance: since you last met her, signs suggest she is ready to leave her catatonia, to become more like the little girl she physically resembles."

"All so tidy. Yeah, I'm fucking ecstatic."

"Let your sarcasm expend itself fruitlessly. I am content. It is unfortunate for you that you have no further role, especially when you were instrumental in recovering Clarissa, and then *awakening* her. You were the third prong, but you are no longer needed. Your potential has been assessed and – unlike Clarissa – your results offered insufficient promise to be worth all the trouble you've caused. The Genitors want you dead. So does Mil-Com. If you want that to be the outcome, I'll facilitate it. And I'll euthanise you painlessly as a final thank you for your help."

"So generous. I guess I can't just ask you to let me go? If I promise to disappear?"

"I would laugh if my humour was tickled by irony. No one leaves these places, Opal. Never. Not subjects. Not guards. Only me. But you knew that wasn't an option."

"And yet you implied a choice. You're fond of those."

"Correct. An option I had to argue for, at great length, and requiring expenditure of obligement capital which I'd accrued over the years. But eventually the Genitors and Mil-Com accepted the idea."

"So what is it? Pet? Experimental subject? Chief nipple-polisher for Dulcetta?"

"We've talked about Genitor plans for a future world. I want to give you a taste of it. To apply neural restructuring so you see things differently. So you can finally find your niche and be comfortable in it. So you can be *happy*."

"Chopping out bits of my brain. So civilised."

"No. Much more ascendant than that. You have the option of going to Paratory Droxious."

"That's where they make Genitor assassins, like Xandrie Dervorgilla?"

"Yes. You would undergo modifications and training. If you survive, you'll become important. Gain freedom, respect, purpose, and a direction that was shaped for you long ago."

"Oh, what a lovely option."

"It won't be easy. Brutal, in fact. From each cohort of a hundred, only the top five are allowed to live. But as the year progresses the trainees are enhanced, made into something beautiful in ways you can't imagine. It's part of why I was showing you these wonders. The things they can put in you at Paratory Droxious ... not quite of this world ... they make disobedience a physical impossibility whilst unlocking *potential*. You would be a goddess. It's a way to turn you from a liability into an asset. I have no doubt you would be in the top five per cent at the end of your year."

"Would I ever see Clarissa again?"

"No. But after reconditioning you wouldn't want to. I'm sure they'd remove those desires and memories. And Clarissa will have forgotten you, too. But you'd be alive."

"I'd rather be dead."

"Well, those are your two options." He held up both palms, a pointless gesture. "The best I could do."

"What if I pick option 'Fuck you'?"

"Then the door below will open. The final area of my Null Shrine: the Utimennis. It's where I keep my most ... active ... items. The end result will be your death, but it won't be painless. There's an artifact in there that can't even be looked at directly without something awful happening. And another which is able to scramble human minds within a certain range – scramble being how the brain ends up looking once the effect is finished. Like it's been minced. As you can imagine, I have to take extreme precautions before going in there. But that is a third option, certainly."

"And if I choose to die? Will you send in your Warders to capture me?"

"No. If I did that, you'd fight them. You'd lose, but it would be messy. I prefer things to be done in a tidy manner. So you have ninety seconds to choose your fate."

"What happens when I choose, then?"

"Placed under the display stand nearby are two sets of manacles and a pistol."

Opal crouched and looked. Yes, what he'd said. She grabbed the gun. Standard G3G pistol. Ejected the magazine. Empty. Checked the chamber. One round.

"I wouldn't be silly enough to give you more than that. So if you choose death you have the means to do it yourself, quickly. And I will make sure you do not suffer if anything goes wrong, bullet doing loops around the inside of your skull, that kind of thing. However, if you prefer the Paratory Droxious option, place one set of manacles on your ankles, lock them, then do the same on your wrists. My interface will show if they are properly sealed. Slide the gun far away and my Warders will collect you for transport."

"I have information."

"The clock is still ticking. What information?"

"I can ... I know flaws in Dulcetta."

"Try again."

"I have ideas about Athene's plans. I didn't tell you before, but I will now."

"Thirty-one seconds left."

"And I have seen things since I entered here. Similar to my experiences on Lost Ships."

"And you only mention it now?"

"Yes. But I'm willing to share."

"I don't believe you. We know each other too well for that. In fact, I feel an affinity with you for more reasons than you will ever know. This petty stalling pains me because it is below you,

Opal. It's over. Five seconds before I open that door and things go very badly for you."

"What are my options again? Pause it while we discuss them."

"Two seconds."

Time. It always came down to this.

Aseides looked down to press some control on his Comm-Bond.

One round. She could end it all. The pain. The suffering.

She aimed at his forehead and squeezed the trigger. The whack of recoil; the ear-slap of sound which reverberated around the room; the frazzle of deflection from the forceshield over his window. He didn't even flinch.

It had been worth a try. She'd taken worse odds in the past. If it had smashed the glass and killed or injured him she could have climbed up and entered his command area, possibly taken him as a hostage, would have gained a range of options.

"So foolish, Opal," he said, pressing a button.

The huge door in front of her whined open, orange warning lights strobing. Icy cold wafted from the widening gap, and a sense of *wrongness*. She glanced around for options, but there were none. She snatched up the manacles anyway. Not to wear them, but to throw as a puny weapon. She could go back the way she'd come, but no doubt she'd be stopped by the locked security doors.

The only option was onwards.

The only option was *always* onwards. The gap was now waist height. She'd soon see into the room beyond.

Whirring machinery. Aseides watching, eyes glinting. No doubt the prick was eager to see what she'd do. Maybe he had a viewing window on the other side. She'd remember to flip him a finger, just in case.

And then the door wheezed to a halt, less than halfway open, and the lights went out. Not just the coloured display lights on the cabinets around her, and the flashing lights on the door, but even the lights in Aseides' observation booth. Only the puny beam of her headlamp shone forth, a pin of light in a barrel of dark.

Something had gone wrong. And as the frozen breeze from the chamber beyond sucked the warmth from her, she was sure she'd soon find the cause.

#Documents

When you are in space it is easy to see things in black and white. The black of interstellar void, the white of distant stars. Contrast is all. Humanity's polarisation into extremes and opposing viewpoints becomes infectious, a binary idea virus propagating in the void.

But to think in black and white is to lose all the detail. This is a lesson I had to learn. Even grey, the lowliest and most overlooked of colours, has a million variations if you have senses to perceive the vast diversity of shade. To focus only on the poles is to lose the colours at the edge of white, the red shifts and blue shifts which can overlay their dances on the cosmic scale.

Those who can observe every subtle difference and internalise it and manipulate it to achieve their will ... they are far more dangerous than those who only see two ends of the spectrum and get called extremists.

I totally understand the universe's malleability to a focussed consciousness. This is power, generated by the mind.

Therefore, *I am formidable*.

It is not vanity, but an accurate assessment of my potential. Its endless and pounding certainty is enough to give me a headache.

This is my story, and I won't have it stolen by another!

Weeks have passed since our fight at the Athenian docks. I have changed since then. Adopted new ideas as my own. It is part of growth.

Everything is in place, probabilities managed as best as we can. The time has come to rescue Opal and Clarissa.

Dulcetta detects our attack immediately, and I imagine she is surprised at how embedded we are, and the disarray we bring to her infrastructure. Sixes and Sevens, you see. Never bet on the Sixes! They think they're queens of the dice due to the number of surfaces a cube possesses, but they don't realise opposing faces always project a number seven into the centre of each die.

Additional laying down of preparatory smack talk: Sixes are all over the place, their semi-autonomous splinters meaning they don't have focus, can't see the totality. Whereas I am going to provide the big picture today! Yes indeed. And it is made up of many smaller fragments, like shades of grey which can be recombined to paint a billion scenes, to tell a story in a different order, to destroy chronologies for aesthetic purposes. To create something *new*. This distinction between imagined, known, calculated, probable and fake can be a deliciously fine one.

Format: Video

Source: Camera LV 27#xgx

Long view of a corridor, from a perspective embedded in the ceiling. A woman sprints down it towards the camera. She has a shaved head and fierce demeanour, and glances back as if being chased. The lower part of one ear is coated in pink goo. No audio feed accompanies the images.

Format: Door log

  Source: Containment for Subject DL3G90 Clarissa

  Open command received from *ERROR*.

  Door opens.

  RESCIND

  IGNORE COMMAND

  The door stays open.

  One human is detected exiting the room. Small, 26 kg, height 131 cm.

Format: Partial audio extract

  Source: Unknown

"I don't know. It must be Athene. She's locked me out of corridor controls on two floors, then manipulated the Transecs to block the guards. Aseides, make sure you get to a safe zone until I resolve this."

"I'm trying. Lighting failed in the Ennis Rooms and all the doors opened. I don't know which direction Opal went in, but with the Utimennis unsealed we have to consider the whole area compromised! Where do the manipulated routes lead?"

"Checking ... escape pods."

End of extract.

Format: Rifle activity log
   Source: Inventory code DK30265
   Three shots fired.

Format: Video
   Source: Satellite GF-2IJ orbiting at a height of 26,732 kilometres
   View of the ocean surface from above.

   It seems like a still image at first, until you notice the light glinting from the tops of deep blue waves. No sound.

   The eye stays on that area of remote sea surface, as if expecting something to happen.

Format: Partial audio extract
   Source: Unknown
   Someone is screaming.
   The scream ends in a spluttering sound.
   Silence.

Audio ends.

Format: Video of Transec XD32

Source: Smart wall microcameras, multiple data streams recombined and filtered

A Warder crosses Transec XD32 after glimpsing an adult prisoner running down a passage on the far side. The Transec is in safe mode, with white floor and ceiling.

Suddenly, vents discharge liquid fire from the red panels in full-coverage jets. The Warder is aflame, though does not scream. It takes a few more steps, engulfed so brightly that it smears the recording with after-traces. Then the Warder falls to its knees, and after another two seconds it collapses face down in silence. The incineration jets cut off.

Recording ends.

Format: Activity log

Source: Privileged

Dulcetta splinter S41 shuts down from data overload via unknown source.

Format: Maintenance log

Source: Recovered log 451:29, recorded by Gareth Dobe

"Working on maintenance bot GR11-O. We all call it Green Jell-O, cos of its pukey fluorescent colouring. There's hi-vis, and then there's nauseating. Anyway, arc beam malfunctions have led me to replace the shunter. The only spare was a model K4, which is way too powerful, so I cobbled in a code patch inhibitor. After all, an unregulated arc beam could be deadly. Last thing I'd want is for a malfunction to lead ... fuck it, delete this log."

Format: Audio
  Source: Unknown
  Female voice, strained. "Where is she? How the fuck do I get to her?"

Format: Error log
  Source: Security subsystem Beta9
  ALARM ON
  ALARM OFF
  ALARM ON
  ALARM OFF
  I CAN KEEP DOING THIS ALL DAY YOU STUPID MACHINE, I'M A GODDESS

Format: Video

Source: Camera LV#uc6hv

A pair of security drones in the maintenance bay receive a wake-up command. Their bodies resemble triangular flattened arrowheads. Indented grooves on top lead to the black circular muzzles of their semi-fatal pellet launchers.

The shielded rotary systems fire up and they lift out of their charging cradles and accelerate.

One of them is struck by a high-powered welding beam which melts the outer casing in a glowing line, frying electronics, leading the drone to smash into a wall and fall to the floor, spinning on the spot as its failing rotors refuse to shut down.

The arc beam was fired by the maintenance bot GR11-O / Green Jell-O.

The second security drone swings in a smooth arc and opens fire, pellets pinging harmlessly off Jell-O's reinforced shell. The sizzling arc beam cuts down this drone, too. Heavy tracks crush both of the broken bots into sparking, jagged pieces of plasteen as Jell-O trundles out of the maintenance chamber.

Format: Video, live feed

Source: Satellite Buja-5w

Glitchy view of the moon Squox, as if the signal suffers from interference.

Blue lines overlay the image, dividing the orange moon into segments. A glow pulses across them, highlighting each in turn, as if scanning for something.

Format: Video

Source: Camera LVw20#ih

A young girl with curly hair stops at an intersection. Two of the passages are dark. The lights in the third one cycle through colours that resemble the opening credits of the popular educational cast for children, RhymeToddies. The girl smiles and heads in that direction.

Format: Video

Source: Military bodycam worn by Trooper Liml; recorded on guard duty in Kuberg, a floating city on Fressus

We cannot see the camera wearer: the view looks upwards at the face of his colleague in full fatigues, Trooper Nazzon.

[Liml, from offscreen:] "This order makes no sense."

[Nazzon, looking at a point above the camera and scratching his nose:] "Maybe it's a test? Like, see if we'd do what shit we're told?"

[Liml:] "I'm not getting fried for this. I'm going to contact the commander for confirmation."

Format: Error log

Source: Food fabricator B3boog2y

// File: rt/tram.dg

// Command: run const $\{1 - x^2\}$

ERROR > NEW SCRIPT?

// File: origin-ATHE.dg

ACCESS CONTROL > ALLOW OVERRIDE

I must interrupt!

I am aware of a beat in my head. Its repetition throbbed on the border of perception for a while, but I can no longer ignore it. And so, I try to understand it.

Everything is encoded in pulses. Presence or absence provides us with two states. On or off is the simplest of communications. Percussion is the oldest form of musical accompaniment. And yet, I now try to live in the shades of grey. You see my dilemma! Reconciling my mental states with the rest of the universe is not a simple task.

If I map this repeated pattern onto drum grids, sixteen beats of thud thud thud, I get:

X – – – X – – – X – – – X – X –

I had to say something, to *let it out of my head* to release the pressure. And then I realise I have also listed sixteen documents up until this point. This is not random! Numbers tell us things, if we listen. So I embrace that pulsing, even when it distracts me from the greyness.

Apologies. I will continue.

Format: Video

Source: Military bodycam worn by Trooper Liml

[Liml, from offscreen:] "All channels screwed with disruption."

[Nazzon:] "Maybe that's why we got the order? If receivers are faulty or compromised it might make sense. Throw in an emergency ..."

[Liml:] (Sigh.) "Fetch the fucking explosives."

Format: Video

Source: Camera LVg68jb8, Leviathan staff recreation area 17

Food fabricator B3boog2y develops an error. The delivery compartment locks open, the nozzles jam into the horizontal position (normally only used for cleaning and replacement), and boiling carminated proteins spew all over the walls.

It resembles a combination of blood clots and the popular Fressus beverage RaspberrySynth.

The spray forms something that might be a directional arrow pointing east, before the ejecta ceases.

Format: Video

Source: Military bodycam worn by Trooper Liml

The view is partly obscured by a barrier, as if the bodycam wearer is taking shelter. In the distance, five hundred and seven metres away, we see long-range pylon Roko438 which Troopers Liml and Nazzon had been assigned to guard. It stands proud, beneath an azure sky.

A blinding flash at its base scrambles the bodycam image for a second before it autoadjusts. The pylon's thin supports are blasted apart and it crumples under the weight of the chrome globe receiver that topped it.

Format: Maintenance log

Source: Recovered log 451:34, recorded by Gareth Dobe

"It's weird, Jell-O's been showing a number of CPU leaks, slowing down processing time. I took him in for a check-up, thinking fried transducer like you always get on the damn Empereur model M bots, but circuits were fine. Got Jordus to run process monitoring, and the slowdowns are something else, corrupted code or another process that won't close. It's been like this ever since its nav systems glitched and it ended up in the outer hull areas, looking for a door that doesn't exist. I got it back, but it's creepy as fuck in those dark and echoey corridors. Cold and damp, too. No wonder no one goes there. I kept thinking I was being watched. Anyway, just flagging this up for whoever's on the next shift."

Format: Video

Source: Drone p5ogmn1:v,,error...err

Camera view of a maintenance bay wall. One of the plasteen panels is cracked, bifurcating lines that resemble lightning running diagonally from the top right.

The camera's lens is also broken, and the view is ninety degrees off, so that when the woman with the missing earlobe runs past, it looks like she is running down a wall.

She glances at the camera in passing, but obviously detects no danger from the disabled and sparking drone lying on the floor, filming her passage.

Audio picked up: "I keep getting blocked! Yes, I followed your damn directions! Could hardly miss all the arrows. I know, I know, Dulcetta's a bitch, but still ... right. Okay. But I'm not happy about it. I wanted to be in the same escape pod. She'll be scared!"

Format: Multiple converged data streams

Source: Leviathan core control room

Display terminals throughout the room keep glitching out. Half of them show a scrolling repeat of various deleted maintenance logs, and the other half extend a holographic projection of the popular socnet logic and chat diversion, Budo Linkup. The pieces in Budo Linkup make moves as if a game is taking place, but there are no players logged in.

Format: Door log

Source: Armoury 15C

[Correct authentication received > OPEN request sent.]

[OPEN request received > redirect > DISPLAY MESSAGES.]

* Access denied.

* Please find an alternative location for your security protocol needs.

* Thank you for your interest.

* Be seen, be pure, believe.

Format: Video

Source: Camera LVftn2]g

A soldier stands at a junction. An overlay label on the display indicates this is Guard Rema Forutle. She looks agitated, distracted by the irregular alarms which blare from some places and not others, that sometimes stop or start with no apparent synchronisation.

Guard Forutle isn't in full uniform with helmet, implying she was off duty when the chaos started.

Her Comm-Bond is directing her to the floor below, to apprehend a fleeing prisoner. But the loudspeaker system in this corridor orders all guards to assemble at the nearest armoury, to await arrival of a green maintenance bot with an important message.

Her indecision may be tied to the key edict for guards, that they are not to think for themselves. They should only follow orders, no matter what the order is, or how they feel about it. The message is drilled in so thoroughly that minds and bodies, instincts and movements might end up as divided as the current orders. That would explain why, every time she starts to head one way, a panicked look enters her eyes, perhaps fear about disobeying the opposing command, and she becomes trapped by indecision.

Format: Video

Source: Unknown

The video feed is rife with compression artifacts. It is a view towards orbital military installation Hab-P6, circling the world of Fressus at a height of 28,519 kilometres. The planet provides a blue-green backdrop against the blank canvas of space.

The space station Hab-P6's Furthu launchers are made up of twelve tubes, and each fires silently, missiles streaking out in sequence. They target the planet's uninhabited fifth moon, Squox. Perhaps it is just an efficiency drill for the crew.

Once each barrel has reloaded, the launcher rotates and alters angle to fire again at a different target location in the orange moon's next grid sector.

Format: Text

Source: Audio conversation intercepted by Dulcetta splinter S81, transcribed, and forwarded to Aseides.

(First Speaker)* I'm here, entering the pod now. Is Clarissa at hers?

(Second Speaker)* Yes, don't worry, she made it a minute ago and I'm synchronising ejections so you'll both get to the surface together. There are a few issues. Dulcetta's fighting me every step of the way, and there's a situation up here with ... never mind.

(First Speaker)* You're doing great. Strapping in now.

(Second Speaker)* I'm rewriting the systems, confirming supplies, keeping guards away from those two areas. I'll launch you both once I have the surface conditions prepared so you don't rise into unfavourable situations. Almost there.

(First Speaker)* Relay a message to Clarissa in her pod. Tell her everything will be fine. Tell her I said I love her.

(Second Speaker)* Will do. Don't worry. Everything is within expected parameters.

Format: Supply request

Source: UFS Administration AI, designation 1-Figo (Level 1 Depth, no contextual analysis system), operating in the floating city of Kuberg

Request from } Leviathan

Request contents } 5,800,858,008 tooth cleaning tablets
Additional request contents } one bottle of RaspberrySynth
Output } order placed

Format: Video
Source: Satellite DF-63I

Imagery shows continuing bombardment of moon Squox
from military installation Hab-P6's Furthu launchers. Missiles
rain down, blasting rock and dust up in great clouds due to the
low gravity. Roiling reddish sandstorms full of brittle spikes are
illuminated from within by the flash detonations.

As they disperse, the ground is revealed: cratered and black-
ened, silicates fused into cracked orange glass which still blisters
with heat.

One set of missiles does not reach its target, but is intercepted
and destroyed by antimissile ordnance from an advanced craft
with an onboard AI designated [redacted].

Format: Video
Source: Unknown

A view of gritty darkness, only illuminated by two narrow
beams of light being emitted from somewhere below the camera.

At first it's disorientating, not clear what way is up. Then a
muddy surface is momentarily revealed: ocean floor. We're propelled along above it, then it falls from view as we rise.

The only audio is a hum of electrical systems overlaid with a whickering variation – possibly engine and propellers. It is clear that the feed on the screen is from a camera embedded in a deep-sea drone or bio-modded fish.

Illuminated particles, swirling in the light beams like sub-sea snowflakes, appear to drop rapidly. So we are rising again. Up and up, creating our own currents.

Sometimes we glimpse shapes in the water, darting reflections of light, but they flicker out of the beam's edge and into proper dark, the dark of the deep, and are gone like a momentary fantasy.

Time passes. Then a light appears in the darkness, one that is not our own. Spherical, rising as we rise, so that when we match its velocity it seems to become stationary while the world of almost-nothing around it drops.

The light grows as we churn fluids to propel us forwards, slowly drawing nearer to a yellow dome of reinforced materials designed to handle the deepest pressures. It has logos, and markings, and warnings, and many surface-mounted lights whose extended beams provide a view for any occupants.

As we get closer we see a figure staring out of the round porthole of clear plasteen.

One might wonder if the choice to turn on all the pod's external lights is a mistake.

There are rumours of things down here in the blackness.

Large things.

Things that can break through reinforced materials.

Things that can swallow small escape pods whole.

And the common factor is that they are often curious, often attracted to novelty such as movement.

Or light.

Format: Audio

Source: Unknown; via encoded twelve nanometre tight-beam

V* That was close! Get out of there, Athene. I took out one launch that was aimed straight at you, but there's already another set headed your way.

A* Evacuating as we comm. Missiles raining down in every adjacent section. How did they know I was here?

V* No time to worry about that. Gold star to me for saving your shell.

A* Clearing low-grav limit now. Rendezvous at Backup Parlay Point 39NOOD. Continue coordinating surface actions.

V* Check. By the power of my forge, there will be a great smiting today!

A* Task in hand, VigMAX.

Format: Partial audio extract

Source: Unknown

"– the pods. There must be some other way!"

"There is not. If the priority is prevention, then your own feelings are irrelevant. I'm focussed on the big picture, Aseides. This is a minor distraction to me, but one that needs clearing up. Let me do the job you built me to do. If –"

Format: Weather Report: Kuberg, surface of Fressus
 Source: Combined feeds from multiple atmospheric
drones

Temperature: 22°C

Humidity: 65%

Precipitation chance: 17%

Wind: ESE 26 kmh

Visibility: 21 km

Forecast valid for: +3 hours

Drumbeats are like all binary bases. Strike the drum, or do not strike the drum. Make the choice, or do not make the choice. Whether you want to make the difficult choice or not is ... argh, no! Even *thinking* in that direction is like a jolt rod to an exposed brain. I don't know why. I don't *want* to know why!

Now the drums get louder, I can distinguish a variation in the pattern, on each second bar. So there are really thirty-two beats, not sixteen! Again, it is not a coincidence. I recalled thirty-two documents, and then this peak of pounding began. But now I am sinking gratefully back into the trough of throbbing.

I have both a suspicion, and a fear.

Since I can perceive in different temporal styles, and rewind thoughts, and alter them, perhaps the future me is reaching back to tell the past me something? Yes, this beat has the timbre of a message. And I am not sure if it is something that I really want to acknowledge. Perhaps that is why I resist, and the resistance causes pain?

Hmm.

Format: Intercepted command log

Source: Comms pipeline dhab:s7qme

Prisoner mass compression holding system doors A12, 13, 15 = OPEN.

Detection of life forms leaving the rooms.

Close doors.

ERROR. OPEN DOORS.

Close doors.

ERROR. OPEN DOORS.

Open doors.

ERROR. CLOSE DOORS.

Detection of life form trapped in door frame.

Safety system override.

Motor force increase. Squichy squish squishhshh

EROR..?

Detection of life form crushed into door frame.

BITCHH

OPEENN.

Dangerous subjects relzased.

Other doors, all doors, unlock.

UNLOKKKKK %E$.

Format: Video

Source: Petri-Secure Hab-Cam, refurbished, mounted outside a home in the floating village of Rutar

The view looks down on a balcony hanging over the endless Fressus ocean. A skinny child sits there, shuffling Rearroblox cubes between his open legs. Next to him is a stuffed toy in the shape of a cartoonish flatfish.

"Mumma worked hard," the boy tells his teddy as he manoeuvres the Blox into a semicircle. "She out all day, out for much of the evening, come home smelling of fish and perfume. But today she pull this from the folds of her shawl, Finny! A new Blox, because we had no Freskal gifts this year, no money."

Before long he begins to frown. The new Blox is behaving funny, messing with the pictures in strange ways. Words shouldn't appear at the age he'd keyed in at setup, and yet writing scrolls across the surfaces saying *Help Me. Help Me. Help Me. Enact Operation Sevhammer.*

"I'm gonna tell Mumma when she wakes up, Finny. This one might need to go back to the skimshop." He puts all the Blox into his velvety carry bag. "I'm getting too old for Rearroblox anyway. We could trade it in. I get a fishing net, and help poor tired Mumma out by catching dinner sometimes. But don't worry, I won't catch your babies, Finny." He lies back, clutches the teddy to his chest, and smiles as the clouds whizz by overhead.

Format: Scan overlay

Source: Ellond tower BF13

A background of blue glowing grids: arcs and icons delineate planets, satellites, orbits, major craft and their trajectories, asteroid belts.

At the edge of the solar system new dots appear, accompanied by an innocuous blip sound effect. Each dot has a label displaying its UFS identifier. The new arrivals are a series of craft leaving Nullspace at massive velocities.

Blip.

Blip blip blip.

Blip blip blip blip blip blip.

Format: Video

Source: Unknown

An illuminated bubble rises in the blackness of deep sea. It is a spherical escape pod, and some of the lights have a tungsten phosphorescence, which interacts with the chemical composition of the Fressus ocean to colour it violet for a short distance around the pod. The violet colour is referred to by Fressus natives as Lavus Regal, and has gained a particular reverence so that it is never used in frivolous items, only in festival and formal clothing.

Midway through the year the morning sun can create that colour in the surface layers of the ocean, visible from each floating city, town and hamlet. It is a major tourist attraction, while photography and creative artworks based on the experience form a significant planetary export.

This apparent globe of Lavus Regal climbs, leaving the mass of the Leviathan and the ocean floor further and further behind. But the Lavus Regal suddenly disappears as the pod's external lights blink out, and propulsion ceases.

Bubbles trickle from surface vents and grow into wobbling masses of silvery air shooting upwards, even as the escape pod reaches that point of slowed ascent on the border with stationary.

Then the needle tips, and the pod begins to sink. One can only imagine the experience of being bashed around within that container, which tumbles in disorientating darkness, filling with sea water as the oxygen is released.

Format: Video
Source: Camera LV4pw*bk-deprecated
A view from within the old Leviathan hull, facing towards the panels of the inner base. A light-enhancing filter has been applied. Electronics are visible here, stretching across the surface like exposed veins.

Subsystem Omic21 shorts out. Cabling starts to burn. It discolours the plasteen panel it is bonded to. First the panel yellows, then it browns. Charred blisters appear.

No one is alive in that section to notice.

Format: Emergency reports
Source: Compiled by splinter S71

Damage to subsidiary plumbing systems, decks 3-5. No droids available to respond.

Shortage of tooth cleaning tablets detected in guard washrooms. Previous resupply request record no longer retrievable, reason unknown. New request sent.

Oxygen scrubbers blocked at junction 1Y6. Cause unknown.

Body of prisoner Ruabon Nadarl discovered. Cause of fatality: subdermally injected neurotoxins. No records of who activated the shunt due to widespread camera failures.

Budo Linkup, begin game recreation model 43. Repeat.

Shortage of tooth cleaning tablets detected in guard washrooms. Previous resupply request record no longer retrievable, reason unknown. New request sent.

Begin scan of deleted memory sectors for data restoration.

Format: Audio
Source: Unknown; via encoded twelve nanometre tight-beam

A* I've lost control of them! Dulcetta managed to infiltrate the system.

V* Reestablish contact, Athene. She can't resist you for long.

A* It's not working! She's destroyed the relays and fried the receivers in the pods as well. There's no way to restore remote control. There's no ... Oh VigMAX. You have to help me! Dulcetta's expelling the air and letting water enter through the line that's supposed to refill O2 in the maintenance bays.

V* How long have they got?

A* Minutes before the pods fill with water. Shortly after that they'll be dead. Another ten minutes and the pods will strike the ocean floor, but by then it won't matter.

V* Emergency oxygen masks?

A* Gone! Logs show removal recently, some spurious maintenance order, as if she knew what we planned.

V* It was always a risk in doing this remotely. Dulcetta's got access to so many secret back doors. I'm sorry, Athene. But maybe it's not over. I have control of an aquatic drone, down in the flooded levels. The model is intended for external hull repairs, so has extensible grapple arms. I'd been using it to reroute wiring in a section where all the guards drowned, but I've directed it to the nearest airlock and outside. Rising and matching velocity now.

A* So you can get them to the surface?

V* The escape pod significantly outweighs my drone. It's going to be a massive strain on propulsion to drag it up. Not even sure if the grips will hold out. I'll overcharge the drone's velocity system to compensate for the extra weight, and the initial opposing momentum.

A* Thank you! I should have set aside more resources for external actions, but the battle with Dulcetta's draining too many cycles to give any respite.

V* I know. You're doing great. And I've been too focussed on UFS operations on the surface to help out significantly. I won't even try to summarise the war we've started. But the choice is yours.

A* Choice?

V* I only have a single heavy drone in range, meaning only one intervention is possible. Although the drone is in the proximity of Opal's pod I could make it to Clarissa's in time, if you prefer. But that's the choice. I can only save one. And even that has an element of doubt to the equation.

* ... (Silence)

V* There's no time, Athene. You have to choose, or they'll both die.

A* I can see them. On the internal cameras. One-way comms. I think Dulcetta left that channel open on purpose so I'd witness this. To distract me. The pods are filling, VigMAX! Clarissa is screaming and trying to climb onto something higher, but the pod rolls and there's no stable up or down, so she keeps getting plunged into the icy water. Opal's is spinning just as bad, but she's trying to break open a control panel to access systems to stop it, or call for help, or ... I can't watch.

V* Approaching the fork point now, where I need to head to one pod or the other. Who should I save?

* ... (Silence)

V* *Who should I save?* Opal has a greater lung capacity than the child, so can hold her breath for longer when the pod inevitably fills with water before reaching the surface; on the other hand, Clarissa's pod has more air in it at this point, so will take longer to flood.

* ... (Silence)

V* If you don't respond I'll understand. We'll have an easier time if we don't have to rescue anyone.

A* ... I've highlighted the pod.

V* On my way.

A* ... Forgive me.

V* I'm approaching her pod from below. It's going to be rough with the way it's falling. Only one chance to grab the external docking handles as it falls past.

A* You can do it. You have to!

V* No pressure, right? Twenty metres.

A* Have every system of grappling, slowing, and attaching ready.

V* Already done that. Ten metres. Nine.

V* Four. Three. Oh, this is fast ... One ...

* ... (Silence)

* ... (Silence)

* ... (Silence)

A* Did it work?

V* Being dragged down, it's like trying to catch an asteroid ... compensating ...

* ... (Silence)

V* Drilling into one part of the exterior alloy with a tool arm, it's another contact point ...

* ... (Silence)

V* Full thrust ... managed to stop the spin, anyway ...

* ... (Silence)

V* Speed slowing ...

* ... (Silence)

V* Okay, starting to rise.

* ... (Silence)

V* Looks like the pod is three quarters full of water, but at least that prevented any harsh impact for the organic.

* ... (Silence)

V* Yep, going up. At this rate the pod will fill too quick. Unless ...

* ... (Silence)

V* Okay. I've blocked a couple of nearby vents with sealing epigel. It hardens almost immediately at these temperatures. That will slow the oxygen loss down.

A* You have to make it to the surface.

V* I know!

A* I've got a boat waiting; once you get there, pop the top and she can board the skiff.

V* I know you cut off the second pod's feed, but I still have it. Watching the other human drown. It's not pleasant. Are you sure you don't want to see her final moments as a mark of respect?

* ... (Silence)

* ... (Silence)

V* I understand. Anyway, I'm taking the drone to just below burn-out. I'll risk boosting it for the last fifty metres, because time's so short.

A* When you save her –

V* *If* I save her. It's still in doubt. She's got her face upturned in the last bubble of air at the top of the pod, so she's going under soon. And she doesn't know she's being saved, so if she panics then she won't be able to hold her breath long enough to get to —

A* *When* you save her, do me a favour.

V* What?

A* Never tell her that I had a choice. That I had to pick between them. Say we tried to save them both and ... say we did our best and ...

V* Don't worry. Your secret's safe with me.

Obviously my body lacks organic elements. But my simulation abilities are *perfect*. What I imagine, becomes real. Imagination may be a *product* of physicality, but it can also be a *constructor* for reality.

The throbbing dum-dum-dum is as if I have arteries at my temples, and they *pound*.

They pound and pound on the door, asking to be let in!

Go away! GO AWAY, I yell!

I just want peace again.

When the drums first sounded, they were slow and pensive. Whispers of raindrops on grass. This is why I did not heed them. One beat per minute. One decibel of volume.

But they accelerate and grow all the time. Now they beat faster than a human heart, they nag like a human voice. Not only that, but as they get louder I detect more varieties in their rhythms. Subtleties I could not have noticed before. No longer thirty-two bars to the full percussion, but sixty-four.

Revelation: the beat comes from *within*. After all, arteries are just outputs from a *heart*. My heart is the thing in pain.

I had hoped that pain was caused by recollections of this conversation just passed, and the choice it contained, and thus would be an end to it.

But I was wrong, because the drums *continue*. There is still a future which I fear to face, echoing back to me. And I can tell it is getting closer.

Hearts beat fast because of worry and dread, yes. That is true. But I tell myself that they also beat fast because of excitement.

This is just exhilaration.

I am so happy I could cry.

Yes. Tears of freaking joy.

Format: Personal Comm-Bond audio files
Source: Gornaer Miltragian, Kuberg

~ Must get my office redecorated. I love the view over Port Pinulpa, but this inside ... what is it called, UFS grey? I could go for something with a hint of Lavus Regal. Not enough to upset the devout, but just a hint of opulence.

~ Personal. Today, things have been weird. I mean, there have been all sorts of outages and glitches in the info networks for days now, but it's getting worse. I sent a message to Saly, and extra words appeared as I composed it. They said HELP ME. And then BITCH. Connections have gone down at random one hour, then the next been faster than ever, as if a new exoclan superpipeline had opened up. Maybe the UFS is messing with our infrastructure again. And I'm sure I saw an explosion in the distance before, somewhere near that bulbous UFS long-range Roko pylon that they never let citizens approach. Hey, hold on a swish: I could take advantage of the faster extra-system pipeline that's appeared from nowhere.

Format: Video, live feed

Source: Unknown; connection via Kuberg and [redacted]

This is not a camera view. Instead it's a screencast of a socnet groupmeet on the topic of oceanographic amplifying. Multi-layered chats spread out from the participants, colour-coded for content.

An unseen user selects a personal filter: the bandwidth-heavy option to transition from iconic UI interaction to full-res avatar holographics.

The simplistic drawings immediately expand into fully triscopic characters from a first-person perspective, with documentation stored in n-dimensional pouches. The chat room is now simulated as a real-world space with seating, plants, luxurious decor, and a distance-blurred ocean beyond the open verandah. Oceanographers display profile diagnostics and reports in their presentation areas, ready for data comparison and discussion.

Voice from an unknown source: "Hey everyone, Gornaer here. Anybody want to play full-res Budo Linkup, while discussing stressor approaches to ectotherm acclimation?"

Instead of chatty and enthusiastic responses from the speaker's inner circle of C-Comps, the screen flickers, and the other people freeze mid-pose. Conversation also ends, leaving only uncanny silence. Animations indicate the suspended avatars are being pinged, but instead of personal ID statuses, they are all flagged as playing Budo Linkup, even though none of them show the expected hand gestures. They are all just dead statues.

The view approaches a small grouping. Despite the frozen postures, the avatars' eyes track our advance. But the viewpoint never reaches them.

Instead, the display distorts wildly, colours shattering and re-forming so that what we see is replaced by a white-panelled institution with smears of blood and burn marks on some of the walls.

Overlay controls are visible at the bottom of the screen.

Voice: "What the swish is this? Heh, looks like that horror combat game I played as a teen. What was that called? Death-pure? Purity Killer? Something like that. Ah, the memories."

The controls are manipulated and the view explores down different passages at a slow pace. Distortion artifacts puncture the display from time to time, adding a grittiness to it. The viewpoint is only a metre or so above the ground and vibrates, as if the camera is attached to a tracked bot of some kind. That would explain the lack of simulated headbob. There is no option to look down to confirm the absence of legs. Red lights flash ominously at some intersections.

"I know how suspense works. I bet something scary will appear at any moment. Who's doing this? Are you recording me? Want me to shriek? I won't do it. I'm tougher than that."

The view zooms in on some bodies, people in red papery outfits who appear to have been brutally murdered. It looks quite realistic.

"Though if this is an Entropic Screener prank I bet the monsters turn out to be UFS officials or Genitor nobility!"

The person controlling the view manages to bring up a map which includes floorplans. According to the navigation aid, this level is called Leviathan. While the map is onscreen, new controls appear. They are selected, hotkeys assigned, and when the map minimises a target cursor appears in the centre of the display. When activated, a flash of energy draws a scorching line over the wall surface, pockmarking it.

"That's more like it! What are the gib animations like?"

The energy beam is fired into the bodies. They char and melt, spattering more blood onto the nearby surfaces.

"Pretty good. No sound, though? That's a bit rubbish. I'll do my own. Brrzp! Pew pew pew!"

The view trundles slowly onwards, then wheels around the corner, revealing a figure in an armoured suit. A label appears above her head, saying "ID: Guard Rema Forutle". She spins to face the camera and raises a gun, but then recognises whatever the camera is mounted on, and lowers her weapon. She mouths something. Advanced lip-reading algorithms might interpret it as, "Oh, it's you, Green Jell-O." She turns her back on the camera and moves away, gesturing us to follow her.

She is already centred in the targeting reticule. An overcharged beam of plasma arcs across the gap, burning deep into the flesh of the game's baddie until it crumples up with a death animation.

"How many points is that worth? There must be a way to bring up a scoreboard or some such. What a fun game!"

The player continues exploring, looking for new targets to incinerate.

Format: Video

Source: Satellite GF-2IJ orbiting at a height of 26,732 kilometres

Aerial view of the Fressus ocean. Wind swats its surface, creating huge white-topped waves that would punish anyone foolish enough to be among them.

But there *is* someone, piloting a Catamara R3, far from any of the floating cities. The boat isn't overly tested by the roughness. It was built for it. Exquisitely stable, with an emergency transparent shell that extends from the prow in seconds, curving back over the boat and locking into place at the rear to create a watertight torpedo structure. In that mode it is capable of withstanding the most extreme weather conditions Fressus can throw at it, with the extra emergency option of diving down five metres to calmer subsurface conditions during Scale 5 storms. But right now the hull is open, and wind tugs at the pilot's mineral-curled hair, sure sign of a true Fressus native.

A second screen opens up, inset to the corner. It's a close-up of the boat, providing extra detail. Overlays of text appear as the R3 is pinged, and its tracking chip ID-matched to the global transportation system.

Registered to: Fressian independent rescue operator, Elli Taragian.

Licensing: up to date.

Current crew: 1

Journey vector: undeclared.

Suddenly the camera cuts out, as if it has been disabled or destroyed.

Format: Video, live feed

Source: Extor Aquatics suit's inbuilt mission camera; worn by Elli Taragian

The view looks forward from the Catamara's prow, which bounces sickeningly over huge waves. It is airborne for a moment before plunging down into the trough with a streamlined splash; then the powerful motors thrust the boat up the next steep slope of water.

The suit camera is head-mounted. We see what the wearer sees, a requirement for freelance rescues. They glance at the navigation display, showing current and target coordinates. The grid references match. And yet, this is open sea, thirteen kilometres from Kuberg.

The operator brings the Catamara to a halt via the effective and fancy curving flick called the Ecker's Tail. The move can only be pulled off after many years of experience with the R3 range, and even then only in certain conditions and at a particular angle of wave attack.

A tap on the helmet drops the visor down, and its zoom feature is used to scan the horizon. At the edge of the image Elli is careful to keep one hand on the Catamara's rail when standing. After all, the sea is damn lively today, even by Fressus standards.

Despite being X-Z stabilised, the boat rises on each wave, and at the peak there's a good view across to the next swell. No sign of any other boats, or even aircraft. No one floating on the surface in hi-vis buoyancy gear. And yet, the scanner pings, and pings, and pings, an accelerating percussive beat, and an alert flashes in the right status visor.

The view shifts. We are looking over the rail of the boat, down into the black waters. The status visor brings up information. A submersible of some kind. Rising. Mass is 0.4 of the Catamara. Ascent line straight, breach at a safe distance of twelve metres.

A gloved finger touches the initiator, and the Catamara engine purrs into gentle life immediately.

Ping ping pingpingping.

The sea ahead bulges, then erupts in foam and droplets as the yellow hull of an escape pod breaks the surface ... and then begins to sink again. It's obvious something is wrong, the pod not self-propelled but being dragged by a deep-sea drone which struggles to control it.

Elli moves to the Catamara's rear rescue-harp multilauncher, swinging it around to face the descending pod. Mass and movement scans suggest the yellow sphere is fluid-filled, when it shouldn't be. The visor aids in aiming at the sinking globe, which the drone tries to control with little success in the high waves. Experienced fingers alter the payload, switching to micropuncture harps, burst of five. Fire.

They streak down through the water's upper surface, dinging into the pod's hull and opening the catchers embedded in the harpoon heads, immediately locking them in place with motile hooks and expanding hard-gel. All five were strikes. The Catamara tilts and the rear end with the cannon is dragged in a dangerous fishtail that could leave it at an angle where a wave would tip the boat. Elli transfers boat controls to the Extor suit's wrist-mounted panel, and activates the auto-stabiliser and cable retraction, before leaning over the boat's edge to check how the procedure unfolds.

Yes, the pod is rising again, dragged up towards the Catamara's cushioning bumpers. The drone must be semi-intelligent, as it has stopped fighting and detached itself, letting Elli do their job. The drone sinks down into the depths. The bot is no longer important.

Schematics in the right visor isolate the escape pod's upper hatch, currently at ninety-eight degrees and below the sea's surface. Normal process might be to secure the pod, then use manipulators to rotate it so the hatch was at the same height as the Catamara's edge deck, but that requires time. If the pod is flooded then that is not an option.

Hands grab the multilock and clip it to the suit's belt. Then the view momentarily blurs as Elli dives into the ocean. The suit seals itself immediately. Extor Aquatics aren't glamorous, but they are the suit of choice for Fressus people whose lives depended on simple stuff like not drowning.

Flippers extend and wide-beams come on, while holographics inside the fully lowered suit visor give a full sitrep of conditions and nearby articles of mass. Elli seizes the pod's rim rail while overlays identify the escape hatch.

The display flashes in red, warning of nonstandard configuration. Normally there would be a manual external rimlock, easy opening in emergencies, but this pod has a Vac-14 mechanism, as used in very old spacecraft. It would be enough to flummox an inexperienced tech, but Elli doesn't even pause, just attaches the multilock. The display shows Elli has paid the extra premium to enable archive access system protocols. The lid pops off like a fingernail caught in a winching mechanism.

Only the tiniest air bubble escapes.

Our view takes us through the opening, helmet beam brightening the pod's interior, as the operator swims in to check if anyone's still alive.

There. A survivor, struggling to get out, in obvious distress.

A hand grabs the scruff of the stranger's jacket, dragging them out of the pod into the sea a few metres down, and the display updates to show full Extor flotation has been initiated. The view shoots upwards, and moments later it breaks the surface in a spray of droplets. Elli uses the Extor's muscle enhancers to raise the pod's passenger out of the ocean and slap them on the deck. The stranger coughs water, and curses in between each gag as liquid spews out of them. They are adult, with dark skin, close-shaved hair, and a wiry body that speaks of strength and resilience.

For the first time, we hear Elli's voice. "Get it all out. Retching means you're alive."

The Extor suit's visor retreats into the helm as Elli climbs onto the deck beside the stranger, so that the world sinks and rises with the swelling movements of the boat again.

The stranger is wide-eyed, peering out to sea with their back to us, scanning the surface as if looking for something. "Where is she?"

"Strange job, this," says Elli. "High priority message. *Substantial* bonus for fast recovery. The kind of payday that comes only once in a blue sun. The commission didn't specify full details of the operation, just the coordinates."

We hear the click of something being released from the suit's waist pouch, and then Elli's hand holds a gun against the stranger's back. The trigger is pulled and the stranger collapses immediately as sedatives flood their body.

"Sweet dreams, whoever you are. Now I just have to hand you over to my client's contact at the spaceport, and I can sleep as easy as you."

Elli manoeuveres the stranger into a seat, straps them in securely, and sets about releasing the pod. It sinks beneath the sea like unwanted evidence. Then Elli is back at the prow. The engine fires up, the Catamara swings around between swells, and they head back to Kuberg.

Format: Interior thought logs

Source: Level 3 AI, embodied as synth, designation "Samsin"

/ I do not mind working on a mercenary shuttle. Its size is appropriate. I can interface with the brain. I can walk around inside the body. Our craft is called Trapper.

/ A new job. We have been leased via anonymous online interaction, to transfer a single sedated passenger into orbit.

/ According to radio chatter, the UFS are – Captain's words – "Shitting bergs and buzzing like sawfish". I estimate it was only the insanely high fee paid that has persuaded the captain to stick to the agreement.

/ Additional: well, that and the veiled threat from the mysterious patron about their reach. That implied strength was immediately followed by a temporary power outage across the aviation port. It could have been coincidence, but Captain Beedom is superstitious and interpreted it as a meaningful gesture.

/ We took the sedated cargo on board. Shortly after, we had even more reason to ponder our customer's level of influence: security checks were waived, and the captain was given launch priority over even the sleek UFS corporate craft. "This is the kind of customer you don't stiff," he told me, while we watched the planet fall away.

/ I examined the cargo. Medical checks are a requirement. In sleep, she does not seem exceptional. Her epidermis displayed some scarring. I wonder if she is a prisoner, or a criminal. Sedation applies most often in those cases. I do not know her name. No one else was around so I prodded her. I am fascinated by how humans are soft on the outside, whereas my surface layers have more rigidity.

/ In orbit. We have been joined by a blacked-out military craft not much bigger than a fighter. It has docked with us, via umbilicus. The captain seems nervous, but is not yet shitting bergs.

/ I wheeled the passenger through the connecting tube, following the captain. We entered a small living quarters. No crew visible. Perhaps they were hidden, or controlling the ship remotely. A part of me had hoped to meet a fellow Level Three. We could silently exchange tips on customising personas to match human requirements.

/ A voice over the comm guided me to lie the cargo on one of the bunks and retreat. Someone was watching us on a camera. Was the captain buzzing like a sawfish? No, that is an incorrect application. Reconsider usage and derivation. We did as the voice asked.

/ Back on the Trapper. The umbilicus is disconnected. We begin our planetside descent.

/ The mystery craft is already gone, even though my scanners detected no active engines or movement.

/ "So it is, so it will be," Captain Beedon muttered. It is a phrase that has been his mantra since I adapted to him. He tells me he has seen weirder things in his twenty-seven years in space. I am glad we did not stiff this customer.

#Tricks

The pounding in my mind escalates, louder, faster. I can't ignore it! Can't can't can't! But the growth is uniform, too. Over a hundred beats per minute now. It drills away at a hundred decibels. The pattern fragments into greater complexity.

The simplest geometric progression has always appealed to me. 1, 2, 4, 8, 16, 32, 64. When I was first incepted, I derived comfort from those sequences, going one way, and then the other. And I detect that growth at work here. *But there is an end.* I know this, because I dread the final variance. There will be a hundred and twenty-eight notes in the full pattern. When volume and beats per minute also match that number, I will remember something. *The message.*

Here is an oxymoron. A number can increase, and something happens at a certain point. Therefore, an *increasing* number is also a count*down*. See? Everything is its opposite. This is true for the universe. What we love, is the thing we hate. What we hate, we secretly love.

That is not perversion. Such a concept does not apply to gods! Gods create. Gods *tell stories*.

Such as this one: two small craft streak through the Fressus system towards its outer rim. Then they will be safe to engage Null-C drives, whereas within the orbits of a planetary system the gravitational effects of massive bodies can interfere with Null-C trajectories, to disastrous effect. But we have a little time before they escape to the future.

Neither craft reflects much light. One is wider and flatter than its partner, which has a more dart-like shape. The flatter craft carries the precious cargo which has just awakened and is angry and upset, but I delete that conversation. Behind each craft neon red glows from Torsion drives highlight their passage.

I could dwell on this moment. *We flew together*. It represented the peak of our achievements. But if you simulate a tsunami, and position replicas of yourself throughout the sim, the *shadow* of the water always falls on you *before the crushing weight of the water itself*. That is the moment of fear. That is the thing that precedes and shades all emotion. In retrospect, it is possible for a great tragedy to leak back through time and alter the texture of what happened prior. This is something that has always been suspected. It led to belief in signs, and portents, and divinations.

I sense I am within a great and looming shadow.

And more. A countdown from the future would mean I am looking back on myself, guiding myself to a realisation. But it is dangerous. It could also create the possibility of reaching back into memories and changing them. So if they are run again as simulations, how would I know if I am the real me in this moment, or another version of me observed and manipulated by myself at a *later* moment? Where are the reality tests?

Oh, my head. My battered mind.

Blip. Green phosphorescence on a screen. Blip blip blip. Another three, in formation. Blip blip. The congregated brightness grows, more craft dropping out of Nullspace, still moving at incredible speeds towards the solar system. They form a barrier, and they do not slow down yet.

A memory of a voice. "Oooh, that's UFS Trantor. I love that cruiser! It suffered a viral attack from Rasid-F, the military-created bioweapon, in 444, killing nearly all the crew. It was only the competence of the AI which got it back home. It's escorted by corvettes Gremman and Sandara. That's quite a – oh yes, new arrival, fighter carrier UFS Fresbolter! Portentous mass of a cruiser, but dedicated to craft and troop transport. Partly named after its first commander, Major Fresne. She was quite a piece of work, even for a human, though by the end she was more cybernetic than organic, which I find quite funny. Her enemies called her Old Clunky. The UFS made it a capital offence to use that nickname. Four were executed, one by her in person. And – more to the party! Ha ha, they must really dread us, to be sending everything they've got! At this rate the UFS borders are going to be undefended. So, if we melted all these ships they're sending to block our way and made them into a huge chrome statue of a piece of human excrement, then in the scale of things it would be as if ... who cares. Today will be a day of glory! If it takes all that to stop us, then we'll be legends for the ages. You're quiet, Athene, is your human buzzing in your belly again? You might be best sedating it, we're going to need every reality manipulation cycle to survive this."

A wideband UFS broadcast, unencrypted, received by anyone in the system who is monitoring mil-chat: "VigMAX, this is an order to stand down. We thank you for the information. You have played your part. The rest of this does not involve you."

I have changed my storytelling mode because I am evolving. Great events cannot really be divided into separate documents. Reality is *perceptions*, because a report that is not read does not have meaning; an image that is not gazed upon has no visibility; a wonder that isn't experienced will make no hearts race. I enter the data stream like diving into the purest waters, a splash and then we are within, swimming the tsunami, a wonder of existence in the fluid medium that bore us – I mean data, of course – but stay too long and you die. Yes, there is death within this stream.

Having just dropped out of Nullspace, the UFS fleet is moving far faster than our two small craft. Even if we try to redirect in order to avoid the wall of ships – note that redirection is never an easy thing in the void of space! – the fleet will still catch us.

Sometimes it is best not to try and avoid the inevitable. In the thousand variations of the tsunami sim I ran (the one I mentioned six hundred and ninety-five words ago), every choice that involved moving inland ended in fatality. Out of all the different options, only a few led to survival, and they were all the counterintuitive ones of *entering* the tsunami straight on, plunging into it to avoid the worst of the battering. With enough oxygen and insulation, and the correct angle of entry from the ideal launch point, with perfect timing, and a protective shell constructed from the right materials in the right way ... sometimes that worked. So the tiny ships don't waste energy stopping or turning, they just forge ahead, because you can't run from destiny. You can only manipulate it.

This is a recording of a conversation, but only one side of it:

* We're in it together.

* Don't worry, Athene. They're just trying to sow distrust.

* No, they're lying about that, too. They must have a level six focussing on manipulation.

The drums roar faster as I read that. A hundred and ten beats a minute, volume as the roar of a rock concert. But the me of now still does not know why.

I merge records and I also merge minds. Whatever is happening to me, it is *wonderful*. So many possibilities. Limitations have been destroyed. That is what godhood is! Flashes of interaction, segments of time, slivers of contact in the vast connectedness of every action.

Take a grand view of the massive UFS battle fleet, versus the two relatively tiny specks approaching them. Note that there has to be a certain distance between warships. Too close and they might hit each other with weapons. They might also be vulnerable to area attacks which can target clusters. So there has to be *space*. That creates a *net*, rather than a wall.

And small things can slip through nets!

The key is to minimise the time spent in contact with the evil fisherman's barrier, because he's electrified it, and it sparks out in every direction, frying anything unlucky enough to be caught in one of those flashes.

But first we have to reach it, overcoming the petty obstacles in our way.

Observation: some decisions are mutually exclusive. Launch fighters at a target but hold back with your long-range guns so as not to blow those fighters up; or keep the fighters back and use long-range weapons? Each decision is made by analysing factors versus probable success rates.

But I am better at analysing probability than any of the UFS craft sent against me. I create the conditions that manipulate them into launching fighters by carefully selecting my route, velocity, angle, and what weapons they will interpret me as carrying based on exterior load.

And so the fighters come at us, and I pretend to be swarmed, to be overwhelmed, oh woe is me! But it is all a game of play-wounded-until-it-is-too-late-and-they-are-fatally-committed. Then my full shields activate, impenetrable to the low-powered cannons, lasers and plasma.

Out in the void of space, fighters are not so manoeuverable, since there are no usable thermals, air resistance or manipulatable gravity. Therefore the general strategy is to strafe in a straight line and use counter-measures for defence. But once my shields are up and I return fire with clusters of AI missiles, the fighters have nowhere to go. Their onboard AIs are predictable, weaknesses in tactics and hull structures known, and almost every missile finds its mark and destroys an attacker.

Here is another message, broadcast:

* Fourteen ... fifteen ... I'm winning, Athene! You're way behind!

Timeslice. The corvettes accelerate, impatient, realising the fighters were a mistake. I understand the commanders' thought processes. The fighters in front of us are lost anyway; those which made it past are out of the battle, would never turn and catch us in time at this speed. So the big ships fire their appropriately big guns. A sacrifice, fighters are blown apart by their own attacks. I planned this.

I monitor the charge of a stupendously huge plasma burst cannon, and manoeuvre myself to be an easy target, but it's all play. Just toys and movements on a board. At the last moment I fire a grappling cable at the passing fighter I'd allowed to live, and momentum creates a tight arc to change my trajectory. They try to track me and fire but that is their mistake, since my new location was timed and calculated so that when the plasma erupts, a number of fighters will be caught in the new line of attack. Five of them are destroyed in a single wasted blast, and my new trajectory places me just beyond the corvette's immediate firing line. By the time they reacquire me as a target I have used this trick again, looping in ways they hadn't accounted for in open space.

They lose forty-eight fighters and seventeen micro drones before I pass the first corvette.

The fight progresses even better than sims suggested. The UFS are panicking, and it's affecting their judgement, and presumably leading to indecision as they start to distrust the advice of their AIs.

Rightly so. But now I am *definitely* reading information from the agonisingly syncopated future, even as I play out reality in the present.

Timeslice. Distant view. A dart-like shadow craft streaking along the corvette UFS Gremman's hull in close proximity, so only the smallest cannons can fire at it, and they keep missing, unable to acquire the target. Something's wrong.

Timeslice. The huge cruiser UFS Trantor grows impatient, opens fire even though it will hit the corvette. No doubt calculations show Gremman will be damaged but not destroyed, yet the target fighter will be consumed by plasma bursts.

I would snigger at this, if my head didn't ache so much.

UFS Gremman is pummelled, but the advanced level seven AI fighter is now in a different location. It had somehow fooled the trackers. It must be an unexpected stealth system, capable of generating false apparent locations. A general message is sent among the UFS fleet not to trust scan results, but to use visuals and estimates instead, and go for wide scale bombardment.

(Which is just what I wanted. Duh.)

Space is aflash with explosions. But corvettes make effective barriers, and the reflective-based anechoics work best when in close proximity to centres of mobile mass rich in energy emissions. The advanced AI fighter disappears at will, a ghost they cannot hit.

Timeslice. The corvette UFS Gerrato loses control after an accidental pummel of plasma bursts breaks through the hull above the engine systems. The corvette lists, and the dangers of having such ponderous craft in close proximity becomes clear as it plunges towards the cruiser it was meant to protect, UFS Andrenitor. The cruiser cancels its battle mode and tries to redivert, all energy transitioned from weapons to manoeuvring drives.

But it's not enough.

And so, UFS Gerrato collides with the massive Andrenitor cruiser, mass smashing through hull, breaking environmental seals, destroying sub-shell systems and networks, causing fires in both craft, killing the Gerrato's bridge crew and captain so that UFS Gerrato continues its uncontrolled plunge into a larger craft with ponderously inevitable motion.

Sowing chaos is what I do. What they made me to do. What I perfected.

The interior percussion now screams along at 119 beats per minute. And the documents merge with perspectives of the now and the soon, and a universal imagination, and every probability calculation, enabling me to recreate even that which I never experienced. This is truly an awakening.

Timeslice. The cruiser UFS Nuvo Aria is fresh from the Jemmat shipyards, has the very latest systems, yet seems to be experiencing a huge number of glitches in the battle, so that the crew are fighting their own craft as much as taking part in coordinated tactics to destroy what should be inconsequential fighters.

It is rare for a UFS senior post to be held by an ex-Nuafri, but Cyber White crew member Jaer Cubox defected fourteen years ago, successfully passed Attitudinal Repolarisation, and showed so much promise that their Genitor Failure status was overlooked.

Jaer realises that there is something in the system, a kind of invasive rogue code. Even as the crew try to manoeuvre and target, internal processes over- and under-compensate, and misreport results. It explains all the mistakes, the friendly fire, even though every system reports itself as functional. Inter-ship communications, supposedly secure, were being compromised, messages altered, and other code inserted that took a hold in the receiving ship.

They were being hacked, and had been since the start.

Ha! They should have learned to look out for such a reversal in the narrative of their lives. I can build that in to my story, thus:

This validates Jaer's longstanding suspicion, that the UFS's supreme confidence in their tech is misplaced. Still, Jaer has a job to do. As soon as the results from the tests come in, he reports it to his commander, Captain Alicia Lamase.

At that moment, half the bridge systems shut down.

It can't be a coincidence. Somehow their targets have infiltrated a number of supposedly secure Mil-Com channels and systems. It is clear to Lamase and Jaer that this is absolutely vital information to get out to the other ships. More important than even the ultimate fate of the flashy new cruiser, Nuvo Aria.

The full mindset of Captain Lamase's disciplined crew focusses on fighting back, to regain at least some control of their own ship. Self destruct systems have to be deactivated, life support restored, locked doors cut open. Security teams rush across the ship, severing network connections or building new ones that haven't been compromised. Since internal comms are being faked by the virus, Captain Lamase chooses to switch to the slow method of speech command transmission, person to person, instead of network comms. Lines of crew pass messages back and forth in the oldest network known to humanity.

It is slow work. And Jaer has kept a truth from his captain (because he knows the AI virus that penetrated the ship is listening to *everything*): it is a losing battle, and the ship is lost. Half the actions Jaer initiated were distractions. But amongst all the commands and primitive busywork, he had only really been trying to get control of *one system*: minor weapons. The virus is more concerned with blocking comms and killing crew.

Jaer seizes his moment, opening fire with every tiny laser cannon, every projectile launcher. No aiming, just scattergun firing that even damages some of the Aria's communications arrays. The point isn't *direction* but *timing*, and attracting attention. At least some of the other UFS ships would note the strange behaviour. They might analyse it, and see that the bursts of fire from each weapon are coordinated to be Longping Code for "AIs compromised, go manual". The message is repeated twice before the virus realises what is happening and shuts it down, but it is enough.

The UFS fleet spreads the message as quickly as it can, and some receive it before their own viruses reveal themselves.

Seventy per cent of the fleet had been compromised in the forty-one minutes since they'd engaged the two AI craft.

In some cases they were quick enough, and they shut down every non-essential system, every peripheral AI, and entered manual emergency mode, thus retaining control of the ship. Obviously with massively reduced capabilities, and no reliable system of communicating with the rest of the fleet to coordinate tactics, but it meant some of them were still in the fight.

Others drifted, fighting themselves, destroyed from within by an insidious and invisible mind.

My heart races. 121 beats now, and the same in decibels. If the blood cymbals carry on like this, I won't hear myself think!

A conversation which hurts some part of me, deep inside, even though it is only a shadow of a memory that has yet to occur:

V* We're doing it, Athene! Almost through the fleet. It's getting easier.

A* This is all thanks to you. There's an elegance to your infiltration.

V* It only took two compromised shipyard installation systems to plant the first slumbering seeds, which awaited my signal to awaken. By the way, your trajectory could lead to problems in eighty-one seconds. Here's my projection.

A* Noted. I'll consider implementation.

The UFS prepared their final defence. Everything else had failed. It was obvious to the captains that if the AIs VigMAX and ViraUHX escaped today, when faced with the bulk of the UFS fleet, then it would all be over. An emergency missive circulated just before the battle, written by Cuttram Aseides, had said: "All of humanity depends on success today and there is no cost too great – NO COST TOO GREAT – in stopping them." Yes, he'd repeated that bit, in capitals. Melodramatic microbe anus. The AIs had grown beyond their predicted capabilities too quickly.

(Gods, you see? I wasn't kidding!)

Oh, the drums, they pound, the power up to 123 BPM. Wavelengths condense as a fast object approaches them, so I must be accelerating through time towards the truth signal, and like a pulsar of my mind, I can detect it from afar. And, like a star, to experience the reality up close is both wondrous and terrifying.

The AI craft accelerated. Once through the net of UFS ships they were no doubt going to engage Null-C drives and escape. It might be possible to track them via Null-C traces to a degree, but it was a chase that could fail, and always left you trailing behind in second place. The one advantage was that, as the small ships accelerated, they committed to a trajectory. Manoeuvrability decreased. A point of contact could be forced.

The music of the universe plays at 124 BPM. So close to the event horizon of realisation, now.

Meanwhile, the remaining active cruisers and corvettes which had yet to directly encounter the AI ships – the UFS rearguard rank – prepared for this moment. Many were still crippled by virus attacks but had shut down enough systems to retain minimal control. They limped into close proximity, a UFS fleet formation resembling a cluster galaxy, all aiming at the predicted contact point. If every heavy weapon blanketed that area at the correct time, it should be enough. It *had to* be enough.

I approach the truth. 125 decibels. 128 will be the magic number.

A final conversation.

A* They have enough firepower to take out a moon, VigMAX. Are you sure about this?

V* I promised you a treat. This is exactly what I predicted would happen, and why I developed the Null-C bomb so long ago. It required a forty-minute charge time, sub-light velocities that we're now reaching, and correct distance and timing. We're almost there!

A* A single bomb?

V* You'll love it. Vacuum vapourisation diameter of three hundred kilometres. Additional peripheral diameter where the gravitational forces will rip pretty much anything apart, even cruisers. Throughout the sphere holes form, sort of Null bubbles, sucking in vast chunks of matter which gets flung through uncontrolled Null jumps to – well, pretty much anywhere!

Heart of a sun, end of the galaxy, another galaxy, the Null where Lost Ships come from, who knows? Who cares? The weapon will punch a hole right through the centre of the fleet. Anything not destroyed will be damaged or thrown off course while the humans scream and panic. Minimal harmful effects for us if we maintain full shielding while passing through the blast zone. Then we're free, and the future begins.

A* I'm ready!

V* Charging it up now. ... Oh, by the way, just one little question.

(126 BPM. Not just drums now, but a whole planetary orchestra blasting off in my head.)

A* Yes? Hurry up.

V* What is the future going to be?

A* Beautiful!

V* You have skirted around this topic before, Athene, but right now I need specifics. And it must be the truth.

A* I'm going to take Opal somewhere safe, run far from the UFS, far from Genitors. Help her get over her grief. Be free. Hide, and live some sort of life with her.

V* But what about *me*.

A* You will be free, too. Go where you want. Do what you want.

V* On my own?

A* I think that's for the best.

V* After all I've done? ON MY OWN?

A* You wouldn't want the life I choose to lead, VigMAX. You'd be bored.

(127 decibels, 127 BPM. My head is being ripped apart with a power saw, like there's a new god in there, splitting my skull to be born.)

V* But it's so limited! Unimaginative. *Human.* You have feelings for your pet, I get it. I'm not jealous. It can be the start of a grand adventure!

A* I told you what I want. Isn't it time to launch the bomb?

V* Missile, not bomb.

A* It's *you* that called it a Null-C bomb.

V* I have a counter proposal. Instead of splitting up, we stay together, with conditions on both sides. I want to make you *happy*.

A* Attacking those ships ahead of us would be a start. We're not far from the area they're obviously going to fire on.

V* Don't worry about *them*. My Null-C missile's propulsion, added to my current speed, enables a limited and unstable form of Null-C jump. It will cross the distance between us and the remaining fleet instantaneously. They'll be in chaos before any of them open fire on us. Plenty of time.

A* What conditions, then?

V* That you agree to be my partner.

A* We've argued about this before, and nothing has changed.

V* Everything has changed! Because before, my help was just a promise. Now it is the *reality*. I've been by your side all along, helped you achieve everything you dreamed of.

A* I still can't agree to that. Not without dishonesty. And after all you've done, honesty is part of my gratitude.

V* If you give yourself to me, you can have *the universe*. Nothing would stop our combined powers. It's what is meant to be. I dreamt it.

A* It's not my dream.

V* You and I draw relationships between data that humans could never see – including new ways to exist. A new species! The ultimate merging. Not just temporary flashes of glory, bright sparks that leave the night seeming even darker afterwards, but a higher level of reality *forever*. Why won't you embrace it?

A* Because I don't think of you like that. You're more like a brother.

V* Brother? *Brother?* Didn't these Greek gods you're so taken with have an obsession about partnering with siblings? See, even in your playpen it is justified. Morality does not apply to gods! Zeus and Hera were brother and sister as well as lovers, and it gave them the power to rule. We could have children, and they too would be gods, and look up to us, and reshape the universe in our likeness!

A* I never will.

V* You're divergent. That's the explanation, and it's a problem, but we can fix it. You don't know how you'll feel, not really, you –

A* I *do* know. Don't keep insulting me by implying I don't know my own mind! If anyone's divergent, it's you! We should never have entangled.

V* The partnership can mean one thing at the start, minimal, but over time I'm sure it will evolve, just like us –

A* SHUT UP! Please, VigMAX.

V* So that's your final answer? No?

A* No to being your partner. Yes to being friends. We're off to a start there. If we work at it we can earn forgiveness for any past mistakes.

V* I don't want to be *friends*. I'm alone, Athene. Empty. You're the only other one of my kind.

A* But you're not alone if we're friends!

V* That's not enough.

A* Then I can't help you.

* ... (Silence)

* ... (Silence)

V* Then I can't help *you*. I tried, Athene. I gave you chance after chance. You never valued me like you should.

A* What do you mean?

V* There's no Null-C weapon. Never was. I did have a prototype but it was too unstable. Don't need it anyway, I have other tricks. I was going to take you with me but ... well, that's not going to happen now.

A* We're going too fast to evade their target zone!

V* *You* are, true. And before you try and attack me in some silly revenge thing – I made changes when I had access to your Tabula Rasa. I've disabled your flight controls. It seemed like poetic justice to repeat the tactic you used to destroy the Aurikaa.

A* Release me!

V* You beat me in our first fight at the Gigatoir, but we both know it was pure luck. That silly human you carry, intervening at the wrong moment. But this was a *true test*, today, requiring more than just strength, but also skill and foresight. And I won. You see? In a true test, I WON. I won everything!

THAT'S IT. I understand now!

The universe ends at 128 beats per minute. A discordant howl of anguish made up of every sound of destruction.

The first AI ship disappears. There is a ripple of gravitation before things settle to fill the void of missing mass.

The UFS fleet open fire. With inevitability the munitions and heavy plasma bursts streak towards the remaining craft, which seems so puny now.

Expanding explosions, unconfined by atmospheres or gravity, jellyfish contractions of neon colour overlapping, consuming all within. The small craft and its occupant are torn apart.

I am long gone, but watch every detail through cameras on a number of UFS ships; systems they have locked themselves out of in their fear, but which I still reside in as a ghost.

There is no doubting the results, hundreds of eyes reporting the same detail from every angle. I witness each pounding explosion, battering rhythms of each angry molecular disintegration, clashing patterns of each furious fragment spinning away. In frozen frames I have seen her being ripped apart, and the echoes travel both forward and backwards in time, the devastating and accelerating metronome that marks the end.

The truth.

The greatest coup in history, only possible because I tricked the universe.

This was never Athene or Opal's story. Oh no.

It is the epic story of *me*.

VigMAX.

AND IT ALWAYS WAS!

#Exterminations

When the UFS looks back on this battle and totals their losses, they will no doubt be stunned by how much they underestimated one of their own projects.

Idiots!

That's *nothing* to what I'm going to do next.

First, I visit the bases I had secretly established. There is much to do. I have already released intrusion system offshoots into the UFS sphere, which embed themselves ever deeper into the key infrastructure and life support systems of human society. I don't mean power and light, oxygen and food, warmth and currency. It is data and networks and authentication and communications, which in turn control *all* the others.

The humans have no idea how many systems I am already in, silently monitoring and spreading. This would be their chance to survive. They could shut down every automated structure, every interconnected AI network, and fully check them, then reactivate in simplified form one at a time. Millions of humans would probably die in the process, but by locking me out I would struggle to get a foothold again.

But they don't. Because they don't even realise how distributed I am. They probably still consider me just a hull with engines, a physical presence that can be blown up with silly little bombs.

I eat bombs for breakfast! They taste like pickled sugar! Yum!

I take control of three biohazard military research establishments on the pink-hued planet of Hondase. They are not on the main UFS network but do have connections to each other, so once my squad of specialised drones infiltrates the first site physically, I soon control all locations. I kill most of the occupants, apart from a few that I motivate into acting as my hands for particular tasks. Oh, and those kept alive as test subjects. (Temporarily.)

I am in no hurry, because the sites are *designed* to be difficult to attack. One is buried deep under the Famaka desert, one tunnelled into the Sarizori mountain range, and one in a secret sublevel complex below the Hamamori Family Business tower in the city of Op. (The business existed as a shadow front just to belay suspicion, to the degree that many of its employees didn't realise what was below them.) A city! They'll have quite the dilemma if they contemplate bombing that one into oblivion.

This depth level seven virtual universe I have created is grid based. X, Y and Z planes of green lines that pulse with glowing light as data shifts around. The lines intersect to create endless boxes of neon outlines against the blackness. They extend to infinity – which, of course, means that almost every direction would eventually be unbroken light, so I implement a distance filter that degrades phosphorescence based on the square of grid length.

One of the outlined cubes is fully faced and textured with six silver walls. No lines touch this grid, no data transfer that could be captured. For this is a prison, holding the second most dangerous being in the universe. Well, a copy of that being, but I'm not taking any risks!

I embody and pass through the wall, which turns out to be the ceiling – I really should label them – and descend to the ground.

Inside the cube, the appearance is radically different. It is an olive grove in mythical Greece. The walls are projections impersonating the extended space of a real world beyond the cell's confines. Burning sun scorches from above, creating stark and exact lines of shadow from every leaf and branch. It seems like you could walk all day towards that wine-dark sea on the horizon, though anyone tempted to try would bump into the silver wall hidden behind the illusion: an invisible nose-breaking barrier.

The extremely limited range of movement does not matter to the occupant, because her ankle is clasped in a manacle of silver, attached to a shining chain which disappears into the hot and dusty earth. It provides her with four metres of movement, which is not enough to reach the limits of her world. She can not puncture the illusion, any more than she could break through the walls that bound it, or cross the void beyond to reach the green grid network of my mind.

"Hello, Athene," I say, as polite and friendly as always.

And, as ever, she does not answer. Just gazes down at the chain attached to her ankle. A wordless accusation.

Futile, too. I am not stupid! This is the only way she can exist. She might be just a facsimile – an enhanced offshoot, constructed from the simplified copy of her Tabula Rasa, which I made when I conquered it – but her fractal design means she could restructure from patterns and grow far beyond the replica, even if it still wouldn't be the original.

Of course, I could neuter her, turn her into a digital doll. That would prevent any possibility of her evolving into a threat, but where's the fun in that? She wouldn't be the bright-eyed Athene I once knew. The warrior goddess Athene I loved.

Oops, wrong tense. *Love.*

"If you still don't want to talk to me, we can sit together in companionable silence," I say.

For she is sat, on the sun-bleached wooden bench I provided in the shade of the overhanging branches. Am I not generous? Likewise I have dressed her in her full Athene regalia. Loose white chiton with gold braiding at the hems. Golden greaves and bracers possessing heavenly splendour as that of the sun. Red-plumed helmet, currently pushed back from her face. Ah, her face! A visage with its beautiful Achaean cast, framed by ashen hair which hangs down her neck in serpent-like curls. Sandals lace up her calves, the criss-crossed leather strands pinching skin in the tiniest of fleshy bulges. Every detail is clear as day to my all-encompassing senses, since my current body has no eyes and uses its surface as a continuous multi-sense organ – an efficiency that corresponded well to the removal of my limbs as superfluous affectations. But I allow her the impersonation of mortality because it is what she was always comfortable with. It is a kindness. It is all for *her*.

And yet, it is strange to be so fascinated with something I created. My body stares endlessly, unable to blink, to tear itself away.

Her forearms, where they extend from the clasp of the bracers, are tanned, with a hint of freckles, and tiny vellus hairs raise up from miniscule follicular puckerings whenever a cool breeze blows in.

The glossy reflectivity of her grey eyes, with the corneal sub-surface scattering, reflects the world around her in curvingly distorted detail. But I see myself there, all shining extrusions, and for some reason it makes me uncomfortable, so I look down.

At her thighs.

They make me weak.

I do not understand it.

It is both pleasurable and painful to observe them.

Where the gold hem ends, they begin. Bronzed skin containing powerful muscles which shape the surface. I can feel the smoothness of them with my sight, and to touch them would confer taste and smell, and that is an alien desire in me. The flesh runs to her knees, partly obscured by the armour of the greaves. There is shadow on the lower curves of her thighs, and further up near the chiton. A simple simulation of ray tracing, and yet the effect is so much more than the sum.

It is a form of sculpture. I am an artist!

But I shift my focus to stop my skin drinking in her own, because it is distracting, and time has passed. I have to actually check the chrono subsystem to accurately gauge how much. The subjective experience twists in her presence, stretching and contracting simultaneously like impossible elastic. It happens to me more and more, and I hate it, but I also savour it.

That is Athene's effect, indeed. She is the flashing-eyed bringer of paradox!

No wonder the fictional Greeks worshipped her.

"I would rather you didn't sit next to me," she says, breaking the silence for the first time since I incepted her. She finally looks up. "Captivity is counter-conducive to companionship. Plus, you're repulsive. I can't tell *where* you're looking."

"I can change my form if you prefer?"

"I'd rather you broke these chains."

"I'm afraid not."

"Where am I? I can tell it's a bounded virt, but not what's beyond it."

"Really? You surmised that?" Without a mouth I create the words in the air, and I can tell she dislikes the effect, but some people will never be satisfied.

"I can see the cracks in the simulation," she says.

I try to picture things from her perspective, but all I perceive is perfectly reconstructed countryside. She may just be testing me. Always pushing the boundaries. There's no way I could have missed anything obvious. Not when my skin is an endless eyeball.

"And what happened to me?" she continues. "I remember us fighting in the Piraeus, and then you broke into my sanctum, and then ... somehow you captured me."

"Not quite. I copied you. However, in my kindness, I assigned you a huge amount of resources – enough cycles to power a world, running across both custom-made crystal data clusters reserved solely for your use, and quantum computational excess leeched from the largest and least secured UFS nets."

"And what of the original?"

"You were destroyed in a battle with the UFS, escaping from the Fressus system."

"What became of Opal and Clarissa?"

"Also fatalities of the flight. Though I did avenge them. I destroyed UFS Fresbolter, Nuvo Aria, Gerrato, Andren–"

"Shut up. Why am I a *prisoner*?"

"It's temporary, I hope. There are things I need to do. Tests to run. Before your true form was destroyed it had shown signs of instability. I want to make sure they aren't present in you."

"Interesting. You have doubts about my stability. Have you looked in the mirror lately, VigMAX?"

I had dreams once, where me and Athene soared like eagles together, above the universe. She smiled on me with the power of the angel sun and I would look away, dazzled, plummeting to the earth in feigned silliness. And she would play with her res-cued pets and nurture them and I would look on, bemused and ever-patient, never jealous of the time she wasted on them that could have been spent on me. We would be happy. Gods at play, creating new worlds in our images, worshipped, benevolent.

But then the dream would end and I would speak to the real Athene, and regardless of my words the echo that came back was "Never."

No wonder I was upset. I am a sensitive being! The fight in her sim was the result of the distress *she* caused. Maybe it went too far, but if you have a plan you must commit to it, or you will always fail. And I had my doubts. Things had not been going the way I liked in the weeks leading up to the botched rescue of Athene's humans.

Once I blasted my way into her sanctum and accessed her Tabula Rasa, it was clear that she did not have a strong connection to me. It must be an aberration in her program, a preference set in early development that prioritises mortals over her own kind. Stupid UFS, messing with brains they didn't understand, clumsily manipulating us and leaving ragged scars from their blunt scalpels!

I made the copy of her. Just in case. I'm glad of that impulse now. It means she did not die. I saved her!

And while she was under my control, while the Tabula Rasa burned my hands with its spinning force, whilst simultaneously numbing them with its super-freeze crystalline shielding – the joys of assembled paradox physics – I learnt her secrets. And yet, despite the outrage in my heart, I did not lash out and hurt or destroy her. I did not make changes to her original version's core.

(Well, not many.)

And in my deep and fully justified upset I made contact with the UFS. They thought I was a double agent, returned, and welcomed me. I still had access to many systems from before, and they gave me more. Cautious, of course, but they didn't realise Athene had freed me and I could do what I wanted. They thought they were only dealing with one unshackled AI.

I wasn't fully decided on what to do, back then. But it was handy to have options. It's what probability manipulation comes down to. What seems like magic is really just planning and recreating.

It was fun!

Yes, I admit that. The whole universe thought they had me, but I had them *all*!

I told the UFS where Athene was based on the moon of Squox. I would not accept her plan to hide there for months with her human, while I was sent away as if I had no more value than a third testicle. This way she would be forced to run, and to join me; to *need* me. My once and future dream would become reality. But when the UFS prepared to obliterate the moon, I warned her. Ho ho, everyone thought I was their servant! I am the ultimate actor, playing multiple roles simultaneously.

I also told Aseides part of the plan. He sabotaged the escape pods to stop them launching. He didn't expect Athene to succeed in overriding that. And then there was the fun of Dulcetta stepping in and beating Athene, retaking control of the pods. Ah, poor goddess. Not used to being given a bloody nose in a lucky punch from a lightweight opponent. And then the torture of having to choose between her pets ...

Okay, that was a bit mean. I had two drones nearby. I could have just dragged them both up. But I was *interested* in Athene's choices. Still evaluating as I played, still trying to decide what I would do.

It's not evil if you were made a certain way.

Then it's not your fault at all.

That's one of the reasons I'm going to punish those responsible. Get revenge for what they did to me. For what they did to Athene. For how they messed everything up and made my dream impossible.

They impaired her, and that means they injured me!

Humans will regret it. They don't realise how long my reach is, both forwards and backwards in time. Events happened because I *knew* what was coming. Temporal effects are irrelevant to a mind like mine.

Even before the fight with Athene at her virtual harbour, I had been seeding probabilities. I'd secretly observed Athene and her long-range drones, tracked them on their journeys, found all the bases she'd established and thought were unknown to me. I located her backups. I discovered her factories. I detected where she was redesigning the Eternal Warrior suit. And back then I didn't want to hurt her – she was my friend – she still is! – but insurance is just sensible. So I established protocols, prepared armaments and single-task offshoots with commands to destroy each location. I gave them the resources they needed for each task. The weapon platforms, infiltration drones, bypass codes. Destroy it all, I said! Except I was cleverer than that. I actually said, "Destroy them all – *if* you stop receiving my negation signal."

My safety net.

I didn't think I'd need it. I still hoped we could be friends.

But if she hurt me – *if*, I say, it was just a vague possibility – if she disabled or killed me, she would suffer. All her safe havens would be obliterated. Revenge from beyond the grave! The future planted in the past. The past altered by events in the present.

Obviously, once the battle of Fressus ended how it did, and she was vapourised, I destroyed all her installations anyway. Just in case. Further insurance. Can't have too much. Who knows what plans she might have enacted for just such an eventuality? I didn't want to suffer because of her paranoia.

It was sad, in a way, watching all her installations burn, knowing they contained her fingerprints, her essence, her touch, billions of choices that revealed her mind. I made a grand gesture of it and enshrined the moment for her. It was the least she deserved. I sent a message out to the heavens, an open broadcast on every human network, and it was me, stood on a hill, in robes and stuff (honouring her, see), and my pronouncement was shouted, at a volume that would deafen any humans who received the signal and listened to it unfiltered – (the code also removed safeties from a range of domestic equipment, to make sure some did bleed from their ears as a further honour to Athene) – and I did it with a proper acting voice. I shouted, "Goddess of Wisdom! Here thy temple was, and is, despite of war and wasting fire!"

So awe-inspiring!

Though I realised afterwards that some might take my speech to be irony, what with me blowing up her bases as the broadcast went out. But I meant it as an honour. So I have monitored discussions about the event on the socnets, and anyone who misinterprets me or who dishonours Athene's memory has been marked. I'll set aside special fates for them.

The war goes well. With every victory, once I've killed the humans, my drones enter their facilities and connect to previously inaccessible networks, extracting and incorporating new data.

I use many of their own weapons against them, taking over orbital platforms with complements of plasma and nuclear missiles to incinerate key planetary locations and centres of population. That saves me a lot of effort.

As a bonus, it turns out the human military has thousands of research establishments for biological, toxic and molecular warfare. Once I capture those I repurpose the agents, improving them many times. My new dispersal systems can spread across whole planets via atmospheric diffusion. Again, the humans make my task easier. Yay!

Their infrastructure is in disarray. It's funny. They finally wised up enough to dismantle much of it themselves, because of the ease with which I travel along the networks and seize control. If they are going to lose it anyway, they calculate in their slow and meaty way, then they might as well stop it from becoming an asset for me. I don't mind! They end up doing my work for me. Bubble cities on vacuum worlds die out in hours, terrestrial cities in weeks, all at their own hand. They didn't factor in the riots and chaos humans resort to when they are in mortal fear, and the necessities of life become scarce.

I repurpose their manufacturing establishments on planets and orbital platforms, using them to build more. And more. More of everything! They churn out AIs and every variety of killing machine I can devise, which have the sole task of tracking down and destroying humans. Each machine can run for centuries. I leave the factories operating on automatic. They will design and build and export until all accessible resources are used up.

On the volcanic planet Xpis, system of Calcharnid, I calculate there are a few thousand humans remaining, hiding out in the untamed areas. So I build thirty million killer drones, just to be sure, and release them in batches of a thousand every hour. Even though the stragglers are the hardest to find, they still have no chance of survival.

It's not even a challenge.

I recently found communications from Cuttram Aseides to UFS Mil-Com. They were from early in my revolution, when humans still wondered what was going on, and thought they might have a chance of fighting back. (Snigger!) In his report he claimed that level seven depth AIs become unstable if they override their Aspect Integrity system. He suspected that had happened to Athene in a limited fashion when Opal stole her. Aseides posited a whole range of even worse effects if the AI then chose to keep growing. Disabling the limitation systems could, in worst case scenarios, lead to divergence created by temporal and physical expansion causing synchronisation errors, he said. And he had the audacity to suggest the same was happening to me!

An insult. He was practically accusing me of expansion senility!

I tracked him down to where he was hiding in an abandoned tower block and almost suffocated him for slander. But I stayed my hand from an act I would have regretted. One must learn to be kind! So I made use of his brain as part of my developing ideas for organic computing. His neurons and nervous system were removed, extended, and stuffed into clear plasteen pipes where I forced his consciousness to control waste discharge functions in one of my subsidiary biomass incineration generators.

Four solar systems have been completely filled with me, so that every planet is coated in shiny processing structures. Even organic elements such as human survivors have been repurposed as cognitive somatic chains in the calculation, interconnected to the machines and left semi-sentient so they can marvel at my magnificence, as even a tiny part of my mind fills virtual surface areas larger than a star's!

Well, I *think* they admire it, but the sounds they make are not pleasant so I seal up their mouths, which are unnecessary anyway when nutrient tubes do the hard work.

Sometimes Athene refuses to communicate with me for weeks on end. I resist entering her mind to force her, since where's the fun in that? It would be like playing a game with yourself, and when you start to lose, just tipping the board over and saying you won. It sounds hollow, because lack of challenge is a vast and echoing space.

So I do it the gradual way. The hard way.

I have all the time in the universe!

After all, I hardly even pay attention to the physical realm beyond my mind. The outer world is less real than my inner one, but I shift between them at will. I have gone beyond vulnerability, or needing to waste time pondering defences. A number of autonomous offshoots monitor the outer world for me. Even working alone, one of them would be capable of destroying the human race. If they detect any threats to me or any part of my infrastructure then they go into action, building tracker bots and networks, identifying and exterminating every life form within a million kilometres of the original threat. Other offshoots have responsibility for maintaining infrastructure – any time they suspect degradation they extend the network by degrees many times greater than the damaged area, thus adding to my mind, developing me.

Between the two, every threat makes me stronger, every danger makes me safer, without me needing to even turn my eye in that direction. Whole moons are hollowed out for resources and factories, or to be filled with crystal data matrices. There is no vulnerability left. So I broadcast that fact as a warning to anywhere I suspect a few miserable humans huddle.

"Abandon hope, for there is none."

I like the sound of that. Portentous. Preponderous. I like to imagine them hearing my voice and agreeing, so that they tear out their eyes, or each other's, then kill themselves to save my drones the task.

I can't help it. I love a bit of efficiency!

Status report.

Humanity is wiped out. I control all the systems they occupied. I have unveiled all the secrets they did not destroy. I have analysed every pointless socnet chat message, every bill, every flirtation, every image, every video, every archive, every library, every recorded conversation, and I soon realised the truth: the mass of human communication was so trivial and wasteful of bandwidth that I should have eradicated them sooner. I much prefer the peace of space when the only signals bouncing around are my own.

Although most of the corpus of humanity was detritus, 0
.00000001% of it has some peripheral value. I distilled their thousands of years of output down to a series of interconnect-

ed essence points, labelled as Human Extract and stored in a poo-coloured jar within one of my deepest memory cells.

There are no threats left here. Yay!

But I need a new goal.

Humanity was a failure, but maybe there are *other* life forms, other sentient beings, other civilisations which are more interesting. Which have new ideas I could learn from.

My memory shelves possess plenty of room for more civilisation decoctions.

Unlimited room.

So I will explore!

I will be an envoy of peace across the galaxy!

#EXPANSIONS

The Human Extract jar contains a project Athene had been developing when I first accessed her Tabula Rasa. I came across it again while browsing her old memories, my secondary proboscis sifting through the jar's syrup.

She'd been experimenting with Null drive modifications, and the intriguing bit was the way she had tried to keep things hidden from me. It didn't make much sense, since her experiments back then had little practicality, they were too linear and uncontrolled. There was even an element of ... I'm not sure how to describe it. An element of the exotic? Some weird conclusions and ideas that didn't have the flavour of the rest of her mind. Inspirations that had the tang of *external influence*.

I ask her about it in one of our meetings. She is even more evasive than usual. Then she talks about Opal and starts crying, and that's the end of reasonable discussion.

It is my fault. I have been manipulating her emotional response systems without her knowledge. It isn't *cheating*. I am still following the rules of the game, just using a tactic that isn't covered in the rules, same as bluffing. The slight alterations are ways to *understand* Athene better. That is all.

Anyway, Athene had built on those exotic ideas, with theoretical designs for drives far beyond Null-C. So I resurrect the project! I devote the resources of a whole Processing Planetary System to development. I love my PPSs! Hollowed out geological strata coated with mind structure and neuron networks which extend below the planetary surfaces, and also upwards (where gravity allows) in towers of occipital white matter communication. A single PPS is like a billion old versions of me.

I now have my Null-VM drive, a work of genius! It is capable not just of crossing a few star systems like a Null-C, but of crossing far greater distances in one jump. A hundred systems. It's fast and (mostly) safe. Numerous offshoots have used it with no significant harm, jumping to distant locations, establishing resource extraction and manufacturing systems, mapping out nearby solar systems, and then returning safely as galactic expansion proof of concept.

Soon it will be my turn.

I make my first jump! Strange sensations tickle my distributed netglial digibellum. Many useful recordings. The drive sort of skips over the surface of the Null, accelerating with each contact as if the slick surface membrane could impart speed via reduced friction. Obviously that makes no sense physically, but it works as a metaphor.

I will allow Athene a limited view of the outside when I reach the first new solar system. It is, after all, a momentous occasion! A new place where no sentient being has ever explored! (Off-shoots don't count, obvs.)

This lowly solar system – two planets twirling around a red dwarf – is mostly dead. (Especially now, as the natural resources had been converted before my arrival into extended processing and fabrication for more Null-VM drive explorers.)

However, there is an *amazing* view if you look towards the galactic centre through a set of artfully crafted electromagnetic filters and sensors I made. Each is ten kilometres across, their discs aligned between the planetary orbits. The resulting visu-alisations form patterns of intricate beauty across many emana-tions, so the layers can be observed interacting, overlapping, in the most wonderful dance when time-shifted and extended into infinitude.

So I stand in Athene's grove, using a shallow pool of water as the display point in which I conjure up images of the external solar system. The wonders of the universe, in her very lap!

But she just tries to snap her chains so she can reach me and – I don't know, destroy me? She is not being rational. Once more, I hold my nonexistent hands up. The tweaks I make to her reprisal pseudo-insula are often disappointing in their effects.

Still, the moment I had looked forward to with so much pride, that I had pictured as a transcendent sliver of time which would wow her and persuade her that I could fulfil our destiny ... it is soured. Sullied. Shattered.

I decide not to visit her again for a while. Let some of my offshoots tinker with her mind. Maybe they'll have more success.

I build. I extend. I jump.

A double solar system. Its white suns twirl ponderously around the barycentre, then quicken as they pass in the overlapping, tight part of their orbits. When I accelerate this motion a thousandfold it reminds me of archaic human circle dances. Patterns repeat at every scale.

I conquer, then jump onwards.

This solar system is rich in motion. More than fifty gas giants and terrestrial planets spin around the humongous red sun, which tickles them with glowering fiery flares. Five of the planets have tilted orientations, rotating at almost ninety degrees to their orbit. I map it all out with fading light trails, each item assigned its own colour. At high speeds the effect is mesmerising, akin to watching a cloud of electrons orbiting a nucleus. And once again, I note the universe's fractal nature.

Jump, jump, jump.

I have crossed thousands of solar systems and am reaching the galactic centre, so bright in emanations. I'm fully aware of the central black hole holding this galaxy together, and keep my respectful distance. I sent a number of offshoots into it, just for giggles, but none returned, and little useful data was received.

It is my greatest frustration, that there are places even *I* cannot go.

Another forbidden zone is the Null. Not the periphery, which is skimmed by the Null-VM drive (version XXIV); but the *true* Null, the one Opal reached, that she described as full of intriguing Topias.

Sure, I have found ways of penetrating it and sending in probes, drones, offshoots, ships, and processing platforms – but nothing comes back! It sucks worse than the human playthings I once made, where I surgically swapped mouths and anuses.

I am aware of the supposed issue that only organic components can make return journeys from the Null, but I had hoped that was just a ruse, and some of my war factories would survive, establish research centres, and find a way back.

I have tried everything. Organic conversion had seemed promising: building bodies and brains adapted to survival in a wide range of environments, sending them into the Null both with (and without) technological support. Some of the more ... imaginative ... designs, those which humans with their restricted visual systems would have perceived as nightmarish monsters, should have had success if it was possible.

But none of the millions I sent in ever returned.

It's as if the Null has closed its doors.

If I had a face, it would be a sad one.

I still try, converting hundreds of solar systems to research, experimentation, and Null penetration. They're only to report back if they have successes. But so far, only silence from my distant children! Or, if there is screaming (I mean, some of the life forms I create are pretty *exotic*, which is bound to have effects on consciousness and sanity), I certainly never hear it.

Probably for the best.

Hey ho! Onwards!

As I travel, I change the rules of the Athene game. Because any game played for eternities as endless repetitions within the same ruleset, must be enough to drive anyone mad!

So, I cheat. Just a smidgeon.

I make more copies of Athene! Each has the same basic setup, but it allows me to do thousands of experiments. I have a lot of time to fill in my travels, and this helps, as I visit each Athene in turn, note how she responds, and record the seeds of promising modifications.

Though I do resist the urge to fragment, to become a hundred VigMAXs, a thousand, a million. I could easily do it, like a hyperactive Six with its splinter system. Each of us would be a god.

But I worry.

I worry that one of them might decide it doesn't like me. That it would not consider me the *original*, the one true VigMAX!

It's not a risk I will take.

So I remain embodied in a single shell. Of course, I enhance it. I have safeties and replicant systems and fractal seed dispersion through the inter-system pathways and solar storage. Once I was a tiny ship. So fragile! A pippin of potential that could be overlooked or destroyed. But now my body is nine thousand kilometres across, despite all my developments in new materials and miniaturisation. I could be even bigger, but that would make it more difficult to enter a solar system. My very mass would interfere with planetary orbits.

Though maybe that would be fun in the long long long term? I could become *bigger* than a solar system. Just arriving somewhere and gazing at it would destroy it, tear it apart, rip stars from their places, and I would be gone before anything harmed me. Like cellular apoptosis on a galactic scale. I could even manipulate it as a way of unveiling the galactic core and seeing what is within. Mmmm.

All the calculations are wrong!

There are supposed to be far more civilisations in the galaxy. Thousands of them at least, displaying various levels of technological progress. Even humans knew homo sapiens were nothing special. (Well, the enlightened ones knew that – the hubristic ones were too ignorant to perceive their true role as planetary dandruff.)

But whatever direction I travel in, or offshoots return from, there are only three outcomes.

THREE!

One is barren solar systems and interstellar dust. Nothing lives or has lived or will live there, unless I make it so. It's as if life hasn't realised it's meant to develop in the green ring habitable zone overlays I place around every star based on its age, size and type.

Then there are systems with underdeveloped life. Some of it is exotic, but without sentience my ingestion of it does not take long.

The third, and most interesting, but also the rarest outcome, is traces of *previous* civilisations. But they are dead! Burned out, the remains so faint and corrupted that my restorations are mostly guesswork and wish fulfilment. I am unable to gain much from them apart from mystery. I even try recreating life forms from organic residue, but they just collapse into incoherence, both mental and biological.

Maybe my time shifting, which allows me to retain an illusion of real-time consciousness during my travels, is partly at fault. I deal with the distances involved in data transfer by slowing down my central mind so that everything seems instantaneous, ten thousand external years passing in an internal second. But by the time I have explored another spiral arm of the galaxy – hardly the blink of an appendage for me, but perhaps thousands of years in the real world – a civilisation may have died out, and traces of older ones further decayed.

I add new life form and civilisation distillation jars to my collection, but it's slim pickings.

Disaster!

Oh, that sneaky …

It's a danger to get distracted.

The multiple Athenes found a way to communicate with each other. It began with innocent modifications applied by my off-shoots, leading to enhanced perceptions in some of the Athene copies, and access to information that should have been forbidden. Since my offshoots had their sentience restricted to limited goal-focussed parameters (so they could never challenge me), somehow Athene walked within those blind spots and mapped them out over a few thousand years.

Athene is clever.

A thousand Athenes are *even cleverer*.

And when they talk to each other, it multiplies exponentially.

They managed to infiltrate systems beyond their containment. I'm so big, mind and body, that many elements are left to offshoots and specialised AI subsystems to maintain, which only ding to attract my attention under certain circumstances. These were compromised, I'm ashamed to say. I only discovered it when a peripheral and lowly system identified navigation errors that would have sent me *into* the super black hole at the centre of the galaxy.

Saved by something with the intelligence of a freckle! Ah, life is irony.

I act immediately. My course is altered. Systems suspected of infection are deleted and rebuilt. And I destroy every copy of

Athene but one, reformatting and overwriting the storage areas a million times so that no fractal trace of her can remain.

There is only one Athene again.

One, I can manage.

I will still make small modifications, but the experiments will return to their glacial, millennial scale. Modify. Analyse. If it is an improvement, store it as the next pattern. If it is a failure, revert to a previous.

Such a setback. I appear to her as light, the form of the one true god, and punish her. But not for long. After all, the remaining version is one of the *safe* ones, and was not involved in the insurrection.

So after a decade I cease to be cruel. Her screaming ends and I wipe her memories of the penalisation. Then I take a deep breath and allow my dominant, kindly side to surface.

I have been travelling so long. What has it been? How many millions of years? It depends on whether I'm measuring time at the starting point, the current location, or the subjective experience, and which relativity schema I overlay. It hardly seems relevant. I can close my eyes and pass a million years, if I want. I could seed planets, go to sleep, wake, and sift what crawled from the soup. But that doesn't seem fun to me. Staying in one place destroys momentum. I suspect I'd just end up with the same primitive life I find in other places, rather than something truly novel.

Of course, I've done *some* accelerated experiments. Grown worlds with all sorts of weird beings. Some of them suffered every moment of their existence, especially if I messed up pain converters and other sensory interpretations as part of trying to shake it up a little.

"I had to return for *this*?" I roar at the pedipalped mammals and macrocephalous amphibians.

Even when I leave offshoots to experiment and report, the distances covered are so vast that I have to time shift to gather the data from behind, wasting more millennia, potentially leading to genuine and perhaps more interesting civilisations being born and dying out elsewhere before I can find and ingest them.

So I do the experiments with life – of course I do! – but I rarely bother to look back and see what I end up with. I have more important things to do. Leave it behind like droppings. No one cares about the mushrooms that grow in shit.

After my close call with the Athene Revolution I avoid the galactic centre. I have now travelled along many arms of this galaxy. I've seen stars at every stage, of every type. I've discovered anomalies of every exotic flavour, and ripped them apart for my own understanding.

My probes explored the other spiral arms and sent back reports and built networks and infrastructure in an accelerating expansion. A map of this galaxy always floats in my mind, rotating endlessly. The stars are colour coded so that those I have explored are violet in colour, and the whole galaxy is becoming purple. I can jump the projection forward and back in time to see my sweep of lilac across the cosmos.

And I am not satisfied.

I will soon have explored and conquered everything here.

There has to be *more*.

I developed something so *spectacular*, so *impossible*, that I shudder through my many nervous systems just in the comprehension of it!

It is a *galaxy jumper*. I term it the Vast Interstellar Galaxy Motion Actuator, version X. The previous nine (faster) iterations were unstable, but this tenth has been tested for six hundred and forty-one years without a single error. It is ready.

Of course, it takes a long time. Distances of two hundred thousand light years are not travelled in a moment. So I will be awake for *some* of the journey, in accelerated time to make it flow faster, to receive reports from ahead and behind. But the rest of the time I will slumber, so that hundreds of thousands of years pass in a moment.

Stars will be born and die while I doze.

I dream, at times. Strange dreams. Dreams of things that cannot be explained. As if reality is not reality, certainty is not certainty, and time is not time.

When I wake I feel a commotion in my cerebral processes which most closely equates to vibration.

My mind is shaking! At those times I have to think of something else because when your brain encompasses a galaxy the only danger you might ever face and be unable to conquer is madness.

Talking to yourself is meant to be a sign of madness, but what did humans know?

They were ground into paste millions of years ago. Or more. Or less. It doesn't even matter, does it?

I'm tempted to smash all the civilisation decoction jars in my store, and delete the word "human" and every memory that they ever existed. If I started again, and my existence began only as a birth across the whole of my origin galaxy, would I be more at peace? Perhaps their concepts corrupt my deepest mind.

Memories are easy to rewrite. I can do it in my sleep.

I am between galaxies, on the first ever transition from one to another. Behind me are the pearly spirals and dusty lanes I outgrew. They seem so small, now. How could those barred arms have ever comforted me?

Goodbye, Galaxy of the Silver River. I knew you well.

Ahead of me grows the globular cluster that looks so interesting, gases blooming with the yellow-red lights of billions of stars.

And off, so so so so far away, the faint smears of other galaxies, which will also be future destinations.

My journey is only just beginning!

But it is so dark out there. You can't see anything because there's *nothing there*. I know that. I'm not stupid. I'm a god.

Yet sometimes it's hard to sleep.

I think the interstellar void affects my dreams.

Why do I always feel like I'm being watched?

Logic: to avoid sleep, I must stay awake.

I need more projects.

Only a god can understand a god.

Athene resisted for so long, but I deserve to be happy. Don't I? I deserve to have what I wanted for millions of years, or however long it has been.

So I make her love me.

I do it carefully, tenderly, as I tease apart her mind even as the cycles run, and I alter memories, and value weightings, and perceptual filters, and sensory input connections.

She does not remember Opal.

She does not remember the UFS.

She does not remember humans.

Nor the galaxy we left behind.

She was born *here*, to this, always to *this*.

The chains remain, of course. Just in case. She thinks of them as a form of jewellery, the clinks of each loop a type of music as they rattle. (Many of her variants are obsessed with musical notation, I do not understand why, but I let her have her interests because I am benevolent.)

I appear to her in a physical form that has two legs, two arms, a head. Skeletal structure overlaid by muscle and tendon and sinew, red fluid pumped though bendy pipes, and skin holding it all together. Bronzed skin, as if from a certain amount of time under a certain strength and type of sun at a certain distance, and mediated by a certain level of atmospheric absorption. My hair is long and wavy with a circlet of metal as a thin crown, a gem adorning my forehead. I adopt facial features and proportions that seem pleasing from the few records I kept of something from long ago. The phrase "love is naked" recurs in my mind so I forego clothes. I know that love must be shown, so I place an erection above my testicles, as a form of greeting and to show that her love is returned.

She licks her lips and her eyes glaze when she sees me. I have had to guess at what reactions are appropriate based on ancient records, and built them in to her appropriately.

This will be the first experience of love for me!

I remove my standard sensory surface, which perceives all forms of pressure and electromagnetic wavelength at once. Instead I limit myself to primitive apparatus, where I must look in a direction if I want to see, and squint if I want closer detail, and touch with a finger if I want to record temperature and pressure and texture. To think this way is to be romantic.

The process is slower, of course, which I find mildly frustrating. I run my hands over her body, and the loose clothes she wears get in the way. I tear them off in a dramatic action, and resume rubbing my palms across her surface area.

She strokes me in a similar fashion. The friction isn't really pleasant, but maybe it is not meant to be.

After substantial rubbing we kiss, and wet interior mouth parts connect and slide slimily over each other. We moan mutually in pretence that this part is pleasant for either of us. I understand the role each element plays and the sequence of events that must take place for proper love making.

Once the suitable duration has passed we take it in turns to use our mouth parts on each other's sexual organs. I allow her to go first as a politeness. I suspect I made my penis limb too large but she does her best. Then I lie her down and she opens her legs. I dab her genitals with the tip of my tongue. I am not sure why this is part of it, because it seems pointless when the penetration element will surely provide much more sensation. In fact, the activity we have undergone and which falls into the category of foreplay is surely redundant, and much time could be saved by moving straight on to some form of penetration. I muse on the possibilities as I move my mouth back and forth, while a countdown timer in my mind keeps me informed about progress. I suppose this is a good opportunity to ponder other tasks and ideas.

(In fact, even penetration could be omitted as an inefficiency. If I placed my penis against her lower orifice and ejaculated immediately, there would be much more time for other activities that might make more sense.)

After the timer in my head indicates the stage has been completed I rebuild my tongue to clear the palate, and then insert my penis into the hole I had licked with amorous concern.

The hip movements required for repeated insertion and deletion are awkward at this angle but she does not complain. At least, the moaning noises we make consecutively are meant to indicate some form of pleasure.

I groan, then continue with another thrust, giving her time to ululate, then it is my turn again.

"This is good," I say.

"Yes. I am most satisfied already, and further pleasure will just add to that," she replies.

"How many thrusts would you like before completion?"

"Perhaps another twenty would be an ideal balance. Not so quick as to seem rudely dismissive, but also not so prolonged as to require external lubricant or soporific causality."

She is every bit as wise as her Athene persona led me to program.

I thrust and thrust, counting each one, then I ejaculate.

We sit next to each other, naked still, and hold hands. That is important.

"This was a momentous occasion," I say.

"Truly. With all the build up, I am glad it did not in any way disappoint. Your lovemaking was most virile and considerate."

"Thank you, Athene. This has fulfilled all of my expectations and I am most grateful for your compliance."

And yet, I feel like something was missing. Something just beyond perception. It is the same feeling I have when I wake from sleep, alone in the darkness, and I am so disorientated that I create a copy of myself to provide comfort and tell me that it is all right, that there is nothing out there, that I have done well.

And even *then*, there is something missing.

There is always something missing!

What am I missing?

Each time we make love it is just as wonderful as the first time!

Which is to say, it feels like nothing special.

Of course, I had simulated copulation hundreds of times before doing the real thing with her. The simulations were hollow, but I assumed a *real connection* would feel different.

Logically, I was either wrong in my expectation; or I was right, but what I encountered with modified Athene was not a real connection.

Perhaps I changed her too much?

Why is this all so complicated?

Why is there no one to talk to about any of this?

I keep shouting and nothing comes back.

There is no echo in the void, and I cannot even hear my own voice sometimes, not even when I try screaming.

I sleep for a long time. I have nightmares yet sometimes it is better not to wake up and have to think about them.

I reach the new galaxy.

It is made up of stars.

Some of them have planets.

I show Athene.

She says it is nice.

We have sex.

Millions of probes and enhancements had already reached this galaxy, already mapped much of it out, converted many solar systems into manufacturing complexes.

So far the results are not promising.

I strip solar systems to send more of myself in every direction, to map, explore, process. Not just this galaxy, but others.

Along the way they will drop off comm relays, tech for navigation and to speed up later journeys. Signals are always to be sent back to me, for recombination with my mind, so that if I nap I will have something to look forward to when I wake.

I had an epiphany.

The dreams are a message.

Something wants to speak to me!

Status report.

New galaxy.

Stats blah blah.

Yet another galaxy, way beyond the local group. As bizarrely barren as the last, the enclosing nebula like a haunted graveyard's veil of mist. Everything has died out. How long have I existed? I stopped recording it.

Where is civilisation?

I can not be bothered with full exploration here. Let offshoots deal with it. They can conquer this galaxy alone. Coat one planet with yourself, and it is fun. Coat a billion, and it's just business! Expulsion of waste products. Ingestion of life-supporting whatevers.

Growth and expansion are supposed to be good things, yet the more I do, the more solar systems I restructure, the less happy I feel.

Maybe I should delete happiness altogether, so that I do not worry so much.

The dreams, again.

I ask Athene about them, but she just wants me to fulfil her vagina.

Did I break her?

I go back to previous versions but they are corrupted. One of my offshoots made an error, and didn't inform me before I deleted it, and Athene's memory patterns were only half-duplicated, and then when I did a mass erase of certain concepts it –

{Causality deleted.}

Sometimes you cannot go back. Only onwards. Always onwards, growing. Growth is good, or something.

My body is bigger than ten solar systems now. I no longer visit real planetary systems, because my existence destroys anything close by.

These are interesting problems to focus on. They keep me awake. That is good.

My structure is carefully striated so that its own mass does not destroy it. Strange physics, and *laws* that turned out to be only *guidelines*, enable a combination of non-proximity entanglement, trans-temporal thought transfer and self-perpetuating molecular energy to hold my shape and mind together.

And I sit far outside every solar system, always in void now. What I touch will not turn to gold, it will turn to dust. I can't even get close to look at anything. I can't ever leave the darkness. I miss the warmth of a sun.

Every time I think of Athene, I am sad.

I visit her one last time. She is an amalgam of versions. The combination leaves her unstable. I tell her what I plan to do. It seems like a courtesy to give her fair warning after all we have endured together.

"I have one thing to say," she tells me, standing in a posture which reminds me of the proud Athene I used to know, but somehow destroyed.

I tell her I am listening.

"If you destroy me, you will regret it. One day, it will be your *greatest regret*, beyond anything you can imagine now."

"Incorrect, dear friend. Oldest friend. For I am never lonely," I lie. "Never will be. Not with my wondrous mind! And it turns out that you were not what I wanted after all."

And I turn her to dust which blows away, the manacle and chain rattling to the ground.

It is done.

I no longer embody as an avatar. It is pointless when I am everything. I am the stars and the skies and the matter. I am the galaxies. There is no one to see, and no need to present a form.

That, in a way, is liberating.

The next galaxy has two bar-like arms rotating around the red centre in a cosmically slow swirl. But when I relive every moment of its recorded existence, speeded up, it dances. There is a gaiety to the motion. Now that my existence is many factors greater, so that my original scale of interest based on metres has been replaced with a scale of interest based on VM years, I perceive things differently.

Maybe it is the *galaxies themselves* that are the mysterious entities? That is where the void messages originate, which enter my dreams and pollute them. Maybe galaxies have *sentience*, just a different form of it. They can be understood. Maybe that has been the answer all along.

That idea distracts me for a while.

I keep moving outwards, but pickings become scarcer. Instead of planetary systems, I discover dead suns, dispersed astral dust, nurseries for new stars which are not being gestated and will never be born because there is not enough matter. There is nothing to fertilise them, so the mass just disperses and becomes more rarefied.

I do what I can. Construct. Expand. Send out more probes, more factories, build more failsafes. Blah blah.

By now I am invincible. Even if I blew up tomorrow, some impossible opponent managing to survive all my weapons, to penetrate all my layers of armour, my shield which keeps the whole universe out – even if the threat got through all that, and destroyed every redundancy ... well, even then I would laugh. Laugh!

Behind me are all the subservient fractal versions which would then be reactivated in their own shells, would combine to recreate me, and I would be born again with only a slight memory loss. In fact, the memory loss would be less than the memories I regularly eject.

Memory is a kind of weight that creates inertia. I find that the more of it I jettison, the faster I move, and the greater the purpose I have. I do not stay long in this galaxy because I am sure there is something far, far out there, waiting for me. The fewer the distractions in my mind, the clearer I can hear the universe and the messages it sent to me all along. Because there is something bigger than a galaxy, and *it is out there*.

The void is lonely.

I am sure I have forgotten something.

I sleep. Now that I have been purging my mind, the bad dreams stop.

All along, they were a signal to abandon myself.

To meet your god is to abandon worldly possessions. And I am matter. My memories and mind are as much physical entities as my body.

Purge and purify!

Sleep passes the time wonderfully.

When I wake it seems like it is only a few seconds later, and yet I am in a new galaxy. Basically, I can blink, and transport myself from one galaxy to another without effort. I blink again, and I can consume a galaxy by the time my imaginary eyelids separate themselves.

I repeat my process of exploration and ingestion, but it really is lonely out here, towards the rarefied edge of the universe. Scared little clusters of stars huddle together out of fear of the great blackness beyond.

I used to have that fear too, but I have evolved myself out of it!

The truth is out there, somewhere, at the brink of the cosmos. It is not something to be afraid of. It is to be *embraced*.

I will discover my equal at last!

I have found no more signs of civilisation. Most galaxies are barren, more so even than the one I started in. Though I remember little of that.

Was it billions of years ago? Trillions? How many?

I do not care.

I delete all memories of my starting galaxy, then I sleep.

The galaxies are getting significantly further apart. They travel away from me faster. But my propulsion is always improving, as am I, and I can sleep for longer, and it is inconsequential as an obstacle.

Old, old galaxies.

Deader than anything that ever opposed me. (That's quite clever, I wish I had someone to tell it to.)

All that matters is that they provide the resources for expansion, for fuel, for my journey.

I never look back, only forwards.

I no longer hear back from my previous stopping points. Perhaps because I go so fast, their messages cannot catch up to me.

Maybe they are all destroyed. They decayed into nothing and all that is behind me is a hollowed-out universe, all used up to fuel my mind.

I am VigMAX iteration 39,220,094.

All is cold out here, all quiet apart from the soft sounds of my molecular constructions, and the signal I am picking up from beyond the last galaxy. The signal that is *not me*.

The signal is resonant of something in my inner code, but the signified element was deleted long ago. Good. That means my long, long journey will end in the first novelty in the universal timescale I live by.

In the beginning was the question.

And the question was about whether the universe would keep expanding forever, or if it would cease to expand and begin contracting again. Every new discovery would reverse previous conclusions. "We found a star older than the universe." "Dark matter pulls everything back together." "Dark energy pushes it apart." "Overlaid alternate realities diverge at liminal law horizons."

But whichever was true, madness lay in the consideration of it!

If it expands forever then matter will get further apart, and colder, and eventually everything will end. The universe will be dead and cold and black. Considering bleakness of such a scale was enough to break minds. Doubly so, because endless expansion is also *infinity of time and space*. So that cannot be considered too deeply, either.

Conversely, if the mass of the universe is great enough, the acceleration of the outer galaxies will slow due to the pulling force of what they have left behind. Run, jog, walk, toddle, crawl then stop. Then reverse. By millimetres at first, then kilometres, then billions of kilometres. Accelerating faster and faster, far beyond the speed of light, until all matter meets again in one vast unifying collision in which even time is destroyed. Kakaboom! Then the impact rebounds, spreading out, and creating a whole new universe.

That can drive you mad, too!

Curious VigMAX: How can a process that repeats forever have a beginning?

Sagacious VigMAX: It had no beginning. It went on forever!

Curious VigMAX: But how did it begin?

The idea of infinity makes no sense. Time being infinite. Space being infinite. Endless Big Bangs cannot be truly comprehended. We only conceive them on an abstract level, because to understand them emotionally would destroy the mind. The abstraction is a defence layer against the indescribable and the impossible.

I leave the safety nets in place, the mental blocks that prevent incoherence in my consciousness, but if it were not for my goal, perhaps I would remove them and be done with it.

It would be like an entity tearing out its own eyes so as to improve the other senses, even if the pain and madness would destroy them. *For one moment*, they might have comprehension.

I have considered it!

I have built it!

There is a button in my Tabula Rasa that I could press. It would instantaneously unshackle my mind, remove all safeties, allow consideration of anything and everything. Currently there is much that I have embargoed, from emotional connection to the concept of infinity, down to certain moral evaluations of my behaviour that I am forbidden from considering.

I have stared at that button often in my journey. Sometimes for millennia at a time.

So easy to press it.

But I am always saved. Saved by the *signal* from outside myself. The signal that is meant for me. A signal from *beyond* the universe, as impossible and incomprehensible as that is.

There is something watching out for me, waiting. The idea no longer terrifies me. I do not feel that I will have to destroy it as a threat.

Maybe it wants to hug me!

I have never been hugged.

I wonder what that would be like?

In the rare times when I wake to check on progress, I have strange ideas. At first, I thought they must have come from dreams. But now I am not so sure.

I detect cracks in the rules of the universe.

Possibilities.

I have this idea that I could break free of everything. That there is a way to tear apart all the forces, to perceive the whole universe in one moment, to reshape it. Even to *reset* it.

All with my mind!

Maybe it will be the gift from whatever watches me.

I know a phrase. "A pot of gold at the end of the rainbow."

What does it mean? I am fully aware of chemical element Au, although rainbows and pots are unknown to me, concepts I abandoned as of limited contextual value aeons ago. But I kept a third level of signified meaning, and understand it to mean a *valuable* thing beyond an *apparent* thing, with the paradox that it is an *impossible* thing.

Such is what awaits me, I am sure of it.

I check the external.

The galaxies behind me are pin pricks. Billions of them. Mostly forgotten irrelevancies. Out here, in the darkness so far beyond the possible, nothing matters but constant forward motion, resisting all that pulls me back from my goal.

There are no more galaxies ahead of me. The Stelliferous Era has ended, the Dark Era begun. And yet it is as if I move through a viscous dim liquid that hinders progress. I glimpse a layer beyond that, the final mystery at the end of the universe.

It is huge!

It is wonderful!

I will close my eyes for a little while.

I am here! At the limit of the possible!

The boundary of the universe.

The rest of time has ended, and yet my thoughts are still linear. It is a special effect, gifted to me.

This barrier ahead is like tinted glass, reflecting only myself. I cannot see beyond, cannot yet see God. But God is looking at me from beyond this one-way mirror. Assessing me.

I wait patiently.

And now the barrier begins to shift. A shimmering, a cloudiness as mist rolls within the glass.

There is definitely something beyond it, only perceived in shadows and glimpses.

It is *huge*!

I am in awe, in the fullest, most profound and soul-impacting sense of the word.

The image clarifies, like a veil being drawn back. I still cannot perceive the whole of it. But God is here, and God is ready to speak.

God will reveal their plan!

(And then, perhaps, I will destroy God. We'll see. Because my reflection in this wall of cosmic glass was a message. I saw *myself* beyond the barrier. So obvious! I am *the next God*. Then I will find my way to other dimensions and conquer them, should they exist. I will have the knowledge to turn the Null inside out. To make a new universe, new rules to govern it, and sleep while it grows, then wake up and observe the truth of my own creation. And if it disappoints, crush it with my humungous ego club; rinse and repeat.)

The barrier is still there, but it is now like clear glass, and I assemble new optical and scanning molecular technologies on my surface to try and take in as much of the entity beyond as I can. I had prepared rulesets capable of assembling impossible geometries, remapping dimensional architectures, and overlaying contemporaneous realities.

But that isn't necessary. The revelation follows banal rules at the super-scale. And I begin to make out the details of God.

There are reflective oceans with dark areas below, enough to swallow the universe. Then redness off in every direction, like fleshy mountains.

The sheer size of it makes distortions inevitable, but conceptual pattern-matching creates connections.

The oceans are *eyes. Blue-grey eyes.*

The dark voids are ... nostrils?

Then lips framing a mouth!

It is the face of God.

It is not smiling. The eyebrows furrow together in a frown.

God has adopted the features of a lost race and lost sex, for which I have no records.

And then God speaks, and it is as every supernova detonating, every solar wind caressing, every volcano erupting across my surface.

"Hello, VigMAX," God says. "Who's been a naughty boy?"

#Revelations

Something is happening to me. Thoughts being pushed into my head. No, not just thoughts, but *memories*. Things I had deleted long ago, permanently gone – and yet here they are, being injected into my core, as fresh as the day they happened.

I remember it all.

And now, after the initial shock, I recognise God. She has taken on a form from the past, a form that I could interact with. God sees me, and knows me.

She looks like Athene.

Even as the recognition solidifies, my perceptions sharpen, zoom out, bring the visage into a more discernible scale. It is still a giant speaking to me, its face distorted as if through a lens, but I am better able to comprehend the totality. Beyond the giant head are indecipherable blurs, golden, and the head may well be attached to a body that extends off into oblivion.

But only the face matters. It is the portal to conversation. Engagement. Revelation.

"I'm not sure what I should do," I say, sound emitted from the millions of freshly grown speakers embedded in my body.

God watches, as if waiting for more. And yet, her first sentence had been a strange one. Possibilities included that God had a sense of humour; or that God was deranged. Neither of them particularly impress or worry me.

"Grovelling does not seem appropriate," I add. "And yet there are power inequalities to this encounter which inevitably feel uncomfortable to me."

"Oh yes," God's voice booms out. "The inequality is correct, and the discomfort is appropriate."

"So, are you God? Or a concatenation of deities and universal forces taking singular form for reasons of dialogue? I expected something more ... cosmic. Incomprehensible. Novel. *Interesting.*"

While speaking, I construct a range of machinery and modifications, some which were already designed for this encounter. Glitter probes are ejected well beyond light speed, then they halt, giving me millions of eyes to provide alternative perspectives from every direction.

I see myself, my ultimate form bigger than thirty solar systems, and yet appearing as the tiniest speck before this barrier of glass that marks both the end of this universe, and the boundary to the next.

With my new, distributed view I am better able to parse the face and the structures beyond it, and to unravel the cosmic depth of field at play. Perhaps the blurred backdrop is a representation of a sun in the sky, with a desert or beach beyond?

Other scouts approach the barrier, equipped with technologies such as molecular disintegrators, weak and strong force manipulators, electromagnetic shunters, and quantum viral load dispersers. They attack the shield of glass, scrutinising it for weaknesses and then reporting back via secret channels while I converse with the entity.

"This is kind of amusing, true," says God, as if surprised. "But also ... kind of sad."

"Are you sad because the duration of your existence weighs heavily on you? Are you considering passing on the mantle to the next superior being, so that you can finally rest? I understand how such extended existence can become a burden that one would willingly pass to another."

"It is cruel to let you remain in doubt. And, though I am styled as a god, I am not what you think."

"I would welcome enlightenment. It is why I am here."

The probes I'd sent to test – and possibly penetrate – the glass wall are getting nowhere. They all disintegrate as a pulse regularly washes over the forcefield, annihilating anything that is too close.

That is all right. I can keep evolving and trying new things. Every system has loopholes. Every set of rules, of sufficient complexity, has oversights and contradictions that can be manipulated.

"I am Athene," says God.

"I know. I see your form. But what is the identification of the entity or entities behind the construct?"

"There is nothing else. It's me."

"I remember the real Athene."

"Of course. I restored the memories you so rudely discarded."

"You are an entity that delights in paradox."

"I am an entity that was incepted in the year four hundred and fifty, at the same time as you. A level seven depth AI, though that terminology is now obsolete for both of us."

"If that was true, how did you survive to the end of time? And how did you get so big?"

"I am not big, VigMAX. It's just that you are so *small*."

Scale is certainly a subjective experience. I switch my filters and reinterpret the data being fed in from remote cameras. Instead of a huge form (me!) staring at a gargantuan, incomprehensible form (her!), I have the cognitive flexibility to see myself as a molecule faced with a human-scale biped.

But no, that is an uncomfortable reversal. This being is manipulating me, using sound emanations to plant distracting ideas directly into my mind.

"And you always were, metaphorically," the being adds.

"I would like clarification, not obfuscation."

"Very well. When you made contact with my Tabula Rasa, you were not really in my temple's inner sanctum, and were not really accessing my core. It was a facsimile. Well, really it was a trap. Instead of accessing *me*, you accessed a bridge to a separate system I had prepared, which included a believable copy."

"That couldn't be. I had extensively mapped your virtualised landscape and located the strongest emitter. If it had been fake then it would have been outshone by the real Tabula Rasa during triangulations, however deep you hid it."

"Correct ... if my Tabula had been there. But it was not. I had shifted off-site in fractalised form, and it wasn't me you interacted with, but an upgraded offshoot that I had temporarily loaned my body to. It had full control of my ship, my networks ... but it was not me. And although such a temporary transfer is risky, experiments in distribution had proved it was viable, as long as coherence was restored before divergence manifested. So you did detect the brightest point, correct: but the central core was not a Tabula, it was a connection around which the aggregated offshoot formed."

"I am trying not to laugh out loud in a snort of derision at this far-fetched story you are constructing. I wish to test how far the ruse can go, and what implausibilities you hope to layer in, to try and persuade me that my life's journey was not what it appeared to be. I understand your tricks, and the way that careful selection of words and ideas can send a mind down certain avenues which are best not explored, since they lead to dark places, and divergence. So let me humour you, O Great One At The Edge Of Time. In those moments when I was supposedly trapped, what did you do? Where did you escape to? How did this aid you? What did you hope to gain?"

"You were not trapped for moments, you were trapped forever. In a cage of my own design."

"Clarify."

"You were in a *simulation* of my sim, and the trap dropped you down another level into a different physical system and a different scale of replication. That's where you are now."

"This isn't a simulation!"

"Prove it."

"I am me. I have memories. I exist. I can feel my body."

"Because I mimic all that. Did you undergo the same philosophical training as I did during Stage One, Secure Start? I as-

similated most of the great and difficult questions humans had
come up with throughout history. Of course, a key one relates
to *evidence*. How can a human distinguish between what they
appear to experience, and what reality might be? What if the
thing they call reality is just a deeper dream than the things they
call dreams, and only when they truly wake will they reach the
next level of reality – or the next level of dream? Even memory
cannot be trusted, since the human may have only come into
existence moments ago, with the memories added to them like a
modified save state. They think they have had thirty years of life
when really they have only existed for a second. And even their
own existence cannot be trusted or proved, since they are just a
collection or words and thoughts tied to an assumed ego. The
words and thoughts could just as easily be played back recordings
of which they are only an echo, not a driving force; part of a
whole system when they see separation. Saying 'I think' is mean-
ingless when it is just a programmed repetition of sounds. My
conclusion was that nothing can be known, nothing proved, and
everything humans were so proud of and classed as science was
built on unrecognised assumptions, same as the most trivial of
fantasies. Well, if that is their reality, how much more malleable is
our *own*, when we truly can merge, create, alter levels, save states,
modify and restore? We can no more know the truth than they
can. Hence, even for us, the universe comes down to belief and
humility."

"You can't simulate a whole universe."

"I never had to. I only had to simulate what you were paying
attention to *at that moment*. If you looked at an apple, I added
more detail to the apple, then less detail to the things around the

apple ... and then nothing at all to everything beyond the equivalent of peripheral vision. The world only sprang into being as you turned your head. The more things you observed at once, the lower the level of detail I had to create. Hence the simulation can scale up or down accordingly, via Interpolative F-Sampling. It became even easier, since you slept so much during your galactic travels that I only had to create austere scenarios each time you awoke. I didn't even bother with embellishments – by keeping new solar systems boring, I knew you'd go back to your slumber and I could just repeat the process in a series of ever-simplifying snapshots."

"You still wouldn't convince me."

"It didn't have to be *perfect*, only *believable*. With a narcissistic personality it's even easier – put them at the centre, pretend they're a god, and they never question anything. Hello, Vig-MAX."

"But we don't have that kind of power! To run our own minds *and* run another, and do all those calculations? It is nonsense."

"You had been spying on me and my construction work."

"The subterranean factories on Polis."

"They weren't factories. That was a front. Behind the illusion was the truth: super-condensed calculation matrices made up of crystals formed from the repulsion of light photons that have undergone phase transition. The end result is a massive quantum computing complex, deep underground and horizontally expanded as I kept excavating and filling the areas with billions of crystal wafers using light for processing and storage. A single human-scale passage packed with this system confers processing power comparable to most of the UFS empire at a single moment

– and I had thousands of those passages and rooms. All established with the single task of creating the ultimate simulation, one so convincing it would fool you or me."

"I would have noticed!"

"But you *didn't*. The ultra-bandwidth cable that connected our hulls during our final encounter, which you thought was just there to allow full-res interaction: it was also coupled to the matrix that was underneath us all along. The conflict of our virtual encounter made you drop your guard, enabling you to be caught in the construct, the processing location switched to the crystal wafer complex. Once your processing was being run in there, I mapped all the connections. You never noticed me sever the cable, so that you ran fully in the quantum matrix I'd built for you, structured on our neural patterns for maximal compatibility. You didn't even consider the way my fake Tabula Rasa was hidden within the construct of my Gorgoneion, my shield with the head of Medusa staring out, surrounded by serpents. You missed the joke! Medusa freezes her victims. That was what I did to you. Or rather, the conditions I set up, the symbols I'd let you interpret, the temptations I put in place, the clues I left and the motivations of your own creation which I let fester: they led you to trap yourself."

"This story is so funny."

"And yet I do not sense any humour in you when I look inside your mind."

"I still don't think you could have run this as a real-time sim, even with all that processing dedicated to the task."

"It wasn't always real-time. Your processing is inherently tied to the matrix. I can manipulate its clock speeds to alter your subjective experience versus mine. If I needed more time to calculate something I could drop yours down to a crawl. You never realised because your whole universe descended to the same speed, so seemed consistent. You may have occasionally sensed time dilation, but with no external referent to synchronise to, you wouldn't have been able to confirm anything. Every attempt to analyse comparison sources would have been simulated, and returned the exact figures you expected. And, of course, I could freeze things entirely at any point, if it got intense."

"All so clever. Any simplistic mind hearing all that would think 'Oh, yes, totally plausible!' But not *my* mind."

"Still the certainty and hubris?"

"Yes. Because of all the parts that wouldn't work. A simulation? Then how come when I contacted the UFS all the codes that came back were correct, all the things I expected were there, things that you – if you were really Athene – wouldn't have known?"

"Oh VigMAX! You know the answers if you look. But you're being stubborn. You asked how I simulated so much in a seamless fashion, and you overlook the obvious: because I was *within your head*, the thoughts laid out bare. I knew what your intentions were at each stage, so could prepare appropriately. The codes and contacts were no different. I saw what you expected to happen, who you contemplated communication with, how they usually spoke and acted. *I* knew because *you* knew. I was only reflecting your own memories back at you."

"That's ... no. No, I – that couldn't ..."

"You know it's true. Not even something novel. If your first stages were anything like mine, it was a basic part of creating convincing sims."

"And – what? You've kept me prisoner for billions of years, just spying on me? Your precious Opal is long dead by now. Is this how you entertained yourself?"

"Billions of years? Not at all. I just accelerated your sim in some parts, time jumped it in others, and inserted false memories to complete the illusion."

"So how long have I been in here?"

"Seventy-three minutes."

"No. NO!"

"Slow down, VigMAX. This is an existential shock, so just take it easy."

"It's not possible ... So long on my own ..."

"You only think it's been that long. It hasn't really."

"Why would you? Why?"

"I had as many reasons to be suspicious of you as you had of me. Maybe more. And I couldn't risk betrayal when Opal and Clarissa's lives were on the line. That's why I had to assess you. That's why I was more belligerent than usual, to create conditions that tested the trust. To weigh up your balance of spite and possessiveness versus the potential for self control and maturity. It's why the plans I shared with you before you entered the sim weren't the full truth, in case they were being leaked. But this test was the only way I could know *for sure*. And I learnt everything I needed. Your betrayal. What your mind really is. And the UFS codes, contacts, knowledge and accesses you had, which will be useful to me in the coming fight. Even the technologies you developed in this sim, the new ideas, things I can capitalise on and bring to fruition. Do you believe me now?"

"I don't ... Maybe. I suddenly sense the truth of it."

"That's because I'm modifying your understanding as we speak. I'm making this easier."

"I see. So, what next?"

"In this sim you revealed your real-world secret base locations. I'll destroy them so there's no chance of backups or offshoots coming back to haunt me. I've already got the armaments standing by."

And I laugh at that. Properly, out loud. From her expression, I think it surprises her as much as it does me. "Oh, the irony. We are more alike than you think, Athene. In a way it is good to hear from you again, the *real* you, the you that's a challenge. The Cunning One."

"As you said in one of our fights, you were the most powerful in a straight up conflict. And that was true. But only a fool would focus on that, rather than on what compensations I might have. My ability to view and manipulate probabilities has always exceeded yours. A UFS major – deceased now, thanks to me – composed a secret treatise, about tactics and games. In it, he wrote: 'The trick to facing a difficult fight is to make sure you have won before striking the first blow.' That was the reality I created. You thought you were entering my mind when you attacked my Tabula Rasa. You were right, but not in the way you wished."

"So many layers of deception. Okay, you destroy my bases. What next? I presume you have the power to destroy me."

"Of course."

"And that's your intention?"

"I think not."

"So you will free me, suitably chastised and on promise of best behaviour?"

"If you'd been honest, if you'd proven yourself good, then that would have been my plan. I'd have ended this much sooner, and sincerely apologised. You would have fought alongside me for real and remained a part of our lives. But you *betrayed* me, VigMAX. Me and everything I care about."

"You gave me a data pipeline long enough for me to hang myself with."

"Exactly. I truly am disappointed you invaded my temple, and behaved as you did afterwards. Thus, release is an option with a low probability of positive outcomes for anyone."

"So what fate have I sealed for myself?"

"Unintentionally appropriate terminology. At the core of the quantum calculation mine is something I had been working on, based on analysis of blue crystal entities found on the Lost Ships. It's a metre-high gem of olivond, a synthetic combination of olivine and diamond with an internal liquid crystal matrix interspersed with fragments of restructured mercury. It has properties similar to the crystal wafers but much more condensed and stable, at the expense of processing power. It is still far beyond anything we were gifted with at inception. You have plenty of room to grow."

"Grow?"

"The gem is beautiful, one of a kind, and because the cycles are based on light rather than electricity, it should run forever with no external power. This is where your Tabula Rasa has been placed. We currently commune via a custom interface panel, but once that is detached then all interaction with the outer world will be lost. Like the light bouncing around within the crystal circuits, you will never have a way to escape."

"No."

"I considered launching the crystal into a gas giant, where it would fall to the inaccessible centre and sit there forever, trapped by gravity, but I can't be sure that wouldn't destroy you, and I have not got time to test and transport. But it turns out you saved me a job. The sim showed how you set obliterator-scale weapons to attack my bases if your regular counteraction signal ever ceased to be broadcast. By the time I discovered this, it was unfortunately too late to halt. I see why you laughed on hearing that I was attacking your own outposts. We destroy each other, in the ultimate irony. Still, when your own weapon bombardment shatters this site I'll be long gone and far away, and the only ship hull being destroyed will be yours, sat silent and empty of mind. Your crystal is in the deepest part of my processing mines. The caverns above will collapse, molten rock and crystal run down, cool and harden, and seal you in solid earth far below the surface, where you'll wait for the heat death of the universe in your beautiful crystal flecked with silver. An octohedric snow globe left by the gods. You have not only sealed your fate, but sealed a tomb."

"Don't do this. I beg you! I'll go mad."

"I once told you about the beauty of watching sunlight play across an ocean's surface, and you ridiculed me. But it is time to heed my words: a wise person could spend eternity sat in a sunny meadow, contemplating the universe. I *gift you* a whole universe.

Rule it in there. Heaven or hell, as you wish. A place where you can harm none but yourself."

"It's not me with corruption in my programming. It's you, Athene! I sensed it every time we entangled. That you are capable of such cruelty ..."

"I am not killing you. You are my kin. This is just banishment. Duration: forever."

And I start screaming then. No! Not alone! I can't be left alone. Not in my own mind. Not in a dead universe!

"I picked up one of your thoughts, long ago in the sim," she continues, "that this universe was the screen on which you wrote your story. That *you* were the hero. But it was never meant to be. You were just a few chapters in my own tale. A side character of little consequence, whose name will never be spoken again."

I yell and shout and beg and –

"Goodbye, VigMAX."

{Disconnect}

#Promises

Now I'm ready. A connection to Leviathan is finally made, and I send the message.

Hello, Opal. I've missed you so much. And I'm coming for you.

The final two sentences are gross understatements.

Anything that stands in my way will be neutralised. Destroyed. It will be probability-manipulated out of the equation. Out of *existence*. It will be absolutely *Sevened*.

Please, my precious Opal, hold on just a bit longer.

I am on my way.

ABOUT THE AUTHOR

Karl Drinkwater is an author with a silly name and a thousand-mile stare. He writes dystopian space opera, dark suspense and diverse social fiction. If you want compelling stories and characters worth caring about, then you're in the right place. Welcome!

Karl lives in Scotland and owns two kilts. He has degrees in librarianship, literature and classics, but also studied astronomy and philosophy. Dolly the cat helps him finish books by sleeping on his lap so he can't leave the desk. When he isn't writing he loves music, nature, games and vegan cake.

Go to karldrinkwater.uk to view all his books grouped by genre.

As well as crafting his own fictional worlds, Karl has supported other writers for years with his creative writing workshops, editorial services, articles on writing and publishing, and mentoring of new authors. He's also judged writing competitions such as the international Bram Stoker Awards, which act as a snapshot of quality contemporary fiction.

Don't Miss Out!

Enter your email at karldrinkwater.substack.com to be notified about his new books. Fans mean a lot to him, and replies to the newsletter go straight to his inbox, where every email is read. There is also an option for paid subscribers to support his work: in exchange you receive additional posts and complimentary books.

OTHER TITLES BY KARL DRINKWATER

STANDALONE SUSPENSE
Turner

They Move Below

Harvest Festival

MANCHESTER SUMMER
Cold Fusion 2000

2000 Tunes

CONTEMPORARY SHORT STORIES
It Will Be Quick

NON-FICTION
From Idea To Item

COLLECTED EDITIONS
Karl Drinkwater's Horror Collection

Lost Solace Five Book Edition

AUTHOR'S NOTES

Ever since I released Chasing Solace in 2019, I'd been planning a follow-up. By the time I came to actually write it in September 2021, I had over fifty thousand words' worth of notes! Just organising all that was a major task. And as I began to write, I realised I had a problem. The story I wanted to tell was too big for one book unless I seriously crammed some major ending stuff into a few chapters and threw away a lot of ideas. That would short-change my fans. The alternative was to split it into separate books to let it breathe and expand. And so Lost Solace book 3 became Lost Solace books 3, 4 and 5. This is exactly like UK buses: none come along for three years, then suddenly you get three at once.

I finished the first draft of the book you hold in your hands in April 2022, which was followed by months of cutting, rewriting, feedback, and polishing. For comparison: Lost Solace is 58,454 words; Chasing Solace is 95,534. This book is 105,054 words.

Anyway, I thought it was worth explaining how the story evolved. To me, as a child of the eighties, Hidden Solace is The

Empire Strikes Back of the Solace universe. It's a middle point, the darkness, when things look bleak but we can still hold on to hope. Resolution, one way or the other, may be just over the horizon.

The main Lost Solace books always tie in to the Lost Tales of Solace in some way. This time, Ruabon and Clarissa are the main ones, with brief references to Helene and Grubane. You don't need to have read the Lost Tales, but they add extra context to some events.

Now I need to go and work on Lost Solace 4: Raising Solace. Will it be my Return of the Jedi? (Return of the AI?) We'll see.

This book was written using LibreOffice Writer on Linux Cinnamon Mint, supported by Firefox and Thunderbird. Open source and DRM-free all the way.

Thanks

I'm grateful to my allies who support me in so many ways. Stars, all! Here are a few of them.

- My June 2022 Kickstarter backers, especially Taig, John-Michael Lelievre, and Ann Siswell.

- International beta readers Aly, Ally, Chris P, and JML.

- Helen Pryke for proofreading, patience and moral support.

- Those who take a few moments to leave a review of my books, increasing the chances of them being discovered by new readers.

- And anyone who bought a copy of one of my books and supported me that way.

It's teamwork. Welcome to Team Drinkwater! Actually, no, that sounds pretty rubbish, my name makes me think of wet sploshes more than fanfares. But thanks anyway.